OXFORD WORLD'S CLASSICS

FRANKENSTEIN

MARY WOLLSTONECRAFT SHELLEY was born in London in 1797, sole child of William Godwin, author of *Political Justice* and *Caleb Williams*, and Mary Wollstonecraft, author of *A Vindication of the Rights of Woman*; her mother died a few days after her birth.

She met the poet Percy Bysshe Shelley in 1812 and eloped to the Continent with him in July 1814. They spent the summer of 1816 with Lord Byron near Geneva, and it was there that *Frankenstein* was begun. They married in London at the end of the year following the suicide of Percy Shelley's first wife, and *Frankenstein* was completed a few months later and published in 1818. The Shelleys returned to the Continent; however, their two infant children died on these travels and Percy Shelley was drowned in Italy in 1822. Shelley returned to England where she continued to write, and where she raised their remaining son. She published another five novels—*Valperga* (1823), *The Last Man* (1826), *Perkin Warbeck* (1830), *Lodore* (1835), and *Falkner* (1837)—as well as many short stories, reviews, and biographical essays, and editing the works of her husband (1839). She resumed her travels in the 1840s, and when her father-in-law died in 1844 her son Florence inherited the Shelley title and she shared in the estate, leaving her financially secure. Mary Shelley died in 1851 and is buried in Bournemouth.

NICK GROOM is Professor in English at the University of Exeter, and a founding member of the Wellcome Centre for Cultures and Environments of Health. He has published widely for both academic and popular readerships, and among his many books are *The Forger's Shadow* (2002), *The Union Jack* (2006, rev. edn 2017), *The Gothic: A Very Short Introduction* (2012), *The Seasons: A Celebration of the English Year* (2014), *The Vampire: A New History* (2018), and editions of a variety of eighteenth-century texts, from crime writing to Shakespeare. He has edited Horace Walpole's *The Castle of Otranto* (2014), Matthew Lewis's *The Monk* (2016), and Ann Radcliffe's *The Italian* (2017) for Oxford World's Classics.

OXFORD WORLD'S CLASSICS

*For over 100 years Oxford World's Classics have brought
readers closer to the world's great literature. Now with over 700
titles—from the 4,000-year-old myths of Mesopotamia to the
twentieth century's greatest novels—the series makes available
lesser-known as well as celebrated writing.*

*The pocket-sized hardbacks of the early years contained
introductions by Virginia Woolf, T. S. Eliot, Graham Greene,
and other literary figures which enriched the experience of reading.
Today the series is recognized for its fine scholarship and
reliability in texts that span world literature, drama and poetry,
religion, philosophy, and politics. Each edition includes perceptive
commentary and essential background information to meet the
changing needs of readers.*

OXFORD WORLD'S CLASSICS

MARY SHELLEY

Frankenstein

or

The Modern Prometheus

THE 1818 TEXT

Edited with an Introduction and Notes by
NICK GROOM

OXFORD
UNIVERSITY PRESS

OXFORD

UNIVERSITY PRESS

Great Clarendon Street, Oxford, OX2 6DP,
United Kingdom

Oxford University Press is a department of the University of Oxford.
It furthers the University's objective of excellence in research, scholarship,
and education by publishing worldwide. Oxford is a registered trade mark of
Oxford University Press in the UK and in certain other countries

Editorial material © Nick Groom 2018

The moral rights of the author have been asserted

First published 2018
First published as an Oxford World's Classics paperback 2019

Impression: 9

Published in the United States of America by Oxford University Press
198 Madison Avenue, New York, NY 10016, United States of America

British Library Cataloguing in Publication Data

Data available

Library of Congress Control Number: 2017952460

ISBN 978-0-19-884082-4

Printed and bound in Great Britain by
Clays Ltd, Elcograf S.p.A.

ACKNOWLEDGEMENTS

I AM extremely grateful to my editor Luciana O'Flaherty, her assistant Kizzy Taylor-Richelieu, my copy editor Rowena Anketell, proofreader Peter Gibbs, and project manager Lisa Eaton: their sure hands and the team at OUP have guided this edition from conception to publication. I am indebted to the Leverhulme Trust, who generously funded me to research the early history of the Gothic—research that has proved to be invaluable for this edition. As I edited the text I very much appreciated the obliging assistance I received from the staff of the British Library, the Codrington Library, and the Weston Library; the staff of the Bodleian Library and University of Exeter Library were equally helpful in providing critical materials. As I was writing the Introduction I was invited to speak at the Albert-Ludwigs-Universität Freiburg, and the discussions at an international workshop on authenticity there also proved to be very timely for my thinking; I would therefore like to thank all the participants, especially Monika Fludernik, Frederick 'Jeff' Karem, and Stephan Packard. Among the other individuals who have directed my thoughts and ideas I would particularly like to thank Lora Fleming, Peter Gilliver, Roger Luckhurst, Robert Marshall, Fiona Stafford, Joanne Parker (and my ever gracious family), and especially my old friend Steve Matthews. I first discussed *Frankenstein* with Steve when we were undergraduates together, and as I was preparing this edition we met again in the graveyard of St Pancras Old Church to talk further about Mary Shelley and the Gothic. It seems fitting, then, to dedicate this volume to you, Steve. Thank you: we got it right—in the words of your beloved Maturin, 'It is better to hear the thunder than to watch the cloud.'

CONTENTS

INTRODUCTION

Readers who are unfamiliar with the plot may prefer to treat the Introduction as an Afterword.

Afterlife

Mary Shelley's *Frankenstein* can be summed up in one short sentence: a mad scientist loses control of a daring experiment with devastating consequences. It is a contemporary myth, comparable to those of *Dr Faustus, Robinson Crusoe, Dr Jekyll and Mr Hyde*, and *Dracula*: the definitive modern parable of the dangers of scientific and technological progress.[1] Indeed, *Frankenstein* seems, uncannily, to become more and more relevant with every generation, being invoked in debates ranging from politics and environmentalism to biotechnology, cloning, genetic modification, and artificial intelligence—indeed any instance of experts supposedly 'playing God'.[2] Pioneering medical break-throughs are swiftly 'Frankensteinized'. Dr Christiaan Barnard himself described the first human heart transplant in 1967 as a Frankenstein experiment:

I began by reporting the patient looked much better—even though he thought he was a new Frankenstein. Amid the laughter, Bossie noted Dr. Frankenstein was the man who created the monster—which meant I was the Frankenstein of Ward C-2. This led to more laughter.[3]

But of course this popular image of *Frankenstein* is not so much driven by Shelley's novel as by multiple retellings of the story's rich tradition in films and the media—notably Boris Karloff's iconic por-trayal of the Monster, complete with neck-bolts to enable him to keep his head attached to his body, in James Whale's 1931 production. It is as if the central idea of the book—the Monster—has escaped its pages and run amok through the nineteenth, twentieth, and now the

---

[1] See Chris Baldick, *In Frankenstein's Shadow: Myth, Monstrosity, and Nineteenth-Century Writing* (Oxford: Clarendon Press, 1987), 1–2.

[2] See Kim Hammond, 'Monsters of Modernity: *Frankenstein* and Modern Environ-mentalism', *cultural geographies* 11/2 (2004), 181–98, at 182.

[3] Christiaan Barnard and Curtis Bill Pepper, *One Life* (New York: Macmillan, 1969), 335.

twenty-first centuries. In doing so, the Monster has also taken on the identity of his creator, Dr Victor Frankenstein. 'Frankenstein' is at the same time the scientist and the Monster, as it is simultaneously Shelley's novel and its afterlife.

Any introduction to the novel should therefore be aware of the book's extraordinary capacity for weaving myths: as one critic puts it, '*Frankenstein* has attained the status of myth—endlessly reproducible, promiscuously applicable, yet always recognizable—in part because it seems monstrous in itself.'[4] In other words, reading the book in the twenty-first century should not merely be an exercise in literary history but affords an unparalleled opportunity for an urgent engagement with the key challenges of our time. Certainly much recent research has investigated the novel's relationship with its immediate political, scientific, and technological contexts rather than treating it as a universal parable, but although the novel does have a 'restless, arguably indiscriminate engagement with a wide variety of urgent cultural and intellectual issues', that does not mean that it is trying to resolve them—rather, *Frankenstein* seems to generate more discussion: it is a textual machine that produces meaning.[5] The book is being constantly reinvented, insistently refitted by critics and commentators: everyone seems to want a *Frankenstein* of their own. *Frankenstein* remains a—perhaps *the*—novel for our time.[6]

Critics have accordingly proposed test-case appraisals using psychoanalytic, feminist, and queer theory; Freudian interpretations are also popular, covering such themes as love and the death drive, incest and Oedipal desire, narcissism, uncanny doubles and doppelgängers, alter egos, language acquisition, and the interpretation of dreams.[7]

[4] David Armitage, 'Monstrosity and Myth in Mary Shelley's *Frankenstein*', in Laura Lunger Knoppers and Joan B. Landes (eds.), *Monstrous Bodies / Political Monstrosities in Early Modern Europe* (Ithaca, NY: Cornell University Press, 2004), 200–26, at 201.

[5] William Christie, *The Two Romanticisms and Other Essays: Mystery and Interpretation in Romantic Literature* (Sydney: Sydney University Press, 2016), 264.

[6] Frankenstein has an extraordinarily pervasive, fantastically rich, and intriguingly complex presence in popular culture, although the manifold instances of the Frankenstein myth are well beyond the scope of this Introduction (see Select Bibliography). There is also prolific digital activity in numerous websites and on social media.

[7] See Lester D. Friedman and Allison B. Kavey, *Monstrous Progeny: A History of the Frankenstein Narratives* (New Brunswick, NJ: Rutgers University Press, 2016), 4–14; Fred Botting points out that much *Frankenstein* criticism is authorial / psychoanalytic: see *Making Monstrous: Frankenstein, Criticism, Theory* (Manchester: Manchester University Press, 1991), 74.

Entertaining and diverse as these readings are, though, they tend to be circular arguments because literary critics are as much products of their time as writers and artists, and so critical approaches emerge moulded in part by the questions already raised by *Frankenstein*; unsurprisingly, such analyses then prove to be particularly applicable to the novel. All the same, there are recognizable trends in the perpetual rethinking and reworking of *Frankenstein*, which are succinctly exemplified by a shift in critical terminology. The being that Victor Frankenstein creates is never named. As the critic Lawrence Lipking has remarked, whereas earlier generations saw a 'Monster', we now see a 'Creature', which he puts down to 'our collective identification with victims'.[8] However, 'Creature' is hardly a less complicated or partisan word than 'Monster'. A better term would be 'Being': it is used in the novel, it is how Mary Shelley's husband the poet Percy Bysshe Shelley described the nameless character (presumably with her approval: see Appendix C, pp. 199–200), and it is a reminder that the novel is deeply concerned with questions of existence, sentience, and essence—questions that have been dramatically contested, rethought, and remodelled in the twenty-first century. Two hundred years after the first publication of the novel, it is time that the word 'Being' was reinstated, as it is in this introduction.

Birth

Mary Shelley was the daughter of two radical firebrands: the political scientist and novelist William Godwin, and the trailblazing feminist theorist and author Mary Wollstonecraft.[9] Shelley was born in the international turbulence of the 1790s: the decade of the French Revolution and Napoleonic Wars. Mary Wollstonecraft Godwin bore both her paternity and her maternity in her name—but her birthright went deeper still, and the writings of her parents would saturate her own work.

---

[8] Lawrence Lipking, 'Frankenstein, the True Story; or, Rousseau Judges Jean-Jacques', in Mary Shelley, *Frankenstein*, ed. J. Paul Hunter (2nd edn., London and New York: W. W. Norton and Company, 2012), 416–34, at 419, 423.

[9] Throughout this edition I refer to the author as Shelley, occasionally as Mary Shelley, despite the fact that she began work on *Frankenstein* before she was married on 30 December 1816; her husband is identified as Percy or Percy Shelley.

Godwin was the darling of the English Jacobins (supporters of the French Revolutionaries). His *Enquiry Concerning Political Justice and its Influence on Morals and Happiness* was published in February 1793, and established him as a champion of extreme intellectual liberalism and ultra-rational politics. In the *Enquiry*, Godwin makes the case for a new economy of knowledge that would develop individual responsibility and personal judgement, and in doing so promote communal benevolence while overturning moribund and tyrannical institutions— from centralized government and organized religion to marriage and monogamy. Godwin was an idealist and a utopian, believing in the perfectibility of humanity. He argues that there are 'no innate principles' and that humans are 'neither virtuous nor vicious as we first come into existence'; indeed, one of the central issues in *Frankenstein* is whether character and morality are instinctive or socially conditioned.[10]

For Godwin, education is consequently the crucial part of socio-cultural training: education (in the widest sense—'the most comprehensive sense that can possibly be annexed to that word') trains 'the characters of men . . . in all their most essential circumstances'. This covers political values ('the modification our ideas receive from the form of government'), schooling ('impressions which [one] intentionally communicates'), and incidental impressions ('the education of accident').[11] The acquisition of knowledge is for Godwin continuous, enabling humans to progress towards perfection—if never actually achieving absolute perfection. Rather, the learning process is 'the faculty of being continually made better and receiving perpetual improvement'.[12] It was also an imaginative exercise: Godwin was not satisfied with promoting his thinking solely through philosophical works or discussion at radical meetings, and so in the course of his career he also wrote six major novels examining personal conduct and visionary duty. Of these, *Caleb Williams* (1794), *St Leon* (1799), and *Fleetwood* (1805) all predate *Frankenstein* and made a particular

---

[10] William Godwin, *An Enquiry Concerning Political Justice and its Influence on Morals and Happiness*, 2 vols. (London, 1793), i. 12 (bk. 1, ch. 3).

[11] Godwin, *An Enquiry Concerning Political Justice*, 2 vols. (2nd edn., London, 1796), i. 46–7 (bk. 1, ch. 4).

[12] Godwin, *An Enquiry Concerning Political Justice*, 2 vols. (3rd edn., London, 1798), i. 93 (bk. 1, ch. 5). Godwin continues, 'The term perfectible, thus explained, not only does not imply the capacity of being brought to perfection, but stands in express opposition to it. If we could arrive at perfection, there would be an end to our improvement.'

impression on his daughter Mary (the last, like parts of *Frankenstein*, is moreover set in Switzerland). He inevitably took a keen and practical interest in his daughter's education.

Mary Wollstonecraft was easily Godwin's equal as an innovative and hugely influential thinker as the author of, among many other works, *A Vindication of the Rights of Woman* (1792; pointedly inspired by Thomas Paine's *Rights of Man*, 1791). Like Godwin, Wollstonecraft was committed to rigorous and enlightened education in order to reform corrupt and archaic social attitudes, especially those that denied opportunities to women. In particular, Wollstonecraft fiercely condemned the literary cult of sentimentality, which she saw as an insidious form of cultural indoctrination that encouraged women to be domestic and docile, unpolitical and powerless.[13]

In addition to her irresistible case for female equality, Wollstonecraft also shared Godwin's rejection of state and social institutions, arguing against the fallen nature of humankind:

We must get entirely clear of all the notions drawn from the wild traditions of original sin: the eating of the apple, the theft of Prometheus, the opening of Pandora's box, and other fables, too tedious to enumerate, on which priests have erected their tremendous structures of imposition, to persuade us, that we are naturally inclined to evil.[14]

A Vindication of the Rights of Woman is uncompromising in its ambition for female emancipation and became an immediate international bestseller. It is the founding statement of British feminism.

Mary idolized her father—'Until I knew [Percy] Shelley I may justly say that he [Godwin] was my God'—and he in turn described her as 'singularly bold, somewhat imperious, and active of mind. Her desire of knowledge is great and her perseverance in everything she undertakes, almost invincible.'[15] But she knew her mother only through her writings. To the surprise of their radical friends and acquaintances, Godwin and Wollstonecraft had married in March 1797; Mary

[13] See Horace Walpole's *Correspondence*, ed. W. S. Lewis (London: Oxford University Press, 1937–83), vol. xxxi (1961), p. 397 (letter to Hannah More, 26 Jan. 1795).

[14] Mary Wollstonecraft, *An Historical and Moral View of the Origin and Progress of the French Revolution; and the Effect it has produced in Europe* (London, 1794), i (single volume published), 17.

[15] *The Letters of Mary Wollstonecraft Shelley*, ed. Betty T. Bennett, 3 vols. (Baltimore: Johns Hopkins University Press, 1980–8), i. 296 (5 Dec. 1822); see Betty T. Bennett, 'Mary Shelley', *ODNB*.

was born five months later on 30 August; within eleven days her mother was dead of puerperal fever. Four years later Godwin married Mary Jane Vial, a translator and children's writer, but the new Mrs Godwin had little time for her predecessor's children: Shelley wrote in 1817 that 'somthing [*sic*] very analogous to disgust arises whenever I mention her'.[16] Neither were things helped by the fact that none of the five children growing up together in the Godwin household shared two parents: Fanny was Wollstonecraft's first illegitimate daughter, fathered by the diplomat and adventurer Gilbert Imlay, Mary her second child by Godwin, William was the son of Mary Jane and Godwin, and Mary Jane had also arrived with two children by previous relationships—a son, Charles, and a daughter, Clara Mary Jane (later known as Claire Clairmont and a few months younger than Shelley).

Mary was in the habit of reading Wollstonecraft's work at her mother's grave in the churchyard of St Pancras Old Church, often while actually sitting on her tomb. It was here that she was wooed by Percy Bysshe Shelley—young, dashing, heir to a baronetcy, a devotee of her father's philosophy, and an obligingly affluent family friend. Unfortunately Percy was also impetuous, reckless, utterly unreliable, a married father, and five years her senior. Nevertheless, in 1814 the 16-year-old Mary eloped with the still-married 21-year-old Percy.[17] They fled to Europe, accompanied by Claire Clairmont, and although they returned just a few weeks later (and it would be years before her father forgave them), such wanderings through a continent ravaged by the Napoleonic Wars would characterize their life together. These journeys deliberately followed in both the literal and theoretical footsteps of Shelley's parents, characterized by a nostalgia for her mother's own Continental travels and the re-enactment of her father's individualistic philosophy: effectively a 'concrete, lived realization of Godwin's and Wollstonecraft's political treatises'.[18]

It was during her elopement tour that Shelley began keeping a brief daily journal, a record that she maintained until the 1840s—and although not all of these volumes survive they nevertheless provide

[16] *Letters of Mary Wollstonecraft Shelley*, ed. Bennett, i. 43 (26 Sept. 1817).

[17] Miranda Seymour speculates that they first made love in the churchyard (*Mary Shelley* (London: Faber and Faber, 2000), 93).

[18] Elisabeth Bronfen, 'Rewriting the Family: Mary Shelley's *Frankenstein* in Its Biographical/Textual Context', in Stephen Bann (ed.), *Frankenstein, Creation and Monstrosity* (London: Reaktion Books, 1994), 16–38, at 24.

a significant insight into her intellectual habits through the books she read. In 1815 these included Beckford's oriental Gothic tale *Vathek*; Brockden Brown's American Gothic *Wieland, or The Transformation*; Chatterton's poems; Goethe's *Sorrows of Young Werther*; Lewis's Gothic *Tales of Wonder*; Milton's *Paradise Lost, Paradise Regained* (twice), and *Areopagitica*; Ovid's *Metamorphoses* in Latin; Plutarch's *Lives of the Noble Greeks and Romans*; Radcliffe's canonical Gothic novel *The Mysteries of Udolpho*; Richardson's monumental epistolary narrative *Clarissa*; and Shakespeare's plays (some of which Percy read aloud); Percy also read Ossian in the same year.[19] But while this reading may have laid the foundations for *Frankenstein*, Shelley was also coping with profound events in her personal life that would have a more intimate and lasting impact.

At the time of her elopement—or very soon after—she became pregnant. The baby was born on 22 February 1815, some two months premature. On 6 March 1815 she wrote in her diary, 'find my baby dead'.[20] This heartbreakingly blunt entry is accompanied by a note recording that she read the 'Fall of the Jesuits' that evening, which surely gives an unnerving insight into the strange intellectualism of the Shelley household; moreover, nowhere in her journal is there mention of the baby's name.[21] Less than a fortnight later on 19 March 1815 she wrote in one of the most personal, if still exceedingly terse, entries:

Dream that my little baby came to life again—that it had only been cold, & that we rubbed it by the fire—& it lived—I awake & find no baby—I think about the little thing all day—

The next day, 'Dream again about my baby'.[22]

As the feminist critic Ellen Moers has persuasively argued, 'Death and birth were . . . as hideously intermixed in the life of Mary Shelley as in Frankenstein's "workshop of filthy creation".' By focusing on the death of Shelley's baby in 1815, Moers argues that *Frankenstein* is a 'birth myth'. The novel tells the 'horror story of Maternity': bodies are physically abject and emotionally treacherous things—which explains

---

[19] *The Journals of Mary Shelley: 1814–1844*, 2 vols. ed. Paula R. Feldman and Diana Scott-Kilvert (Oxford: Clarendon Press, 1987), i. 88-93.

[20] *Journals of Shelley*, ed. Feldman and Scott-Kilvert, i. 68.

[21] The baby appears to have been known as Clara. The 'Fall of the Jesuits' was possibly Abbé Augustin Barruel's *Memoirs Illustrating the History of Jacobinism* (1797): see Explanatory Notes, note to p. 25.

[22] *Journals of Shelley*, ed. Feldman and Scott-Kilvert, i. 70.

the revoltingly corporeal detail in the novel of Victor Frankenstein's undertakings in creating the Being.[23] Although it would be well over a year before she began *Frankenstein*, the trauma of a newborn's death should obviously not be treated lightly—strangely, however, she and Percy did make a sardonic joke about infant mortality. Shelley jotted down a recipe for medication to treat a baby's convulsions; Percy then Gothicized the formula by turning it into a potion of regeneration:

> [Mary] a table spoonful of the spirit of aniseed with a small quantity of spermaceti—
>
> [Percy]—9 drops of human blood—7 grains of gunpowder
> ½ an oz. of putrified brain   13 mashed grave worms—[24]

The macabre ingredients of this concoction of medieval sorcery prefigure Victor Frankenstein's later necromantic researches. In any case, within two months of losing her child Shelley was pregnant again.

If rebellion, the death of their baby, and a rigorous regime of reading combined to create the mood under which *Frankenstein* would be composed, inspiration did not strike until the Shelleys travelled to Switzerland in 1816, the 'Year Without a Summer'. The weather everywhere was atrocious—the result of a massive volcanic explosion in April 1815 on the Indonesian island of Tambora that had sent dust into the stratosphere and dramatically affected climatic patterns across the globe. The Shelleys, with Clairmont again in tow (and now pregnant herself), arrived at Geneva in May 1816 and met the renowned and rakish poet Lord Byron on the 25th—Byron being the father of Clairmont's unborn child; also in attendance was Byron's cantankerous physician, John Polidori. Within a few days the Shelleys had moved into Maison Chappuis in the village of Cologny on Lake Geneva, while Byron rented the Villa Diodati, where Milton had purportedly once stayed. The residences were just a short walk apart, past a vineyard.

Shelley's journals for the first part of this stay have not survived (though she did later write an account of the genesis of *Frankenstein*

---

[23] Ellen Moers, *Literary Women* (New York: Doubleday, 1976), 95–7.

[24] *Journals of Shelley*, ed. Feldman and Scott-Kilvert, i. 80; see Timothy Morton, *Shelley and the Revolution in Taste: The Body and the Natural World* (Cambridge: Cambridge University Press, 1995), 71, in which Morton claims that this is a medieval recipe.

in 1831), but Polidori's diary does.[25] Clearly the conversation—between the three men at least—was audacious stuff. Polidori was an expert on somnambulism and had introduced that topic to the company soon after the Shelley party arrived; a week later on 15 June 1816 he recounts talking with Percy Shelley: 'a conversation about principles,—whether man was to be thought merely an instrument' (that is, whether or not humans were free moral agents—a quintessentially Godwinian issue).[26] Meanwhile Byron had acquired *Fantasmagoriana*, a scarce collection of German spine-chillers translated into French, with which he regaled his guests during the wet and dreary nights. On 16 June, enthralled by these tales, they seem to have dared each other to write their own ghost stories. Over the next few evenings the conversation became increasingly disturbing.[27] The night of 18 June was particularly strange. Percy Shelley became transfixed by Coleridge's description of a female vampire, stunned by the revelation of her reptilian breasts. Polidori takes up the tale:

Twelve o'clock, really began to talk ghostly. L[ord] B[yron] repeated some verses of Coleridge's *Christabel*, of the witch's breast; when silence ensued, and [Percy] Shelley, suddenly shrieking and putting his hands to his head, ran out of the room with a candle. Threw water in his face and gave him ether. He was looking at Mrs. S[helley], and suddenly thought of a woman he had heard of who had eyes instead of nipples, which, taking hold of his mind, horrified him.[28]

Polidori began writing his own story, 'The Vampyre', the very next night.[29]

As for Shelley, she claimed that her 'ghost story' was inspired by a nightmare she experienced at about the same time, following another late-night conversation between Byron and Percy Shelley:

During one of these, various philosophical doctrines were discussed, and among others the nature of the principle of life, and whether there was any probability of its ever being discovered and communicated. . . . Perhaps a corpse would be reanimated; . . . perhaps the component parts of

---

[25] Shelley's account was prefaced to the 3rd edn. of 1831 (see Appendix A, pp. 173–7).

[26] *The Diary of Dr. John William Polidori, 1816: Relating to Byron, Shelley, etc.*, ed. William Michael Rossetti [his nephew] (London: Elkin Mathews, 1911), 123.

[27] *Diary of Polidori*, ed. Rossetti, 125.   [28] *Diary of Polidori*, ed. Rossetti, 127–8.

[29] *Diary of Polidori*, ed. Rossetti, 132; he had already started *Ernestus Berchtold* on 18 June.

a creature might be manufactured, brought together, and endued with vital warmth.

Night waned upon this talk, and even the witching hour had gone by, before we retired to rest. When I placed my head on my pillow, I did not sleep, nor could I be said to think. My imagination, unbidden, possessed and guided me, gifting the successive images that arose in my mind with a vividness far beyond the usual bounds of reverie. I saw—with shut eyes, but acute mental vision—I saw the pale student of unhallowed arts kneeling beside the thing he had put together. I saw the hideous phantasm of a man stretched out, and then, on the working of some powerful engine, show signs of life, and stir with an uneasy, half-vital motion . . . He sleeps; but he is awakened; he opens his eyes; behold, the horrid thing stands at his bedside, opening his curtains and looking on him with yellow, watery, but speculative eyes. (Appendix A, pp. 175–6)

Galvanized by the experience, haunted by her dream, Shelley worked at the story with feverish tenacity, the talk at Villa Diodati and her exacting regime of reading feeding her imagination. Then Matthew Lewis, author of the lurid horror novel *The Monk* (1796) and a prolific dramatist, visited Diodati, and on 18 August Percy engaged Lewis on the subject of ghosts—a conversation that quickly turned into a theological quarrel:

We talk of Ghosts. Neither Lord Byron nor M. G. L[ewis]. seem to believe in them; and they both agree, in the very face of reason, that none could believe in ghosts without believing in God. I do not think that all the persons who profess to discredit these visitations, really discredit them; or, if they do in the daylight, are not admonished by the approach of loneliness and midnight, to think more respectfully of the world of shadows.[30]

Unabashed, Lewis then went on to tell five ghost stories.

Over the following months Shelley wrote, discussed her story with Percy, and sometimes he read aloud to her—*Paradise Lost*, *Gulliver's Travels*, *Pamela*, chapters of Gibbon's *Decline and Fall of the Roman Empire*, *Castle Rackrent*, and the fateful 'Christabel'.[31] By the time of their return to England, Shelley was writing nearly every day. She read *Don Quixote* and reread her father's *Caleb Williams*. Her novel

---

[30] *Journals of Shelley*, ed. Feldman and Scott-Kilvert, i. 126 (in Percy's hand); the text is from Percy Bysshe Shelley, *Essays, Letters from Abroad, Translations and Fragments*, ed. Mary Wollstonecraft Shelley, 2 vols. (London: Edward Moxon, 1840), ii. 96.

[31] *Journals of Shelley*, ed. Feldman and Scott-Kilvert, i. 145–7, 131.

took shape as a series of letters written by Capt. Robert Walton, an Arctic explorer, who rescues Victor Frankenstein from the Arctic wastes. He records Frankenstein's unbelievable confession—that he has created a living being from dead cadavers—and the awful price he has paid for this terrible and unholy deed. Walton himself eventually comes face-to-face with the Being, apparently verifying Frankenstein's incredible tale.

But even as Shelley was writing, life with Percy was never far from some dreadful crisis. In October, he received 'a very alarming letter' from Fanny Godwin, Shelley's half-sister.[32] By the time Percy got to Bristol, Fanny had committed suicide through an overdose of laudanum. Two months later came the news that Percy's estranged wife Harriet had been found dead in the Serpentine in Hyde Park, heavily pregnant (though probably not with Percy's child).[33] It was only eighteen months since Shelley's baby had died—eighteen months of birth and bereavement. *Frankenstein* thus cannibalizes Shelley's life, preying upon her reading and her society, to produce a text in which themes of life and death, identity and disintegration, dominate the characters and the action. She certainly seems consciously to have introduced a motif of pregnancy, for instance, into the text using words such as 'confinement' for Victor's researches (p. 34), a term usually reserved for women preparing for childbirth. Moreover, the narrator Capt. Walton spends nine months on his account (coincidentally the same amount of time Shelley spent writing the second draft), and, if Walton's letters are dated to 1796–7, they virtually cover Wollstonecraft's term of pregnancy preceding the birth of her daughter Mary and her own death shortly afterwards.[34] Such possibilities begin to reveal how inextricable Shelley's life—in all its Romantic extremes—is from the composition of the novel, and from its themes.

[32] *Journals of Shelley*, ed. Feldman and Scott-Kilvert, i. 139.

[33] *Journals of Shelley*, ed. Feldman and Scott-Kilvert, i. 150.

[34] According to this biological arithmetic, Walton's first letter is dated 11 Dec. 1796, and his last 12 Sept. 1797; Shelley was born on 30 Aug. 1797, and Wollstonecraft died on 10 Sept. 1797; see Anne K. Mellor, 'Making a "Monster": An Introduction to *Frankenstein*', in Esther Schor (ed.), *The Cambridge Companion to Mary Shelley* (Cambridge: Cambridge University Press, 2003), 9–25, at 12; see also Charles Robinson (ed.), *The Frankenstein Notebooks: A Facsimile Edition of Mary Shelley's Manuscript Novel, 1816–1817 . . .*, 2 vols. (New York: Garland, 1996), vol. i, pp. lxv–lxvi.

Science

Shelley's account of the genesis of *Frankenstein* published in 1831 confirms that she was an attentive listener while Percy was discussing natural science with Byron and Polidori. She already had some familiarity with practical science: in 1812 her father had taken her to hear the chemist and inventor Humphry Davy lecture, and while writing *Frankenstein* she read Davy's 'Discourse Introductory to Lectures on Chemistry', combining elements of Davy's thinking into the novel via the lectures of Monsieur Waldman.[35] She also spent several weeks studying the psychological philosophy of John Locke.[36] But Shelley had a more immediate informant in Percy. Having been sent down from Oxford University for co-writing a pamphlet on atheism, Percy's attention had turned to surgery and in 1811 he had dabbled in anatomical science for a few months, attending John Abernethy's anatomy lectures and his demonstrator William Lawrence's postmortems at St Bartholomew's Hospital in London (the same Lawrence was part of Godwin's circle and later became Shelley's own physician).[37]

The study and teaching of anatomy lay at the less reputable end of natural philosophy because of the difficulty in obtaining human cadavers. By the Murder Act of 1752, for 'better Preventing the horrid Crime of Murder', the bodies of executed criminals could be given up for public dissection as an alternative to gibbeting.[38] But not only was this supply wholly inadequate for the sixteen-month medical course in surgery that required students to dissect three such specimens, it also tarnished the whole practice of surgery by associating it with the gallows. As an alternative, Astley Cooper, a colleague of Abernethy's at Bart's who in 1801 had famously performed a public dissection (or 'articulation') on an elephant, advocated comparative anatomy—dissecting animal rather than human corpses, on the assumption that there was sufficient similarity between the two. Another

[35] *Journals of Shelley*, ed. Feldman and Scott-Kilvert, i. 142–3.

[36] She read Locke's *Essay Concerning Human Human Understanding* from late Nov. to early Jan.: see *Journals of Shelley*, ed. Feldman and Scott-Kilvert, i. 146–53.

[37] See Sharon Ruston, *Shelley and Vitality* (Houndmills: Palgrave Macmillan, 2005), 75–86; and Seymour, *Mary Shelley*, 71. In her introduction to *Frankenstein* (1994), Marilyn Butler ingeniously argues that the novel is an ironic dramatization of debates in the natural sciences, notably vitalism, in which Lawrence played a key role.

[38] Tim Marshall, *Murdering to Dissect: Grave-Robbing,* Frankenstein *and the Anatomy of Literature* (Manchester: Manchester University Press, 1995), 20–1.

alternative was to use waxwork models. These, often built around actual skeletons, were horribly lifelike—not least because they were modelled on dissections of executed criminals and included such details as rope burns around the neck where the hangman's noose had chafed: a sign of posthumous authenticity. Meanwhile the French anatomist Honoré Fragonard preserved and exhibited human and animal body parts by flaying his specimens—these *écorchés* were simultaneously examples of scientific research and, like anatomical waxwork models, strangely carnal art objects. Moreover, despite being synthetic and expensive, waxworks and *écorchés* at least had the advantage of not decomposing. Operating theatres were foetid places: medical cadavers were already putrefying by the time they were dissected, and their stench attracted hordes of vermin—one reason Shelley describes Victor's laboratory as 'filthy' (p. 35).[39] For all this, following the publication of *Frankenstein* Shelley seems to have sustained a somewhat ghoulish interest in anatomy. She researched the subject in April 1819 and read Joseph Forsyth's account of his visit to an anatomical museum, and in January the next year visited the Wax Anatomy of the Gabinetto Fisico, a leading collection of medical models in Florence.[40]

There were of course more sinister options for those requiring cadavers. In September 1813 *The Times* reported that a dead body had been stolen from St Pancras Burying Ground, and by the time *Frankenstein* was published bodysnatching was a growing problem. Come the 1820s it appeared to reach epidemic proportions—at least in the public imagination—and this fear of unlawful exhumation eventually led to the Anatomy Act of 1832. Grave-robbing haunts *Frankenstein*. Victor's researches lead him to collect bones from charnel houses and to ransack dissecting rooms and slaughterhouses. He skulks in graveyards at night, half-admits to stealing carcasses,

---

[39] The musician Hector Berlioz (1803–69) trained as a medical student and described his first day in the dissecting room in shocking terms: 'When I entered that fearful human charnel-house, littered with fragments of limbs, and saw the ghastly faces and cloven heads, the bloody cesspool in which we stood, with its reeking atmosphere, the swarms of sparrows fighting for scraps of lungs, and the rats in the corners gnawing bleeding vertebræ, such a feeling of horror possessed me that I leapt out of the window, and fled home as though Death and all his hideous crew were at my heels' (*Autobiography of Hector Berlioz, Member of the Institute of France, from 1803 to 1865*, trans. Rachel (Scott Russell) Holmes and Eleanor Holmes, 2 vols. (1870; London: Macmillan and Co., 1884), i. 22).

[40] Now known as La Specola at the Museo Zoologico in Florence.

imagines his fingers as 'profane' disturbers of the human body (p. 35), and is, plainly, a 'resurrection' man—animating the dead with new life. Walton describes Victor as a revived corpse; Victor describes himself as a walking memento mori; and the Being is a 'demoniacal corpse' (p. 38). Chillingly, when Victor discovers that his bride Elizabeth has been murdered by the Being, her body is laid out like a cadaver about to be dissected, a grotesque set-piece that draws attention to the sexual undertones of anatomical examination. Indeed, the risk that Elizabeth's body will be posthumously violated hangs over her corpse like an unspeakable nightmare because of the threat that Victor himself has posed to the dead.

Victor's original ambition is to be useful to humanity—'what glory would attend the discovery, if I could banish disease from the human frame, and render man invulnerable to any but a violent death!' (p. 23). His great medical discovery is not, however, immunity to all sickness, or even the reanimation of the dead, but 'handywork', as Shelley later described it (Appendix A, p. 176). Victor prepares a 'frame', for the 'reception' of life (p. 33). Such thinking was part of a revolutionary trend in materialist science that had developed from the associationist psychological theories of John Locke and the mechanistic philosophy of Julien Offray de La Mettrie, author of the self-explanatory *L'Homme machine* (1748), whose provocative thesis that 'man is a machine' was reflected into the popular craze for anthropic contraptions such as talking heads and mechanical marionettes. The Automaton Chess Player ('The Turk') was first exhibited in 1770 and appeared in London in 1783 alongside the Speaking Figure, a doll that answered questions; it returned to the capital in 1819.[41]

While the narrowing of distinctions between the human and the mechanical in one sense reduced the body to a reflex-driven machine, this materialist trend at the same time presented the opportunity to improve the human physique—in effect applying Godwin's theory of intellectual perfectibility to flesh and bone. Medical scientists had been seriously investigating transplantation since the end of the seventeenth century, but the idea goes back much further into Christian

[41] See Mark Sussman, 'Performing the Intelligent Machine: Deception and Enchantment in the Life of the Automaton Chess Player', in John Bell (ed.), *Puppets, Masks, and Performing Objects* (Cambridge, MA, and London: MIT Press, 2001), 71–86, at 77–8; both were, of course, fakes.

tradition: the twin Arabian saints Cosmas and Damian, often later adopted as patrons of medical schools, performed a miraculous transplant by removing the cancerous leg of a patient and replacing it with that of a deceased Ethiopian, thereby creating a hybrid human with one white leg and one black one.[42] In the field of dentistry, barber-surgeons in Britain had been accomplishing comparable feats on a regular basis since at least the reign of Henry VIII. Tooth transplantation became increasingly popular and eventually attracted the attention of the eighteenth-century physician and antiquary John Hunter, who became the first to publish a treatise on the subject.[43] Hunter preferred 'live' teeth (vivisected from living donors), and also favoured young female teeth—which were usually forcibly taken from servants.[44] However, to counter ethical concerns about exploiting living donors he also recommended keeping a collection of dead teeth, and many of those killed at Waterloo had their teeth removed, with individual specimens being sold to dentists at £2 each.

Interest spread in cosmetic surgery too in London in the early 1800s, reviving earlier procedures for skin grafts developed in fifteenth-century Sicily and taking inspiration from the Indian subcontinent, where representatives of the East India Company encountered ancient techniques of grafting and reconstruction. The most significant of these researchers was the anatomical surgeon Joseph Carpue, who specialized in rhinoplasty (nose reconstruction), and who was connected with both the galvanist Giovanni Aldini and the anatomist William Lawrence.[45] Carpue's first human subjects were successfully treated in 1812 and 1815, and in 1816 he published his monograph *An Account of Two Successful Operations for Restoring a Lost Nose*—'the starting point of modern plastic surgery'.[46] In response to the vogue for these cosmetic treatments, *Frankenstein* Gothicizes medical procedure, imagining a body brought into being through dismemberment and amalgamation—an enforced union of parts. The horror of

[42] Sts Cosmas and Damian were patron saints at the University of Ingolstadt Medical School, where Victor studies.

[43] John Hunter, *The Natural History of the Human Teeth* (London, 1771).

[44] David Hamilton, *A History of Organ Transplantation: Ancient Legends to Modern Practice* (Pittsburgh: University of Pittsburgh Press, 2012), 34–45: the satirist Thomas Rowlandson depicted the grim scene.

[45] Carpue also incidentally worked with Aldini on his 1803 electrical experiments on a human corpse (discussed later in this section).

[46] Hamilton, *History of Organ Transplantation*, 58.

Victor's science lies in rendering the human body utterly alien and monstrous by breaking down distinctions between the living and the dead, the animate and inanimate, the self and the 'other'.

Comparative anatomy similarly bred fears that human distinctiveness was being eroded. If there was sufficient similarity between humans and animals to allow animals to be used in dissection, then operations could be demonstrated on animals, and cross-species surgery might even be possible. Descartes had distinguished humans from animals by arguing that animals were effectively clockwork machines with no soul or capacity to reason, and he went on to claim that pain could only be felt through the faculty of understanding. By this logic animals did not experience discomfort in the same way as humans, and so Cartesian thinking permitted animal vivisection. As early as 1656 the architect Christopher Wren had pioneered hypodermic injections by inebriating his dog with wine introduced directly into its veins, and in 1818—the year of *Frankenstein*—James Blundell published his accounts of experimental blood transfusions given to dogs.[47] There were however objections to such experimentation. In 1789, the utilitarian Jeremy Bentham declared, 'the question is not, Can they *reason*? nor, Can they *talk*? but, Can they *suffer*?', thus raising and critiquing the issue of 'natural rights'.[48] In the context of the French Revolution, this was a fundamental political matter: what was the relationship of rights based on specific human wants to those based on general utility, or the common good? To put it another way, were animals somehow protected by the same values that were symbolically enshrined in the 1688 Glorious Revolution and which were being ferociously endorsed in France during the Revolutionary decade of the 1790s—or was this simply 'rhetorical nonsense, nonsense upon stilts'?[49] Although the Neoplatonist philosopher Thomas Taylor satirized Paine and Wollstonecraft in *A Vindication of the Rights of Brutes* (1792), the question of the rights of men, women, and human

[47] See N. S. R. Maluf, 'History of Blood Transfusion', *Journal of the History of Medicine*, 9/1 (1954), 59–107; the first plausible account of blood transfusion was at Coburg, Saxony, in 1615 (59). Blundell had previously lectured on animal vivisection and subsequently went on to work with human subjects; in 1828 *The Lancet* reported that he had successfully transfused blood into a human patient.

[48] Jeremy Bentham, *An Introduction to the Principles and Morals of Legislation* (London, 1789), p. cccix.

[49] See Philip Schofield, 'Jeremy Bentham's "Nonsense upon Stilts"', *Utilitas*, 15 (2003), 1–26.

slaves was actually brought into sharp relief when considering animals.[50] Indeed, William Wilberforce, the campaigner for the abolition of slavery, was among the founders of the Society for the Prevention of Cruelty to Animals in 1809.[51]

But the most notorious medical reports of the time concerned cross-species inoculation. In *An Inquiry into the Causes and Effects of the Variolae Vaccine* (1798), Edward Jenner had examined the spread of cowpox infection from horses to cows to humans. This was not simply a case of animal-to-human infection, for Jenner pointed out that 'what renders the Cow-pox virus so extremely singular is, that the person who has been thus affected is for ever after secure from the infection of the Small Pox'.[52] Deliberately infecting human subjects with animal diseases was highly controversial, even if it resulted in immunity, and fears that inoculated persons would grow horns and tails, develop leather hides, and chew the cud lingered for years, exacerbated by wonderfully fanciful scare stories.[53] One report, for instance, concerned 'a child at Peckham, who, after being inoculated with the cowpox, had its former disposition absolutely changed to the *brutal*, so that it ran upon all fours like a BEAST, bellowing like a cow, and butting with its head like a bull'.[54] It is no accident then that Victor constructs the Being from both human and animal remains—it is an inter-species crossbreed.

Arguments about transplantation, vivisection, and hybridity were part of a wider debate on 'vitalism' (or the life force), which was stimulated by mechanistic theories of the body, and which preoccupied scientists and poets such as Humphry Davy and Erasmus Darwin, as well as the anatomists John Abernethy and William Lawrence. This matter hinged on whether life was essentially metaphysical (and, by extension, whether divine agency was evident in the design of the

[50] Taylor did, however, later translate Aristotle's *History of Animals* (1809), the founding work of comparative biology.

[51] See Sharon Ruston, 'Natural Rights and Natural History', in Sharon Ruston (ed.), *Literature and Science*, vol. 61 (Essays and Studies, 2008) (Cambridge: D.S. Brewer for The English Association, 2008), 53–71, at 55.

[52] Edward Jenner, *An Inquiry into the Causes and Effects of the Variolae Vaccine* (London, 1798), repr. in Tim Fulford (ed.), *Romanticism and Science, 1773–1833*, 5 vols. (London and New York: Routledge, 2002), i. 103–6, at 104.

[53] See 'Pamphlets on Vaccination' from the *Edinburgh Review*, 15 (1810), 324–51, in Fulford (ed.), *Romanticism and Science*, i. 131–56.

[54] Fulford (ed.), *Romanticism and Science*, i. 145.

natural world), or whether life was engendered by material effects. Much ink has been spilt in trying to determine Shelley's position in the 'vitalist row', but *Frankenstein* is not a manifesto for either vitalists or materialists. As historian Ludmilla Jordanova comments more generally, the novel is not a 'direct critique of science' but an investigation of its 'instability, uncertainty, ambiguity', an 'exploration of the internal conflicts felt by practitioners in a variety of fields'.[55]

Abernethy, under whom Percy Shelley had briefly studied anatomy, was a vitalist, believing that the life force was electrical and linked to the notion of soul. Darwin, whose work was certainly familiar to Shelley (see Appendix A, p. 175), was, like Davy, also an avowed vitalist: in an essay appended to his poem *The Temple of Nature* (1803), he described how spontaneous life was the consequence of decay: 'the most simple animals and vegetables may be produced by the congress of the parts of decomposing organic matter, without what can properly be termed generation, as the genus did not previously exist; which accounts for the endless varieties, as well as for the immense numbers of microscopic animals'.[56] Victor's declaration that 'To examine the causes of life, we must first have recourse to death' (p. 32) appears to confirm that he is a vitalist, and a successful one at that, even if the consequences of his success are calamitous; his language too is vitalist in how he can 'bestow', 'endue', 'infuse', and 'give' life.[57]

The most striking demonstrations of apparent vitalism were displays of electrical power. Benjamin Franklin (who later played chess with the Automaton Chess Player) had famously electrified the world of science in 1752 with his account of flying a kite during a thunderstorm and harvesting lightning in a jar. This was a risky business. In 1753 the *Gentleman's Magazine* carried reports of three separate incidents in which four investigators were electrocuted during thunderstorms, one of whom had been instantly struck dead (admittedly it was also reported that four mute people had regained their speech

---

[55] Ludmilla Jordanova, 'Melancholy Reflection: Constructing an Identity for Unveilers of Nature', in Bann (ed.), *Frankenstein, Creation and Monstrosity*, 60–76, at 60.

[56] Erasmus Darwin, 'Additional Notes. Spontaneous Vitality of Microscopic Animals', in *The Temple of Nature; or The Origin of Society: A Poem, with Philosophical Notes* (London: J. Johnson, 1803), [new pagination] 1–11, at 8; for Davy, see, for example, Explanatory Notes, note to p. 34.

[57] See Sharon Ruston, *Creating Romanticism: Case Studies in the Literature, Science and Medicine of the 1790s* (Houndmills: Palgrave Macmillan, 2013), 125.

following doses of electricity).[58] By 1767, such experiments were a thrilling form of parlour magic: 'the present race of electricians', observed the philosopher Joseph Priestley, are 'drawing lightning from the clouds into a private room, and amusing themselves at their leisure, by performing with it all the experiments that are exhibited by electrical machines'.[59] Chief among this 'race of electricians' were Luigi Galvani (who gave his name to the science of chemically generated bioelectricity) and his nephew Giovanni Aldini. Aldini visited London in January 1803 and applied his galvanic apparatus to the body of George Foster, who had been hanged for murder. Aldini's account of his very first experiment was astonishing—and a direct inspiration for *Frankenstein*: 'On the first application of the arcs the jaw began to quiver, the adjoining muscles were horribly contorted, and the left eye actually opened.'[60] Foster appeared to look narrowly out of one, lifeless eye—half alive, half undead.

The young Percy Shelley was exhilarated by such accounts and proceeded to electrocute his own family. As his sister Hellen recalled,

When my brother commenced his studies in chemistry, and practised electricity upon us, I confess my pleasure in it was entirely negatived by terror at its effects. Whenever he came to me with his piece of folded brown packing-paper under his arm, and a bit of wire and a bottle (if I remember right), my heart would sink with fear at his approach; but shame kept me silent, and, with as many others as he could collect, we were placed hand-in-hand round the nursery table to be electrified.[61]

When Percy went up to Oxford, his rooms were scattered not only with books, clothes, and pistols, but also 'phials innumerable, . . . crucibles. . . . An electrical machine, an air-pump, the galvanic trough, a solar microscope, and large glass jars and receivers'.[62] This is the locus classicus of Victor Frankenstein's laboratory.

---

[58] *Gentleman's Magazine*, 23 (1753), 430–2, at 431.

[59] Joseph Priestley, *The History and Present State of Electricity, with Original Experiments* (2nd edn., London, 1769), 519. For Davy on electricity, see 'Historical Sketch of Electrical Discovery', 'LECTURE I.—Introductory to Electro-Chemical Science', and 'LECTURE II.—Electro-Chemical Science', in *The Collected Works of Sir Humphry Davy, Bart. LL.D., F.R.S.*, ed. John Davy, 9 vols. (London: Smith, Elder, and Co., 1839-40), viii. 256–305.   [60] Fulford (ed.), *Romanticism and Science*, i. 288.

[61] Thomas Jefferson Hogg, *The Life of Percy Bysshe Shelley*, ed. Edward Dowden (London: George Routledge & Sons, 1906), 21.

[62] Hogg, *Shelley*, 88; he also rigged up a kite to electrocute a cat during a thunderstorm, and threatened to electrocute his college scout's son.

Capt. Walton's expedition that frames Victor Frankenstein's narrative is also part of the same spectrum of electromagnetic experimentation as Victor's galvanic vitalism: he is in quest of the magnetic North Pole, as well as seeking the North-West Passage—a fabled searoute connecting the northern Atlantic Ocean with the Pacific that would revolutionize trade and communications within the British Empire. In 1773 Daines Barrington had proposed Arctic exploration to the Royal Society Council to ascertain whether the polar sea could be navigated to open a route to the East Indies, prompting an expedition to the Arctic Circle led by John Phipps and Skeffington Lutwidge. Charles Duncan attempted the same voyage in the early 1790s before his crew mutinied, and in 1817 John Barrow, Second Secretary to the Admiralty, published his accounts of Arctic exploration in the *Quarterly Review*.[63] By the time *Frankenstein* was published there was a government bounty of £20,000 available for traversing the passage and a £5,000 prize for reaching within one degree of the North Pole, and in that year two Admiralty voyages involving four ships set sail on such an expedition. *Frankenstein*, like Samuel Taylor Coleridge's poem 'The Rime of the Ancyent Marinere' (1798), is implicated in contemporary maritime politics: it is written at sea, and driven by the needs of imperial commerce.

Myth

Crucially, Shelley's engagement with vitalism in *Frankenstein* presents modern science and natural philosophy not as separate from the past, but as part of a continuing—if mysterious—history that has its roots in ancient mythology and magic. Chief among these arcane influences was the figure of Prometheus. In his play *Prometheus Bound*, the ancient Greek tragedian Aeschylus had described Prometheus *pyrphoros*—the bringer of fire—who was punished for stealing fire from the gods by being chained to a rock and having his liver torn out by an eagle. Every night the organ regenerated so by the next morning he could again be disembowelled. The Roman poet Ovid developed this myth as Prometheus *plasticator*—the maker—in which

---

[63] *Quarterly Review* (Oct. 1816, published 1817): see Adriana Craciun, *Writing Arctic Disaster: Authorship and Exploration* (Cambridge: Cambridge University Press, 2016), 82–5, 91–101.

Prometheus crafts a man from clay and then steals celestial fire to bring his creation to life. The two myths blended in third-century Neoplatonism, which linked fire to love and the soul as well as to life, and the myth was later taken up by writers such as the early eighteenth-century Whig philosopher the Earl of Shaftesbury, who described poets as 'a second *Maker*; a just PROMETHEUS, under JOVE'.[64] Literary composition thereby corresponded to mythic creation—and archetypal rebellion.

Shelley was familiar with the Prometheus myths from her childhood. Her father had written two children's guides to classical mythology: *Fables Ancient and Modern Adapted for the Use of Children* (1805) and *The Pantheon, or, Ancient History of the Gods of Greece and Rome* (1806). Godwin related the Ovidian fable of Prometheus *plasticator* in *The Pantheon*: 'with this [fire] he animated his image: and the man of Prometheus immediately moved, and thought, and spoke, and became every thing that the fondest wishes of his creator could ask'.[65] He also elucidated the story by relating it to the Christian creation myth in the book of Genesis:

The fable of Prometheus's man, and Pandora, the first woman, was intended to convey an allegorical sense . . . it is impossible not to remark a considerable resemblance between the story of Pandora's box, and that of the apple with which Eve in the Bible *tempted* her husband, *and he did eat*.[66]

This cocktail of mythology and Christianity was not new (Milton, for instance, had alluded to Aeschylus' *Prometheus Bound* in *Paradise Lost* in the 'adamantine chains' that bind Satan), but it was to prove intoxicating for Shelley in composing *Frankenstein*, who sutured the book together out of different texts, disparate literary traditions, and various scientific systems.[67]

Prometheus was also a dominant figure in the occult tradition. Directly before discussing Prometheus in his philosophical dialogue 'The Moralists' (1709), Shaftesbury presents alchemy as a craft: 'it

---

[64] Earl of Shaftesbury, 'Advice to an Author' [1710], in *Characteristicks of Men, Manners, Opinions, Times*, 3 vols. (5th edn., London: 1732), i. 207; Shelley read Ovid's *Metamorphoses* in 1815, though she did not record reading Shaftesbury until 1825.

[65] 'Edward Baldwin' [William Godwin], *The Pantheon: or Ancient History of the Gods of Greece and Rome* (London: Thomas Hodgkins, 1806), 95.

[66] 'Baldwin' [Godwin], *The Pantheon*, 97–9.

[67] John Milton, *Paradise Lost*, ed. Alastair Fowler (London and New York: Longman, 1971), i. 48.

promises such Wonders, and requires more the Labour of Hands than Brains'. Alchemy is practical philosophy, a creative art:

For with some of these [Alchymists] it has actually been under deliberation how to make *Man*, by other Mediums than Nature has hitherto provided. Every Sect has a *Recipe*. When you know it, you are Master of Nature: you solve all her *Phænomena*: you see all her Designs, and can account for her Operations.[68]

For Shaftesbury, Prometheus is a tragic alchemist who in creating a living being bears the blame for all the world's ills: he is '*Chance*, *Destiny*, . . . or an *evil Dæmon*'; an 'Artist, with his unlucky Hand'.[69] This depiction of alchemy as a dextrous and creative artistry—and as a potentially catastrophic enterprise—is clearly evident in *Franken-stein*, despite Victor's rejection of the mystical tradition. Indeed, Victor emphasizes that he uses his own hands, not tools, in his manu-facture—'Cursed . . . be the hands that formed you!' (p. 71)—and in a ghastly counterpart to Victor's handicraft the Being's hands leave murderous marks on the necks of his victims William and Elizabeth.[70]

Byron and Percy Shelley were both fascinated by Prometheus as the stealer of divine fire and both wrote about him while they were at the Villa Diodati: Byron composed his poem 'Prometheus' and began the Promethean drama *Manfred*, and Percy began planning *Prometheus Unbound*.[71] This neo-Prometheanism was in part simply an excitable response to the thunderstorms that played across Lake Geneva that summer (and which were incorporated into *Frankenstein* when Victor sees an oak tree struck by a thunderbolt and when the Being is illuminated by lightning), but they were also representative of a more widespread recuperation of supernatural mythology. The Romantic essayist William Hazlitt had claimed that as a consequence of the French Revolution,

All the common-place figures of poetry, tropes, allegories, personifications, with the whole heathen mythology, were instantly discarded; classical allu-sion was considered as a piece of antiquated foppery . . . kings and queens

---

[68] Shaftesbury, 'The Moralists', in *Characteristicks*, ii. 190.

[69] Shaftesbury, 'The Moralists', in *Characteristicks*, ii. 203, 201.

[70] See Peter J. Capuano, *Changing Hands: Industry, Evolution, and the Reconfiguration of the Victorian Body* (Ann Arbor: University of Michigan Press, 2015), 30–2.

[71] Byron also worked on Canto III of *Childe Harold's Pilgrimage*, and Percy Shelley wrote 'Hymn to Intellectual Beauty' and 'Mont Blanc' while there.

were dethroned from their rank and station in legitimate tragedy or epic poetry as they were decapitated elsewhere.[72]

Yet in fact 'the whole heathen mythology' straightaway returned. Mythological figures became embodied in the satirical political prints of James Gillray and the young George Cruikshank, and, in addition to Byron and Percy Shelley, poets such as John Keats developed a 'Romantic Hellenism' that blended classical myth with mystical English folklore.[73]

The overriding reason for this revival of classical mythology was that it provided a frame of reference, both comprehensible and irresistible, for the mystifying operations of the new science.[74] Benjamin Franklin's kite-flying exploits had frequently been compared to the divine enterprise of Prometheus *pyrphoros*, and the electrocutions of investigators during thunderstorms reported in 1753 led one correspondent to warn that 'we are come at last to touch the celestial fire, which, if thro' our ignorance, we make too free with, as it is fabled *Prometheus* did of old, like him we may be brought too late to repent of our temerity'.[75] Prometheus *plasticator* was also present throughout anatomical science. 'In a word,' wrote the taxidermist Charles Waterton, 'you must possess Promethean boldness, and bring down fire, and animation as it were, into your preserved specimen'.[76] It is overly simplistic to suggest that by subtitling her book *The Modern Prometheus* Shelley is merely criticizing the overreaching ambition of Victor as dangerously egotistical, oblivious of wider implications and responsibility. Rather, by invoking the Promethean myths, she is

---

[72] William Hazlitt, 'On the Living Poets', in *Lectures on the English Poets* (2nd edn., London: Taylor and Hessey, 1819), 319.

[73] Modernizations of myths and legends included Maria Edgeworth, *The Modern Griselda: A Tale* (1805); Selina Davenport, *The Hypocrite, or, The Modern Janus* (1814); Barbara Hofland, *Patience and Perseverance, or The Modern Griselda* (1816); and Hazlitt himself wrote *Liber Amoris; or The New Pygmalion* (1823): see Armitage, 'Monstrosity and Myth', 205–10; see also Martin Aske, *Keats and Hellenism: An Essay* (Cambridge: Cambridge University Press, 1985), and Jennifer Wallace, *Shelley and Greece: Rethinking Romantic Hellenism* (Houndmills: Palgrave, 1997).

[74] See Simon Schaffer, 'Experimenters' Techniques, Dyers' Hands, and the Electric Planetarium', *Isis*, 88 (1997), 456–83.

[75] *Gentleman's Magazine*, 23 (1753), 430–2, at 431.

[76] Charles Waterton, 'On Preserving Birds for Cabinets of Natural History', in *Wanderings in South America, the North-West of the United States, and the Antilles, in the Years 1812, 1816, 1820, & 1824* (London: J. Mawman, 1825), 307–26, at 308.

connecting her novel to a complex tradition of human origins and contemporary life sciences—the whole discourse of existence.

As such, Victor Frankenstein is very much the Prometheus of the story. His apprenticeship is in occult alchemy, and although his scientific career follows the latest thinking, his mystical supernaturalism never leaves him: not only does he call on the 'spirits of the dead' for aid, they supposedly hover around him (pp. 154, 158). He is an artist with a thirst for fame and glory; he is a craftsman with the spark of Romantic genius. Indeed, the identification of the Promethean Victor with Percy Shelley is tempting, and in fact 'Victor' was the name under which Percy published his first collection of poems, along with those of his sister, Elizabeth. For Percy, the poet is a seeker of truth. In 'Alastor' he imagines nature as an archive of forbidden and dazzling knowledge, to be taken by seduction, or be spirited away by stealth:

> Mother of this unfathomable world!
> Favour my solemn song, for I have loved
> Thee ever, and thee only; I have watched
> Thy shadow, and the darkness of thy steps,
> And my heart ever gazes on the depth
> Of thy deep mysteries.
>
> (ll. 18–23)

But if these lines, written in 1815, can be read as a prototype for Victor, Shelley also unmasks the dark side of artistic creativity. Victor is neglectful of his friends, family, and fiancée. Despite being a cosmopolitan European—born in Geneva, working in Germany, and a traveller through Britain and the Continent—he is a recluse who shuns society. He is forever on the verge of madness—brilliant, fanatical, possessed, and delusional; he suffers several breakdowns in the course of the narrative and displays the symptoms of severe melancholia, a psychiatric condition linked to the creative imagination and tellingly defined in the *Edinburgh Physical and Medical Dictionary* (1807) as 'characterized by erroneous judgment . . . from imaginary perceptions or recollection influencing the conduct, and depressing the mind with ill-grounded fears'.[77] Shelley mockingly suggests that the whole novel can be read as a gigantic symptom of madness.

---

[77] Definition in Robert Morris, James Kendrick, et al., *The Edinburgh Medical and Physical Dictionary*, 2 vols. (Edinburgh: Bell & Bradfute, and Mundell, Doig, & Stevenson, 1807), vol. ii, n.p.: entry for 'MELANCHOLIA'.

Gender

The portrayal of 'Mother Nature' in 'Alastor'—'Mother of this unfath-
omable world'—is both familiar and proverbial and at the heart of
gender issues in the novel. Gender is writ large in *Frankenstein*—
a novel by a woman, daughter of a renowned feminist, and written
while she was pregnant and raising a young baby.[78] And yet the novel
describes a man's attempt to create human life without women—
a patriarchal procreative utopia, a definitively unmotherly nature. The
female characters are all passive, inert in their gendered categories of
wives, mothers, nurses, and servants, while the men do the serious
intellectual work. In the third edition, Elizabeth is even objectified as
a 'gift' to Victor—she is angelic, 'heaven-sent . . . celestial' (pp. 184,
183). Elizabeth also inadvertently kills Victor's silent mother, who
contracts scarlet fever from her, while the dead mother's insentient
image brings about the death of William. In an intensely claustropho-
bic overlap of female kinship roles Elizabeth is simultaneously Victor's
cousin, sister, mother, fiancée, and plaything, and like nearly all the
other female characters, she dies. Neither do women have a voice in
the novel. Safie, despite receiving an education and having a name
linked to *sophia* (wisdom), actually speaks a foreign language, and
Justine's defence at her trial following William's death is overruled.
Most ironically, Elizabeth's testimony in favour of Justine turns the
court against her and sends her to her death, leading Justine to make
a false confession. And then there is the half-character and utterly
silent Margaret Walton Saville, recipient of her brother Capt. Walton's
letters, whose initials are, tellingly, shared by Mary Wollstonecraft
Shelley. Walton and Victor both leave women (sister and fiancée respec-
tively) to follow their masculine ambitions, and in the course of their
conversations Victor argues that power is incompatible with feminine
domesticity. Victor is responsible for both the figurative and literal murder of his family; another family, the De Laceys—which also lacks
a mother—is destroyed by the Being, and Safie's mother, a feminist
thinker, is already dead.

Victor's relationships with women are Oedipal and necrophiliac, as
shown by his macabre hallucination in which he embraces a fetch of
Elizabeth:

---

[78] William was born on 24 Jan. 1816; Clara on 2 Sept. 1817.

I thought I saw Elizabeth, in the bloom of health, walking in the streets of Ingolstadt. Delighted and surprised, I embraced her; but as I imprinted the first kiss on her lips, they became livid with the hue of death; her features appeared to change, and I thought that I held the corpse of my dead mother in my arms; a shroud enveloped her form, and I saw the grave-worms crawling in the folds of the flannel. (p. 37)

There is also a strong, if covert, homosexual theme running through the novel. In the classical myth of Pygmalion and Galatea, Pygmalion sculpts a beautiful woman, and after he falls in love with the statue it comes to life with a kiss. Victor creates a male Being who repeatedly overshadows his thoughts of his fiancée Elizabeth and who strangles her on the night of their wedding in the nuptial bed. Victor's most passionate relationship is undoubtedly with his Being, underlining his acute self-obsession and pathological narcissism.[79]

By presenting women as perpetual victims, the novel delineates a society defined by men. But Shelley goes far further in exposing the politics of gender relations, and it has been suggested that *Frankenstein* has been more influential in feminist literary theory than any other novel.[80] Ellen Moers, for instance, reads the novel as a critique of male attitudes to the female body and reproduction (the 'birth myth') in themes such as hysteria and madness, sexual violence, and captivity and enslavement. Though this approach may encourage readers to see Victor as a character disempowered and feminized by his predicament, prone as he is to hysterics, these themes taken together rework the whole relationship between women writers and the Gothic. Earlier authors, notably Ann Radcliffe, have been identified as exponents of a characteristically 'female Gothic' through their emphasis on education and the powers of reason (especially in explaining apparently supernatural occurrences), as well as the moral effects of beauty (notably the sublime), an emphasis on reading and literature, an emancipatory political edge, their valuing of the domestic sphere and nurture, and a poetics of *terror* rather than of *horror*. Radcliffe's own influential distinction between terror and horror—the former 'expands the soul,

[79] Shelley had read 'Pygmalion et Galatée, ou La Statue animée depuis vingt-quatre heures', in Stéphanie-Félicité Du Crest Genlis's *Nouveaux contes moraux et nouvelles historiques*, vol. iv (Paris: Maradan—imprimerie de Cellot, 1805).

[80] At least with the possible exception of Charlotte Brontë's *Jane Eyre*: see Diane Long Hoeveler, '*Frankenstein*, Feminism, and Literary Theory', in Schor (ed.), *Cambridge Companion to Shelley*, 45–62, at 45.

and awakens the faculties to a high degree of life', the latter 'contracts, freezes, and nearly annihilates them'—was a deliberate attempt to distinguish her intellectually aware writing from the loathsome sensationalism of 'Monk' Lewis.[81] But in *Frankenstein* the emphasis is precisely on the visceral and physiological, and Shelley writes horror back into the 'female Gothic'. But rather than endorsing horror as a vehicle for the lurid male sexual fantasies aroused by writers such as Lewis, Shelley's novel confronts the reader with repellent images of abjection used for centuries to vilify, oppress, and censor the female body.

The Being himself is unnervingly described as 'the filthy mass that moved and talked'—even as an 'abortion' (pp. 108, 170)—but Shelley's female horror writing is most powerful in the creation and immediate destruction of the She-Being. Victor is repeatedly 'sickened' by the work, which he finds far more odious than his original male creation. Incomplete and embryonic, the terminated She-Being is an atrocity of unutterable revulsion: a female monstrosity. Victor is nauseated. He rips the thing apart: 'The remains of the half-finished creature, whom I had destroyed, lay scattered on the floor, and I almost felt as if I had mangled the living flesh of a human being' (p. 129). The She-Being never lives, though in an uncanny moment it does emit a strangled cry: when Victor casts the mutilation into the sea, weighted down with stones, it exudes a 'gurgling sound as it sunk' (p. 130).

Other feminist critics have examined the ways in which *Frankenstein* rewrites canonical literature, most emphatically Milton's *Paradise Lost*. According to the groundbreaking feminist critics Sandra Gilbert and Susan Gubar, Shelley 'cast her birth myth—her myth of origins—in precisely those cosmogenic terms to which her parents, her husband, and indeed her whole literary culture constantly alluded: the terms of *Paradise Lost*'. They christen this, 'bibliogenesis', and argue that *Frankenstein* exposes the misogyny implicit in the biblical Fall.[82] Remarkably, despite reading *Paradise Lost*, the Being never mentions Eve, not even in requesting a mate. But, like the She-Being, Eve is acutely present through her non-existence. Such telling absences and

[81] See Ann Radcliffe, 'On the Supernatural in Poetry' [1826], in *The Italian, or The Confessional of the Black Penitents*, ed. Nick Groom (Oxford: Oxford University Press, 2017), 403.

[82] Sandra Gilbert and Susan Gubar, *The Madwoman in the Attic: The Woman Writer and the Nineteenth-Century Literary Imagination*, 2nd edn. (New Haven and London: Yale University Press, 2000), 224.

suggestive gaps in the text lay bare that this is a dysfunctional world and that reading the novel with gender relations in mind can reveal its bizarre and abnormal geometry. As the critical theorist Gayatri Chakravorty Spivak perceptively points out, *Frankenstein* is 'a text of nascent feminism . . . [that] remains cryptic . . . simply because it does not speak the language of feminist individualism which we have come to hail as the language of high feminism within English literature'.[83] Just as she resists the temptation to answer imponderable questions of identity, science, and myth, Shelley does not proselytize about women and their rights in the novel but rather presents her female characters as perplexingly inaccessible.

Taking the politics of gender into the novel's scientific context demonstrates the remarkable capacity of the novel *Frankenstein* to target fundamental issues that remain contemporary concerns today. 'Mother Nature' is, in the context of feminist thinking, an unstable proposition, full of patriarchal assumptions and contradictions. To gender the environment as female presupposes that the secrets of the natural world are passively supine, awaiting their discovery by active researchers. In the seventeenth century Francis Bacon, the modern father of empirical scientific investigation, had straightforwardly described nature as female, the quarry of natural philosophers, who were naturally male and bent on plundering 'still laid up in the womb of nature many secrets of excellent use'.[84] This rhetoric continued in the eighteenth and nineteenth centuries through the work of Davy and others, and in the novel is taken up by Monsieur Waldman, who describes to Victor the disturbingly invasive practices of natural philosophers: 'They penetrate into the recesses of nature, and shew how she works in her hiding places' (p. 29).[85]

Masculine science is defined by such an exercise of 'power over nature, described in metaphors of sexual penetration and phallic creativity . . . for public acclaim and glory'.[86] Victor ignores all taboos in his quest for knowledge and craves celebrity; Walton too is a glory-hunter

---

[83] Gayatri Chakravorty Spivak, 'Three Women's Texts and a Critique of Imperialism', *Critical Inquiry*, 12 (1985), 243–61, at 254.

[84] *The Philosophical Works of Francis Bacon*, ed. Robert Leslie Ellis and James Spedding (1905); ed. John M. Robertson (Abingdon: Routledge, 2011), 292.

[85] See further Davy in Explanatory Notes, note to p. 29.

[86] Brian Easlee, *Fathering the Unthinkable: Masculinity, Science, and the Nuclear Arms Race* (London: Pluto Press, 1983), 36.

putting the lives of his crew at risk in attempting to realize his ambition. The novel shows how masculine norms structure not only
domestic and sexual relationships, but also whole intellectual dis-
ciplines and practices—'the entangling of science with ego, power
and status'.[87] The very fact that Victor works in secret and alone
brings into question his ethical credibility: as is evident in the name
'operating theatre', science in the Enlightenment was a public performance, a visible process, and students usually dissected cadavers
as part of a group.[88] Victor, however, defines himself (and his masculinity) not with the advance of his reasoning but only the final out-
come of his labours—indeed, he maintains that his discovery 'was so
great and overwhelming, that all the steps by which I had been progressively led to it were obliterated, and I beheld only the result'
(p. 33). His focus on outputs then enables Victor to abdicate any
responsibility or liability. This is bad science—detached and amoral. To
put it bluntly, science without accountability is not only dehumanizing,
it is also ultimately potentially lethal.

   Frankenstein shows that these questions about scientific culpability
are 'wicked problems'—difficult to define and impossible to contain;
restlessly changing and contradictory in their nature; inextricable
from other, equally wicked, problems; and requiring unique solutions
from multiple perspectives. But if ethical questions about scientific
experimentation, or sociocultural problems concerning the status of
women, cannot be resolved, they can at least be better understood by
turning to the Being. What exactly is it that Victor creates?

Being

The Being is a composite man-beast, a hybrid of the living and the
dead. It is made of body fragments from different corpses, gleanings
from dissection rooms and abattoirs, parts from 'tortured' animals—
a literal chimera, a fusion infused with a 'spark of being' (pp. 34, 36),
though he is not properly undead as he has never actually lived.[89] His

---

[87] Hammond, 'Monsters of Modernity', 190.

[88] See Susan Catherine Lawrence, ' "Desirous of Improvements in Medicine": Pupils
and Practitioners in the Medical Societies at Guy's and Bartholomew's Hospitals, 1795–
1815', *Bulletin of the History of Medicine*, 59 (1985), 89–104.

[89] See Maria Beville, *The Unnameable Monster in Literature and Film* (New York and
London: Routledge, 2014), 83.

origins are mixed and broken; as the Marxist literary critic Franco Moretti has suggested, he is a '*collective* and *artificial* creature', like a proletarian worker.[90] Victor forms him out of disparate pieces of the poor, the dispossessed, and possibly the criminal too, rather than from a single cadaver. But while the Being is a living embodiment of Victor's achievements in bio-scientific research, he is also horrendously flawed—the Being's gigantic stature is, for example, the direct result of Victor's impatience: since 'the minuteness of the parts formed a great hindrance to my speed', he resolves to deal with that inconvenience by making him eight feet tall (p. 34).[91] Victor also selects his features as 'beautiful' (p. 37) in an attempt to create an exquisite form. Instead, what results is 'body horror': twisted physiognomy and hideous physiology substituting for the broken ruins and blasted landscapes in which Gothic fiction is more often played out.[92] The resulting Being has a less-than-animal status. He is not a freak or 'sport of nature', but artificial, prosthetic, inauthentic life; at best a walking evisceration. Thus Victor clearly thinks that killing the Being is not murder, and neither is dismembering his mate—it is simply ending an experiment, dismantling a project over which he has absolute power.

There is a lack of clarity in naming the Being just as there is a lack of cohesion and totality in the descriptions of him. He twice refers to himself as a 'creature' ('I am thy creature', p. 70), though he also admits he is a 'monster'. 'Creature' disguises the fact that the Being is manufactured, not created—yet Victor does not hesitate to think in those terms, naming and renaming the Being: 'I beheld the wretch— the miserable monster whom I had created' (p. 37); he is also a 'devil' and occasionally a 'daemon'. When Shelley saw the theatrical adaptation *Presumption* in 1823, she wrote, 'The play bill amused me extremely, for in the list of dramatic personæ came, —— by Mr T. Cooke: this nameless mode of naming the un[n]ameable is rather

[90] Franco Moretti, *Signs Taken for Wonders: Essays in the Sociology of Literary Forms*, trans. Susan Fischer, David Forgacs, and David Miller (London: NLB, 1983), 85.

[91] As Peter Brooks puts it, he is 'an exotic body with a difference, a distinct perversion from the tradition of desirable objects' (*Body Work: Objects of Desire in Modern Narrative* (Cambridge, MA: Harvard University Press, 1993), 199).

[92] Despite inaccuracies, see Judith Halberstam, *Skin Shows: Gothic Horror and the Technology of Monsters* (Durham, NC: Duke University Press, 1996), 28–9.

good.'[93] But she had purposefully not named the Being, and the constellation of terms used to describe him are calculated to create a hazy obscurity; the confusion and collapse of language. The Being is then an early example of 'weird' rather than representational realism, in which Shelley portrays the fleshly form of the Being 'even while cancelling the literal terms of the description'.[94] He/it is an unrepresentable impossibility, horribly visceral yet indescribable, provoking a sublime terror. Like a revenant he rides on the wings of storm and tempest, and is often encountered in spectacular landscapes of vertiginous mountains, impenetrable forests, or outlandish ice-fields—geographies of strangeness, estrangement, and excess that alienate rather than humanize characters.

As much as he is manufactured, though, the Being is also part-animal. Indeed, one of Victor's insults is to call him a 'vile insect', promising to stamp him out (p. 70). This is an extreme instance of making the Being bestial. The tendency of animal rights at the time Shelley was writing was increasingly anthropomorphic. Nineteenth-century defences of animal rights focused on intelligence: animal 'sagacity' being defined as obedience to humans, domestication and compliancy, and expressing familial instincts.[95] Not only are these the aspirations of the Being, but he actually adopts the language of animal intelligence in admitting that he is not human: 'I had *sagacity* enough to discover, that the unnatural hideousness of my person was the chief object of horror' (p. 97, my emphasis). If the Being is admitting he is animal, then this is in the context of an emerging sense of animal emancipation, which has led to the current debate on animal rights in law today. What is more, this debate also engages with theories of human racialization and—because the Being is denied a mate and Victor is endeavouring to exterminate him—with eugenics and even ethnic cleansing. The Being stands for the oppressed whenever it is considered to be 'sub-human'.

[93] Betty T. Bennett and Charles E. Robinson (eds.), *The Mary Shelley Reader* (New York and Oxford: Oxford University Press, 1990), 404: letter to Leigh Hunt (9–11 Sept. 1823).

[94] Graham Harman, *Weird Realism: Lovecraft and Philosophy* (Winchester and Washington: Zero Books, 2012), 17.

[95] See Rob Boddice, 'The Historical Animal Mind: "Sagacity" in Nineteenth-Century Britain', in Julie A. Smith and Robert W. Mitchell (eds.), *Experiencing Animal Minds: An Anthology of Animal–Human Encounters* (New York: Columbia University Press, 2012), 65–78.

The word 'Being' also pinpoints the question of existence that so troubles *Frankenstein*. However he is named, the Being does not claim to be comprehensively human. Not only does he recognize his own deformity—'I was not even of the same nature as man' (p. 87)—but is he even a life form at all, or a purely man-made product painfully aware of his own eerie nature?[96] He is both physically mature and mentally infantile, and although he has lustrous black hair and lupine teeth he is also initially foetal in his appearance with 'watery eyes' and a 'shrivelled complexion' (p. 37). The Being does not grow in bodily stature through the novel (from the outset he possesses superhuman strength and agility), but he does make supernatural advances in intelligence, emotions, and even wisdom. He also evidently develops independence of thought and action, particularly in envisaging situations and planning ways of bringing them into being. Hence his social ambitions for friendship, or, failing that, noble savagery with a mate and helpmeet.

Throughout *Frankenstein* the human and the 'other', or non-human, are not in a static, anchored relationship; instead the non-human repeatedly comes into intimate proximity with the human, then recedes. How close does the 'other' need to get to be assimilated as human? Victor truly knows the Being inside out, but once the Being is animate he becomes radically unfamiliar and colossally threatening. But the Being's demands are not unreasonable: he requests that Victor act humanely. If Victor does so, the Being will be humanized by the transaction and can reciprocate in a civilized fashion. But of course Victor cannot do so—his own humanity is drained from him and he actually becomes less than human, reinforcing the fear that in fabricating the Being he has become monstrous himself: 'often did my human nature turn with loathing from my occupation' (p. 35). The distinction between human and non-human 'other' is reversed. Critics have grappled with how human the Being is, but perhaps the point is not to insist that he is either human or non-human, rather he is near human (*very* near human). Yet having come within touching

---

[96] Northrop Frye bizarrely asserts that the Being is 'an ordinary human being isolated from mankind by extreme ugliness' (*A Study of English Romanticism* (New York: Random House, 1968), 44). Apart from being made out of both human and animal carrion, the Being is also fully 8 feet tall; it is therefore a surprise that some critics claim that Shelley 'never suggested that he was other than fully human' (Anne K. Mellor, *Mary Shelley: Her Life, Her Fiction, Her Monsters* (New York and Abingdon: Routledge, 2009), 63).

distance of the human, the Being then turns malign: the wanton destruction of the De Laceys' cottage and garden is surely meant to be shocking—even indefensible—and the Being then wilfully murders three people and ensures a fourth is executed.

Although the Being develops consciousness, does it follow that he also acquires a sense of good and evil, and a resultant awareness of rights, responsibility, culpability, integrity, and moral standards? As he is artificial these principles are clearly not innate to the Being, but are they impossible for him to attain? He is surely humanized by acquiring speech, powerfully implying that language and literature make humanity, and not vice versa, and in that sense *Frankenstein* is a *Bildungsroman* or narrative of cultural formation.[97] The Being is no Caliban, who in Shakespeare's *The Tempest* scoffs at Prospero, 'You taught me language, and my profit on 't | Is I know how to curse' (I. ii. 365–6); rather, the Being eavesdrops to learn language and acquire culture, hears Volney's *Ruins* read aloud, and then finds copies of *Paradise Lost*, *The Sorrows of Young Werther*, and a volume of Plutarch's *Lives of the Noble Greeks and Romans* from which he teaches himself to read—becoming, in the process, both 'phoneticized and alphabeticized'.[98] These four texts bring the consciousness of the Being into being.

Paradise Lost is key to making him near human, not only feeding his intellect but also stirring his passions: '*Paradise Lost* excited different and far deeper emotions' (p. 94). He describes himself in Miltonic terms, identifying first with Adam (who is moulded from clay) and thereby interpreting his own condition as a fall from grace, as expulsion and wandering—reminding the reader that this is a novel of home, exile, and migration, in which the Being refers to his own 'emigration' (p. 75). But he then models himself on Satan, as a diabolical agent of revenge. There is no question as to whether the Being has a soul: despite being underwritten by Milton's great Christian epic, *Frankenstein* (especially in the 1818 version) is set in a world abandoned by God, and the divine is only mentioned in exclamations and as a figure of speech. But the cosmogony of *Paradise*

---

[97] The term was first used in 1819: see Helena Feder, *Ecocriticism and the Idea of Culture: Biology and the Bildungsroman* (London and New York: Routledge, 2016), 19 n.

[98] Maureen McLane, *Romanticism and the Human Sciences: Poetry, Population, and the Discourse of Species* (Cambridge: Cambridge University Press, 2000), 97.

Lost does nevertheless generate the emotional landscape of the Being and fires his imagination, providing him with characters he can assume and a plot that he can re-enact: the poem serves as a manual for his identity. Reading (as Wollstonecraft would have agreed) is essentially character-forming.

In one way, then, the Being can be seen as a 'thought experiment' on the uses of literature and how it creates personality. In an instant of self-awareness, the Being attempts to consolidate his outsider status by proposing that Victor has a duty to grant him rights: 'Do your duty towards me, and I will do mine towards you and the rest of mankind' (p. 70). If Victor will comply and provide him with a mate 'of the same species' (p. 106), the Being offers to remove himself from society and disappear into South America—even being an outsider can endow him with a social role. But he also desires to be a species, not a monster: not to be singular but part of a community (even though that community does not yet exist—his rights might be termed 'anticipatory rights').[99] Against this, Victor fears the Being's potency and the global threat that a 'race of devils would be propagated upon the earth' (p. 125). His anxiety that he would initiate a species of incarnate giants that would place humanity at risk through competition and overpopulation places the novel within a long-standing dispute between Thomas Malthus (author of *An Essay on the Principle of Population*, 1798) and Godwin, who eventually replied in 1820 with *Of Population*. Victor appears to reason as a Malthusian, believing that the principle of population is inexorable increase (although he is also of course frantically trying to justify to himself his change of heart over the She-Being).[100] The population issue is perhaps a red herring, though; what is really at stake is that a Being and his mate on the loose would pose the combined threat of male and female sexual abuse and miscegenation—a much more tangible and immediate danger. Victor therefore denies the Being conjugal rights. This means that the Being's death is also the extinction of Victor's emergent

[99] See Diana Reese, 'A Troubled Legacy: Mary Shelley's *Frankenstein* and the Inheritance of Human Rights', *Representations*, 96 (2006), 48–72, at 58–9.

[100] See McLane, *Romanticism and the Human Sciences*, 103–4; see also Robert Mitchell, 'Population Aesthetics in Romantic and Post-Romantic Literature', in Jacques Khalip and Forest Pyle (eds.), *Constellations of a Contemporary Romanticism* (New York: Fordham University Press, 2016), 267–89, esp. at 269.

'new species' (p. 34).[101] But although the Being dies alone, he is not forgotten.

Plots

The Being is not forgotten because, like Victor, he survives in Walton's letters, both directly and indirectly. The whole narrative structure of *Frankenstein* is another Shelleyan experiment—this time investigating authenticity in writing. This experimentation is both dazzling and dizzying in conception and execution. What are sometimes called stories-within-stories, or nested or concentric narratives, are inadequate ways of elucidating Shelley's sophisticated mapping of literary methods and media. The structure of the novel is in fact built of several interlocking levels, all contained in Capt. Walton's letters to his sister Margaret Saville (her initials 'MS' implying 'manuscript'). These letters, sent from the ends of the earth, contain Victor's account, which includes the Being's life story in direct speech, and which in turn has within it the De Lacey story and the history of Safie as corroborated by the letters of Felix and Safie; these are copied by the Being, given to Victor to authenticate his version of events, and shown to Walton by Victor. But that is not all. Henry Clerval's words are given in direct speech, making him—as Victor's confidante—a posthumous co-narrator, while Walton comes before the Being to take down his daemonic confession from his own mouth. These spiralling and proliferating and criss-crossing accounts make *Frankenstein* a hallucinatory text—not least because they are mirrored by doubled characters (two professors at Ingolstadt, two adopted daughters, two ailing fathers) and overlapping selves (Elizabeth is both Victor's sibling and his betrothed, Victor and Walton are twinned, the Being is a demon brother) so that identities waver and coalesce throughout. The interlaced plots are not so much stories-within-stories as visions-within-dreams-within-tales, and present the alarming possibility that the whole thing is Walton's delirium brought on by the chilling cold—a possibility made all the more plausible by Walton's hollow assurances that he is transcribing

[101] Natural history taxonomies are abstract concepts: see Sandra Swart, 'Zombie Zoology: History and Reanimating Extinct Animals', in Susan Nance (ed.), *The Historical Animal* (Syracuse, NY: Syracuse University Press, 2015), 54–71, at 64–5.

Victor's story 'as nearly as possible in his own words' (p. 18) and that he is writing to the very moment:

I am interrupted. What do these sounds portend? It is midnight; the breeze blows fairly, and the watch on deck scarcely stir. Again; there is a sound as of a human voice, but hoarser; it comes from the cabin where the remains of Frankenstein still lie. I must arise, and examine. (p. 167)

There are other documents in the book too: Victor's letters of introduction and much correspondence from his friends and family, as well as his fragmentary logbook detailing the formation of the Being (which the Being himself reads). The text is also rich in quotation and allusion—quoting from, for example, Coleridge's 'Rime of the Ancyent Marinere' and furthermore integrating elements of that work such as the description of the frozen north as well as the over-powering need of characters to tell their stories. This yearning to narrate oneself or textually shape one's own life means that the book is a palimpsest of biographies and autobiographies: it includes three life stories of male characters, plus Safie's history. But these relations of events are not inherently trustworthy: as Walton states at the outset, he is a (failed) poet whose daydreams are becoming 'more fervent and vivid'; and as Victor warns at the end, the Being 'is eloquent and persuasive . . . once his words had even power over my heart' (pp. 7, 160). This in spite of the Being being hampered by having to use Victor's human language whereas he actually needs his own idiolect, an exclusive voice. His fluency cannot be trusted by Victor because to speak true would make the Being (more) human. Victor challenges the sincerity of the Being's speech not in order to question his honesty, but rather—by the extreme tactic of sacrificing his faith in language—to remind Walton that the Being is not human.

Storytellers are inherently untrustworthy, and last in this line of unreliable narrators is Shelley herself. While the book is ostensibly about the origin of life, it is also a creation myth about the origin of stories, and with the veracity—or otherwise—of those tales. If *Frankenstein* is a story about 'the experience of writing *Frankenstein*' it is by extension also Shelley's own covert female memoir about literary composition, a defining personal history in which she gives birth to herself as a novelist.[102]

---

[102] Barbara Johnson, 'My Monster/My Self', *Diacritics*, 12 (1982), 2–10, at 7–8.

There are other media too: lectures, songs and music, sentimental gestures, and looks. Indeed, seeing is everywhere. *Frankenstein* is, according to one critic, 'thick with images of eyes and elaborately described acts of seeing'.[103] From the moment the Being rouses, Victor is transfixed by his eyes. Like Eve in *Paradise Lost* he sees himself in a pool, but unlike the beautifully narcissistic Eve ('What thou seest, | What there thou seest fair creature is thyself, | With thee it came and goes'), the Being is terrified by the all-too clear image ('I was in reality the monster that I am', p. 82)—a monstrosity he sees reflected in the faces of victims.[104] Victor has a sixth sense that he is being watched when the Being spies on him; he fears being in the Being's line of sight, being objectified or 'caught' in his gaze: being perceived by the Being as 'other'.[105]

Capt. Walton, Victor, the Being, and of course the reader are all puzzling out evidence, all investigators and detectives. Indeed, rather than Edgar Allan Poe's character Auguste Dupin (who first appeared in the short story 'The Murders in the Rue Morgue', 1841), the Being should really be recognized as the inaugural literary detective, raking over evidence to discover who or what he might be only to find himself at the heart of a blasphemous crime. Likewise Victor is effectively a cryptographer, ransacking crypts to solve the riddle of life; he is moreover an 'author' (p. 169), the 'author of unalterable evils' (p. 64), and his assembly of sources and body parts can be seen as a form of 'editing'—a term now used in genetic engineering. From a contemporary perspective, then, the novel is concerned with information technology. At the University of Ingolstadt Victor is fixated with gathering 'information', repeating the word several times. For Victor, 'real information' (p. 31) is literally cutting-edge knowledge, secularized by natural science. Thus the Being is a walking information system: a flesh-and-blood example (the first example) of 'Romantic biomedia'.[106]

The Being too collects and sifts knowledge and information. In particular, he values language as a 'godlike science' (p. 80) and rightly

---

[103] Tony E. Jackson, *The Technology of the Novel: Writing and Narrative in British Fiction* (Baltimore: Johns Hopkins University Press, 2009), 70.

[104] Milton, *Paradise Lost*, iv. 467–9.

[105] See Eleanor Salotto, 'Frankenstein and Dis(re)membered Identity'), *Journal of Narrative Technique*, 24 (1994), 190–211, at 195.

[106] Andrew Burkett, 'Mediating Monstrosity: Media, Information, and Mary Shelley's *Frankenstein*', *Studies in Romanticism*, 51 (2012), 579–605, at 586.

equates words with identity and power. Although, unlike Adam, the Being does not name things himself, he is stirringly eloquent, his vocabulary reaped from Milton and Goethe: just as a dissected corpse is 'articulated' so language can be carved up and reassembled. Reading is another critical linguistic activity: whether for Victor, who begins by reading the wrong books (Agrippa, Paracelsus, and Magnus), or the Being, whose discovery of Victor's case notes effectively constitutes his 'birth certificate' (if ironically far from authenticating him this dossier reveals that he is artificial). But the Being does inscribe his sense of selfhood from printed books, and learns to write too—becoming, in effect, 'embodied writing'.[107] The Being even entertains an 'education fantasy' in which he conceives of training the 'unprejudiced' child William 'as my companion and friend' (p. 105)—an experiment that rapidly proves disastrous and results in William becoming his first victim.[108] In fact, the Being is not the only one in the novel to find education problematic: Walton has neglected his education and M. Krempe rebukes Victor over his reading. Even the De Laceys, who successfully teach Safie to speak French, are not able to keep their faith in language when they face the Being, despite his desperately candid conversation with their blind father.

In conversation with old M. De Lacey the Being is shown to be a prime example of artificial intelligence: he clearly interacts as sentient and the Turing test would pose no problem to him, even if he cannot actually pass as human because of his frightful appearance and seesawing principles. This appearance is the result of Victor's manufacture, which has produced an appalling hybrid. But purity and hybridity are themselves slippery concepts. In her 'Cyborg Manifesto', the radical philosopher Donna Haraway has questioned the assumed integrity of the human body and reasons that 'we are all chimeras, theorised and fabricated hybrids of machine and organism; in short, we are cyborgs'.[109] Extreme as this polemic is, it does present an argument that resonates insistently with a Being that is man-made and synthetic. Haraway contends that, like the Being, 'the cyborg has no

[107] Jackson, *Technology of the Novel*, 75–6.

[108] McLane, *Romanticism and the Human Sciences*, 99.

[109] Donna Haraway, 'A Cyborg Manifesto: Science, Technology, and Socialist-Feminism in the Late Twentieth Century', in Neil Badmington (ed.), *Posthumanism* (Houndmills: Palgrave, 2000), 69–84, at 70; see Jay Clayton, 'Frankenstein's Futurity: Replicants and Robots', in Schor (ed.), *Cambridge Companion to Shelley*, 84–99.

origin story in the Western sense' and that what is at stake for human-ity is 'production, reproduction, and imagination'—which of course are core themes of *Frankenstein*.[110] Although the Being does in no way exhibit all of the features of Haraway's postmodern cyborg, the point is that being in part artificial—part-built—does not diminish human identity; rather, it is now inevitable. In that sense, the Being is actually *more* than human in twenty-first-century terms—and, bearing in mind eighteenth- and nineteenth-century tooth transplants and cos-metic surgery, hybridity and body-modification have plainly been part of many cultures for centuries, and may even (if counter-intuitively) be a defining characteristic of the human.

So it is that the Being insistently poses existential questions. Three times (pp. 87, 88) he asks, 'What was I?'

Who was I? What was I? Whence did I come? What was my destination? These questions continually recurred, but I was unable to solve them. (p. 94)

In one case he answers himself with inarticulate groans—an agoniz-ingly cogent response to his predicament. But there are other answers too. One answer is that the Being is *people*, is plural: his name is Legion. As the philosopher Peter Steeves contends, if the Being is 'a new creation, a new kind of individual, brought into being by the conglomeration of parts from various donors—both human and non-human', then Shelley's work looks forward to radical new definitions of the human, encompassing both the extreme hybridity of *Homo sapiens* DNA, 90 per cent of which is shared with animals, and also the proposition that humans are ecosystems consisting of many different species—bacteria in the gut, microscopic parasites, fungi, viruses, and so forth. In this sense, the Being, being explicitly a multifarious amalgam of the non-human, represents (like the cyborg) the 'true nature' of humanity.[111]

The Being's deceptively straightforward questions about existence and being become unsettling through their insistent repetition, and they also suggest that human assumptions regarding their own place in the world may be gravely mistaken. Shelley hints at this in her description of the 'mighty Alps, whose white and shining pyramids

---

[110] Haraway, 'Cyborg Manifesto', 71, 70.
[111] H. Peter Steeves, 'Animal Animal Animal Animal', *CR: The New Centennial Review* 11, *Animals . . . In Theory* (2011), 193–221, at 204, 206.

and domes towered above all, as belonging to another earth, the habitations of another race of beings' (p. 66). These mountains are imagined as an alternative and unearthly environment, comparable to the remote wilds of South America where the Being believes he can lead an independent and sustainable life outside human society. But that is not all. The seemingly cyclopean architecture of the Alps conjures up the possibility that there are other beings on earth, displacing the human from the centre of the novel. Just as Victor fears that the Being and She-Being will generate an incestuous 'race of devils' in the Amazonian depths, so Shelley, having radically questioned and undermined what it is to be human—and given no answer to this eternal riddle—now sidelines the human, defying anthropocentric primacy. *Frankenstein* foreshadows the speculative realist turn in philosophy, 'an antihumanist orientation that challenges universal human supremacy and rethinks the relation of the human to the nonhuman'.[112] Thus at the last the Being is not non-human or even near human, rather, by exposing the inadequacies of the human, it is beyond human, with its own subjectivity and agency. The novel is both an elegy to the waning of the human and at the same time an epitaph to the new flesh, the 'unhuman'.

Afterbirth

Frankenstein is not a static text, but exists in a vital and mutually challenging relationship with criticism and theory, and also crucially with changing human values and social attitudes—it is itself a 'wicked text': edgy, changeable, untrammelled, and resistant to explanation. Indeed the Gothic, for all its supernaturalism and sensationalism, is fundamentally an intense encounter with what it is to be human. *Frankenstein* exemplifies this, and is almost unparalleled in the way that it has become a totemic parable of scientific progress and an omen of the threats that technology poses to humanity.

Within six years of first publication the basic premise of *Frankenstein* was already well known enough for it to be used by the Foreign Secretary George Canning in 1824 to configure the parliamentary debate on slavery:

---

[112] Carl H. Sederholm and Jeffrey Andrew Weinstock (eds.), *The Age of Lovecraft* (Minneapolis: University of Minnesota Press, 2016), 4.

In dealing with the negro, Sir, we must remember that we are dealing with a being possessing the form and strength of a man, but the intellect only of a child. To turn him loose in the manhood of his physical strength, in the maturity of his physical passions, but in the infancy of his uninstructed reason, would be to raise up a creature resembling the splendid fiction of a recent romance; the hero of which constructs a human form, with all the corporeal capabilities of man, and with the thews and sinews of a giant; but being unable to impart to the work of his hands a perception of right and wrong, he finds too late that he has only created a more than mortal power of doing mischief, and himself recoils from the monster which he has made.

Such would be the effect of a sudden emancipation, before the negro was prepared for the enjoyment of a well-regulated liberty.[113]

It subsequently featured in political cartoons in *Punch* magazine on the Crimean War ('The Russian Frankenstein and his Monster', 1854), working-class protests ('The Brummagem [Birmingham] Frankenstein', 1866), and Irish Home Rule and the Phoenix Park Murders ('The Irish Frankenstein', 1882).[114] It was a major hit on the nineteenth-century stage and inspired dozens of twentieth-century films, including James Whale's epoch-making productions *Frankenstein* (1931) and *Bride of Frankenstein* (1935). Alongside Bram Stoker's *Dracula* (1897) and the rage for vampires, *Frankenstein* set the agenda for the popular horror genre and its fascination with, among many other things, the body and monstrosity, sex and gender, outsiders and otherness, dreams and the supernatural, contagion, social oppression and rebellion, death and killing, and technophobia—all of which feature in the original novel. More recently, the book has engendered a lexicon of popular scientific 'frankenfear' terminology in concepts such as 'frankenstein ecosystems', genetically modified 'frankenfoods', and even cross-bred 'frankencats'.[115]

The Being himself has escaped the pages of the text to become a multifaceted figure, a warning from the past on abuse of power in

[113] *Parliamentary Debates* (series 4), vol. x, col. 1103 (16 Mar. 1824); slavery is discussed by Marie Mulvey Roberts, *Dangerous Bodies: Historicizing the Gothic Corporeal* (Manchester: Manchester University Press, 2016), 52–91.

[114] See Baldick, *In Frankenstein's Shadow*, 95, 85, 90. 'Frankenstein' is cited by *OED* as both a noun (1838) and a verb (1827).

[115] See *New Scientist* (20 Feb. 1999), 4–5; Luiz G. R. Oliveira-Santos and Fernando A. S. Fernandez, 'Pleistocene Rewilding, Frankenstein Ecosystems, and an Alternative Conservation Agenda', *Conservation Biology*, 24 (2010), 4–5; Friedman and Kavey, *Monstrous Progeny*, *passim*, esp. 64; 'Ligers and Tigons: Activists Aim to Outlaw "Inhumane" Breeding of Frankencats', *Guardian* online (19 May 2017).

the future. It is a commonplace to describe *Frankenstein* as the first science-fiction novel. Shelley herself put it in the context of ghost stories although it contains no ghosts (except in Victor's imaginings) or even any supernatural effects, explained or otherwise, and the central character is a modern natural scientist rather than a medieval sorcerer. 'Science fiction', like the 'Gothic', is of course a retrospective classification of genre, and at the time the novel was regarded as a 'romance', meaning a modern fiction with fantastical elements. Yet *Frankenstein* is science fiction in that the plot is driven by a technical hypothesis based on speculative biology; this is proven by experimental method and leads in turn to a consistent logic of cause and effect. *Frankenstein* is also Gothic insofar as it bares (or autopsies) the grisly workings of philosophy and identity politics to demonstrate how the progressive discourse of human rights has depended on ruthless distinctions between the human and non-human, and how these divisions have in turn normalized attitudes to such things as social oppression and animal experimentation; the ghastliness of these exposures is expressed in supernatural language. So although the devils and daemons in the novel may be figures of speech, they are pervasive, darkly testifying to Victor's way of making sense of the dreadful, baffling, and murderous world in which, through his own folly, through his dream coming true, he finds himself. And if the novel bears an unspeakable secret, it is this Gothic nightmare later divulged by Mary Shelley in her essay 'On Ghosts' (1824): that 'the earth is a tomb, the gaudy sky a vault, we but walking corpses'.[116] The novel ends with the Being disappearing into the night to build his funeral pyre, to deliver himself from life. *Frankenstein* is a compelling reminder that we the readers, like Victor and the Being, like Mary and Percy Shelley, are merely the passing dead: 'Time to die.'[117]

[116] 'Σς' [i.e. Mary Shelley], 'On Ghosts', *London Magazine*, 9 (1824), 253–6, at 254.
[117] Last words spoken by the replicant Roy Batty in Ridley Scott's film *Blade Runner* (1982), a film deeply indebted to Mary Shelley's *Frankenstein*.

NOTE ON THE TEXT

FRANKENSTEIN was published on 1 January 1818 in a standard print run of 500 copies. A second edition followed five years later, and Shelley subsequently substantially revised the text for a new third edition in 1831. Until the end of the twentieth century the 1831 text was the preferred version, but this orthodoxy was overturned by three major editions in the 1990s, all of which were based on the original 1818 *Frankenstein*. The present edition also favours 1818 over both 1831 and other possible versions. The reasons for doing so are best explained by outlining the composition and editorial history of the book.

The familiar tale that *Frankenstein* was inspired by a morbid challenge to write a ghost story around 16–17 June 1816 is described in the Introduction (pp. xvii–xviii; see also Appendix A, pp. 173–7). Although her journals for 14 May 1815 to 20 July 1816 are missing, the records we do have show that Shelley was working on her novel consistently from at least July 1816 to April 1817, and that from the outset it involved Percy Shelley as well. From 29 July 1816 and throughout August, Shelley wrote on most days. On 12 August 1816, for instance, she recorded 'Write my story', and on the twenty-first of the same month 'Shelley [i.e. Percy] & I talk about my story . . . Shelley reads Milton' (which he did for the next three days).[1] They travelled through most of September, but come October and November she was again writing (or 'working') nearly every day, sometimes while Percy read aloud to inspire her—*Castle Rackrent*, *Gulliver*, *Pamela*, and *Paradise Lost* across four evenings: on 17 November 1816, for instance, 'he reads Paradise Lost—aloud in the evening—I work'.[2] She wrote to Percy from Bath on 5 December 1816 (he was looking for a house for them in Marlow, Buckinghamshire): 'I have . . . finished the 4 Chap. of Frankenstein which is a very long one & I think you would like it.'[3]

Shelley appears to have finished the first full draft by 10 April 1817, the next week 'Correct[ed] F[rankenstein].' every day, and from 18

---

[1] *The Journals of Mary Shelley: 1814–1844*, 2 vols. ed. Paula R. Feldman and Diana Scott-Kilvert (Oxford: Clarendon Press, 1987), i. 124, 130.

[2] *Journals of Shelley*, ed. Feldman and Scott-Kilvert, i. 146.

[3] *The Letters of Mary Wollstonecraft Shelley*, ed. Betty T. Bennett, 3 vols. (Baltimore: Johns Hopkins University Press, 1980–8), i. 22.

April to 13 May transcribed (and doubtless revised) the entire text.[4] The day after that Percy spent further time on the book: 'S[helley]. . . . corrects F. write Preface—Finis.'[5] It was immediately sent to the publisher John Murray, who despite his initial enthusiasm decided not to take it.[6] Percy then sent it to Charles Ollier and evidently at least one other publisher, before trying Lackington, Allen & Co., who specialized in magic and the supernatural, on 22 August.[7] After some bargaining at the beginning of September Percy brokered a deal and began making arrangements for receiving proofs and advertising the new novel.[8] Percy's letters reveal that he steered the book through production and was keen to see it before the public, enquiring on 23 December 'On what day do you propose to publish it?'[9] The Shelleys received their copies on 31 December, Mary inscrutably recording the event in her journal in the last entry for 1817: 'Fran^{tein} comes'.[10] The book was published a day later and by 2 January Percy was already sending out copies.[11] The first edition of *Frankenstein* outsold all the works of Percy Shelley put together, and made more money than he would make in his lifetime.[12] But without Percy the book may never have found a publisher.

Charles E. Robinson, *Frankenstein*'s most assiduous editor, argues that there were eleven lifetime renderings of the novel, from a lost original 'ur-text' through Shelley's manuscript, Percy Shelley's revisions, fair copy, proofs (corrected by Percy), revises, and the first edition itself. This was followed by Shelley's annotations to a copy of the first edition for a projected second edition (but not followed), second edition proofs (corrected by Godwin), and the fully revised edition of

[4] *Journals of Shelley*, ed. Feldman and Scott-Kilvert, i. 166, 168–9.

[5] *Journals of Shelley*, ed. Feldman and Scott-Kilvert, i. 169.

[6] *Journals of Shelley*, ed. Feldman and Scott-Kilvert, i. 171, 174.

[7] *The Letters of Percy Bysshe Shelley*, ed. Frederick L. Jones, 2 vols. (Oxford: Clarendon Press, 1964), i. 549; i. 551, 553.

[8] *Journals of Shelley*, ed. Feldman and Scott-Kilvert, i. 180.

[9] *Letters of Percy Bysshe Shelley*, i. 556, 558, 564, 565, 572, 583, 585; see also William St Clair, *The Godwins and the Shelleys: The Biography of a Family* (London: Faber and Faber, 1989), 554 n. 25.

[10] *Journals of Shelley*, ed. Feldman and Scott-Kilvert, i. 189.

[11] Charles E. Robinson, '*Frankenstein*: Its Composition and Publication', in Andrew Smith (ed.), *The Cambridge Companion to* Frankenstein (Cambridge: Cambridge University Press, 2016), 13–25, at 13; *Letters of Percy Bysshe Shelley*, i. 590.

[12] William St Clair, *The Reading Nation in the Romantic Period* (Cambridge: Cambridge University Press, 2004), 360.

1831.[13] Several of these states no longer exist (such as proofs and revises), though it is not unreasonable to infer that they did. The 1831 third-edition text was reprinted throughout the nineteenth and twentieth centuries, gradually becoming a composite that included elements of the 1818 version. However, in 1982 James Rieger's edition of the 1818 text (first published in 1974) was republished by the University of Chicago Press and drew serious attention to the 1818 text. This was followed by Marilyn Butler's edition in 1993, republished by Oxford World's Classics a year later, in which she made a strong case for favouring the 1818 text over that of 1831 (notably that of her Oxford stablemate M. K. Joseph's edition of 1969, by then an old warhorse); Butler also helpfully provided an appendix giving the substantive changes made in 1831. Also in 1994 D. L. Macdonald and Kathleen Scherf edited the 1818 text for Broadview Press, likewise listing the 1831 variants and relegating them to an appendix. Two years later in 1996, J. Paul Hunter's Norton edition similarly reprinted the 1818 text, and in the same year Robinson edited *The Frankenstein Notebooks* in two volumes. Subsequently editions have appeared that reproduce both 1818 and 1831, such as *The Annotated Frankenstein* (2012) by Susan J. Wolfson and Ronald L. Levao. Since the 1990s, with the 1818 *Frankenstein* readily available, there has been little appetite to return to the 1831 revision, and there are convincing critiques of the inferiority of the 1831 text—which, for example, introduces religious themes inconsistent with the godless mood of the novel.[14] But bearing in mind this intricate editorial history and engagement with other texts and technologies, *Frankenstein* has inevitably proved appealing to digital treatments, from Stuart Curran's heavily annotated hypertext for *Romantic Circles Electronic Editions* (2009) and the immersive and interactive *FrankenMOO* project.[15]

Robinson's scholarship next led to his edition of *The Original Frankenstein* in 2008, which gave two texts of the novel: not the 1818 and 1831 versions, but the earliest manuscript draft, written by Shelley and revised by Percy Shelley, and a restoration of Shelley's

---

[13] Robinson, '*Frankenstein*: Its Composition and Publication', 15; see E. B. Murray, 'Changes in the 1823 Edition of *Frankenstein*', *The Library*, 6th ser., 3 (1981), 320–7.

[14] See e.g. Peter J. Capuano, *Changing Hands: Industry, Evolution, and the Reconfiguration of the Victorian Body* (Ann Arbor: University of Michigan Press, 2015), 37–41. www.sonstroem.com/frankmoo/

[15] http://homes.lmc.gatech.edu/~broglio/rc/frankenstein/: see Andrew Burkett, 'Mediating Monstrosity: Media, Information, and Mary Shelley's *Frankenstein*', *Studies in Romanticism* 51/4 (2012), 579–605, at 579–81.

draft that strips Percy Shelley's changes from the text. The suggestion is that Mary Shelley's own version, without the meddling hand of her husband, is the more authentic text. Percy Shelley's revisions certainly add elements of artifice, mannered archaism, and restraint to a story that is otherwise impetuous and turbulent, and Anne Mellor in particular has championed the first (if incomplete) Shelley draft, noting that among Percy's changes are revising colloquialisms to a more formal diction, substituting words derived from Anglo-Saxon to those with a Latin heritage, introducing atheistic elements, and softening the depiction of Victor while making the Being more monstrous.[16]

Percy was responsible for about 4,000 of the first draft's 72,000 words (5½ per cent of the text), and clearly had an impact on the tone of the novel.[17] Yet should those adjustments be disregarded? Like most authors today dealing with editors, Shelley herself witnessed and clearly endorsed these amendments. Yet in reviving an early, cancelled draft editors and critics risk the accusation that they are rewriting the novel to conform to their own predilections. Tellingly, the plot of the novel itself is effectively co-produced—a mutual and collaborative editing together of disparate texts—and so to inscribe in *Frankenstein* the figure of Mary Shelley as a singularly creative Romantic artist actually undermines the status of the work as a cooperative enterprise. Percy Shelley did not rewrite *Frankenstein* (and was certainly not the novel's co-author); he simply acted as Shelley's hands-on line-editor, production assistant, and publicist. The text printed in 1818 accordingly represents Shelley's intentions when the book was first published, and is therefore the basis of the present edition. Following Butler's Oxford edition (reissued in 1998 and 2008) the substantive changes made in the third edition of 1831 are included in Appendix B.

The present edition has been re-edited from the 1818 edition and several inaccuracies in Butler's edition have been emended. Shelley's use of the apostrophe has been retained, as have her minor inconsistencies in spelling (for example, 'avelânche'/'avelanche', and later 'avalanche': pp. 67, 68, 117). Obvious errors have been silently corrected, such as 'his native country' for 'her native country' (p. 20); a rogue

---

[16] Anne K. Mellor, 'Choosing a Text of *Frankenstein* to Teach', in Stephen C. Behrendt (ed.), *Approaches to Teaching Shelley's* Frankenstein (New York: Modern Language Association of America), 31–7.

[17] The MS of Frankenstein has been digitized by the Shelley-Godwin Archive and is available online at shelleygodwinarchive.org/contents/frankenstein. A facsimile of the MS was published in 2018 by SP Books (Cambremer: Éditions des Saints Pères).

quotation mark on p. 24; 'Ingoldstadt' (p. 73); a missing full stop (p. 118); and so forth. A misprint for 'obliged' (p. 72) is present in the Codrington copy (LR.4.e.44–46; vol. 2, p. 32) but is rectified in the Bodleian copy (Arch. AA e.167), indicating that stop-press corrections were made during printing.

Like all editors, I owe a debt to those who have preceded me, and have made grateful use of their scholarship and critical insights. The introductions and notes to all the editions mentioned here and in the Select Bibliography have contributed to my understanding of the novel.

SELECT BIBLIOGRAPHY

Selected Editions of Frankenstein

Frankenstein; or, The Modern Prometheus, 3 vols. (London: Lackington, Hughes, Harding, Mavor, & Jones, 1818).

Frankenstein; or, The Modern Prometheus (London: Henry Colburn and Richard Bentley, 1831).

Butler, Marilyn (ed.), *Frankenstein or The Modern Prometheus: The 1818 Text* (London: William Pickering, 1993; repr. Oxford: Oxford University Press, 1994).

Curran, Stuart (ed.), *Frankenstein, Romantic Circles Electronic Editions* (online, hosted by Romantic Circles, 2009: https://romantic-circles.org/editions/frankenstein).

Hindle, Maurice (ed.), *Frankenstein* (London: Penguin, 2003).

Hunter, J. Paul (ed.), *Frankenstein; or, The Modern Prometheus* (2nd edn., London and New York: W. W. Norton & Company, 2012).

Joseph, M. K. (ed.), *Frankenstein* (Oxford: Oxford University Press, 1969).

Macdonald, D. L., and Scherf, Kathleen (eds.), *Frankenstein; or, The Modern Prometheus* (Ontario: Broadview, 1994).

Rieger, James (ed.), *Frankenstein or The Modern Prometheus: The 1818 Text (with Variant Readings, an Introduction, and Notes)* (Chicago: University of Chicago Press, 1982) (derives from earlier 1974 edition).

Robinson, Charles E. (ed.), *The Frankenstein Notebooks: A Facsimile Edition of Mary Shelley's Manuscript Novel, 1816–1817 (with Alterations in the Hand of Percy Bysshe Shelley) as it survives in Draft and Fair Copy Deposited by Lord Abinger in the Bodleian Library, Oxford (Dep. c. 477/1 and Dep c. 534/1–2)*, 2 vols. (New York: Garland, 1996).

Robinson, Charles E. (ed.), *Frankenstein or The Modern Prometheus: The Original Two-Volume Novel of 1816–1817 from the Bodleian Library Manuscripts* (Oxford: Bodleian Library, 2008).

Wolfson, Susan J. (ed.), *Mary Wollstonecraft Shelley's Frankenstein; or, The Modern Prometheus* (New York: Longman, 2003) (1818 text).

Wolfson, Susan J., and Levao, Ronaldo L. (eds.), *The Annotated Frankenstein* (Cambridge, Mass.: Belknap Press, 2012).

Other Works Written or Edited by Mary Shelley in Chronological Order

Mounseer Nongtongpaw; or, The Discoveries of John Bull in a Trip to Paris (London: M. J. Godwin & Co., 1808).

[Attrib. Percy Bysshe Shelley,] *History of a Six Weeks' Tour through a Part of France, Switzerland, Germany, and Holland: With Letters Descriptive of a Sail round the Lake of Geneva and of the Glaciers of Chamouni* (London: T. Hookham, Jun., and C. and J. Ollier, 1817).

Valperga; or, The Life and Adventures of Castruccio, Prince of Lucca, 3 vols. (London: G. and W. B. Whittaker, 1823).

[Ed.,] *Posthumous Poems of Percy Bysshe Shelley* (London: John and Henry L. Hunt, 1824).

The Last Man, 3 vols. (London: Henry Colburn, 1826).

The Fortunes of Perkin Warbeck, A Romance, 3 vols. (London: Henry Colburn and Richard Bentley, 1830).

[Ed., with Thomas Moore; attrib. to Moore,] *Letters and Journals of Lord Byron: With Notices of His Life*, 2 vols. (London: John Murray, 1830).

'Proserpine: A Mythological Drama, in Two Acts', in *The Winter's Wreath for 1832* (London: Whittaker, Treacher, and Arnot [1831]), 1–20.

Lodore, 3 vols. (London: Richard Bentley, 1835).

[With James Montgomery and Sir David Brewster,] *Cabinet of Biography: Lives of the Most Eminent Literary and Scientific Men of Italy, Spain and Portugal*, 3 vols. (vols. 86–8 of *Cabinet Cyclopædia*, ed. Revd Dionysius Lardner) (London: Longman, Rees, Orme, Brown, Green, & Longman; and John Taylor, 1835–7).

Falkner: A Novel, 3 vols. (London: Saunders and Otley, 1837).

Lives of the Most Eminent Literary and Scientific Men of France, 2 vols. (vols. 102–3 of *Cabinet Cyclopædia*, ed. Lardner) (London: Longman, Orme, Brown, Green, & Longman; and John Taylor, 1838–9).

Ed., *Poetical Works of Percy Bysshe Shelley*, 4 vols. (London: Edward Moxon, 1839).

Ed., *The Poetical Works of Percy Bysshe Shelley* (London: Edward Moxon, 1840).

Ed. [attrib. to Percy Bysshe Shelley], *Essays, Letters from Abroad, Translations and Fragments*, 2 vols. (London: Edward Moxon, 1840).

Rambles in Germany and Italy, in 1840, 1842, and 1843, 2 vols. (London: Edward Moxon, 1844).

Proserpine & Midas: Two Unpublished Mythological Dramas, ed. André Koszul (London: Humphrey Milford, 1922).

Mathilda, ed. Elizabeth Nitchie (Chapel Hill, NC: University of North Carolina Press, 1959).

Mary Shelley: Collected Tales and Stories, with Original Engravings, ed. Charles E. Robinson (Baltimore: Johns Hopkins University Press, 1976).

Life and Background

Bennett, Betty T. (ed.), *Letters of Mary Wollstonecraft Shelley*, 3 vols. (Baltimore: Johns Hopkins University Press, 1980, 1983, 1988).

Bennett, Betty T., and Robinson, Charles E. (eds.), *The Mary Shelley Reader* (New York and Oxford: Oxford University Press, 1990).

Feldman, Paula R., and Scott-Kilvert, Diana, *The Journals of Mary Shelley: 1814–1844*, 2 vols. (Oxford: Clarendon Press, 1987).

Gittings, Robert, and Manton, Jo, *Claire Clairmont and the Shelleys* (Oxford and New York: Oxford University Press, 1992).

Lawson, Shanon, *The Mary Shelley Chronology & Resource Site* (online, hosted by Romantic Circles, https://romantic-circles.org/reference/chronologies/mschronology).

St Clair, William, *The Godwins and the Shelleys: The Biography of a Family* (London: Faber and Faber, 1989).

St Clair, William, *The Reading Nation in the Romantic Period* (Cambridge: Cambridge University Press, 2004).

Seymour, Miranda, *Mary Shelley* (London: Faber and Faber, 2000).

Shelley, Percy Bysshe, *The Letters of Percy Bysshe Shelley*, ed. Frederick L. Jones, 2 vols. (Oxford: Clarendon Press, 1964).

General Studies and Collections of Critical Essays

Bann, Stephen (ed.), *Frankenstein, Creation and Monstrosity* (London: Reaktion Books, 1994).

Fisch, Audrey A., *Frankenstein* (Hastings: Helm, 2009).

Groom, Nick, *The Gothic: A Very Short Introduction* (Oxford: Oxford University Press, 2012).

Horton, Robert, *Frankenstein* (New York: University of Columbia Press, 2014).

Knoppers, Laura Lunger, and Landes, Joan B. (eds.), *Monstrous Bodies/ Political Monstrosities in Early Modern Europe* (Ithaca, NY: Cornell University Press, 2004).

Levine, George, and Knoepflmacher, U. C. (eds.), *The Endurance of* Frankenstein: *Essays on Mary Shelley's Novel* (Berkeley and Los Angeles: University of California Press, 1979).

Morton, Timothy (ed.), *A Routledge Literary Sourcebook on Mary Shelley's* Frankenstein (London and New York: Routledge, 2002).

Smith, Andrew (ed.), *The Cambridge Companion to* Frankenstein (Cambridge: Cambridge University Press, 2016).

Townshend, Dale (ed.), *Terror and Wonder: The Gothic Imagination* (London: British Library, 2014).

Townshend, Dale, and Wright, Angela (eds.), *Romantic Gothic: An Edinburgh Companion* (Edinburgh: Edinburgh University Press, 2016).

Literary Criticism

Bate, Jonathan, *Song of the Earth* (London: Picador, 2000).

Braudy, Leo, *Haunted: On Ghosts, Witches, Vampires, Zombies, and Other*

Monsters of the Natural and Supernatural Worlds (New Haven: Yale University Press, 2016).

Brooks, Peter, *Body Work: Objects of Desire in Modern Narrative* (Cambridge, MA: Harvard University Press, 1993).

Capuano, Peter J., *Changing Hands: Industry, Evolution, and the Reconfiguration of the Victorian Body* (Ann Arbor: University of Michigan Press, 2015).

Christie, William, *The Two Romanticisms and Other Essays: Mystery and Interpretation in Romantic Literature* (Sydney: Sydney University Press, 2016).

Clemit, Pamela, *The Godwinian Novel: The Radical Fictions of Godwin, Brockden Brown, Mary Shelley* (Oxford: Oxford University Press, 1993).

DeLamotte, Eugenia, *The Perils of the Night: A Feminist Study of Nineteenth-Century Gothic* (Oxford: Oxford University Press, 1990).

Feder, Helena, *Ecocriticism and the Idea of Culture: Biology and the Bildungsroman* (London and New York: Routledge, 2016).

Gilbert, Sandra, and Gubar, Susan, *The Madwoman in the Attic: The Woman Writer and the Nineteenth-Century Literary Imagination* (2nd edn., New Haven: Yale University Press, 2000).

Hoeveler, Diane Long, *Gothic Feminism: The Professionalization of Gender from Charlotte Smith to the Brontës* (Liverpool: Liverpool University Press, 1998).

Khalip, Jacques, and Pyle, Forest (eds.), *Constellations of a Contemporary Romanticism* (New York: Fordham University Press, 2016).

McLane, Maureen, *Romanticism and the Human Sciences: Poetry, Population, and the Discourse of Species* (Cambridge: Cambridge University Press, 2000).

Mellor, Anne K., *Romanticism & Gender* (New York and London: Routledge, 1993).

Moers, Ellen, *Literary Women* (New York: Doubleday, 1976).

Moretti, Franco, *Signs Taken for Wonders: Essays in the Sociology of Literary Forms*, trans. Susan Fischer, David Forgacs, and David Miller (London: NLB, 1983).

Mulvey-Roberts, Marie, *Dangerous Bodies: Historicising the Gothic Corporeal* (Manchester: Manchester University Press, 2016).

Medicine and Science

Aldiss, Brian W., with Wingrove, David, *Trillion Year Spree: The History of Science Fiction* (New York: Atheneum, 1986).

Desmond, Adrian, *The Politics of Evolution: Morphology, Medicine, and Reform in Radical London* (Chicago: University of Chicago Press, 1989).

Easlee, Brian, *Fathering the Unthinkable: Masculinity, Science, and the Nuclear Arms Race* (London: Pluto Press, 1983).

Fulford, Tim (ed.), *Romanticism and Science, 1773–1833*, 5 vols. (London and New York: Routledge, 2002).

Golinski, Jan, *Science as Public Culture: Chemistry and Enlightenment in Britain, 1760–1820* (Cambridge: Cambridge University Press, 1992).

Holmes, Richard, *The Age of Wonder: How the Romantic Generation Discovered the Beauty and Terror of Science* (London: HarperPress, 2008).

Marshall, Tim, *Murdering to Dissect: Grave-Robbing, Frankenstein and the Anatomy of Literature* (Manchester: Manchester University Press, 1995).

Merchant, Carolyn, *The Death of Nature: Women, Ecology and the Scientific Revolution* (San Francisco: Harper Row, 1980).

Pamboukian, Sylvia A., *Doctoring the Novel: Medicine and Quackery from Shelley to Doyle* (Athens, OH: Ohio University Press, 2012).

Richardson, Ruth, *Death, Dissection and the Destitute: The Politics of the Corpse in Pre-Victorian Britain* (2nd edn., London: Phoenix Press, 2001).

Ruston, Sharon, *Creating Romanticism: Case Studies in the Literature, Science and Medicine of the 1790s* (Houndmills: Palgrave Macmillan, 2013).

Ruston, Sharon, *Shelley and Vitality* (Houndmills: Palgrave Macmillan, 2005).

Popular Culture and Films

Baldick, Chris, *In Frankenstein's Shadow: Myth, Monstrosity, and Nineteenth-Century Writing* (Oxford: Clarendon Press, 1987).

Beville, Maria, *The Unnameable Monster in Literature and Film* (New York and London: Routledge, 2014).

Frayling, Christopher, *Frankenstein: The First Two Hundred Years* (London: Reel Art Press, 2017).

Friedman, Lester D., and Kavey, Allison B., *Monstrous Progeny: A History of the Frankenstein Narratives* (New Brunswick, NJ: Rutgers University Press, 2016).

Haining, Peter (ed.), *The Frankenstein Collection* (London: Artus Books, 1994).

Hitchcock, Susan Tyler, *Frankenstein: A Cultural History* (New York and London: W. W. Norton & Company, 2007).

Horton, Robert, *Frankenstein* (New York: University of Columbia Press, 2014).

Murray, Robin L., and Heumann, Joseph K., *Monstrous Nature: Environment and Horror on the Big Screen* (Lincoln, NE: University of Nebraska Press, 2016).

Rigby, Jonathan, *English Gothic: A Century of Horror Cinema* (3rd edn., London: Reynolds & Hearn, 2004).

Warner, Marina, *Managing Monsters: Six Myths of Our Time, The 1994 Reith Lectures* (London: Vintage, 1994).

Young, Elizabeth, *Black Frankenstein: The Making of an American Metaphor* (New York: New York University Press, 2008).

Horror

Asma, Stephen T., *On Monsters: An Unnatural History of Our Worst Fears* (Oxford: Oxford University Press, 2009).

Botting, Fred, *Making Monstrous: Frankenstein, Criticism, Theory* (Manchester: Manchester University Press, 1991).

Carroll, Noël, *The Philosophy of Horror or Paradoxes of the Heart* (New York: Routledge, 1990).

Cohen, Jeffrey Jerome (ed.), *Monster Theory: Reading Culture* (Minneapolis and London: University of Minnesota Press, 1996).

Fahy, Thomas (ed.), *The Philosophy of Horror* (Lexington, KY: University Press of Kentucky, 2010).

Fernie, Ewan, *The Demonic: Literature and Experience* (London and New York: Routledge, 2013).

Grunenberg, Christoph (ed.), *Gothic: Transmutations of Horror in Late Twentieth Century Art* (Boston: Institute of Contemporary Art; Cambridge, MA, and London: MIT Press, 1997).

Halberstam, Judith, *Skin Shows: Gothic Horror and the Technology of Monsters* (Durham, NC: Duke University Press, 1996).

Hills, Matt, *The Pleasures of Horror* (London and New York: Continuum, 2005).

McGinn, Colin, *Ethics, Evil, and Fiction* (Oxford: Oxford University Press, 1997).

Articles and Chapters

Cottom, Daniel, '*Frankenstein* and the Monster of Representation', *Substance*, 28 (1980), 60–71.

Crimmins, Jonathan, 'Mediation's Sleight of Hand: The Two Vectors of the Gothic in Mary Shelley's *Frankenstein*', *Studies in Romanticism*, 52 (2013), 561–83.

Hammond, Kim, 'Monsters of Modernity: *Frankenstein* and Modern Environmentalism', *cultural geographies*, 11 (2004), 181–98.

Hindle, Maurice, 'Vital Matters: Mary Shelley's *Frankenstein* and Romantic Science', *Critical Survey*, 2 (1990), 29–35.

Jacobus, Mary, 'Is There a Woman in this Text?', *New Literary History*, 14 (1982), 117–61.

Johnson, Barbara, 'My Monster/My Self', *Diacritics*, 12 (1982), 2–10.

Latour, Bruno, 'Love Your Monsters', in M. Shellenberger and T. Nordhaus (eds.), *Love Your Monsters: Postenvironmentalism and the Anthropocene* (Oakland, CA: Breakthrough Institute, 2011), 17–25.

Spivak, Gayatri Chakravorty, 'Three Women's Texts and a Critique of Imperialism', *Critical Inquiry*, 12 (1985), 243–61.

Further Reading in Oxford World's Classics

Godwin, William, *Caleb Williams*, ed. Pamela Clemit (Oxford: Oxford University Press, 2009).

Lewis, Matthew, *The Monk*, ed. Nick Groom (Oxford: Oxford University Press, 2016).

Shelley, Mary, *The Last Man*, ed. Morton Paley (Oxford: Oxford University Press, 2008).

Polidori, John, *The Vampyre, and Other Tales of the Macabre*, ed. Robert Morrison and Chris Baldick (Oxford: Oxford University Press, 2008).

Wollstonecraft, Mary, *A Vindication of the Rights of Men; A Vindication of the Rights of Woman; An Historical and Moral View of the French Revolution*, ed. Janet Todd (Oxford: Oxford University Press, 2008).

A CHRONOLOGY OF MARY SHELLEY

Life	Historical and Cultural Background
	Henry Boyd translates Dante Alighieri's *Divine Comedy*; Humphry Davy, 'Discourse Introductory to Lectures on Chemistry'; Walter Scott (ed.), *Minstrelsy of the Scottish Border*.
1803 (28 Mar.) William Godwin born to Mary Jane and William Godwin.	Hostilities break out again between UK and the French Republic; acquisition of the Elgin Marbles. Erasmus Darwin, *The Temple of Nature*.
1804	Napoleon proclaimed emperor; a locomotive designed by Richard Trevithick makes the first steam-powered journey. Blake begins *Jerusalem: The Emanation of the Giant Albion*, completed 1820; Edgeworth, *Popular Tales*.
1805 M. J. Godwin & Co. Juvenile Library opens at 4 Skinner Street, Holborn in London.	Nelson defeats a combined French and Spanish fleet at the Battle of Trafalgar, where he is fatally wounded; Napoleonic forces defeat a combined Austrian and Russian army at Austerlitz. Henry Cary translates Dante's *Inferno*; Scott, *The Lay of the Last Minstrel*.
1806	France blockades Continental ports against Britain; first steam-driven textile mill in Manchester. Charlotte Dacre, *Zofloya*; Edgeworth, *Leonora*.
1807 Godwin and his family move to 4 Skinner Street, Holborn.	Abolition of the slave trade in the British Empire. Thomas Bowdler, *The Family Shakespeare*; Charles and Mary Lamb, *Tales from Shakespeare*; Thomas Moore, *Irish Melodies*; Thomas Paine, *The Age of Reason*; Wordsworth, *Poems in Two Volumes*.
1808 MWS contributes to the poem *Mounseer Nongtongpaw; or, The Discoveries of John Bull in a Trip to Paris* published by M. J. Godwin & Co.	Peninsular War begins. Johann Wolfgang von Goethe, *Faust*, 1st part (2nd part 1832); Scott, *Marmion*.
1809	Battle of Corunna and death of General Sir John Moore. Byron, *English Bards and Scottish Reviewers*; Goethe, *Elective Affinities*.

Life	*Historical and Cultural Background*
1810	London riots. Scott, *The Lady of the Lake*; Percy Bysshe Shelley, *Zastrozzi*; Southey, *The Curse of Kehama*.
1811 Attends a school for the daughters of Dissenters in Ramsgate, run by Miss Caroline Petman.	George III declared insane and his son George, Prince of Wales, becomes regent; Luddites begin breaking machines in the North and Midlands. Austen, *Sense and Sensibility*; Percy Shelley, *St Irvyne; or, The Rosicrucian* and *The Necessity of Atheism*.
1812 Writes lecture 'The Influence of Governments on the Character of a People'; (7 June) sent to Scotland to stay with William Baxter and his family in Dundee and forges close friendship with Baxter's youngest daughter, Isabel; (10 Nov.) visits London with another of Baxter's daughters Christina ('Christy'); (11 Nov.) meets Percy Bysshe Shelley and his wife Harriet when they dine with the Godwins.	Byron defends Luddites in the House of Lords, machine-breaking continues; War of 1812 breaks out between USA, Canada, and UK (concludes in 1815); Napoleonic forces retreat from Moscow; Prime Minister Spencer Perceval assassinated; Viscount Castlereagh made Foreign Secretary. Byron, *Childe Harold's Pilgrimage* (cantos i–ii); Cary translates Dante's *Purgatorio* and *Paradiso*; Edgeworth, *The Absentee*; Brothers Grimm, *Grimms' Fairy Tales*, i; Charles Maturin, *The Milesian Chief*.
1813 (3 June) returns to Dundee with Christy Baxter.	Leigh Hunt imprisoned for libelling the Prince Regent; Southey appointed Poet Laureate. Austen, *Pride and Prejudice*; Byron, *The Giaour*; Percy Shelley, *Queen Mab*; Southey, *Life of Nelson*.
1814 (30 Mar.) returns to Skinner Street; (May) encounters Percy Shelley again, after which they regularly meet at her mother's graveside; (28 July) elopes at dawn to France with Percy Shelley, accompanied by Claire Clairmont, leading to her estrangement from Godwin for two and a half	Napoleon abdicates and is exiled to Elba; First Treaty of Paris restores France to 1792 borders; Congress of Vienna commences to re-establish European balance of power. Austen, *Mansfield Park*; Byron, *The Corsair*; Scott, *Waverley*; Southey, *Roderick, The Last of the Goths*; Wordsworth, *The Excursion*.

Life	*Historical and Cultural Background*
years; (July–Aug.) travels through France, Switzerland, Germany, and Holland; (3 Sept.) returns to London; (27 Sept.) moves to St Pancras with Percy Shelley and Clairmont; (23 Oct.–9 Nov.) Percy flees from creditors and lives apart from MWS; (30 Nov.) Harriet Shelley gives birth to a son, Charles.	
1815 (Jan.) death of Sir Bysshe, Percy Shelley's grandfather, leaving him with an annual income of £1,000; (22 Feb.) MWS gives birth prematurely to a daughter, Clara; (6 Mar.) Clara dies; (June–July) visits Devon with Percy; (Aug.) settles with Percy at Bishops Gate, Windsor; (Sept.) visits Oxford, travelling there by river.	Ratification of Treaty of Ghent (1814) ends War of 1812; Napoleon's 'Hundred Days' rule, ending in defeat by Wellington and Blücher at the Battle of Waterloo; restoration of Louis XVIII; Napoleon exiled to St Helena. Austen, *Emma* (dated 1816); Byron, *Hebrew Melodies*; Brothers Grimm, *Grimms' Fairy Tales*, ii; E. T. A. Hoffman, *The Devil's Elixir*; Scott, *Guy Mannering*.
1816 (24 Jan.) gives birth to a son, William; (3 May) leaves England with William and Percy, accompanied by Clairmont, who is pregnant by Lord Byron; (13 May) arrives in Geneva; (27 May) meets Byron and his physician Dr John Polidori; (1 June) moves into Maison Chappuis with William, Percy, and Clairmont; (10 June) Byron takes up residence at the nearby Villa Diodati; (16–17 June) MWS begins *Frankenstein*; (21–7 July) travels to Chamonix and the Mer de Glace; (29 Aug.) returns to England, arriving 8 Sept.; (9 Oct.) suicide	'The Year Without a Summer', following volcanic explosion of Mount Tambora in 1815; post-war recession and repressive domestic legislation; passenger ship the *Medusa* wrecked; Sir Humphry Davy invents the safety lamp. Byron, *Childe Harold*, canto iii; Coleridge, *Christabel and Other Poems*; Hunt, *The Story of Rimini*; Caroline Lamb, *Glenarvon*; William Lawrence, *An Introduction to Comparative Anatomy and Physiology*; Thomas Love Peacock, *Headlong Hall*; Scott, *The Antiquary*; Percy Shelley, *Alastor and Other Poems*.

Life	*Historical and Cultural Background*
of Fanny Imlay (*née* Wollstonecraft), MWS's half-sister; (9 Nov.) suicide of heavily pregnant Harriet Shelley by drowning; (30 Dec.) MWS marries Percy Shelley at St Mildred's Church, Bread Street, London, and is reconciled with Godwin, who stands witness; over the next two and a half months the Shelleys live variously with the Godwins, Leigh Hunt and his family, and Thomas Love Peacock.	
1817 (18 Mar.) moves to Marlow and is joined by Clairmont and daughter; (27 Mar.) Percy Shelley refused custody of his two children by Harriet; (14 May) MWS completes *Frankenstein*; (2 Sept.) gives birth to daughter, Clara Everina; (12–13 Nov.) *History of a Six Weeks' Tour through a Part of France, Switzerland, Germany, and Holland* published anonymously.	Prince Regent mobbed; suspension of Habeas Corpus; Gagging Acts against radical press and seditious assembly; the impostor Princess Caraboo appears; gas lighting introduced to illuminate Covent Garden Theatre. Austen, *Persuasion* (dated 1818); Byron, *Manfred*; Coleridge, *Biographia Literaria*; Moore, *Lalla Rookh*; Peacock, *Melincourt*; Scott, *Rob Roy*; death of Austen; birth of Karl Marx.
1818 (1 Jan.) *Frankenstein; or, The Modern Prometheus* published anonymously in 3 volumes; (11 Mar.) leaves London with Percy, Claire, their children, and servants for France and Italy; (24 Sept.) Clara Everina dies in Venice from dysentery.	Byron, *Childe Harold*; William Hazlitt, *Lectures on English Poets*; John Keats, *Endymion*; Peacock, *Nightmare Abbey*; Scott, *The Heart of Midlothian*; Percy Shelley, *The Revolt of Islam*; death of Matthew 'Monk' Lewis.
1819 (7 June) William Shelley dies in Rome from malaria; (Aug.– Feb. 1820) MWS writes *Mathilda* (pub. 1959); (12 Nov.) gives birth to a son, Percy Florence, in Florence.	'Peterloo' Massacre in Manchester; Lord Liverpool's ministry passes repressive 'Six Acts'. Byron, *Don Juan*, cantos i–ii; John Polidori, *The Vampyre* in *New Monthly Magazine*; Hazlitt, *Lectures on the English Comic Writers*; Scott, *The Bride of Lammermoor* and *Ivanhoe*; Percy Shelley, *The Cenci*; Wordsworth, *Peter Bell*.

Life

Historical and Cultural Background

1820 (Mar.) begins *Castruccio, Prince of Lucca*; (Apr.–May) writes *Proserpine* and *Midas*.

Death of George III, accession of Prince Regent as George IV; public trial of Queen Caroline; Cato Street Conspiracy, a plot to assassinate the Cabinet, is exposed and conspirators executed; Scottish Insurrection of mass strikes, leaders subsequently executed.
Blake, *Jerusalem: The Emanation of the Giant Albion*; Keats, *Lamia, The Eve of St Agnes, Hyperion, and Other Poems*; Charles Lamb, *Essays of Elia* in *London Magazine*; Maturin, *Melmoth the Wanderer*; Scott, *The Abbot* and *The Monastery*; Percy Shelley, *Prometheus Unbound and Other Poems*.

1821 (July) *Frankenstein, ou Le Prométhée moderne* published in Paris, translated into French by Jules Saladin, and attributed to 'Mᵐᵉ. Shelly', niece [*sic*] of William Godwin.

Coronation of George IV, Queen Caroline is evicted from ceremony and dies three weeks later; Greek War of Independence begins (ends 1832); loss of potato crop in West of Ireland creates famine; death of Napoleon.
Byron, *Don Juan*, cantos iii–v; Thomas De Quincey, *Confessions of an English Opium Eater* in *London Magazine*; Scott, *Kenilworth*; Percy Shelley, *Epipsychidion* and *Adonais*; death of Keats; death of Polidori by suicide.

1822 (16 June) suffers near-fatal miscarriage in San Terenzo; (1 July) Percy Shelley and Edward Williams sail to Leghorn in Shelley's yacht (the 'Don Juan') to meet Hunt; (8 July) returning from Hunt, Percy and Williams are drowned in the Gulf of La Spezia; (14 Aug.) Percy Shelley cremated at Viareggio.

Death of Castlereagh by suicide.
Thomas Lovell Beddoes, *The Bride's Tragedy*; Byron, *Werner*; Peacock, *Maid Marion*; Scott, *The Fortunes of Nigel*, *The Pirate*, and *Peveril of the Peak*; Percy Shelley, *Hellas*; Southey, *A Vision of Judgement*.

Life

Historical and Cultural Background

1823   (19 Feb.) *Valperga: or, The Life and Adventures of Castruccio, Prince of Lucca* 'BY THE AUTHOR OF "FRANKENSTEIN"' published in 3 volumes; (28 July) Richard Brinsley Peake's stage adaptation *Presumption: or, The Fate of Frankenstein* opens at the Theatre Royal, English Opera House, Strand, London; (11 Aug.) 2nd edition of *Frankenstein*, corrected by Godwin, published in 2 volumes, naming author as 'MARY WOLLSTONECRAFT SHELLEY'; (18 Aug.) Henry Milner's stage adaptation *Frankenstein; or, The Demon of Switzerland* opens at the Royal Coburg Theatre, London; (25 Aug.) MWS arrives back in London; (28 Aug.) attends performance of *Presumption* with Godwin; (1 Sept.) a burlesque *Humgumption; or, Dr. Frankenstein and the Hobgoblin of Hoxton* opens at the New Surrey Theatre, London, and another anonymous adaptation *Presumption and the Blue Demon* opens at Davis's Royal Amphitheatre, London; (20 Oct.) Peake's stage sequel *Another Piece of Presumption!* opens at the Adelphi Theatre, London; (27 Nov.) MWS receives first annual repayable allowance of £100 from Sir Timothy Shelley for maintenance of Percy Florence (Sir Timothy insists on him being raised in England, though refuses ever to meet MWS).

Byron, *Don Juan*, cantos vi–xiv; Thomas Carlyle, *Life of Schiller*; Hazlitt, *Liber Amoris*; Charles Lamb, *Essays of Elia*; Scott, *Quentin Durward*; Southey, *History of the Peninsular War* (completed 1832); death of Radcliffe.

Life

Historical and Cultural Background

1824   (9 Feb.) Begins writing *The Last Man*; (June) *Posthumous Poems of Percy Bysshe Shelley* published and withdrawn within the month following threats by Sir Timothy that he would cease his payments to Percy Florence; (Aug.) Percy Florence's allowance increased to £200; (13 Dec.) *Frank-in-Steam; or, The Modern Promise to Pay* opens at the Olympic Theatre, London.

Byron, *Don Juan*, cantos xv–xvi, and *The Deformed Transformed*; James Hogg, *The Private Memoirs and Confessions of a Justified Sinner*; Scott, *Redgauntlet* and *St Ronan's Well*; death of Byron.

1825   (Feb.) completes *The Last Man*.

Coleridge, *Aids to Reflection*; Hazlitt, *The Spirit of the Age*; Scott, *The Talisman* and *The Betrothed*; Southey, *A Tale of Paraguay*.

1826   (23 Jan.) *The Last Man* 'BY THE AUTHOR OF FRANKENSTEIN' published in 3 volumes; (10 June) first French stage adaptation *Le Monstre et le magicien* by Jean Toussaint Merle and 'Beraud Antony' [Antoine Nicolas Beraud] opens in Paris (six further productions are staged in Paris before the end of the decade); (3 July) Henry Milner's revised stage adaptation *The Man and the Monster! Or, The Fate of Frankenstein; A Peculiar Romantic Melo-Dramatic Pantomimic Spectacle* opens at the Royal Coburg (now Old Vic) Theatre, London; (14 Sept.) Percy Florence becomes heir to the Shelley baronetcy on the death of Charles Bysshe, Shelley's son by his first wife Harriet; (9 Oct.) James Kerr's translation of *Le Monstre et le magicien* opens at the New Royal West London Theatre.

Radcliffe, 'On the Supernatural in Poetry' and *Gaston de Blondeville*.

Life	Historical and Cultural Background
1827 (May) Sir Timothy increases his annual payments to Percy Florence to £250; (Sept.) MWS begins *The Fortunes of Perkin Warbeck*.	John Clare, *The Shepherd's Calendar*; De Quincey, 'On Murder Considered as One of the Fine Arts', i; John Keble, *The Christian Year*; Johann Friedrich Blumenbach, *A Manual of Comparative Anatomy* (1805), trans. Lawrence; Scott, *Chronicles of the Canongate*, 1st ser.; death of Blake.
1828 (11 Apr.) visits Paris and contracts smallpox; (26 May) returns to England.	Repeal of Test Acts. Scott, *Tales of a Grandfather*, 1st ser., and *Chronicles of the Canongate*, 2nd ser.: death of Francisco de Goya.
1829 (June) Sir Timothy increases his annual payments to Percy Florence to £300.	Catholic Relief Act (culmination of Catholic Emancipation). Carlyle, 'Signs of the Times'; Peacock, *The Misfortunes of Elfin*; Scott, *Tales of a Grandfather*, 2nd ser.; death of Davy.
1830 (13 May) *The Fortunes of Perkin Warbeck, A Romance* 'BY THE AUTHOR OF "FRANKENSTEIN"' published in 3 volumes; *Letters and Journals of Lord Byron: With Notices of His Life*, edited with Thomas Moore (to whom the edition is attributed), published in 2 volumes.	Death of George IV and accession of William IV; July Revolution in France; political demonstrations in Spain, Portugal, and the Italian states. William Cobbett, *Rural Rides*; Scott, *Tales of a Grandfather*, 3rd and 4th ser.; Alfred, Lord Tennyson, *Poems, Chiefly Lyrical*; death of Hazlitt.
1831 (31 Oct.) 3rd revised, corrected, and illustrated edition of *Frankenstein* published in Bentley's Standard Novels series 'BY THE AUTHOR OF THE LAST MAN, PERKIN WARBECK, &c. &c.'; (Nov.) 'Proserpine. A Mythological Drama, in Two Acts' published in *The Winter's Wreath*.	Great Reform Bill passed by House of Commons but defeated by House of Lords leading to nationwide riots; Michael Faraday discovers electromagnetic induction; beginning of cholera epidemic; Commander James Clark Ross reaches the North Pole. Peacock, *Crotchet Castle*; Edgar Allan Poe, *Poems*; Edward Trelawny, *Adventures of a Younger Son*.
1832 (8 Sept.) MWS's half-brother William Godwin dies; (29 Sept.) Percy Florence enters Harrow School.	Great Reform Bill becomes law. Scott, *Tales of My Landlord*, 3rd and 4th ser.; Tennyson, *Poems*; death of Goethe.

Life	*Historical and Cultural Background*
1833	Slavery abolished in British Empire; Shaftesbury's Factory Act regulates child labour. Carlyle, *Sartor Resartus*; Charles Lamb, *Last Essays of Elia*; John Newman, *Tracts for Our Times*.
1834	Poor Law Amendment Act dramatically increases role of workhouses; 'Tolpuddle Martyrs'; beginnings of emancipation of slaves in the West Indies. Lady Blessington, *Conversations with Lord Byron*; Southey, *The Doctor*; death of Coleridge; death of Charles Lamb; death of Malthus.
1835 (7 Apr.) *Lodore*, by 'THE AUTHOR OF "FRANKENSTEIN"', published in 3 volumes; from this year until 1839 MWS contributes nearly all of the essays in the 5 volumes of Revd Dionysius Lardner's *Cabinet of Biography: Lives of the Most Eminent Literary and Scientific Men of Italy, Spain and Portugal* (1835–7) and *Lives of the Most Eminent Literary and Scientific Men of France* (1838–9).	Robert Browning, *Paracelsus*; Charles Dickens, *Sketches by Boz*, 1st ser.; Moore, *The Fudges in England*; Wordsworth, *Yarrow Revisited and Other Poems*; death of Cobbett.
1836 (14 Apr.) Godwin dies and leaves his papers to MWS.	Dickens, *Sketches by Boz*, 2nd ser., and *The Posthumous Papers of the Pickwick Club*.
1837 (Feb.) *Falkner. A Novel*, by 'THE AUTHOR OF "FRANKENSTEIN;" "THE LAST MAN," &c.', published in 3 volumes; (10 Oct.) Percy Florence matriculates at Trinity College, Cambridge.	Death of William IV and accession of Victoria; widespread discontent and demonstration among labouring classes; electric telegraph patented; Fox Talbot develops photographic prints. Carlyle, *The French Revolution*; Dickens, *Oliver Twist*; J. G. Lockhart, *Life of Scott*.
1838	Chartists publish People's Charter inspiring nationwide rallies; Anti-Corn Law League established; Anglo-Afghan War (ends 1842); emancipation of slaves in the West Indies.

Life	*Historical and Cultural Background*
	Elizabeth Barrett, *The Seraphim*; Charles Darwin, *Journal of Researches into the Geology and Natural History of the Various Countries visited by H.M.S. Beagle* (to 1843); Dickens, *Nicholas Nickleby*; Wordsworth, *Sonnets*.
1839 (Jan.–May) MWS publishes her edition of *Poetical Works of Percy Bysshe Shelley* in 4 volumes, with biographical notes; (Dec.) publishes her edition of Percy's *Essays, Letters from Abroad, Translations and Fragments* in 2 volumes.	Chartist riots and rejection by Parliament of first Chartist petition; First China Opium War. De Quincey, 'On Murder Considered as One of the Fine Arts', ii.
1840 (June–Nov.) embarks on a Continental tour with Percy Florence and several of his friends, remaining in Paris until the end of the year.	Queen Victoria marries Prince Albert; Penny Post instituted. Browning, *Sordello*; Dickens, *The Old Curiosity Shop*.
1841 (Feb.) Percy Florence graduates and his allowance is increased to £400; (17 June) Mary Jane Godwin dies.	*Punch* founded. Browning, *Pippa Passes*; Carlyle, *On Heroes, Hero-Worship, and the Heroic in History*; Dickens, *Barnaby Rudge*.
1842 (June) MWS embarks on another Continental tour with Percy Florence and friends.	Mines Act makes employing women and children in mining illegal; second Chartist petition rejected leading to nationwide protests; Britain takes Hong Kong after Opium War. Browning, *Dramatic Lyrics*; Edwin Chadwick, 'Report on the Sanitary Condition of the Labouring Population'; Dickens, *American Notes*; Thomas Babington Macaulay, *Lays of Ancient Rome*; Tennyson, *Poems*; Wordsworth, *Poems Chiefly of Early and Late Years*.
1843 (Aug.) returns to England after visiting Clairmont in Paris.	Expansion of British Empire making Gambia and Natal colonies. Carlyle, *Past and Present*; Dickens, *A Christmas Carol* and *Martin Chuzzlewit*; Macaulay, *Critical and Historical Essays*; John Ruskin, *Modern Painters*, i; death of Southey; Wordsworth appointed Poet Laureate.

Life	*Historical and Cultural Background*
1844 (24 Apr.) Sir Timothy Shelley dies, leaving the encumbered part of his estate to MWS and Percy Florence, with the latter succeeding to the baronetcy; (July) *Rambles in Germany and Italy, in 1840, 1842, and 1843* published in two volumes.	First telegraph line from Paddington to Slough. William Barnes, *Poems of Rural Life in the Dorset Dialect*; Barrett, *Poems*; Robert Chambers, *Vestiges of the Natural History of Creation* (on evolution); Benjamin Disraeli, *Coningsby*; death of William Beckford.
1845	Lunacy Act reforms care of mentally ill; doomed Franklin Expedition in search of Northwest Passage (both ships lost with all hands 1847).
	De Quincey, 'Suspiria de Profundis' in *Blackwood's Magazine*; Dickens, *The Cricket on the Hearth*; Disraeli, *Sybil*; Friedrich Engels, *Condition of the Working Classes in England in 1844*; Poe, *Tales of Mystery and Imagination*.
1846	'Railway Mania' (272 Railway Acts passed); Repeal of the Corn Laws; Irish potato famine (to 1849). Charlotte Brontë, Emily Brontë, and Anne Brontë, *Poems by Currer, Ellis, and Acton Bell*; Dickens, *Pictures from Italy* and *Dombey and Son*; Edward Lear, *A Book of Nonsense*; Ruskin, *Modern Painters*, ii.
1847	Factory Act regulates hours of employment; first medical use of chloroform. Anne Brontë, *Agnes Grey*; Charlotte Brontë, *Jane Eyre*; Emily Brontë, *Wuthering Heights*; Tennyson, *The Princess*; William Makepeace Thackeray, *Vanity Fair*.
1848 (22 June) Percy Florence marries Jane St John; (Aug.) MWS, Percy Florence, and Jane move to Field Place.	Mass Chartist meetings support third petition, which is comprehensively rejected by Parliament leading to nationwide rioting; Public Health Act; 'Year of Revolutions' in Europe taking Louis Napoleon to power in France; cholera epidemic.

Life	*Historical and Cultural Background*
	Anne Brontë, *The Tenant of Wildfell Hall*; Elizabeth Gaskell, *Mary Barton*; Marx and Engels, *Communist Manifesto*; John Stuart Mill, *Principles of Political Economy*; death of Emily Brontë and Branwell Brontë; Pre-Raphaelite Brotherhood formed.
1849 (26 Dec.) William and Robert Brough's burlesque adaptation *Frankenstein; or, The Model Man* opens at the Adelphi Theatre, London (the Being named 'The What Is It').	Charlotte Brontë, *Shirley*; De Quincey, 'The English Mail-Coach' in *Blackwood's Magazine*; Dickens, *David Copperfield*; Macaulay, *History of England*, i–ii; Ruskin, *The Seven Lamps of Architecture*; Thackeray, *Pendennis*; death of Beddoes; death of Anne Brontë; death of Poe.
1850	Public Libraries Act. Beddoes, *Death's Jest-Book*; Elizabeth Barrett Browning, *Poems*; Robert Browning, *Christmas Eve and Easter Day*; Nathaniel Hawthorne, *The Scarlet Letter*; Hunt, *Autobiography*; Tennyson, *In Memoriam*; Wordsworth, *The Prelude*; death of Wordsworth; Tennyson appointed Poet Laureate.
1851 (1 Feb.) MWS dies of a brain tumour at Chester Square, London; the remains of Wollstonecraft and Godwin are disinterred from the churchyard of St Pancras Old Church and MWS is buried at St Peter's, Bournemouth, between the reinterred remains of her parents.	The Great Exhibition at Crystal Palace; William Thomson (Lord Kelvin) establishes principle of the conservation of energy. Henry Mayhew, *London Labour and the London Poor*; Herbert Melville, *Moby Dick*; Ruskin, *The Stones of Venice*, i; death of J. M. W. Turner.

FRANKENSTEIN;

OR,

THE MODERN PROMETHEUS.

❖

IN THREE VOLUMES.

❖

Did I request thee, Maker, from my clay
To mould me man? Did I solicit thee
From darkness to promote me?—

PARADISE LOST.

VOL. I.

═══════

London:

PRINTED FOR
LACKINGTON, HUGHES, HARDING, MAVOR, & JONES,
FINSBURY SQUARE.

1818.

TO

WILLIAM GODWIN,

AUTHOR OF POLITICAL JUSTICE, CALEB WILLIAMS, &c.

THESE VOLUMES

Are respectfully inscribed

BY

THE AUTHOR.

PREFACE.

instantaneous creation of life [handwritten margin note]

THE event on which this fiction is founded has been supposed, by Dr. Darwin,* and some of the physiological writers of Germany,* as not of impossible occurrence. I shall not be supposed as according the remotest degree of serious faith to such an imagination; yet, in assuming it as the basis of a work of fancy, I have not considered myself as merely weaving a series of supernatural terrors.* The event on which the interest of the story depends is exempt from the disadvantages of a mere tale of spectres or enchantment. It was recommended by the novelty of the situations which it developes; and, however impossible as a physical fact, affords a point of view to the imagination for the delineating of human passions more comprehensive and commanding than any which the ordinary relations of existing events can yield.

I have thus endeavoured to preserve the truth of the elementary principles of human nature, while I have not scrupled to innovate upon their combinations. The *Iliad*, the tragic poetry of Greece,—Shakespeare, in the *Tempest* and *Midsummer Night's Dream*,—and most especially Milton, in *Paradise Lost*, conform to this rule; and the most humble novelist, who seeks to confer or receive amusement from his labours, may, without presumption, apply to prose fiction a licence, or rather a rule, from the adoption of which so many exquisite combinations of human feeling have resulted in the highest specimens of poetry.

The circumstance on which my story rests was suggested in casual conversation.* It was commenced, partly as a source of amusement, and partly as an expedient for exercising any untried resources of mind. Other motives were mingled with these, as the work proceeded. I am by no means indifferent to the manner in which whatever moral tendencies exist in the sentiments or characters it contains shall affect the reader; yet my chief concern in this respect has been limited to the avoiding the enervating effects of the novels of the present day, and to the exhibition of the amiableness of domestic affection, and the excellence of universal virtue. The opinions which naturally spring from the character and situation of the hero are by no means to be conceived as existing always in my own conviction; nor is any inference justly to be drawn from the following pages as prejudicing any philosophical doctrine of whatever kind.*

It is a subject also of additional interest to the author, that this story was begun in the majestic region where the scene is principally laid, and in society which cannot cease to be regretted. I passed the summer of 1816 in the environs of Geneva. The season was cold and rainy, and in the evenings we crowded around a blazing wood fire, and occasionally amused ourselves with some German stories of ghosts,* which happened to fall into our hands. These tales excited in us a playful desire of imitation. Two other friends (a tale from the pen of one of whom would be far more acceptable to the public than any thing I can ever hope to produce) and myself agreed to write each a story,* founded on some supernatural occurrence.

The weather, however, suddenly became serene; and my two friends left me on a journey among the Alps, and lost, in the magnificent scenes which they present, all memory of their ghostly visions. The following tale is the only one which has been completed.

FRANKENSTEIN;
OR, THE
MODERN PROMETHEUS.

VOLUME I

LETTER I.

To Mrs. SAVILLE,* *England.*

St. Petersburgh,* Dec. 11th, 17—.*

YOU will rejoice to hear that no disaster has accompanied the commencement of an enterprise which you have regarded with such evil forebodings.
I arrived here yesterday; and my first task is to assure my dear sister of
my welfare, and increasing confidence in the success of my undertaking.

I am already far north of London; and as I walk in the streets of
Petersburgh, I feel a cold northern breeze play upon my cheeks, which
braces my nerves, and fills me with delight. Do you understand this
feeling? This breeze, which has travelled from the regions towards
which I am advancing, gives me a foretaste of those icy climes. Inspirited
by this wind of promise, my day dreams become more fervent and
vivid.* I try in vain to be persuaded that the pole is the seat of frost
and desolation; it ever presents itself to my imagination as the region
of beauty and delight. There, Margaret, the sun is for ever visible; its
broad disk just skirting the horizon, and diffusing a perpetual splen-
dour. There—for with your leave, my sister, I will put some trust in
preceding navigators—there snow and frost are banished;* and, sail-
ing over a calm sea, we may be wafted to a land surpassing in wonders
and in beauty every region hitherto discovered on the habitable globe.
Its productions and features may be without example, as the phænomena of the heavenly bodies undoubtedly are in those undiscovered
solitudes. What may not be expected in a country of eternal light?
I may there discover the wondrous power which attracts the needle;
and may regulate a thousand celestial observations, that require only

this voyage to render their seeming eccentricities consistent for ever. I shall satiate my ardent curiosity with the sight of a part of the world never before visited, and may tread a land never before imprinted by the foot of man. These are my enticements, and they are sufficient to conquer all fear of danger or death, and to induce me to commence this laborious voyage with the joy a child feels when he embarks in a little boat, with his holiday mates, on an expedition of discovery up his native river. But, supposing all these conjectures to be false, you cannot contest the inestimable benefit which I shall confer on all mankind to the last generation, by discovering a passage near the pole to those countries, to reach which at present so many months are requisite; or by ascertaining the secret of the magnet,* which, if at all possible, can only be effected by an undertaking such as mine.

These reflections have dispelled the agitation with which I began my letter, and I feel my heart glow with an enthusiasm which elevates me to heaven; for nothing contributes so much to tranquillize the mind as a steady purpose,—a point on which the soul may fix its intellectual eye. This expedition has been the favourite dream of my early years. I have read with ardour the accounts of the various voyages which have been made in the prospect of arriving at the North Pacific Ocean* through the seas which surround the pole. You may remember, that a history of all the voyages made for purposes of discovery composed the whole of our good uncle Thomas's library. My education was neglected, yet I was passionately fond of reading. These volumes were my study day and night, and my familiarity with them increased that regret which I had felt, as a child, on learning that my father's dying injunction had forbidden my uncle to allow me to embark in a sea-faring life.

These visions faded when I perused, for the first time, those poets whose effusions entranced my soul, and lifted it to heaven. I also became a poet, and for one year lived in a Paradise of my own creation;* I imagined that I also might obtain a niche in the temple where the names of Homer and Shakespeare are consecrated. You are well acquainted with my failure, and how heavily I bore the disappointment. But just at that time I inherited the fortune of my cousin, and my thoughts were turned into the channel of their earlier bent.

Six years have passed since I resolved on my present undertaking. I can, even now, remember the hour from which I dedicated myself to this great enterprise. I commenced by inuring my body to hardship. I accompanied the whale-fishers on several expeditions to the North

Sea; I voluntarily endured cold, famine, thirst, and want of sleep; I often worked harder than the common sailors during the day, and devoted my nights to the study of mathematics, the theory of medicine, and those branches of physical science from which a naval adventurer might derive the greatest practical advantage. Twice I actually hired myself as an under-mate in a Greenland whaler, and acquitted myself to admiration. I must own I felt a little proud, when my captain offered me the second dignity* in the vessel, and entreated me to remain with the greatest earnestness; so valuable did he consider my services.

And now, dear Margaret, do I not deserve to accomplish some great purpose. My life might have been passed in ease and luxury; but I preferred glory to every enticement that wealth placed in my path. Oh, that some encouraging voice would answer in the affirmative! My courage and my resolution is firm; but my hopes fluctuate, and my spirits are often depressed. I am about to proceed on a long and difficult voyage; the emergencies of which will demand all my fortitude: I am required not only to raise the spirits of others, but sometimes to sustain my own, when their's are failing.

This is the most favourable period for travelling in Russia. They fly quickly over the snow in their sledges; the motion is pleasant, and, in my opinion, far more agreeable than that of an English stage-coach. The cold is not excessive, if you are wrapt in furs, a dress which I have already adopted; for there is a great difference between walking the deck and remaining seated motionless for hours, when no exercise prevents the blood from actually freezing in your veins. I have no ambition to lose my life on the post-road between St. Petersburgh and Archangel.*

I shall depart for the latter town in a fortnight or three weeks; and my intention is to hire a ship there, which can easily be done by paying the insurance for the owner, and to engage as many sailors as I think necessary among those who are accustomed to the whale-fishing. I do not intend to sail until the month of June: and when shall I return? Ah, dear sister, how can I answer this question? If I succeed, many, many months, perhaps years, will pass before you and I may meet. If I fail, you will see me again soon, or never.

Farewell, my dear, excellent, Margaret. Heaven shower down blessings on you, and save me, that I may again and again testify my gratitude for all your love and kindness.

Your affectionate brother,
R. WALTON.

LETTER II.

To Mrs. SAVILLE, *England.*

Archangel, 28th March, 17—.

HOW slowly the time passes here, encompassed as I am by frost and snow; yet a second step is taken towards my enterprise. I have hired a vessel, and am occupied in collecting my sailors; those whom I have already engaged appear to be men on whom I can depend, and are certainly possessed of dauntless courage.

But I have one want which I have never yet been able to satisfy; and the absence of the object of which I now feel as a most severe evil. I have no friend, Margaret: when I am glowing with the enthusiasm of success, there will be none to participate my joy; if I am assailed by dis-appointment, no one will endeavour to sustain me in dejection. I shall commit my thoughts to paper, it is true; but that is a poor medium for the communication of feeling.* I desire the company of a man who could sympathize with me; whose eyes would reply to mine. You may deem me romantic,* my dear sister, but I bitterly feel the want of a friend. I have no one near me, gentle yet courageous, possessed of a cultivated as well as of a capacious mind, whose tastes are like my own, to approve or amend my plans. How would such a friend repair the faults of your poor brother! I am too ardent in execution, and too impatient of difficulties. But it is a still greater evil to me that I am self-educated: for the first fourteen years of my life I ran wild on a com-mon, and read nothing but our uncle Thomas's books of voyages. At that age I became acquainted with the celebrated poets of our own country; but it was only when it had ceased to be in my power to derive its most important benefits from such a conviction, that I perceived the necessity of becoming acquainted with more languages than that of my native country. Now I am twenty-eight, and am in reality more illit-erate than many school-boys of fifteen. It is true that I have thought more, and that my day dreams are more extended and magnificent; but they want (as the painters call it) *keeping*;* and I greatly need a friend who would have sense* enough not to despise me as romantic, and affection enough for me to endeavour to regulate my mind.

Well, these are useless complaints; I shall certainly find no friend on the wide ocean, nor even here in Archangel, among merchants and seamen. Yet some feelings, unallied to the dross of human nature, beat even in these rugged bosoms. My lieutenant, for instance, is a man of wonderful courage and enterprise; he is madly desirous of glory. He is an Englishman, and in the midst of national and professional prejudices, unsoftened by cultivation, retains some of the noblest endowments of humanity. I first became acquainted with him on board a whale vessel: finding that he was unemployed in this city, I easily engaged him to assist in my enterprise.

The master is a person of an excellent disposition, and is remarkable in the ship for his gentleness, and the mildness of his discipline. He is, indeed, of so amiable a nature, that he will not hunt (a favourite, and almost the only amusement here), because he cannot endure to spill blood. He is, moreover, heroically generous. Some years ago he loved a young Russian lady, of moderate fortune; and having amassed a considerable sum in prize-money, the father of the girl consented to the match. He saw his mistress once before the destined ceremony; but she was bathed in tears, and, throwing herself at his feet, entreated him to spare her, confessing at the same time that she loved another, but that he was poor, and that her father would never consent to the union. My generous friend reassured the suppliant, and on being informed of the name of her lover instantly abandoned his pursuit. He had already bought a farm with his money, on which he had designed to pass the remainder of his life; but he bestowed the whole on his rival, together with the remains of his prize-money to purchase stock, and then himself solicited the young woman's father to consent to her marriage with her lover. But the old man decidedly refused, thinking himself bound in honour to my friend; who, when he found the father inexorable, quitted his country, nor returned until he heard that his former mistress was married according to her inclinations. 'What a noble fellow!' you will exclaim. He is so; but then he has passed all his life on board a vessel, and has scarcely an idea beyond the rope and the shroud.*

But do not suppose that, because I complain a little, or because I can conceive a consolation for my toils which I may never know, that I am wavering in my resolutions. Those are as fixed as fate; and my voyage is only now delayed until the weather shall permit my embarkation. The winter has been dreadfully severe; but the spring promises well, and it is considered as a remarkably early season; so that, perhaps, I may sail sooner than I expected. I shall do nothing rashly; you know me sufficiently to confide in my prudence and considerateness whenever the safety of others is committed to my care.

I cannot describe to you my sensations on the near prospect of my undertaking. It is impossible to communicate to you a conception of the trembling sensation, half pleasurable and half fearful, with which I am preparing to depart. I am going to unexplored regions, to 'the land of mist and snow;'* but I shall kill no albatross, therefore do not be alarmed for my safety.

Shall I meet you again, after having traversed immense seas, and returned by the most southern cape of Africa or America? I dare not expect such success, yet I cannot bear to look on the reverse of the picture. Continue to write to me by every opportunity: I may receive your letters (though the chance is very doubtful) on some occasions when I need them most to support my spirits. I love you very tenderly. Remember me with affection, should you never hear from me again.

> Your affectionate brother,
> ROBERT WALTON.

LETTER III.

To Mrs. SAVILLE, *England.*

July 7th, 17—.

MY DEAR SISTER,

I write a few lines in haste, to say that I am safe, and well advanced on my voyage. This letter will reach England by a merchant-man now on its homeward voyage from Archangel; more fortunate than I, who may not see my native land, perhaps, for many years. I am, however, in good spirits: my men are bold, and apparently firm of purpose; nor do the floating sheets of ice that continually pass us, indicating the dangers of the region towards which we are advancing, appear to dismay them. We have already reached a very high latitude; but it is the height of summer, and although not so warm as in England, the southern gales, which blow us speedily towards those shores which I so ardently desire to attain, breathe a degree of renovating warmth which I had not expected.

No incidents have hitherto befallen us, that would make a figure in a letter. One or two stiff gales, and the breaking of a mast, are accidents which experienced navigators scarcely remember to record; and I shall be well content, if nothing worse happen to us during our voyage.

Adieu, my dear Margaret. Be assured, that for my own sake, as well as your's, I will not rashly encounter danger. I will be cool, persevering, and prudent.

Remember me to all my English friends.

Most affectionately yours,
R. W.

LETTER IV.

To Mrs. SAVILLE, *England*.

August 5th, 17——.

So strange an accident has happened to us, that I cannot forbear recording it, although it is very probable that you will see me before these papers can come into your possession.

Last Monday (July 31st), we were nearly surrounded by ice, which closed in the ship on all sides, scarcely leaving her the sea room in which she floated. Our situation was somewhat dangerous, especially as we were compassed round by a very thick fog. We accordingly lay to, hoping that some change would take place in the atmosphere and weather.

About two o'clock the mist cleared away, and we beheld, stretched out in every direction, vast and irregular plains of ice, which seemed to have no end. Some of my comrades groaned, and my own mind began to grow watchful with anxious thoughts, when a strange sight suddenly attracted our attention, and diverted our solicitude from our own situation. We perceived a low carriage, fixed on a sledge and drawn by dogs, pass on towards the north, at the distance of half a mile: a being which had the shape of a man, but apparently of gigantic stature, sat in the sledge, and guided the dogs. We watched the rapid progress of the traveller with our telescopes, until he was lost among the distant inequalities* of the ice.

This appearance excited our unqualified wonder. We were, as we believed, many hundred miles from any land; but this apparition seemed to denote that it was not, in reality, so distant as we had supposed. Shut in, however, by ice, it was impossible to follow his track, which we had observed with the greatest attention.

About two hours after this occurrence, we heard the ground sea,* and before night the ice broke, and freed our ship. We, however, lay to until the morning, fearing to encounter in the dark those large loose masses which float about after the breaking up of the ice. I profited of this time to rest for a few hours.

In the morning, however, as soon as it was light, I went upon deck, and found all the sailors busy on one side of the vessel, apparently talking to some one in the sea. It was, in fact, a sledge, like that we had seen before, which had drifted towards us in the night, on a large frag-ment of ice.* Only one dog remained alive; but there was a human being within it, whom the sailors were persuading to enter the vessel. He was not, as the other traveller seemed to be, a savage inhabitant of some undiscovered island, but an European. When I appeared on deck, the master said, 'Here is our captain, and he will not allow you to perish on the open sea.'

On perceiving me, the stranger addressed me in English, although with a foreign accent. 'Before I come on board your vessel,' said he, 'will you have the kindness to inform me whither you are bound?'

You may conceive my astonishment on hearing such a question addressed to me from a man on the brink of destruction, and to whom I should have supposed that my vessel would have been a resource which he would not have exchanged for the most precious wealth the earth can afford. I replied, however, that we were on a voyage of discovery towards the northern pole.

Upon hearing this he appeared satisfied, and consented to come on board. Good God! Margaret, if you had seen the man who thus capitulated* for his safety, your surprise would have been boundless. His limbs were nearly frozen, and his body dreadfully emaciated by fatigue and suffering. I never saw a man in so wretched a condition. We attempted to carry him into the cabin; but as soon as he had quit-ted the fresh air, he fainted. We accordingly brought him back to the deck, and restored him to animation by rubbing him with brandy, and forcing him to swallow a small quantity. As soon as he shewed signs of life, we wrapped him up in blankets, and placed him near the chimney of the kitchen-stove. By slow degrees he recovered, and ate a little soup, which restored him wonderfully.

Two days passed in this manner before he was able to speak; and I often feared that his sufferings had deprived him of under-standing. When he had in some measure recovered, I removed him to my own cabin, and attended on him as much as my duty would per-mit. I never saw a more interesting creature: his eyes have generally an expression of wildness, and even madness; but there are moments when, if any one performs an act of kindness towards him, or does him any the most trifling service, his whole countenance is lighted up, as it were, with a beam of benevolence and sweetness that I never saw equalled. But he is generally melancholy and despairing; and sometimes he gnashes his teeth, as if impatient of* the weight of woes that oppresses him.

When my guest was a little recovered, I had great trouble to keep off the men, who wished to ask him a thousand questions; but I would not allow him to be tormented by their idle curiosity, in a state of body and mind whose restoration evidently depended upon entire repose. Once, however, the lieutenant asked, Why he had come so far upon the ice in so strange a vehicle?

His countenance instantly assumed an aspect of the deepest gloom; and he replied, 'To seek one who fled from me.'

'And did the man whom you pursued travel in the same fashion?'

'Yes.'

'Then I fancy we have seen him; for, the day before we picked you up, we saw some dogs drawing a sledge, with a man in it, across the ice.'

This aroused the stranger's attention; and he asked a multitude of questions concerning the route which the dæmon,* as he called him, had pursued. Soon after, when he was alone with me, he said, 'I have, doubtless, excited your curiosity, as well as that of these good people; but you are too considerate to make inquiries.'

'Certainly; it would indeed be very impertinent and inhuman in me to trouble you with any inquisitiveness of mine.'

'And yet you rescued me from a strange and perilous situation; you have benevolently restored me to life.'

Soon after this he inquired, if I thought that the breaking up of the ice had destroyed the other sledge? I replied, that I could not answer with any degree of certainty; for the ice had not broken until near midnight, and the traveller might have arrived at a place of safety before that time; but of this I could not judge.

From this time the stranger seemed very eager to be upon deck, to watch for the sledge which had before appeared; but I have persuaded him to remain in the cabin, for he is far too weak to sustain the rawness of the atmosphere. But I have promised that some one should watch for him, and give him instant notice if any new object should appear in sight.

Such is my journal of what relates to this strange occurrence up to the present day. The stranger has gradually improved in health, but is very silent, and appears uneasy when any one except myself enters his cabin. Yet his manners are so conciliating and gentle, that the sailors are all interested in him, although they have had very little communication with him. For my own part, I begin to love him as a brother; and his constant and deep grief fills me with sympathy and compassion. He must have been a noble creature in his better days, being even now in wreck so attractive and amiable.

I said in one of my letters, my dear Margaret, that I should find no friend on the wide ocean; yet I have found a man who, before his spirit had been broken by misery, I should have been happy to have possessed as the brother of my heart.

I shall continue my journal concerning the stranger at intervals, should I have any fresh incidents to record.

August 13th, 17—.

My affection for my guest increases every day. He excites at once my admiration and my pity to an astonishing degree. How can I see so noble a creature destroyed by misery without feeling the most poignant grief? He is so gentle, yet so wise; his mind is so cultivated; and when he speaks, although his words are culled with the choicest art, yet they flow with rapidity and unparalleled eloquence.

He is now much recovered from his illness, and is continually on the deck, apparently watching for the sledge that preceded his own. Yet, although unhappy, he is not so utterly occupied by his own misery, but that he interests himself deeply in the employments of others. He has asked me many questions concerning my design; and I have related my little history frankly to him. He appeared pleased with the confidence, and suggested several alterations in my plan, which I shall find exceedingly useful. There is no pedantry in his manner; but all he does appears to spring solely from the interest he instinctively takes in the welfare of those who surround him. He is often overcome by gloom, and then he sits by himself, and tries to overcome all that is sullen or unsocial in his humour.* These paroxysms pass from him like a cloud from before the sun, though his dejection never leaves him. I have endeavoured to win his confidence; and I trust that I have succeeded. One day I mentioned to him the desire I had always felt of finding a friend who might sympathize with me, and direct me by his counsel. I said, I did not belong to that class of men who are offended by advice. 'I am self-educated, and perhaps I hardly rely sufficiently upon my own powers. I wish therefore that my companion should be wiser and more experienced than myself, to confirm and support me; nor have I believed it impossible to find a true friend.'

'I agree with you,' replied the stranger, 'in believing that friendship is not only a desirable, but a possible acquisition. I once had a friend, the most noble of human creatures, and am entitled, therefore, to judge respecting friendship. You have hope, and the world before you,* and have no cause for despair. But I—I have lost every thing, and cannot begin life anew.'

As he said this, his countenance became expressive of a calm settled grief, that touched me to the heart. But he was silent, and presently retired to his cabin.

Even broken in spirit as he is, no one can feel more deeply than he does the beauties of nature. The starry sky, the sea, and every sight afforded by these wonderful regions, seems still to have the power of elevating his soul from earth. Such a man has a double existence: he may suffer misery, and be overwhelmed by disappointments; yet when he has retired into himself, he will be like a celestial spirit, that has a halo around him, within whose circle no grief or folly ventures.

Will you laugh at the enthusiasm I express concerning this divine wanderer? If you do, you must have certainly lost that simplicity which was once your characteristic charm. Yet, if you will, smile at the warmth of my expressions, while I find every day new causes for repeating them.

August 19th, 17—.

Yesterday the stranger said to me, 'You may easily perceive, Captain Walton, that I have suffered great and unparalleled misfortunes. I had determined, once, that the memory of these evils should die with me; but you have won me to alter my determination. You seek for knowledge and wisdom, as I once did; and I ardently hope that the gratification of your wishes may not be a serpent to sting you, as mine has been. I do not know that the relation of my misfortunes will be useful to you, yet, if you are inclined, listen to my tale. I believe that the strange incidents connected with it will afford a view of nature, which may enlarge your faculties and understanding. You will hear of powers and occurrences, such as you have been accustomed to believe impossible:

but I do not doubt that my tale conveys in its series internal evidence of the truth of the events of which it is composed.'

You may easily conceive that I was much gratified by the offered communication; yet I could not endure that he should renew his grief by a recital of his misfortunes. I felt the greatest eagerness to hear the promised narrative, partly from curiosity, and partly from a strong desire to ameliorate his fate, if it were in my power. I expressed these feelings in my answer.

'I thank you,' he replied, 'for your sympathy, but it is useless; my fate is nearly fulfilled. I wait but for one event, and then I shall repose in peace. I understand your feeling,' continued he, perceiving that I wished to interrupt him; 'but you are mistaken, my friend, if thus you will allow me to name you; nothing can alter my destiny: listen to my history, and you will perceive how irrevocably it is determined.'

He then told me, that he would commence his narrative the next day when I should be at leisure. This promise drew from me the warmest thanks. I have resolved every night, when I am not engaged, to record, as nearly as possible in his own words, what he has related during the day. If I should be engaged, I will at least make notes. This manuscript will doubtless afford you the greatest pleasure: but to me, who know him, and who hear it from his own lips, with what interest and sympathy shall I read it in some future day!

CHAPTER I.

I AM by birth a Genevese; and my family is one of the most distinguished of that republic. My ancestors had been for many years counsellors and syndics;* and my father had filled several public situations with honour and reputation. He was respected by all who knew him for his integrity and indefatigable attention to public business. He passed his younger days perpetually occupied by the affairs of his country; and it was not until the decline of life that he thought of marrying, and bestowing on the state sons who might carry his virtues and his name down to posterity.

As the circumstances of his marriage illustrate his character, I cannot refrain from relating them. One of his most intimate friends was a merchant, who, from a flourishing state, fell, through numerous mischances, into poverty. This man, whose name was Beaufort, was of a proud and unbending disposition, and could not bear to live in poverty and oblivion in the same country where he had formerly been distinguished for his rank and magnificence. Having paid his debts, therefore, in the most honourable manner, he retreated with his daughter to the town of Lucerne,* where he lived unknown and in wretchedness. My father loved Beaufort with the truest friendship, and was deeply grieved by his retreat in these unfortunate circumstances. He grieved also for the loss of his society, and resolved to seek him out and endeavour to persuade him to begin the world again through his credit and assistance.

Beaufort had taken effectual measures to conceal himself; and it was ten months before my father discovered his abode. Overjoyed at this discovery, he hastened to the house, which was situated in a mean street, near the Reuss.* But when he entered, misery and despair alone welcomed him. Beaufort had saved but a very small sum of money from the wreck of his fortunes; but it was sufficient to provide him with sustenance for some months, and in the mean time he hoped to procure some respectable employment in a merchant's house. The interval was consequently spent in inaction; his grief only became more deep and rankling, when he had leisure for reflection; and at length it took so fast hold of his mind, that at the end of three months he lay on a bed of sickness, incapable of any exertion.

His daughter attended him with the greatest tenderness; but she saw with despair that their little fund was rapidly decreasing, and that there was no other prospect of support. But Caroline Beaufort possessed a mind of an uncommon mould; and her courage rose to support her in her adversity. She procured plain work;* she plaited straw; and by various means contrived to earn a pittance scarcely sufficient to support life.

Several months passed in this manner. Her father grew worse; her time was more entirely occupied in attending him; her means of subsistence decreased; and in the tenth month her father died in her arms, leaving her an orphan and a beggar. This last blow overcame her; and she knelt by Beaufort's coffin, weeping bitterly, when my father entered the chamber. He came like a protecting spirit to the poor girl, who committed herself to his care, and after the interment of his friend he conducted her to Geneva, and placed her under the protection of a relation. Two years after this event Caroline became his wife.

When my father became a husband and a parent, he found his time so occupied by the duties of his new situation, that he relinquished many of his public employments, and devoted himself to the education of his children. Of these I was the eldest, and the destined successor to all his labours and utility. No creature could have more tender parents than mine. My improvement and health were their constant care, especially as I remained for several years their only child. But before I continue my narrative, I must record an incident which took place when I was four years of age.

My father had a sister, whom he tenderly loved, and who had married early in life an Italian gentleman. Soon after her marriage, she had accompanied her husband into his native country, and for some years my father had very little communication with her. About the time I mentioned she died; and a few months afterwards he received a letter from her husband, acquainting him with his intention of marrying an Italian lady, and requesting my father to take charge of the infant Elizabeth, the only child of his deceased sister. 'It is my wish,' he said, 'that you should consider her as your own daughter, and educate her thus. Her mother's fortune is secured to her, the documents of which I will commit to your keeping. Reflect upon this proposition; and decide whether you would prefer educating your niece yourself to her being brought up by a stepmother.'

My father did not hesitate, and immediately went to Italy, that he might accompany the little Elizabeth to her future home. I have often heard my mother say, that she was at that time the most beautiful child she had ever seen, and shewed signs even then of a gentle and affectionate disposition. These indications, and a desire to bind as closely as possible the ties of domestic love, determined my mother to consider Elizabeth as my future wife; a design which she never found reason to repent. *wait what cousin*

From this time Elizabeth Lavenza became my playfellow, and, as we grew older, my friend. She was docile and good tempered, yet gay and playful as a summer insect. Although she was lively and animated, her feelings were strong and deep, and her disposition uncommonly affectionate. No one could better enjoy liberty, yet no one could submit with more grace than she did to constraint and caprice. Her imagination was luxuriant, yet her capability of application was great. Her person was the image of her mind; her hazel eyes, although as lively as a bird's, possessed an attractive softness. Her figure was light and airy; and, though capable of enduring great fatigue, she appeared the most fragile creature in the world. While I admired her understanding and fancy, I loved to tend on her, as I should on a favourite animal; and I never saw so much grace both of person and mind united to so little pretension.

Every one adored Elizabeth. If the servants had any request to make, it was always through her intercession. We were strangers to any species of disunion and dispute; for although there was a great dissimilitude in our characters, there was an harmony in that very dissimilitude. I was more calm and philosophical than my companion; yet my temper was not so yielding. My application was of longer endurance; but it was not so severe whilst it endured. I delighted in investigating the facts relative to the actual world; she busied herself in following the aërial creations of the poets. The world was to me a secret, which I desired to discover; to her it was a vacancy, which she sought to people with imaginations of her own.

My brothers were considerably younger than myself; but I had a friend in one of my schoolfellows, who compensated for this deficiency. Henry Clerval was the son of a merchant of Geneva, an intimate friend of my father. He was a boy of singular talent and fancy. I remember, when he was nine years old, he wrote a fairy tale, which was the delight and amazement of all his companions. His favourite study consisted in books of chivalry and romance;* and when very young, I can remember, that we used to act plays composed by him out of these favourite books, the principal characters of which were Orlando, Robin Hood, Amadis, and St. George.*

No youth could have passed more happily than mine. My parents were indulgent, and my companions amiable. Our studies were never forced; and by some means we always had an end placed in view, which excited us to ardour in the prosecution of them. It was by this method, and not by emulation, that we were urged to application. Elizabeth was not incited to apply herself to drawing, that her companions might not outstrip her; but through the desire of pleasing her aunt, by the representation of some favourite scene done by her own hand. We learned Latin and English, that we might read the writings in those languages; and so far from study being made odious to us through punishment, we loved application, and our amusements would have been the labours of other children. Perhaps we did not read so many books, or learn languages so quickly, as those who are disciplined according to the ordinary methods; but what we learned was impressed the more deeply on our memories.

In this description of our domestic circle I include Henry Clerval; for he was constantly with us. He went to school with me, and generally passed the afternoon at our house; for being an only child, and destitute of companions at home, his father was well pleased that he should find associates at our house; and we were never completely happy when Clerval was absent.

I feel pleasure in dwelling on the recollections of childhood, before misfortune had tainted my mind, and changed its bright visions of extensive usefulness into gloomy and narrow reflections upon self. But, in drawing the picture of my early days, I must not omit to record those events which led, by insensible steps to my after tale of misery: for when I would account to myself for the birth of that passion, which afterwards ruled my destiny, I find it arise, like a mountain river, from ignoble and almost forgotten sources; but, swelling as it proceeded, it became the torrent which, in its course, has swept away all my hopes and joys.

Natural philosophy* is the genius* that has regulated my fate; I desire therefore, in this narration, to state those facts which led to my predilection for that science. When I was thirteen years of age, we all went on a party of pleasure to the baths near Thonon:* the inclemency of the weather obliged us to remain a day confined to the inn. In this house I chanced to find a volume of the works of Cornelius Agrippa.* I opened it with apathy; the theory which he attempts to demonstrate, and the wonderful facts which he relates, soon changed this feeling into enthusiasm. A new light seemed to dawn upon my mind; and, bounding with joy, I communicated my discovery to my father. I cannot help remarking here the many opportunities instructors possess of directing the attention of their pupils to useful knowledge, which they utterly neglect. My father looked carelessly at the title-page of my book, and said, 'Ah! Cornelius Agrippa! My dear Victor, do not waste your time upon this; it is sad trash.'

If, instead of this remark, my father had taken the pains to explain to me, that the principles of Agrippa had been entirely exploded, and that a modern system of science had been introduced, which possessed much greater powers than the ancient, because the powers of the latter were chimerical,* while those of the former were real and practical; under such circumstances, I should certainly have thrown Agrippa aside, and, with my imagination warmed as it was, should probably have applied myself to the more rational theory of chemistry which has resulted from modern discoveries. It is even possible, that the train of my ideas would never have received the fatal impulse that led to my ruin. But the cursory glance my father had taken of my volume by no means assured me that he was acquainted with its contents; and I continued to read with the greatest avidity.

When I returned home, my first care was to procure the whole works of this author, and afterwards of Paracelsus and Albertus Magnus.* I read and studied the wild fancies of these writers with delight; they appeared to me treasures known to few beside myself; and although I often wished to communicate these secret stores of knowledge to my father, yet his indefinite censure of my favourite Agrippa always withheld me. I disclosed my discoveries to Elizabeth, therefore, under a promise of strict secrecy; but she did not interest herself in the subject, and I was left by her to pursue my studies alone.

It may appear very strange, that a disciple of Albertus Magnus should arise in the eighteenth century; but our family was not scientifical, and I had not attended any of the lectures given at the schools of Geneva. My dreams were therefore undisturbed by reality; and I entered with the greatest diligence into the search of the philosopher's stone and the elixir of life.* But the latter obtained my most undivided attention: wealth was an inferior object; but what glory would attend the discovery, if I could banish disease from the human frame, and render man invulnerable to any but a violent death!

Nor were these my only visions. The raising of ghosts or devils* was a promise liberally accorded by my favourite authors, the fulfil-ment of which I most eagerly sought; and if my incantations were always unsuccessful, I attributed the failure rather to my own inexperience and mistake, than to a want of skill or fidelity in my instructors.

The natural phænomena that take place every day before our eyes did not escape my examinations. Distillation, and the wonderful effects of steam,* processes of which my favourite authors were utterly ignorant, excited my astonishment; but my utmost wonder was engaged by some experiments on an air-pump,* which I saw employed by a gentleman whom we were in the habit of visiting.

The ignorance of the early philosophers on these and several other points served to decrease their credit with me: but I could not entirely throw them aside, before some other system should occupy their place in my mind.

When I was about fifteen years old, we had retired to our house near Belrive,* when we witnessed a most violent and terrible thunder-storm. It advanced from behind the mountains of Jura;* and the thunder burst at once with frightful loudness from various quarters of the heavens. I remained, while the storm lasted, watching its progress with curiosity and delight. As I stood at the door, on a sudden I beheld a stream of fire issue from an old and beautiful oak, which stood about twenty yards from our house; and so soon as the dazzling light vanished, the oak had disappeared, and nothing remained but a blasted stump. When we visited it the next morning, we found the tree shattered in a singular manner. It was not splintered by the shock, but entirely reduced to thin ribbands of wood. I never beheld any thing so utterly destroyed.

The catastrophe of this tree excited my extreme astonishment; and I eagerly inquired of my father the nature and origin of thunder and lightning. He replied, 'Electricity;' describing at the same time the various effects of that power. He constructed a small electrical machine, and exhibited a few experiments; he made also a kite, with a wire and string, which drew down that fluid* from the clouds.

This last stroke completed the overthrow of Cornelius Agrippa, Albertus Magnus, and Paracelsus, who had so long reigned the lords of my imagination. But by some fatality I did not feel inclined to commence the study of any modern system; and this disinclination was influenced by the following circumstance.

My father expressed a wish that I should attend a course of lec-tures upon natural philosophy, to which I cheerfully consented. Some accident prevented my attending these lectures until the course was nearly finished. The lecture, being therefore one of the last, was entirely incomprehensible to me. The professor discoursed with the greatest fluency of potassium and boron, of sulphates and oxyds,* terms to which I could affix no idea; and I became disgusted with the science of natural philosophy, although I still read Pliny and Buffon* with delight, authors, in my estimation, of nearly equal interest and utility.

My occupations at this age were principally the mathematics, and most of the branches of study appertaining to that science. I was busily employed in learning languages; Latin was already familiar to me, and I began to read some of the easiest Greek authors without the help of a lexicon. I also perfectly understood English and German. This is the list of my accomplishments at the age of seventeen; and you may conceive that my hours were fully employed in acquiring and maintaining a knowledge of this various literature.

Another task also devolved upon me, when I became the instructor of my brothers. Ernest was six years younger than myself, and was my principal pupil. He had been afflicted with ill health from his infancy, through which Elizabeth and I had been his constant nurses: his disposition was gentle, but he was incapable of any severe application. William,* the youngest of our family, was yet an infant, and the most beautiful little fellow in the world; his lively blue eyes, dimpled cheeks, and endearing manners, inspired the tenderest affection.

Such was our domestic circle, from which care and pain seemed for ever banished. My father directed our studies, and my mother partook of our enjoyments. Neither of us possessed the slightest preeminence over the other; the voice of command was never heard amongst us; but mutual affection engaged us all to comply with and obey the slightest desire of each other.

CHAPTER II.

WHEN I had attained the age of seventeen, my parents resolved that I should become a student at the university of Ingolstadt.* I had hitherto attended the schools of Geneva; but my father thought it necessary, for the completion of my education, that I should be made acquainted with other customs than those of my native country. My departure was therefore fixed at an early date; but, before the day resolved upon could arrive, the first misfortune of my life occurred—an omen, as it were, of my future misery.

Elizabeth had caught the scarlet fever; but her illness was not severe, and she quickly recovered. During her confinement, many arguments had been urged to persuade my mother to refrain from attending upon her. She had, at first, yielded to our entreaties; but when she heard that her favourite was recovering, she could no longer debar herself from her society, and entered her chamber long before the danger of infection was past. The consequences of this imprudence were fatal. On the third day my mother sickened; her fever was very malignant, and the looks of her attendants prognosticated the worst event. On her death-bed the fortitude and benignity of this admirable woman did not desert her. She joined the hands of Elizabeth and myself: 'My children,' she said, 'my firmest hopes of future happiness were placed on the prospect of your union. This expectation will now be the consolation of your father. Elizabeth, my love, you must supply my place to your younger cousins. Alas! I regret that I am taken from you; and, happy and beloved as I have been, is it not hard to quit you all? But these are not thoughts befitting me; I will endeavour to resign myself cheerfully to death, and will indulge a hope of meeting you in another world.'*

She died calmly; and her countenance expressed affection even in death. I need not describe the feelings of those whose dearest ties are rent by that most irreparable evil, the void that presents itself to the soul, and the despair that is exhibited on the countenance. It is so long before the mind can persuade itself that she, whom we saw every day, and whose very existence appeared a part of our own, can have departed for ever—that the brightness of a beloved eye can have been extinguished, and the sound of a voice so familiar, and dear to the ear, can be hushed, never more to be heard. These are the reflections of the first days; but when the lapse of time proves the reality of the evil, then the actual bitterness of grief commences. Yet from whom has not that rude hand rent away some dear connexion; and why should I describe a sorrow which all have felt, and must feel? The time at length arrives, when grief is rather an indulgence than a necessity; and the smile that plays upon the lips, although it may be deemed a sacrilege, is not banished. My mother was dead, but we had still duties which we ought to perform; we must continue our course with the rest, and learn to think ourselves fortunate, whilst one remains whom the spoiler* has not seized.

My journey to Ingolstadt, which had been deferred by these events, was now again determined upon. I obtained from my father a respite of some weeks. This period was spent sadly; my mother's death, and my speedy departure, depressed our spirits; but Elizabeth endeavoured to renew the spirit of cheerfulness in our little society. Since the death of her aunt, her mind had acquired new firmness and vigour. She determined to fulfil her duties with the greatest exactness; and she felt that that most imperious* duty, of rendering her uncle and cousins happy, had devolved upon her. She consoled me, amused her uncle, instructed my brothers; and I never beheld her so enchanting as at this time, when she was continually endeavouring to contribute to the happiness of others, entirely forgetful of herself.

The day of my departure at length arrived. I had taken leave of all my friends, excepting Clerval, who spent the last evening with us. He bitterly lamented that he was unable to accompany me: but his father could not be persuaded to part with him, intending that he should become a partner with him in business, in compliance with his favourite theory, that learning was superfluous in the commerce of ordinary life. Henry had a refined mind; he had no desire to be idle, and was well pleased to become his father's partner, but he believed that a man might be a very good trader, and yet possess a cultivated understanding.

We sat late, listening to his complaints, and making many little arrangements for the future. The next morning early I departed. Tears gushed from the eyes of Elizabeth; they proceeded partly from sorrow at my departure, and partly because she reflected that the same journey was to have taken place three months before, when a mother's blessing would have accompanied me.

I threw myself into the chaise* that was to convey me away, and indulged in the most melancholy reflections. I, who had ever been surrounded by amiable companions, continually engaged in endeavouring to bestow mutual pleasure, I was now alone. In the university, whither I was going, I must form my own friends, and be my own protector. My life had hitherto been remarkably secluded and domestic; and this had given me invincible repugnance to new countenances. I loved my brothers, Elizabeth, and Clerval; these were 'old familiar faces;'* but I believed myself totally unfitted for the company of strangers. Such were my reflections as I commenced my journey; but as I proceeded, my spirits and hopes rose. I ardently desired the acquisition of knowledge. I had often, when at home, thought it hard to remain during my youth cooped up in one place, and had longed to enter the world, and take my station among other human beings. Now my desires were complied with, and it would, indeed, have been folly to repent.

I had sufficient leisure for these and many other reflections during my journey to Ingolstadt, which was long and fatiguing. At length the high white steeple of the town met my eyes. I alighted, and was conducted to my solitary apartment, to spend the evening as I pleased.

The next morning I delivered my letters of introduction, and paid a visit to some of the principal professors, and among others to M. Krempe, professor of natural philosophy. He received me with politeness, and asked me several questions concerning my progress in the different branches of science appertaining to natural philosophy. I mentioned, it is true, with fear and trembling, the only authors I had ever read upon those subjects. The professor stared: 'Have you,' he said, 'really spent your time in studying such nonsense?'

I replied in the affirmative. 'Every minute,' continued M. Krempe with warmth, 'every instant that you have wasted on those books is utterly and entirely lost. You have burdened your memory with exploded systems, and useless names. Good God! in what desert land have you lived, where no one was kind enough to inform you that these fancies, which you have so greedily imbibed, are a thousand years old, and as musty as they are ancient? I little expected in this enlightened and scientific age to find a disciple of Albertus Magnus and Paracelsus. My dear Sir, you must begin your studies entirely anew.'

So saying, he stept aside, and wrote down a list of several books treating of natural philosophy, which he desired me to procure, and dismissed me, after mentioning that in the beginning of the following week he intended to commence a course of lectures upon natural philosophy in its general relations, and that M. Waldman, a fellow-professor, would lecture upon chemistry the alternate days that he missed.

I returned home, not disappointed, for I had long considered those authors useless whom the professor had so strongly reprobated; but I did not feel much inclined to study the books which I procured at his recommendation. M. Krempe was a little squat man, with a gruff voice and repulsive countenance; the teacher, therefore, did not prepossess me in favour of his doctrine. Besides, I had a contempt for the uses of modern natural philosophy. It was very different, when the masters of the science sought immortality and power; such views, although futile, were grand: but now the scene was changed. The ambition of the inquirer seemed to limit itself to the annihilation of those visions on which my interest in science was chiefly founded. I was required to exchange chimeras of boundless grandeur for realities of little worth.

Such were my reflections during the first two or three days spent almost in solitude. But as the ensuing week commenced, I thought of the information which M. Krempe had given me concerning the lectures. And although I could not consent to go and hear that little conceited fellow deliver sentences* out of a pulpit, I recollected what he had said of M. Waldman, whom I had never seen, as he had hitherto been out of town.

Partly from curiosity, and partly from idleness, I went into the lecturing room, which M. Waldman entered shortly after. This professor was very unlike his colleague. He appeared about fifty years of age, but with an aspect expressive of the greatest benevolence; a few gray hairs covered his temples, but those at the back of his head were nearly black. His person was short, but remarkably erect; and his voice the sweetest I had ever heard.* He began his lecture by a recapitulation of the history of chemistry and the various improvements made by different men of learning, pronouncing with fervour the names of the most distinguished discoverers. He then took a cursory* view of the present state of the science, and explained many of its elementary terms. After having made a few preparatory experiments, he concluded with a panegyric upon modern chemistry, the terms of which I shall never forget:—

'The ancient teachers of this science,' said he, 'promised impossibilities, and performed nothing. The modern masters promise very little; they know that metals cannot be transmuted, and that the elixir of life is a chimera. But these philosophers, whose hands seem only made to dabble in dirt, and their eyes to pore over the microscope or crucible, have indeed performed miracles. They penetrate into the recesses of nature, and shew how she works in her hiding places.* They ascend into the heavens; they have discovered how the blood circulates, and the nature of the air we breathe. They have acquired new and almost unlimited powers; they can command the thunders of heaven, mimic the earthquake, and even mock the invisible world with its own shadows.'*

I departed highly pleased with the professor and his lecture, and paid him a visit the same evening. His manners in private were even more mild and attractive than in public; for there was a certain dignity in his mien during his lecture, which in his own house was replaced by the greatest affability and kindness. He heard with attention my little narration concerning my studies, and smiled at the names of Cornelius Agrippa, and Paracelsus, but without the contempt that M. Krempe had exhibited. He said, that 'these were men to whose indefatigable zeal modern philosophers were indebted for most of the foundations of their knowledge. They had left to us, as an easier task, to give new names, and arrange in connected classifications, the facts which they in a great degree had been the instruments of bringing to light. The labours of men of genius, however erroneously directed, scarcely ever fail in ultimately turning to the solid advantage of mankind.' I listened to his statement, which was delivered without any presumption or affectation; and then added, that his lecture had removed my prejudices against modern chemists; and I, at the same time, requested his advice concerning the books I ought to procure.

'I am happy,' said M. Waldman, 'to have gained a disciple; and if your application equals your ability, I have no doubt of your success. Chemistry is that branch of natural philosophy in which the greatest improvements have been and may be made; it is on that account that I have made it my peculiar* study; but at the same time I have not neglected the other branches of science. A man would make but a very sorry chemist, if he attended to that department of human knowledge alone. If your wish is to become really a man of science, and not merely a petty experimentalist, I should advise you to apply to every branch of natural philosophy, including mathematics.'*

He then took me into his laboratory, and explained to me the uses of his various machines; instructing me as to what I ought to procure, and promising me the use of his own, when I should have advanced far enough in the science not to derange their mechanism. He also gave me the list of books which I had requested; and I took my leave.

Thus ended a day memorable to me; it decided my future destiny.

CHAPTER III.

FROM this day natural philosophy, and particularly chemistry, in the most comprehensive sense of the term, became nearly my sole occupation. I read with ardour those works, so full of genius and discrimination, which modern inquirers have written on these subjects. I attended the lectures, and cultivated the acquaintance, of the men of science of the university; and I found even in M. Krempe a great deal of sound sense and real information, combined, it is true, with a repulsive physiognomy and manners, but not on that account the less valuable. In M. Waldman I found a true friend. His gentleness was never tinged by dogmatism; and his instructions were given with an air of frankness and good nature, that banished every idea of pedantry. It was, perhaps, the amiable character of this man that inclined me more to that branch of natural philosophy which he professed, than an intrinsic love for the science itself. But this state of mind had place only in the first steps towards knowledge: the more fully I entered into the science, the more exclusively I pursued it for its own sake. That application, which at first had been a matter of duty and resolution, now became so ardent and eager, that the stars often disappeared in the light of morning whilst I was yet engaged in my laboratory.

As I applied so closely,* it may be easily conceived that I improved rapidly. My ardour was indeed the astonishment of the students; and my proficiency, that of the masters. Professor Krempe often asked me, with a sly smile, how Cornelius Agrippa went on? whilst M. Waldman expressed the most heartfelt exultation in my progress. Two years passed in this manner, during which I paid no visit to Geneva, but was engaged, heart and soul, in the pursuit of some discoveries, which I hoped to make. None but those who have experienced them can conceive of the enticements of science. In other studies you go as far as others have gone before you, and there is nothing more to know; but in a scientific pursuit there is continual food for discovery and wonder. A mind of moderate capacity, which closely pursues one study, must infallibly arrive at great proficiency in that study; and I, who continually sought the attainment of one object of pursuit, and was solely wrapt up in this, improved so rapidly, that, at the end of two years, I made some discoveries in the improvement of some chemical instruments, which procured me great esteem and admiration at the university. When I had arrived at this point, and had become as well acquainted with the theory and practice of natural philosophy as depended on the lessons of any of the professors at Ingolstadt, my residence there being no longer conducive to my improvements, I thought of returning to my friends and my native town, when an incident happened that protracted my stay.

One of the phænomena which had peculiarly attracted my attention was the structure of the human frame, and, indeed, any animal endued with life. Whence, I often asked myself, did the principle* of life proceed? It was a bold question, and one which has ever been considered as a mystery; yet with how many things are we upon the brink of becoming acquainted, if cowardice or carelessness did not restrain our inquiries. I revolved these circumstances in my mind, and determined thenceforth to apply myself more particularly to those branches of natural philosophy which relate to physiology.* Unless I had been animated by an almost supernatural enthusiasm, my application to this study would have been irksome, and almost intolerable. To examine the causes of life, we must first have recourse to death.* I became acquainted with the science of anatomy: but this was not sufficient; I must also observe the natural decay and corruption of the human body. In my education my father had taken the greatest precautions that my mind should be impressed with no supernatural horrors. I do not ever remember to have trembled at a tale of superstition, or to have feared the apparition of a spirit. Darkness had no effect upon my fancy; and a church-yard was to me merely the receptacle of bodies deprived of life, which, from being the seat of beauty and strength, had become food for the worm. Now I was led to examine the cause and progress of this decay, and forced to spend days and nights in vaults and charnel houses. My attention was fixed upon every object the most insupportable to the delicacy of the human feelings. I saw how the fine form of man was degraded and wasted; I beheld the corruption of death succeed to the blooming cheek of life; I saw how the worm inherited the wonders of the eye and brain. I paused, examining and analysing all the minutiæ of causation, as exemplified in the change from life to death, and death to life, until from the midst of this darkness a sudden light broke in upon me— a light so brilliant and wondrous, yet so simple, that while I became dizzy with the immensity of the prospect which it illustrated, I was surprised that among so many men of genius, who had directed their inquiries towards the same science, that I alone should be reserved to discover so astonishing a secret.

Remember, I am not recording the vision of a madman. The sun does not more certainly shine in the heavens, than that which I now affirm is true. Some miracle might have produced it, yet the stages of the discovery were distinct and probable. After days and nights of incredible labour and fatigue, I succeeded in discovering the cause of generation and life; nay, more, I became myself capable of bestowing animation upon lifeless matter.

The astonishment which I had at first experienced on this discovery soon gave place to delight and rapture. After so much time spent in painful labour, to arrive at once at the summit of my desires, was the most gratifying consummation of my toils. But this discovery was so great and overwhelming, that all the steps by which I had been progressively led to it were obliterated, and I beheld only the result. What had been the study and desire of the wisest men since the creation of the world, was now within my grasp. Not that, like a magic scene, it all opened upon me at once: the information I had obtained was of a nature rather to direct my endeavours so soon as I should point them towards the object of my search, than to exhibit that object already accomplished. I was like the Arabian who had been buried with the dead, and found a passage to life aided only by one glimmering, and seemingly ineffectual, light*

I see by your eagerness, and the wonder and hope which your eyes express, my friend, that you expect to be informed of the secret with which I am acquainted; that cannot be: listen patiently until the end of my story, and you will easily perceive why I am reserved upon that subject. I will not lead you on, unguarded and ardent as I then was, to your destruction and infallible misery. Learn from me, if not by my precepts, at least by my example, how dangerous is the acquirement of knowledge, and how much happier that man is who believes his native town to be the world, than he who aspires to become greater than his nature will allow.

When I found so astonishing a power placed within my hands, I hesitated a long time concerning the manner in which I should employ it. Although I possessed the capacity of bestowing animation, yet to prepare a frame for the reception of it, with all its intricacies of fibres, muscles, and veins, still remained a work of inconceivable difficulty and labour. I doubted at first whether I should attempt the creation of a being like myself or one of simpler organization; but my imagination was too much exalted by my first success to permit me to doubt of my ability to give life to an animal as complex and wonderful as man. The materials at present within my command hardly appeared adequate to so arduous an undertaking; but I doubted not that I should ultimately succeed. I prepared myself for a multitude of reverses; my operations might be incessantly baffled, and at last my work be imperfect: yet, when I considered the improvement which every day takes place in science and mechanics, I was encouraged to hope my present attempts would at least lay the foundations of future success. Nor could I consider the magnitude and complexity of my plan as any argument of its impracticability. It was with these feelings that I began the creation of a human being. As the minuteness of the parts formed a great hindrance to my speed, I resolved, contrary to my first intention, to make the being of a gigantic stature; that is to say, about eight feet in height, and proportionably large. After having formed this determination, and having spent some months in successfully collecting and arranging my materials, I began.

No one can conceive the variety of feelings which bore me onwards, like a hurricane, in the first enthusiasm of success. Life and death appeared to me ideal bounds,* which I should first break through, and pour a torrent of light into our dark world. A new species would bless me as its creator and source; many happy and excellent natures would owe their being to me. No father could claim the gratitude of his child so completely as I should deserve their's. Pursuing these reflections, I thought, that if I could bestow animation upon lifeless matter, I might in process of time (although I now found it impossible) renew life where death had apparently devoted the body to corruption.*

These thoughts supported my spirits, while I pursued my undertaking with unremitting ardour. My cheek had grown pale with study, and my person had become emaciated with confinement.* Sometimes, on the very brink of certainty, I failed; yet still I clung to the hope which the next day or the next hour might realize. One secret which I alone possessed was the hope to which I had dedicated myself; and the moon gazed on my midnight labours, while, with unrelaxed and breathless eagerness, I pursued nature to her hiding places.* Who shall conceive the horrors of my secret toil, as I dabbled among the unhallowed damps of the grave, or tortured the living animal to animate the lifeless clay? My limbs now tremble, and my eyes swim with the remembrance; but then a resistless, and almost frantic impulse, urged me forward; I seemed to have lost all soul or sensation but for this one pursuit. It was indeed but a passing trance, that only made me feel with renewed acuteness so soon as, the unnatural stimulus ceasing to operate, I had returned to my old habits. I collected bones from charnel houses; and disturbed, with profane fingers, the tremendous secrets of the human frame. In a solitary chamber, or rather cell, at the top of the house, and separated from all the other apartments by a gallery and staircase, I kept my workshop of filthy* creation; my eyeballs were starting from their sockets in attending to the details of my employment. The dissecting room and the slaughter-house furnished many of my materials; and often did my human nature turn with loathing from my occupation, whilst, still urged on by an eagerness which perpetually increased, I brought my work near to a conclusion.

The summer months passed while I was thus engaged, heart and soul, in one pursuit. It was a most beautiful season; never did the fields bestow a more plentiful harvest, or the vines yield a more luxuriant vintage: but my eyes were insensible to the charms of nature. And the same feelings which made me neglect the scenes around me caused me also to forget those friends who were so many miles absent, and whom I had not seen for so long a time. I knew my silence disquieted them; and I well remembered the words of my father: 'I know that while you are pleased with yourself, you will think of us with affection, and we shall hear regularly from you. You must pardon me, if I regard any interruption in your correspondence as a proof that your other duties are equally neglected.'

I knew well therefore what would be my father's feelings; but I could not tear my thoughts from my employment, loathsome in itself, but which had taken an irresistible hold of my imagination. I wished, as it were, to procrastinate all that related to my feelings of affection until the great object, which swallowed up every habit of my nature, should be completed.

I then thought that my father would be unjust if he ascribed my neglect to vice, or faultiness on my part; but I am now convinced that he was justified in conceiving that I should not be altogether free from blame. A human being in perfection ought always to preserve a calm and peaceful mind, and never to allow passion or a transitory desire to disturb his tranquillity. I do not think that the pursuit of knowledge is an exception to this rule. If the study to which you apply yourself has a tendency to weaken your affections, and to destroy your taste for those simple pleasures in which no alloy* can possibly mix, then that study is certainly unlawful, that is to say, not befitting the human mind. If this rule were always observed; if no man allowed any pursuit whatsoever to interfere with the tranquillity of his domestic affections, Greece had not been enslaved; Cæsar would have spared his country; America would have been discovered more gradually; and the empires of Mexico and Peru* had not been destroyed.

But I forget that I am moralizing in the most interesting part of my tale; and your looks remind me to proceed.

My father made no reproach in his letters; and only took notice of my silence by inquiring into my occupations more particularly than before. Winter, spring, and summer, passed away during my labours; but I did not watch the blossom or the expanding leaves—sights which before always yielded me supreme delight, so deeply was I engrossed in my occupation. The leaves of that year had withered before my work drew near to a close; and now every day shewed me more plainly how well I had succeeded. But my enthusiasm was checked by my anxiety, and I appeared rather like one doomed by slavery to toil in the mines, or any other unwholesome trade, than an artist occupied by his favourite employment. Every night I was oppressed by a slow fever, and I became nervous to a most painful degree; a disease that I regretted the more because I had hitherto enjoyed most excellent health, and had always boasted of the firmness of my nerves. But I believed that exercise and amusement would soon drive away such symptoms; and I promised myself both of these, when my creation should be complete.

CHAPTER IV.

IT was on a dreary night of November,* that I beheld the accomplishment of my toils. With an anxiety that almost amounted to agony, I collected the instruments of life* around me, that I might infuse a spark of being into the lifeless thing that lay at my feet. It was already one in the morning; the rain pattered dismally against the panes,* and my candle was nearly burnt out, when, by the glimmer of the half-extinguished light, I saw the dull yellow eye of the creature open; it breathed hard, and a convulsive motion agitated its limbs.

How can I describe my emotions at this catastrophe, or how delineate the wretch whom with such infinite pains and care I had endeavoured to form? His limbs were in proportion, and I had selected his features as beautiful.* Beautiful!—Great God! His yellow skin scarcely covered the work of muscles and arteries beneath; his hair was of a lustrous black, and flowing; his teeth of a pearly whiteness; but these luxuriances only formed a more horrid contrast with his watery eyes, that seemed almost of the same colour as the dun white sockets in which they were set, his shrivelled complexion, and straight black lips.*

The different accidents of life are not so changeable as the feelings of human nature. I had worked hard for nearly two years, for the sole purpose of infusing life into an inanimate body. For this I had deprived myself of rest and health. I had desired it with an ardour that far exceeded moderation; but now that I had finished, the beauty of the dream vanished, and breathless horror and disgust filled my heart. Unable to endure the aspect* of the being I had created, I rushed out of the room, and continued a long time traversing my bed-chamber, unable to compose my mind to sleep. At length lassitude succeeded to the tumult I had before endured; and I threw myself on the bed in my clothes, endeavouring to seek a few moments of forgetfulness. But it was in vain: I slept indeed, but I was disturbed by the wildest dreams. I thought I saw Elizabeth, in the bloom of health, walking in the streets of Ingolstadt. Delighted and surprised, I embraced her; but as I imprinted the first kiss on her lips, they became livid with the hue of death; her features appeared to change, and I thought that I held the corpse of my dead mother in my arms; a shroud enveloped her form, and I saw the grave-worms crawling in the folds of the flannel. I started from my sleep with horror; a cold dew covered my forehead, my teeth chattered, and every limb became convulsed; when, by the dim and yellow light of the moon, as it forced its way though the window-shutters, I beheld the wretch—the miserable monster* whom I had created. He held up the curtain of the bed; and his eyes, if eyes they may be called, were fixed on me. His jaws opened, and he muttered some inarticulate sounds, while a grin wrinkled his cheeks. He might have spoken, but I did not hear; one hand was stretched out, seemingly to detain me, but I escaped, and rushed down stairs. I took refuge in the court-yard belonging to the house which I inhabited; where I remained during the rest of the night, walking up and down in the greatest agitation, listening attentively, catching and fearing each sound as if it were to announce the approach of the demoniacal corpse to which I had so miserably given life.

Oh! no mortal could support the horror of that countenance. A mummy* again endued with animation could not be so hideous as that wretch. I had gazed on him while unfinished; he was ugly then; but when those muscles and joints were rendered capable of motion, it became a thing such as even Dante* could not have conceived.

I passed the night wretchedly. Sometimes my pulse beat so quickly and hardly,* that I felt the palpitation of every artery; at others, I nearly sank to the ground through languor and extreme weakness. Mingled with this horror, I felt the bitterness of disappointment: dreams that had been my food and pleasant rest for so long a space, were now become a hell to me; and the change was so rapid, the overthrow so complete!

Morning, dismal and wet, at length dawned, and discovered to my sleepless and aching eyes the church of Ingolstadt, its white steeple and clock, which indicated the sixth hour. The porter opened the gates of the court, which had that night been my asylum, and I issued into the streets, pacing them with quick steps, as if I sought to avoid the wretch whom I feared every turning of the street would present to my view. I did not dare return to the apartment which I inhabited, but felt impelled to hurry on, although wetted by the rain, which poured from a black and comfortless sky.

I continued walking in this manner for some time, endeavouring, by bodily exercise, to ease the load that weighed upon my mind. I traversed the streets, without any clear conception of where I was, or what I was doing. My heart palpitated in the sickness of fear; and I hurried on with irregular steps, not daring to look about me:

> Like one who, on a lonely road,
> Doth walk in fear and dread,
> And, having once turn'd round, walks on,
> And turns no more his head;
> Because he knows a frightful fiend
> Doth close behind him tread.[1]

Continuing thus, I came at length opposite to the inn at which the various diligences* and carriages usually stopped. Here I paused, I knew not why; but I remained some minutes with my eyes fixed on a coach that was coming towards me from the other end of the street. As it drew nearer, I observed that it was the Swiss diligence: it stopped

---

[1] Coleridge's 'Ancient Mariner.'*

just where I was standing; and, on the door being opened, I perceived Henry Clerval, who, on seeing me, instantly sprung out. 'My dear Frankenstein,' exclaimed he, 'how glad I am to see you! how fortunate that you should be here at the very moment of my alighting!'

Nothing could equal my delight on seeing Clerval; his presence brought back to my thoughts my father, Elizabeth, and all those scenes of home so dear to my recollection. I grasped his hand, and in a moment forgot my horror and misfortune; I felt suddenly, and for the first time during many months, calm and serene joy. I welcomed my friend, therefore, in the most cordial manner, and we walked towards my college. Clerval continued talking for some time about our mutual friends, and his own good fortune in being permitted to come to Ingolstadt. 'You may easily believe,' said he, 'how great was the difficulty to persuade my father that it was not absolutely necessary for a merchant not to understand any thing except book-keeping; and, indeed, I believe I left him incredulous to the last, for his constant answer to my unwearied entreaties was the same as that of the Dutch school-master in the Vicar of Wakefield:* "I have ten thousand florins a year without Greek, I eat heartily without Greek." But his affection for me at length overcame his dislike of learning, and he has permitted me to undertake a voyage of discovery to the land of knowledge.'

'It gives me the greatest delight to see you; but tell me how you left my father, brothers, and Elizabeth.'

'Very well, and very happy, only a little uneasy that they hear from you so seldom. By the bye, I mean to lecture you a little upon their account myself.—But, my dear Frankenstein,' continued he, stopping short, and gazing full in my face, 'I did not before remark how very ill you appear; so thin and pale; you look as if you had been watching* for several nights.'

'You have guessed right; I have lately been so deeply engaged in one occupation, that I have not allowed myself sufficient rest, as you see: but I hope, I sincerely hope, that all these employments are now at an end, and that I am at length free.'

I trembled excessively; I could not endure to think of, and far less to allude to the occurrences of the preceding night. I walked with a quick pace, and we soon arrived at my college. I then reflected, and the thought made me shiver, that the creature whom I had left in my apartment might still be there, alive, and walking about. I dreaded to behold this monster; but I feared still more that Henry should see

him. Entreating him therefore to remain a few minutes at the bottom
of the stairs, I darted up towards my own room. My hand was already
on the lock of the door before I recollected myself. I then paused; and
a cold shivering came over me. I threw the door forcibly open, as
children are accustomed to do when they expect a spectre to stand in
waiting for them on the other side; but nothing appeared. I stepped
fearfully in: the apartment was empty; and my bedroom was also
freed from its hideous guest. I could hardly believe that so great
a good-fortune could have befallen me; but when I became assured
that my enemy had indeed fled, I clapped my hands for joy, and ran
down to Clerval.

We ascended into my room, and the servant presently brought
breakfast; but I was unable to contain myself. It was not joy only that
possessed me; I felt my flesh tingle with excess of sensitiveness, and
my pulse beat rapidly. I was unable to remain for a single instant in
the same place; I jumped over the chairs, clapped my hands, and
laughed aloud. Clerval at first attributed my unusual spirits to joy on
his arrival; but when he observed me more attentively, he saw a wildness in my eyes for which he could not account; and my loud, unrestrained, heartless laughter, frightened and astonished him.

'My dear Victor,' cried he, 'what, for God's sake, is the matter? Do
not laugh in that manner. How ill you are! What is the cause of all this?'

'Do not ask me,' cried I, putting my hands before my eyes, for
I thought I saw the dreaded spectre glide into the room; '*he* can
tell.—Oh, save me! save me!' I imagined that the monster seized me;
I struggled furiously, and fell down in a fit.

Poor Clerval! what must have been his feelings? A meeting, which
he anticipated with such joy, so strangely turned to bitterness. But
I was not the witness of his grief; for I was lifeless, and did not recover
my senses for a long, long time.

This was the commencement of a nervous fever, which confined
me for several months. During all that time Henry was my only nurse.
I afterwards learned that, knowing my father's advanced age, and
unfitness for so long a journey, and how wretched my sickness would
make Elizabeth, he spared them this grief by concealing the extent of
my disorder. He knew that I could not have a more kind and attentive
nurse than himself; and, firm in the hope he felt of my recovery, he
did not doubt that, instead of doing harm, he performed the kindest
action that he could towards them.

But I was in reality very ill; and surely nothing but the unbounded and unremitting attentions of my friend could have restored me to life. The form of the monster on whom I had bestowed existence was for ever before my eyes, and I raved incessantly concerning him. Doubtless my words surprised Henry: he at first believed them to be the wanderings of my disturbed imagination; but the pertinacity with which I continually recurred to the same subject persuaded him that my disorder indeed owed its origin to some uncommon and terrible event.

By very slow degrees, and with frequent relapses, that alarmed and grieved my friend, I recovered. I remember the first time I became capable of observing outward objects with any kind of pleasure, I perceived that the fallen leaves had disappeared, and that the young buds were shooting forth from the trees that shaded my window. It was a divine spring; and the season contributed greatly to my convalescence. I felt also sentiments of joy and affection revive in my bosom; my gloom disappeared, and in a short time I became as cheerful as before I was attacked by the fatal passion.

'Dearest Clerval,' exclaimed I, 'how kind, how very good you are to me. This whole winter, instead of being spent in study, as you promised yourself, has been consumed in my sick room. How shall I ever repay you? I feel the greatest remorse for the disappointment of which I have been the occasion; but you will forgive me.'

'You will repay me entirely, if you do not discompose yourself, but get well as fast as you can; and since you appear in such good spirits, I may speak to you on one subject, may I not?'

I trembled. One subject! what could it be? Could he allude to an object on whom I dared not even think?

'Compose yourself,' said Clerval, who observed my change of colour, 'I will not mention it, if it agitates you; but your father and cousin would be very happy if they received a letter from you in your own hand-writing. They hardly know how ill you have been, and are uneasy at your long silence.'

'Is that all? my dear Henry. How could you suppose that my first thought would not fly towards those dear, dear friends whom I love, and who are so deserving of my love.'

'If this is your present temper, my friend, you will perhaps be glad to see a letter that has been lying here some days for you: it is from your cousin, I believe.'

CHAPTER V.

CLERVAL then put the following letter into my hands.

To V. FRANKENSTEIN.

'MY DEAR COUSIN,

'I cannot describe to you the uneasiness we have all felt concerning your health. We cannot help imagining that your friend Clerval conceals the extent of your disorder: for it is now several months since we have seen your hand-writing; and all this time you have been obliged to dictate your letters to Henry. Surely, Victor, you must have been exceedingly ill; and this makes us all very wretched, as much so nearly as after the death of your dear mother. My uncle was almost persuaded that you were indeed dangerously ill, and could hardly be restrained from undertaking a journey to Ingolstadt. Clerval always writes that you are getting better; I eagerly hope that you will confirm this intelligence soon in your own hand-writing; for indeed, indeed, Victor, we are all very miserable on this account. Relieve us from this fear, and we shall be the happiest creatures in the world. Your father's health is now so vigorous, that he appears ten years younger since last winter. Ernest also is so much improved, that you would hardly know him: he is now nearly sixteen, and has lost that sickly appearance which he had some years ago; he is grown quite robust and active.

'My uncle and I conversed a long time last night about what profession Ernest should follow. His constant illness when young has deprived him of the habits of application; and now that he enjoys good health, he is continually in the open air, climbing the hills, or rowing on the lake. I therefore proposed that he should be a farmer; which you know, Cousin, is a favourite scheme of mine. A farmer's is a very healthy happy life; and the least hurtful, or rather the most beneficial profession of any. My uncle had an idea of his being educated as an advocate, that through his interest he might become a judge. But, besides that he is not at all fitted for such an occupation, it is certainly more creditable to cultivate the earth for the sustenance of man, than to be the confidant, and sometimes the accomplice, of his vices; which is the profession of a lawyer. I said, that the employments of a prosperous farmer, if they were not a more honourable, they were at least a happier species of occupation than that of a judge, whose misfortune it was always to meddle with the dark side of human nature. My uncle smiled, and said, that I ought to be an advocate myself, which put an end to the conversation on that subject.

'And now I must tell you a little story that will please, and perhaps amuse you. Do you not remember Justine Moritz? Probably you do not; I will relate her history, therefore, in a few words. Madame Moritz, her mother, was a widow with four children, of whom Justine was the third. This girl had always been the favourite of her father; but, through a strange perversity, her mother could not endure her, and, after the death of M. Moritz, treated her very ill. My aunt observed this; and, when Justine was twelve years of age, prevailed on her mother to allow her to live at her house. The republican institutions of our country have produced simpler and happier manners than those which prevail in the great monarchies that surround it. Hence there is less distinction between the several classes of its inhabitants; and the lower orders being neither so poor nor so despised, their manners are more refined and moral. A servant in Geneva does not mean the same thing as a servant in France and England. Justine, thus received in our family, learned the duties of a servant; a condition which, in our fortunate country, does not include the idea of ignorance, and a sacrifice of the dignity of a human being.

'After what I have said, I dare say you well remember the heroine of my little tale: for Justine was a great favourite of your's; and I recollect you once remarked, that if you were in an ill humour, one glance from Justine could dissipate it, for the same reason that Ariosto gives concerning the beauty of Angelica*—she looked so frank-hearted and happy. My aunt conceived a great attachment for her, by which she was induced to give her an education superior to that which she had at first intended. This benefit was fully repaid; Justine was the most grateful little creature in the world: I do not mean that she made any professions, I never heard one pass her lips; but you could see by her eyes that she almost adored her protectress. Although her disposition was gay, and in many respects inconsiderate, yet she paid the greatest attention to every gesture of my aunt. She thought her the model of all excellence, and endeavoured to imitate her phraseology and manners, so that even now she often reminds me of her.

'When my dearest aunt died, every one was too much occupied in their own grief to notice poor Justine, who had attended her during her illness with the most anxious affection. Poor Justine was very ill; but other trials were reserved for her.

'One by one, her brothers and sister died; and her mother, with the exception of her neglected daughter, was left childless. The conscience of the woman was troubled; she began to think that the deaths of her favourites was a judgment from heaven to chastise her partiality. She was a Roman Catholic; and I believe her confessor confirmed the idea which she had conceived. Accordingly, a few months after your departure for Ingolstadt, Justine was called home by her repentant mother. Poor girl! she wept when she quitted our house: she was much altered since the death of my aunt; grief had given softness and a winning mildness to her manners, which had before been remarkable for vivacity. Nor was her residence at her mother's house of a nature to restore her gaiety. The poor woman was very vacillating in her repentance. She sometimes begged Justine to forgive her unkindness, but much oftener accused her of having caused the deaths of her brothers and sister. Perpetual fretting at length threw Madame Moritz into a decline, which at first increased her irritability, but she is now at peace for ever. She died on the first approach of cold weather, at the beginning of this last winter. Justine has returned to us; and I assure you I love her tenderly. She is very clever and gentle, and extremely pretty; as I mentioned before, her mien and her expressions continually remind me of my dear aunt.

'I must say also a few words to you, my dear cousin, of little darling William. I wish you could see him; he is very tall of his age, with sweet laughing blue eyes, dark eye-lashes, and curling hair. When he smiles, two little dimples appear on each cheek, which are rosy with health. He has already had one or two little *wives*, but Louisa Biron is his favourite, a pretty little girl of five years of age.

'Now, dear Victor, I dare say you wish to be indulged in a little gossip concerning the good people of Geneva. The pretty Miss Mansfield has already received the congratulatory visits on her approaching marriage with a young Englishman, John Melbourne, Esq. Her ugly sister, Manon, married M. Duvillard, the rich banker, last autumn. Your favourite schoolfellow, Louis Manoir, has suffered several misfortunes since the departure of Clerval from Geneva. But he has already recovered his spirits, and is reported to be on the point of marrying a very lively pretty Frenchwoman, Madame Tavernier. She is a widow, and much older than Manoir; but she is very much admired, and a favourite with every body.

'I have written myself into good spirits, dear cousin; yet I cannot conclude without again anxiously inquiring concerning your health.

Dear Victor, if you are not very ill, write yourself, and make your father and all of us happy; or—I cannot bear to think of the other side of the question; my tears already flow. Adieu, my dearest cousin.

'ELIZABETH LAVENZA.
'Geneva, March 18th, 17—.'

'Dear, dear Elizabeth!' I exclaimed when I had read her letter, 'I will write instantly, and relieve them from the anxiety they must feel.' I wrote, and this exertion greatly fatigued me; but my convalescence had commenced, and proceeded regularly. In another fortnight I was able to leave my chamber.

One of my first duties on my recovery was to introduce Clerval to the several professors of the university. In doing this, I underwent a kind of rough usage, ill befitting the wounds that my mind had sustained. Ever since the fatal night, the end of my labours, and the beginning of my misfortunes, I had conceived a violent antipathy even to the name of natural philosophy. When I was otherwise quite restored to health, the sight of a chemical instrument would renew all the agony of my nervous symptoms. Henry saw this, and had removed all my apparatus from my view. He had also changed my apartment; for he perceived that I had acquired a dislike for the room which had previously been my laboratory. But these cares of Clerval were made of no avail when I visited the professors. M. Waldman inflicted torture when he praised, with kindness and warmth, the astonishing progress I had made in the sciences. He soon perceived that I disliked the subject; but, not guessing the real cause, he attributed my feelings to modesty, and changed the subject from my improvement to the science itself, with a desire, as I evidently saw, of drawing me out. What could I do? He meant to please, and he tormented me. I felt as if he had placed carefully, one by one, in my view those instruments which were to be afterwards used in putting me to a slow and cruel death. I writhed under his words, yet dared not exhibit the pain I felt. Clerval, whose eyes and feelings were always quick in discerning the sensations of others, declined the subject, alleging, in excuse, his total ignorance; and the conversation took a more general turn. I thanked my friend from my heart, but I did not speak. I saw plainly that he was surprised, but he never attempted to draw my secret from me; and although I loved him with a mixture of affection and reverence that knew no bounds, yet I could never persuade myself to confide to him that event which was so often present to my recollection, but which I feared the detail to another would only impress more deeply.

M. Krempe was not equally docile; and in my condition at that time, of almost insupportable sensitiveness, his harsh blunt encomiums gave me even more pain than the benevolent approbation of M. Waldman. 'D——n the fellow!' cried he; 'why, M. Clerval, I assure you he has outstript us all. Aye, stare if you please; but it is nevertheless true. A youngster who, but a few years ago, believed Cornelius Agrippa as firmly as the gospel, has now set himself at the head of the university; and if he is not soon pulled down, we shall all be out of countenance.— Aye, aye,' continued he, observing my face expressive of suffering, 'M. Frankenstein is modest; an excellent quality in a young man. Young men should be diffident of themselves, you know, M. Clerval; I was myself when young: but that wears out in a very short time.'

M. Krempe had now commenced an eulogy on himself, which happily turned the conversation from a subject that was so annoying to me.

Clerval was no natural philosopher. His imagination was too vivid for the minutiæ of science. Languages were his principal study; and he sought, by acquiring their elements, to open a field for self-instruction on his return to Geneva. Persian, Arabic, and Hebrew, gained his attention, after he had made himself perfectly master of Greek and Latin. For my own part, idleness had ever been irksome to me; and now that I wished to fly from reflection, and hated my former studies, I felt great relief in being the fellow-pupil with my friend, and found not only instruction but consolation in the works of the orientalists. Their melancholy is soothing, and their joy elevating to a degree I never experienced in studying the authors of any other country. When you read their writings, life appears to consist in a warm sun and garden of roses,—in the smiles and frowns of a fair enemy, and the fire that consumes your own heart. How different from the manly and heroical poetry of Greece and Rome.

Summer passed away in these occupations, and my return to Geneva was fixed for the latter end of autumn; but being delayed by several accidents, winter and snow arrived, the roads were deemed impassable, and my journey was retarded until the ensuing spring. I felt this delay very bitterly; for I longed to see my native town, and my beloved friends. My return had only been delayed so long from an unwillingness to leave Clerval in a strange place, before he had become acquainted with any of its inhabitants. The winter, however, was spent cheerfully;

and although the spring was uncommonly late, when it came, its beauty compensated for its dilatoriness.

The month of May had already commenced, and I expected the letter daily which was to fix the date of my departure, when Henry proposed a pedestrian tour in the environs of Ingolstadt that I might bid a personal farewell to the country I had so long inhabited. I acceded with pleasure to this proposition: I was fond of exercise, and Clerval had always been my favourite companion in the rambles of this nature that I had taken among the scenes of my native country.

We passed a fortnight in these perambulations: my health and spirits had long been restored, and they gained additional strength from the salubrious air I breathed, the natural incidents of our progress, and the conversation of my friend. Study had before secluded me from the intercourse of my fellow-creatures, and rendered me unsocial; but Clerval called forth the better feelings of my heart; he again taught me to love the aspect of nature, and the cheerful faces of children. Excellent friend! how sincerely did you love me, and endeavour to elevate my mind, until it was on a level with your own. A selfish pursuit had cramped and narrowed me, until your gentleness and affection warmed and opened my senses; I became the same happy creature who, a few years ago, loving and beloved by all, had no sorrow or care. When happy, inanimate nature had the power of bestowing on me the most delightful sensations. A serene sky and verdant fields filled me with ecstacy. The present season was indeed divine; the flowers of spring bloomed in the hedges, while those of summer were already in bud: I was undisturbed by thoughts which during the preceding year had pressed upon me, notwithstanding my endeavours to throw them off, with an invincible burden.

Henry rejoiced in my gaiety, and sincerely sympathized in my feelings: he exerted himself to amuse me, while he expressed the sensations that filled his soul. The resources of his mind on this occasion were truly astonishing: his conversation was full of imagination; and very often, in imitation of the Persian and Arabic writers, he invented tales of wonderful fancy and passion. At other times he repeated my favourite poems, or drew me out into arguments, which he supported with great ingenuity.

We returned to our college on a Sunday afternoon: the peasants were dancing, and every one we met appeared gay and happy. My own spirits were high, and I bounded along with feelings of unbridled joy and hilarity.

CHAPTER VI.

ON my return, I found the following letter from my father:—

'*To* V. FRANKENSTEIN.

'MY DEAR VICTOR,

'You have probably waited impatiently for a letter to fix the date of your return to us; and I was at first tempted to write only a few lines, merely mentioning the day on which I should expect you. But that would be a cruel kindness, and I dare not do it. What would be your surprise, my son, when you expected a happy and gay welcome, to behold, on the contrary, tears and wretchedness? And how, Victor, can I relate our misfortune? Absence cannot have rendered you callous to our joys and griefs; and how shall I inflict pain on an absent child? I wish to prepare you for the woeful news, but I know it is impossible; even now your eye skims over the page, to seek the words which are to convey to you the horrible tidings.

'William is dead!—that sweet child, whose smiles delighted and warmed my heart, who was so gentle, yet so gay! Victor, he is murdered!

'I will not attempt to console you; but will simply relate the circumstances of the transaction.

'Last Thursday (May 7th) I, my niece, and your two brothers, went to walk in Plainpalais.* The evening was warm and serene, and we prolonged our walk farther than usual. It was already dusk before we thought of returning; and then we discovered that William and Ernest, who had gone on before, were not to be found. We accordingly rested on a seat until they should return. Presently Ernest came, and inquired if we had seen his brother: he said, that they had been playing together, that William had run away to hide himself, and that he vainly sought for him, and afterwards waited for him a long time, but that he did not return.

'This account rather alarmed us, and we continued to search for him until night fell, when Elizabeth conjectured that he might have returned to the house. He was not there. We returned again, with torches; for I could not rest, when I thought that my sweet boy had lost himself, and was exposed to all the damps and dews of night: Elizabeth also suffered extreme anguish. About five in the morning I discovered my lovely boy, whom the night before I had seen blooming and active in health, stretched on the grass livid and motionless: the print of the murderer's finger was on his neck.

de mongel

'He was conveyed home, and the anguish that was visible in my countenance betrayed the secret to Elizabeth. She was very earnest to see the corpse. At first I attempted to prevent her; but she persisted, and entering the room where it lay, hastily examined the neck of the victim, and clasping her hands exclaimed, "O God! I have murdered my darling infant!"

'She fainted, and was restored with extreme difficulty. When she again lived, it was only to weep and sigh. She told me, that that same evening William had teazed her to let him wear a very valuable miniature that she possessed of your mother. This picture is gone, and was doubtless the temptation which urged the murderer to the deed. We have no trace of him at present, although our exertions to discover him are unremitted; but they will not restore my beloved William.

'Come, dearest Victor; you alone can console Elizabeth. She weeps continually, and accuses herself unjustly as the cause of his death; her words pierce my heart. We are all unhappy; but will not that be an additional motive for you, my son, to return and be our comforter? Your dear mother! Alas, Victor! I now say, Thank God she did not live to witness the cruel, miserable death of her youngest darling!

'Come, Victor; not brooding thoughts of vengeance against the assassin, but with feelings of peace and gentleness, that will heal, instead of festering the wounds of our minds. Enter the house of mourning, my friend, but with kindness and affection for those who love you, and not with hatred for your enemies.

'Your affectionate and afflicted father,

'ALPHONSE FRANKENSTEIN.
'Geneva, May 12th, 17—.'

Clerval, who had watched my countenance as I read this letter, was surprised to observe the despair that succeeded to the joy I at first expressed on receiving news from my friends. I threw the letter on the table, and covered my face with my hands.

'My dear Frankenstein,' exclaimed Henry, when he perceived me weep with bitterness, 'are you always to be unhappy? My dear friend, what has happened?'

I motioned to him to take up the letter, while I walked up and down the room in the extremest agitation. Tears also gushed from the eyes of Clerval, as he read the account of my misfortune.

'I can offer you no consolation, my friend,' said he; 'your disaster is irreparable. What do you intend to do?'

'To go instantly to Geneva: come with me, Henry, to order the horses.'

During our walk, Clerval endeavoured to raise my spirits. He did not do this by common topics of consolation, but by exhibiting the truest sympathy. 'Poor William!' said he, 'that dear child; he now sleeps with his angel mother. His friends mourn and weep, but he is at rest: he does not now feel the murderer's grasp; a sod covers his gentle form, and he knows no pain. He can no longer be a fit subject for pity; the survivors are the greatest sufferers, and for them time is the only consolation. Those maxims of the Stoics,* that death was no evil, and that the mind of man ought to be superior to despair on the eternal absence of a beloved object, ought not to be urged. Even Cato* wept over the dead body of his brother.'

Clerval spoke thus as we hurried through the streets; the words impressed themselves on my mind, and I remembered them afterwards in solitude. But now, as soon as the horses arrived, I hurried into a cabriole,* and bade farewell to my friend.

My journey was very melancholy. At first I wished to hurry on, for I longed to console and sympathize with my loved and sorrowing friends; but when I drew near my native town, I slackened my progress. I could hardly sustain the multitude of feelings that crowded into my mind. I passed through scenes familiar to my youth, but which I had not seen for nearly six years. How altered every thing might be during that time? One sudden and desolating change had taken place; but a thousand little circumstances might have by degrees worked other alterations, which, although they were done more tranquilly, might not be the less decisive. Fear overcame me; I dared not advance, dreading a thousand nameless evils that made me tremble, although I was unable to define them.

I remained two days at Lausanne,* in this painful state of mind. I contemplated the lake: the waters were placid; all around was calm, and the snowy mountains, 'the palaces of nature,'* were not changed. By degrees the calm and heavenly scene restored me, and I continued my journey towards Geneva.

The road ran by the side of the lake, which became narrower as I approached my native town. I discovered more distinctly the black sides of Jura, and the bright summit of Mont Blanc;* I wept like a child: 'Dear mountains! my own beautiful lake! how do you welcome your wanderer? Your summits are clear; the sky and lake are blue and placid. Is this to prognosticate peace, or to mock at my unhappiness?'

I fear, my friend, that I shall render myself tedious by dwelling on these preliminary circumstances; but they were days of comparative happiness, and I think of them with pleasure. My country, my beloved country! who but a native can tell the delight I took in again beholding thy streams, thy mountains, and, more than all, thy lovely lake.

Yet, as I drew nearer home, grief and fear again overcame me. Night also closed around; and when I could hardly see the dark mountains, I felt still more gloomily. The picture appeared a vast and dim scene of evil, and I foresaw obscurely that I was destined to become the most wretched of human beings. Alas! I prophesied truly, and failed only in one single circumstance, that in all the misery I imagined and dreaded, I did not conceive the hundredth part of the anguish I was destined to endure.

It was completely dark when I arrived in the environs of Geneva; the gates of the town were already shut; and I was obliged to pass the night at Secheron, a village half a league to the east of the city. The sky was serene; and, as I was unable to rest, I resolved to visit the spot where my poor William had been murdered. As I could not pass through the town, I was obliged to cross the lake in a boat to arrive at Plainpalais. During this short voyage I saw the lightnings playing on the summit of Mont Blanc in the most beautiful figures. The storm appeared to approach rapidly; and, on landing, I ascended a low hill, that I might observe its progress. It advanced; the heavens were clouded, and I soon felt the rain coming slowly in large drops, but its violence quickly increased.

I quitted my seat, and walked on, although the darkness and storm increased every minute, and the thunder burst with a terrific* crash over my head. It was echoed from Salêve,* the Juras, and the Alps of Savoy; vivid flashes of lightning dazzled my eyes, illuminating the lake, making it appear like a vast sheet of fire; then for an instant every thing seemed of a pitchy darkness, until the eye recovered itself from the preceding flash. The storm, as is often the case in Switzerland, appeared at once in various parts of the heavens. The most violent storm hung exactly north of the town, over that part of the lake which lies between the promontory of Belrive and the village of Copêt. Another storm enlightened Jura with faint flashes; and another darkened and sometimes disclosed the Môle,* a peaked mountain to the east of the lake.

While I watched the storm, so beautiful yet terrific, I wandered on with a hasty step. This noble war in the sky elevated my spirits; I clasped my hands, and exclaimed aloud, 'William, dear angel! this is thy funeral, this thy dirge!' As I said these words, I perceived in the gloom a figure which stole from behind a clump of trees near me; I stood fixed, gazing intently: I could not be mistaken. A flash of lightning illuminated the object, and discovered its shape plainly to me; its gigantic stature, and the deformity of its aspect, more hideous than belongs to humanity, instantly informed me that it was the wretch, the filthy dæmon to whom I had given life. What did he there? Could he be (I shuddered at the conception) the murderer of my brother? No sooner did that idea cross my imagination, than I became convinced of its truth; my teeth chattered, and I was forced to lean against a tree for support. The figure passed me quickly, and I lost it in the gloom. Nothing in human shape could have destroyed that fair child. *He* was the murderer! I could not doubt it. The mere presence of the idea was an irresistible proof of the fact. I thought of pursuing the devil; but it would have been in vain, for another flash discovered him to me hanging among the rocks of the nearly perpendicular ascent of Mont Salêve, a hill that bounds Plainpalais on the south. He soon reached the summit, and disappeared.

I remained motionless. The thunder ceased; but the rain still continued, and the scene was enveloped in an impenetrable darkness. I revolved in my mind the events which I had until now sought to forget: the whole train of my progress towards the creation; the appearance of the work of my own hands alive at my bed side; its departure. Two years had now nearly elapsed since the night on which he first received life; and was this his first crime? Alas! I had turned loose into the world a depraved wretch, whose delight was in carnage and misery; had he not murdered my brother?

No one can conceive the anguish I suffered during the remainder of the night, which I spent, cold and wet, in the open air. But I did not feel the inconvenience of the weather; my imagination was busy in scenes of evil and despair. I considered the being whom I had cast among mankind, and endowed with the will and power to effect purposes of horror, such as the deed which he had now done, nearly in the light of my own vampire,* my own spirit let loose from the grave, and forced to destroy all that was dear to me.

Day dawned; and I directed my steps towards the town. The gates were open; and I hastened to my father's house. My first thought was to discover what I knew of the murderer, and cause instant pursuit to be made. But I paused when I reflected on the story that I had to tell. A being whom I myself had formed, and endued with life, had met me at midnight among the precipices of an inaccessible mountain. I remembered also the nervous fever with which I had been seized just at the time that I dated my creation, and which would give an air of delirium to a tale otherwise so utterly improbable. I well knew that if any other had communicated such a relation to me, I should have looked upon it as the ravings of insanity. Besides, the strange nature of the animal would elude all pursuit, even if I were so far credited as to persuade my relatives to commence it. Besides, of what use would be pursuit? Who could arrest a creature capable of scaling the over-hanging sides of Mont Salêve? These reflections determined me, and I resolved to remain silent.

It was about five in the morning when I entered my father's house. I told the servants not to disturb the family, and went into the library to attend their usual hour of rising.

Six years had elapsed, passed as a dream but for one indelible trace, and I stood in the same place where I had last embraced my father before my departure for Ingolstadt. Beloved and respectable parent! He still remained to me. I gazed on the picture of my mother, which stood over the mantelpiece. It was an historical subject, painted at my father's desire, and represented Caroline Beaufort in an agony of despair, kneeling by the coffin of her dead father. Her garb was rustic, and her cheek pale; but there was an air of dignity and beauty, that hardly permitted the sentiment of pity. Below this picture was a mini-ature of William; and my tears flowed when I looked upon it. While I was thus engaged, Ernest entered: he had heard me arrive, and has-tened to welcome me. He expressed a sorrowful delight to see me: 'Welcome, my dearest Victor,' said he. 'Ah! I wish you had come three months ago, and then you would have found us all joyous and delighted. But we are now unhappy; and, I am afraid, tears instead of smiles will be your welcome. Our father looks so sorrowful: this dread-ful event seems to have revived in his mind his grief on the death of Mamma. Poor Elizabeth also is quite inconsolable.' Ernest began to weep as he said these words.

'Do not,' said I, 'welcome me thus; try to be more calm, that I may not be absolutely miserable the moment I enter my father's house after so long an absence. But, tell me, how does my father support his misfortunes? and how is my poor Elizabeth?'

'She indeed requires consolation; she accused herself of having caused the death of my brother, and that made her very wretched. But since the murderer has been discovered—'

'The murderer discovered! Good God! how can that be? who could attempt to pursue him? It is impossible; one might as well try to over-take the winds, or confine a mountain-stream with a straw.'

'I do not know what you mean; but we were all very unhappy when she was discovered. No one would believe it at first; and even now Elizabeth will not be convinced, notwithstanding all the evidence. Indeed, who would credit that Justine Moritz, who was so amiable, and fond of all the family, could all at once become so extremely wicked?'

'Justine Moritz! Poor, poor girl, is she the accused? But it is wrong-fully; every one knows that; no one believes it, surely, Ernest?'

'No one did at first; but several circumstances came out, that have almost forced conviction upon us: and her own behaviour has been so confused, as to add to the evidence of facts a weight that, I fear, leaves no hope for doubt. But she will be tried to-day, and you will then hear all.'

He related that, the morning on which the murder of poor William had been discovered, Justine had been taken ill, and confined to her bed; and, after several days, one of the servants, happening to exam-ine the apparel she had worn on the night of the murder, had discovered in her pocket the picture of my mother, which had been judged to be the temptation of the murderer. The servant instantly shewed it to one of the others, who, without saying a word to any of the family, went to a magistrate; and, upon their deposition, Justine was appre-hended. On being charged with the fact, the poor girl confirmed the suspicion in a great measure by her extreme confusion of manner.

This was a strange tale, but it did not shake my faith; and I replied earnestly, 'You are all mistaken; I know the murderer. Justine, poor, good Justine is innocent.'

At that instant my father entered. I saw unhappiness deeply impressed on his countenance, but he endeavoured to welcome me cheerfully; and, after we had exchanged our mournful greeting, would have introduced some other topic than that of our disaster, had not Ernest exclaimed, 'Good God, Papa! Victor says that he knows who was the murderer of poor William.'

'We do also, unfortunately,' replied my father; 'for indeed I had rather have been for ever ignorant than have discovered so much depravity and ingratitude in one I valued so highly.'

'My dear father, you are mistaken; Justine is innocent.'

'If she is, God forbid that she should suffer as guilty. She is to be tried to-day, and I hope, I sincerely hope, that she will be acquitted.'

This speech calmed me. I was firmly convinced in my own mind that Justine, and indeed every human being, was guiltless of this murder. I had no fear, therefore, that any circumstantial evidence could be brought forward strong enough to convict her; and, in this assurance, I calmed myself, expecting the trial with eagerness, but without prognosticating an evil result.

We were soon joined by Elizabeth. Time had made great alterations in her form since I had last beheld her. Six years before she had been a pretty, good-humoured girl, whom every one loved and caressed. She was now a woman in stature and expression of countenance, which was uncommonly lovely. An open and capacious forehead gave indications of a good understanding, joined to great frankness of disposition. Her eyes were hazel, and expressive of mildness, now through recent affliction allied to sadness. Her hair was of a rich dark auburn, her complexion fair, and her figure slight and graceful. She welcomed me with the greatest affection. 'Your arrival, my dear cousin,' said she, 'fills me with hope. You perhaps will find some means to justify my poor guiltless Justine. Alas! who is safe, if she be convicted of crime? I rely on her innocence as certainly as I do upon my own. Our misfortune is doubly hard to us; we have not only lost that lovely darling boy, but this poor girl, whom I sincerely love, is to be torn away by even a worse fate. If she is condemned, I never shall know joy more. But she will not, I am sure she will not; and then I shall be happy again, even after the sad death of my little William.'

'She is innocent, my Elizabeth,' said I, 'and that shall be proved; fear nothing, but let your spirits be cheered by the assurance of her acquittal.'

'How kind you are! every one else believes in her guilt, and that made me wretched; for I knew that it was impossible: and to see every one else prejudiced in so deadly a manner, rendered me hopeless and despairing.' She wept.

'Sweet niece,' said my father, 'dry your tears. If she is, as you believe, innocent, rely on the justice of our judges, and the activity with which I shall prevent the slightest shadow of partiality.'

CHAPTER VII.

WE passed a few sad hours, until eleven o'clock, when the trial was to commence. My father and the rest of the family being obliged to attend as witnesses, I accompanied them to the court. During the whole of this wretched mockery of justice, I suffered living torture. It was to be decided, whether the result of my curiosity and lawless devices would cause the death of two of my fellow-beings: one a smiling babe, full of innocence and joy; the other far more dreadfully murdered, with every aggravation of infamy that could make the murder memorable in horror. Justine also was a girl of merit, and possessed qualities which promised to render her life happy: now all was to be obliterated in an ignominious grave; and I the cause! A thousand times rather would I have confessed myself guilty of the crime ascribed to Justine; but I was absent when it was committed, and such a declaration would have been considered as the ravings of a madman, and would not have exculpated her who suffered through me.

The appearance of Justine was calm. She was dressed in mourning; and her countenance, always engaging, was rendered, by the solemnity of her feelings, exquisitely beautiful. Yet she appeared confident in innocence, and did not tremble, although gazed on and execrated by thousands; for all the kindness which her beauty might otherwise have excited, was obliterated in the minds of the spectators by the imagination of the enormity she was supposed to have committed. She was tranquil, yet her tranquillity was evidently constrained; and as her confusion had before been adduced as a proof of her guilt, she worked up her mind to an appearance of courage. When she entered the court, she threw her eyes round it, and quickly discovered where we were seated. A tear seemed to dim her eye when she saw us; but she quickly recovered herself, and a look of sorrowful affection seemed to attest her utter guiltlessness.

The trial began;* and after the advocate against her had stated the charge, several witnesses were called. Several strange facts combined against her, which might have staggered any one who had not such proof of her innocence as I had. She had been out the whole of the night on which the murder had been committed, and towards morning had been perceived by a market-woman not far from the spot where the body of the murdered child had been afterwards found. The woman asked her what she did there; but she looked very strangely, and only returned a confused and unintelligible answer. She returned to the house about eight o'clock; and when one inquired where she had passed the night, she replied, that she had been looking for the child, and demanded earnestly, if any thing had been heard concerning him. When shewn the body, she fell into violent hysterics, and kept her bed for several days. The picture was then produced, which the servant had found in her pocket; and when Elizabeth, in a faltering voice, proved that it was the same which, an hour before the child had been missed, she had placed round his neck, a murmur of horror and indignation filled the court.

Justine was called on for her defence. As the trial had proceeded, her countenance had altered. Surprise, horror, and misery, were strongly expressed. Sometimes she struggled with her tears; but when she was desired to plead, she collected her powers, and spoke in an audible although variable voice:—

'God knows,' she said, 'how entirely I am innocent. But I do not pretend that my protestations should acquit me: I rest my innocence on a plain and simple explanation of the facts which have been adduced against me; and I hope the character I have always borne will incline my judges to a favourable interpretation, where any circumstance appears doubtful or suspicious.'

She then related that, by the permission of Elizabeth, she had passed the evening of the night on which the murder had been committed, at the house of an aunt at Chêne, a village situated at about a league from Geneva. On her return, at about nine o'clock, she met a man, who asked her if she had seen any thing of the child who was lost. She was alarmed by this account, and passed several hours in looking for him, when the gates of Geneva were shut, and she was forced to remain several hours of the night in a barn belonging to a cottage, being unwilling to call up the inhabitants, to whom she was well known. Unable to rest or sleep, she quitted her asylum early, that she might again endeavour to find my brother. If she had gone near the spot where his body lay, it was without her knowledge. That she had been bewildered when questioned by the market-woman, was not surprising, since she had passed a sleepless night, and the fate of poor William was yet uncertain. Concerning the picture she could give no account.

'I know,' continued the unhappy victim, 'how heavily and fatally this one circumstance weighs against me, but I have no power of explaining it; and when I have expressed my utter ignorance, I am only left to conjecture concerning the probabilities by which it might have been placed in my pocket. But here also I am checked. I believe that I have no enemy on earth, and none surely would have been so wicked as to destroy me wantonly. Did the murderer place it there? I know of no opportunity afforded him for so doing; or if I had, why should he have stolen the jewel, to part with it again so soon?

'I commit my cause to the justice of my judges, yet I see no room for hope. I beg permission to have a few witnesses examined concerning my character; and if their testimony shall not overweigh my supposed guilt, I must be condemned, although I would pledge my salvation on my innocence.'

Several witnesses were called, who had known her for many years, and they spoke well of her; but fear, and hatred of the crime of which they supposed her guilty, rendered them timorous, and unwilling to come forward. Elizabeth saw even this last resource, her excellent dispositions and irreproachable conduct, about to fail the accused, when, although violently agitated, she desired permission to address the court.

'I am,' said she, 'the cousin of the unhappy child who was murdered, or rather his sister, for I was educated by and have lived with his parents ever since and even long before his birth. It may therefore be judged indecent* in me to come forward on this occasion; but when I see a fellow-creature about to perish through the cowardice of her pretended friends, I wish to be allowed to speak, that I may say what I know of her character. I am well acquainted with the accused. I have lived in the same house with her, at one time for five, and at another for nearly two years. During all that period she appeared to me the most amiable and benevolent of human creatures. She nursed Madame Frankenstein, my aunt, in her last illness with the greatest affection and care; and afterwards attended her own mother during a tedious* illness, in a manner that excited the admiration of all who knew her. After which she again lived in my uncle's house, where she was beloved by all the family. She was warmly attached to the child who is now dead, and acted towards him like a most affectionate mother. For my own part, I do not hesitate to say, that, notwithstanding all the evidence produced against her, I believe and rely on her perfect innocence. She had no temptation for such an action: as to the bauble on which the chief proof rests, if she had earnestly desired it, I should have willingly given it to her; so much do I esteem and value her.'

Excellent Elizabeth! A murmur of approbation was heard; but it was excited by her generous interference, and not in favour of poor Justine, on whom the public indignation was turned with renewed violence, charging her with the blackest ingratitude. She herself wept as Elizabeth spoke, but she did not answer. My own agitation and anguish was extreme during the whole trial. I believed in her innocence; I knew it. Could the dæmon, who had (I did not for a minute doubt) murdered my brother, also in his hellish sport have betrayed the innocent to death and ignominy. I could not sustain the horror of my situation; and when I perceived that the popular voice, and the countenances of the judges, had already condemned my unhappy victim, I rushed out of the court in agony. The tortures of the accused did not equal mine; she was sustained by innocence, but the fangs of remorse tore my bosom, and would not forego their hold.

I passed a night of unmingled wretchedness. In the morning I went to the court; my lips and throat were parched. I dared not ask the fatal question; but I was known, and the officer guessed the cause of my visit. The ballots* had been thrown; they were all black, and Justine was condemned.

I cannot pretend to describe what I then felt. I had before experienced sensations of horror; and I have endeavoured to bestow upon them adequate expressions, but words cannot convey an idea of the heart-sickening despair that I then endured. The person to whom I addressed myself added, that Justine had already confessed her guilt. 'That evidence,' he observed, 'was hardly required in so glaring a case, but I am glad of it; and, indeed, none of our judges like to condemn a criminal upon circumstantial evidence, be it ever so decisive.'

When I returned home, Elizabeth eagerly demanded the result.

'My cousin,' replied I, 'it is decided as you may have expected; all judges had rather that ten innocent should suffer, than that one guilty should escape. But she has confessed.'

This was a dire blow to poor Elizabeth, who had relied with firmness upon Justine's innocence. 'Alas!' said she, 'how shall I ever again believe in human benevolence? Justine, whom I loved and esteemed as my sister, how could she put on those smiles of innocence only to betray; her mild eyes seemed incapable of any severity or ill-humour, and yet she has committed a murder.'

Soon after we heard that the poor victim had expressed a wish to
see my cousin. My father wished her not to go; but said, that he left it
to her own judgment and feelings to decide. 'Yes,' said Elizabeth,
'I will go, although she is guilty; and you, Victor, shall accompany me:
I cannot go alone.' The idea of this visit was torture to me, yet I could
not refuse.

We entered the gloomy prison-chamber, and beheld Justine sitting
on some straw at the further end; her hands were manacled, and her
head rested on her knees. She rose on seeing us enter; and when we
were left alone with her, she threw herself at the feet of Elizabeth,
weeping bitterly. My cousin wept also.

'Oh, Justine!' said she, 'why did you rob me of my last consolation.
I relied on your innocence; and although I was then very wretched,
I was not so miserable as I am now.'

'And do you also believe that I am so very, very wicked? Do you also
join with my enemies to crush me?' Her voice was suffocated with sobs.

'Rise, my poor girl,' said Elizabeth, 'why do you kneel, if you are
innocent? I am not one of your enemies; I believed you guiltless, notwithstanding every evidence, until I heard that you had yourself
declared your guilt. That report, you say, is false; and be assured, dear
Justine, that nothing can shake my confidence in you for a moment,
but your own confession.'

'I did confess; but I confessed a lie. I confessed, that I might obtain
absolution; but now that falsehood lies heavier at my heart than all my
other sins. The God of heaven forgive me! Ever since I was condemned, my confessor has besieged me; he threatened and menaced,
until I almost began to think that I was the monster that he said I was.
He threatened excommunication and hell fire in my last moments, if
I continued obdurate.* Dear lady, I had none to support me; all
looked on me as a wretch doomed to ignominy and perdition. What
could I do? In an evil hour* I subscribed to a lie; and now only am
I truly miserable.'

She paused, weeping, and then continued—'I thought with horror, my sweet lady, that you should believe your Justine, whom your
blessed aunt had so highly honoured, and whom you loved, was
a creature capable of a crime which none but the devil himself could
have perpetrated. Dear William! dearest blessed child! I soon shall
see you again in heaven, where we shall all be happy; and that consoles
me, going as I am to suffer ignominy and death.'

'Oh, Justine! forgive me for having for one moment distrusted you. Why did you confess? But do not mourn, my dear girl; I will every where proclaim your innocence, and force belief. Yet you must die; you, my playfellow, my companion, my more than sister. I never can survive so horrible a misfortune.'

'Dear, sweet Elizabeth, do not weep. You ought to raise me with thoughts of a better life, and elevate me from the petty cares of this world of injustice and strife. Do not you, excellent friend, drive me to despair.'

'I will try to comfort you; but this, I fear, is an evil too deep and poignant to admit of consolation, for there is no hope. Yet heaven bless thee, my dearest Justine, with resignation, and a confidence elevated beyond this world. Oh! how I hate its shews and mockeries! when one creature is murdered, another is immediately deprived of life in a slow torturing manner; then the executioners, their hands yet reeking with the blood of innocence, believe that they have done a great deed. They call this *retribution*. Hateful name! When that word is pronounced, I know greater and more horrid punishments are going to be inflicted than the gloomiest tyrant has ever invented to satiate his utmost revenge. Yet this is not consolation for you, my Justine, unless indeed that you may glory in escaping from so miserable a den. Alas! I would I were in peace with my aunt and my lovely William, escaped from a world which is hateful to me, and the visages of men which I abhor.'

Justine smiled languidly. 'This, dear lady, is despair, and not resignation. I must not learn the lesson that you would teach me. Talk of something else, something that will bring peace, and not increase of misery.'

During this conversation I had retired to a corner of the prison-room, where I could conceal the horrid anguish that possessed me. Despair! Who dared talk of that? The poor victim, who on the morrow was to pass the dreary boundary between life and death, felt not as I did, such deep and bitter agony. I gnashed my teeth, and ground them together, uttering a groan that came from my inmost soul. Justine started. When she saw who it was, she approached me, and said, 'Dear Sir, you are very kind to visit me; you, I hope, do not believe that I am guilty.'

I could not answer. 'No, Justine,' said Elizabeth; 'he is more convinced of your innocence than I was; for even when he heard that you had confessed, he did not credit it.'

'I truly thank him. In these last moments I feel the sincerest gratitude towards those who think of me with kindness. How sweet is the
affection of others to such a wretch as I am! It removes more than half
my misfortune; and I feel as if I could die in peace, now that my innocence is acknowledged by you, dear lady, and your cousin.'

Thus the poor sufferer tried to comfort others and herself. She
indeed gained the resignation she desired. But I, the true murderer,
felt the never-dying worm* alive in my bosom, which allowed of no
hope or consolation. Elizabeth also wept, and was unhappy; but her's
also was the misery of innocence, which, like a cloud that passes over
the fair moon, for a while hides, but cannot tarnish its brightness.
Anguish and despair had penetrated into the core of my heart; I bore
a hell within me,* which nothing could extinguish. We staid several
hours with Justine; and it was with great difficulty that Elizabeth
could tear herself away. 'I wish,' cried she, 'that I were to die with you;
I cannot live in this world of misery.'

Justine assumed an air of cheerfulness, while she with difficulty
repressed her bitter tears. She embraced Elizabeth, and said, in a voice
of half-suppressed emotion, 'Farewell, sweet lady, dearest Elizabeth,
my beloved and only friend; may heaven in its bounty bless and preserve you; may this be the last misfortune that you will ever suffer.
Live, and be happy, and make others so.'

As we returned, Elizabeth said, 'You know not, my dear Victor, how
much I am relieved, now that I trust in the innocence of this unfortunate girl. I never could again have known peace, if I had been deceived
in my reliance on her. For the moment that I did believe her guilty,
I felt an anguish that I could not have long sustained. Now my heart
is lightened. The innocent suffers; but she whom I thought amiable
and good has not betrayed the trust I reposed in her, and I am
consoled.'

Amiable cousin! such were your thoughts, mild and gentle as your
own dear eyes and voice. But I—I was a wretch, and none ever conceived
of the misery that I then endured.

END OF VOL. I.

VOLUME II

CHAPTER I.

NOTHING is more painful to the human mind, than, after the feelings have been worked up by a quick succession of events, the dead calmness of inaction and certainty which follows, and deprives the soul both of hope and fear. Justine died; she rested; and I was alive. The blood flowed freely in my veins, but a weight of despair and remorse pressed on my heart, which nothing could remove. Sleep fled from my eyes; I wandered like an evil spirit, for I had committed deeds of mischief beyond description horrible, and more, much more, (I persuaded myself) was yet behind. Yet my heart overflowed with kindness, and the love of virtue. I had begun life with benevolent intentions, and thirsted for the moment when I should put them in practice, and make myself useful to my fellow-beings. Now all was blasted:* instead of that serenity of conscience, which allowed me to look back upon the past with self-satisfaction, and from thence to gather promise of new hopes, I was seized by remorse and the sense of guilt, which hurried me away to a hell of intense tortures, such as no language can describe.

This state of mind preyed upon my health, which had entirely recovered from the first shock it had sustained. I shunned the face of man; all sound of joy or complacency was torture to me; solitude was my only consolation—deep, dark, death-like solitude.

My father observed with pain the alteration perceptible in my disposition and habits, and endeavoured to reason with me on the folly of giving way to immoderate grief. 'Do you think, Victor,' said he, 'that I do not suffer also? No one could love a child more than I loved your brother;' (tears came into his eyes as he spoke); 'but is it not a duty to the survivors, that we should refrain from augmenting their unhappiness by an appearance of immoderate grief? It is also a duty owed to yourself; for excessive sorrow prevents improvement or enjoyment, or even the discharge of daily usefulness, without which no man is fit for society.'

This advice, although good, was totally inapplicable to my case;

I should have been the first to hide my grief, and console my friends, if remorse had not mingled its bitterness with my other sensations. Now I could only answer my father with a look of despair, and endeavour to hide myself from his view.

About this time we retired to our house at Belrive. This change was particularly agreeable to me. The shutting of the gates regularly at ten o'clock, and the impossibility of remaining on the lake after that hour, had rendered our residence within the walls of Geneva very irksome to me. I was now free. Often, after the rest of the family had retired for the night, I took the boat, and passed many hours upon the water. Sometimes, with my sails set, I was carried by the wind; and sometimes, after rowing into the middle of the lake, I left the boat to pursue its own course, and gave way to my own miserable reflections. I was often tempted, when all was at peace around me, and I the only unquiet thing that wandered restless in a scene so beautiful and heavenly, if I except some bat, or the frogs, whose harsh and interrupted croaking was heard only when I approached the shore—often, I say, I was tempted to plunge into the silent lake, that the waters might close over me and my calamities for ever. But I was restrained, when I thought of the heroic and suffering Elizabeth, whom I tenderly loved, and whose existence was bound up in mine. I thought also of my father, and surviving brother: should I by my base desertion leave them exposed and unprotected to the malice of the fiend whom I had let loose among them?

At these moments I wept bitterly, and wished that peace would revisit my mind only that I might afford them consolation and happiness. But that could not be. Remorse extinguished every hope. I had been the author of unalterable evils; and I lived in daily fear, lest the monster whom I had created should perpetrate some new wickedness. I had an obscure feeling that all was not over, and that he would still commit some signal* crime, which by its enormity should almost efface the recollection of the past. There was always scope for fear, so long as any thing I loved remained behind. My abhorrence of this fiend cannot be conceived. When I thought of him, I gnashed my teeth, my eyes became inflamed, and I ardently wished to extinguish that life which I had so thoughtlessly bestowed. When I reflected on his crimes and malice, my hatred and revenge burst all bounds of moderation. I would have made a pilgrimage to the highest peak of the Andes, could I, when there, have precipitated him to their base.

I wished to see him again, that I might wreak the utmost extent of anger on his head, and avenge the deaths of William and Justine.

Our house was the house of mourning. My father's health was deeply shaken by the horror of the recent events. Elizabeth was sad and desponding; she no longer took delight in her ordinary occupations; all pleasure seemed to her sacrilege toward the dead; eternal woe and tears she then thought was the just tribute she should pay to innocence so blasted and destroyed. She was no longer that happy creature, who in earlier youth wandered with me on the banks of the lake, and talked with ecstacy of our future prospects. She had become grave, and often conversed of the inconstancy of fortune, and the instability of human life.

'When I reflect, my dear cousin,' said she, 'on the miserable death of Justine Moritz, I no longer see the world and its works as they before appeared to me. Before, I looked upon the accounts of vice and injustice, that I read in books or heard from others, as tales of ancient days, or imaginary evils; at least they were remote, and more familiar to reason than to the imagination; but now misery has come home, and men appear to me as monsters thirsting for each other's blood. Yet I am certainly unjust. Every body believed that poor girl to be guilty; and if she could have committed the crime for which she suffered, assuredly she would have been the most depraved of human creatures. For the sake of a few jewels, to have murdered the son of her benefactor and friend, a child whom she had nursed from its birth, and appeared to love as if it had been her own! I could not consent to the death of any human being; but certainly I should have thought such a creature unfit to remain in the society of men. Yet she was innocent. I know, I feel she was innocent; you are of the same opinion, and that confirms me. Alas! Victor, when falsehood can look so like the truth, who can assure themselves of certain happiness? I feel as if I were walking on the edge of a precipice, towards which thousands are crowding, and endeavouring to plunge me into the abyss. William and Justine were assassinated, and the murderer escapes; he walks about the world free, and perhaps respected. But even if I were condemned to suffer on the scaffold for the same crimes, I would not change places with such a wretch.'

I listened to this discourse with the extremest agony. I, not in deed, but in effect, was the true murderer. Elizabeth read my anguish in my countenance, and kindly taking my hand said, 'My dearest cousin, you must calm yourself. These events have affected me, God knows how deeply; but I am not so wretched as you are. There is an expression of despair, and sometimes of revenge, in your countenance, that makes me tremble. Be calm, my dear Victor; I would sacrifice my life to your peace. We surely shall be happy: quiet in our native country, and not mingling in the world, what can disturb our tranquillity?'

She shed tears as she said this, distrusting the very solace that she gave; but at the same time she smiled, that she might chase away the fiend that lurked in my heart. My father, who saw in the unhappiness that was painted in my face only an exaggeration of that sorrow which I might naturally feel, thought that an amusement suited to my taste would be the best means of restoring to me my wonted serenity. It was from this cause that he had removed to the country; and, induced by the same motive, he now proposed that we should all make an excursion to the valley of Chamounix.* I had been there before, but Elizabeth and Ernest never had; and both had often expressed an earnest desire to see the scenery of this place, which had been described to them as so wonderful and sublime. Accordingly we departed from Geneva on this tour about the middle of the month of August, nearly two months after the death of Justine.

The weather was uncommonly fine; and if mine had been a sorrow to be chased away by any fleeting circumstance, this excursion would certainly have had the effect intended by my father. As it was, I was somewhat interested in the scene; it sometimes lulled, although it could not extinguish my grief. During the first day we travelled in a carriage. In the morning we had seen the mountains at a distance, towards which we gradually advanced. We perceived that the valley through which we wound, and which was formed by the river Arve,* whose course we followed, closed in upon us by degrees; and when the sun had set, we beheld immense mountains and precipices overhanging us on every side, and heard the sound of the river raging among rocks, and the dashing of waterfalls around.

The next day we pursued our journey upon mules; and as we ascended still higher, the valley assumed a more magnificent and astonishing character. Ruined castles hanging on the precipices of piny mountains; the impetuous Arve, and cottages every here and there peeping forth from among the trees, formed a scene of singular beauty. But it was augmented and rendered sublime* by the mighty Alps, whose white and shining pyramids and domes* towered above all, as belonging to another earth, the habitations of another race of beings.

We passed the bridge of Pelissier, where the ravine, which the river forms, opened before us, and we began to ascend the mountain that overhangs it. Soon after we entered the valley of Chamounix. This valley is more wonderful and sublime, but not so beautiful and pictur-esque* as that of Servox,* through which we had just passed. The high and snowy mountains were its immediate boundaries; but we saw no more ruined castles and fertile fields. Immense glaciers approached the road; we heard the rumbling thunder of the falling avelânche, and marked the smoke of its passage. Mont Blanc, the supreme and mag-nificent Mont Blanc, raised itself from the surrounding *aiguilles*,* and its tremendous *dome* overlooked the valley.

During this journey, I sometimes joined Elizabeth, and exerted myself to point out to her the various beauties of the scene. I often suffered my mule to lag behind, and indulged in the misery of reflec-tion. At other times I spurred on the animal before my companions, that I might forget them, the world, and, more than all, myself. When at a distance, I alighted, and threw myself on the grass, weighed down by horror and despair. At eight in the evening I arrived at Chamounix. My father and Elizabeth were very much fatigued; Ernest, who accom-panied us, was delighted, and in high spirits: the only circumstance that detracted from his pleasure was the south wind, and the rain it seemed to promise for the next day.

We retired early to our apartments, but not to sleep; at least I did not. I remained many hours at the window, watching the pallid light-ning that played above Mont Blanc, and listening to the rushing of the Arve, which ran below my window.

CHAPTER II.

THE next day, contrary to the prognostications of our guides, was fine, although clouded. We visited the source of the Arveiron, and rode about the valley until evening. These sublime and magnificent scenes afforded me the greatest consolation that I was capable of receiv-ing. They elevated me from all littleness* of feeling; and although they did not remove my grief, they subdued and tranquillized it. In some degree, also, they diverted my mind from the thoughts over which it had brooded for the last month. I returned in the evening, fatigued, but less unhappy, and conversed with my family with more cheerfulness than had been my custom for some time. My father was pleased, and Elizabeth overjoyed. 'My dear cousin,' said she, 'you see what happiness you diffuse when you are happy; do not relapse again!'

The following morning the rain poured down in torrents, and thick mists hid the summits of the mountains. I rose early, but felt unusually melancholy. The rain depressed me; my old feelings recurred, and I was miserable. I knew how disappointed my father would be at this sudden change, and I wished to avoid him until I had recovered myself so far as to be enabled to conceal those feelings that overpowered me. I knew that they would remain that day at the inn; and as I had ever inured myself to rain, moisture, and cold, I resolved to go alone to the summit of Montanvert. I remembered the effect that the view of the tremendous and ever-moving glacier had produced upon my mind when I first saw it. It had then filled me with a sublime ecstacy that gave wings to the soul, and allowed it to soar from the obscure world to light and joy. The sight of the awful* and majestic in nature had indeed always the effect of solemnizing my mind, and causing me to forget the passing cares of life. I determined to go alone, for I was well acquainted with the path, and the presence of another would destroy the solitary grandeur of the scene.

The ascent is precipitous, but the path is cut into continual and short windings, which enable you to surmount the perpendicularity of the mountain. It is a scene terrifically desolate. In a thousand spots the traces of the winter avelanche may be perceived, where trees lie broken and strewed on the ground; some entirely destroyed, others bent, leaning upon the jutting rocks of the mountain, or transversely upon other trees. The path, as you ascend higher, is intersected by ravines of snow, down which stones continually roll from above; one of them is particularly dangerous, as the slightest sound, such as even speaking in a loud voice, produces a concussion of air sufficient to draw destruction upon the head of the speaker. The pines are not tall or luxuriant, but they are sombre, and add an air of severity to the scene. I looked on the valley beneath; vast mists were rising from the rivers which ran through it, and curling in thick wreaths around the opposite mountains, whose summits were hid in the uniform clouds, while rain poured from the dark sky, and added to the melancholy impression I received from the objects around me. Alas! why does man boast of sensibilities superior to those apparent in the brute; it only renders them more necessary beings.* If our impulses were confined to hunger, thirst, and desire, we might be nearly free; but now we are moved by every wind that blows, and a chance word or scene that that word may convey to us.

> We rest; a dream has power to poison sleep.
>   We rise; one wand'ring thought pollutes the day.
> We feel, conceive, or reason; laugh, or weep,
>   Embrace fond woe, or cast our cares away;
> It is the same: for, be it joy or sorrow,
>   The path of its departure still is free.
> Man's yesterday may ne'er be like his morrow;
>   Nought may endure but mutability!*

It was nearly noon when I arrived at the top of the ascent. For some time I sat upon the rock that overlooks the sea of ice. A mist covered both that and the surrounding mountains. Presently a breeze dissipated the cloud, and I descended upon the glacier. The surface is very uneven, rising like the waves of a troubled sea, descending low, and interspersed by rifts that sink deep. The field of ice is almost a league in width, but I spent nearly two hours in crossing it. The opposite mountain is a bare perpendicular rock. From the side where I now stood Montanvert was exactly opposite, at the distance of a league; and above it rose Mont Blanc, in awful majesty. I remained in a recess of rock, gazing on this wonderful and stupendous scene. The sea, or rather the vast river of ice, wound among its dependent mountains, whose aërial summits hung over its recesses. Their icy and glittering peaks shone in the sunlight over the clouds. My heart, which was before sorrowful, now swelled with something like joy; I exclaimed— 'Wandering spirits, if indeed ye wander, and do not rest in your narrow beds, allow me this faint happiness, or take me, as your companion, away from the joys of life.'

As I said this, I suddenly beheld the figure of a man, at some distance, advancing towards me with superhuman speed. He bounded over the crevices in the ice, among which I had walked with caution; his stature also, as he approached, seemed to exceed that of man. I was troubled: a mist came over my eyes, and I felt a faintness seize me; but I was quickly restored by the cold gale of the mountains. I perceived, as the shape came nearer, (sight tremendous and abhorred!) that it was the wretch whom I had created. I trembled with rage and horror, resolving to wait his approach, and then close with him in mortal combat. He approached; his countenance bespoke bitter anguish, combined with disdain and malignity, while its unearthly ugliness rendered it almost too horrible for human eyes. But I scarcely observed this; anger and hatred had at first deprived me of utterance, and I recovered only to overwhelm him with words expressive of furious detestation and contempt.

'Devil!' I exclaimed, 'do you dare approach me? and do not you fear the fierce vengeance of my arm wreaked on your miserable head? Begone, vile insect!* or rather stay, that I may trample you to dust! and, oh, that I could, with the extinction of your miserable existence, restore those victims whom you have so diabolically murdered!'

'I expected this reception,' said the dæmon. 'All men hate the wretched; how then must I be hated, who am miserable beyond all living things! Yet you, my creator, detest and spurn me, thy creature, to whom thou art bound by ties only dissoluble by the annihilation of one of us. You purpose to kill me. How dare you sport thus with life? Do your duty towards me, and I will do mine towards you and the rest of mankind.* If you will comply with my conditions, I will leave them and you at peace; but if you refuse, I will glut the maw of death, until it be satiated with the blood of your remaining friends.'

'Abhorred monster! fiend that thou art! the tortures of hell are too mild a vengeance for thy crimes. Wretched devil! you reproach me with your creation; come on then, that I may extinguish the spark which I so negligently bestowed.' *You are implicated, you cannot kill*

My rage was without bounds; I sprang on him, impelled by all the feelings which can arm one being against the existence of another.

He easily eluded me, and said,

'Be calm! I entreat you to hear me, before you give vent to your hatred on my devoted* head. Have I not suffered enough, that you seek to increase my misery? Life, although it may only be an accumulation of anguish, is dear to me, and I will defend it. Remember, thou hast made me more powerful than thyself; my height is superior to thine; my joints more supple. But I will not be tempted to set myself in opposition to thee. I am thy creature,* and I will be even mild and docile to my natural lord and king, if thou wilt also perform thy part, the which thou owest me. Oh, Frankenstein, be not equitable to every other, and trample upon me alone, to whom thy justice, and even thy clemency and affection, is most due. Remember, that I am thy creature: I ought to be thy Adam; but I am rather the fallen angel, whom thou drivest from joy for no misdeed. Every where I see bliss, from which I alone am irrevocably excluded. I was benevolent and good; misery made me a fiend. Make me happy, and I shall again be virtuous.'*

'Begone! I will not hear you. There can be no community between you and me; we are enemies. Begone, or let us try our strength in a fight, in which one must fall.'

'How can I move thee? Will no entreaties cause thee to turn a favourable eye upon thy creature, who implores thy goodness and compassion. Believe me, Frankenstein: I was benevolent; my soul glowed with love and humanity: but am I not alone, miserably alone? You, my creator, abhor me; what hope can I gather from your fellow-creatures, who owe me nothing? they spurn and hate me. The desert mountains and dreary glaciers are my refuge. I have wandered here many days; the caves of ice,* which I only do not fear, are a dwelling to me, and the only one which man does not grudge. These bleak skies I hail, for they are kinder to me than your fellow-beings. If the multitude of mankind knew of my existence, they would do as you do, and arm themselves for my destruction. Shall I not then hate them who abhor me? I will keep no terms with my enemies. I am miserable, and they shall share my wretchedness. Yet it is in your power to recompense me, and deliver them from an evil which it only remains for you to make so great, that not only you and your family, but thousands of others, shall be swallowed up in the whirlwinds of its rage. Let your compassion be moved, and do not disdain me. Listen to my tale: when you have heard that, abandon or commiserate me, as you shall judge that I deserve. But hear me. The guilty are allowed, by human laws, bloody as they may be, to speak in their own defence before they are condemned. Listen to me, Frankenstein. You accuse me of murder; and yet you would, with a satisfied conscience, destroy your own creature. Oh, praise the eternal justice of man! Yet I ask you not to spare me: listen to me; and then, if you can, and if you will, destroy the work of your hands.'

'Why do you call to my remembrance circumstances of which I shudder to reflect, that I have been the miserable origin and author? Cursed be the day, abhorred devil, in which you first saw light! Cursed (although I curse myself) be the hands that formed you! You have made me wretched beyond expression. You have left me no power to consider whether I am just to you, or not. Begone! relieve me from the sight of your detested form.'

'Thus I relieve thee, my creator,' he said, and placed his hated hands before my eyes, which I flung from me with violence; 'thus I take from thee a sight which you abhor. Still thou canst listen to me, and grant me thy compassion. By the virtues that I once possessed, I demand this from you. Hear my tale; it is long and strange, and the temperature of this place is not fitting to your fine sensations; come to the hut upon the mountain. The sun is yet high in the heavens; before it descends to hide itself behind yon snowy precipices, and illuminate another world, you will have heard my story, and can decide. On you it rests, whether I quit for ever the neighbourhood of man, and lead a harmless life, or become the scourge of your fellow-creatures, and the author of your own speedy ruin.'

As he said this, he led the way across the ice: I followed. My heart was full, and I did not answer him; but, as I proceeded, I weighed the various arguments that he had used, and determined at least to listen to his tale. I was partly urged by curiosity, and compassion confirmed my resolution. I had hitherto supposed him to be the murderer of my brother, and I eagerly sought a confirmation or denial of this opinion. For the first time, also, I felt what the duties of a creator towards his creature were, and that I ought to render him happy before I complained of his wickedness. These motives urged me to comply with his demand. We crossed the ice, therefore, and ascended the opposite rock. The air was cold, and the rain again began to descend: we entered the hut, the fiend with an air of exultation, I with a heavy heart, and depressed spirits. But I consented to listen; and, seating myself by the fire which my odious companion had lighted, he thus began his tale.

CHAPTER III.

'It is with considerable difficulty that I remember the original æra of my being: all the events of that period appear confused and indistinct. A strange multiplicity of sensations seized me, and I saw, felt, heard, and smelt, at the same time; and it was, indeed, a long time before I learned to distinguish between the operations of my various senses.* By degrees, I remember, a stronger light pressed upon my nerves, so that I was obliged to shut my eyes. Darkness then came over me, and troubled me; but hardly had I felt this, when, by opening my eyes, as I now suppose, the light poured in upon me again. I walked, and,

I believe, descended; but I presently found a great alteration in my sensations. Before, dark and opaque bodies had surrounded me, impervious to my touch or sight; but I now found that I could wander on at liberty, with no obstacles which I could not either surmount or avoid. The light became more and more oppressive to me; and, the heat wearying me as I walked, I sought a place where I could receive shade. This was the forest near Ingolstadt; and here I lay by the side of a brook resting from my fatigue, until I felt tormented by hunger and thirst. This roused me from my nearly dormant state, and I ate some berries which I found hanging on the trees, or lying on the ground. I slaked my thirst at the brook; and then lying down, was overcome by sleep.

'It was dark when I awoke; I felt cold also, and half-frightened as it were instinctively, finding myself so desolate. Before I had quitted your apartment, on a sensation of cold, I had covered myself with some clothes; but these were insufficient to secure me from the dews of night. I was a poor, helpless, miserable wretch; I knew, and could distinguish, nothing; but, feeling pain invade me on all sides, I sat down and wept.

'Soon a gentle light stole over the heavens, and gave me a sensation of pleasure. I started up, and beheld a radiant form rise from among the trees. I gazed with a kind of wonder. It moved slowly, but it enlightened my path; and I again went out in search of berries. I was still cold, when under one of the trees I found a huge cloak, with which I covered myself, and sat down upon the ground. No distinct ideas occupied my mind; all was confused. I felt light, and hunger, and thirst, and darkness; innumerable sounds rung in my ears, and on all sides various scents saluted me: the only object that I could distinguish was the bright moon, and I fixed my eyes on that with pleasure.

'Several changes of day and night passed, and the orb of night had greatly lessened when I began to distinguish my sensations from each other. I gradually saw plainly the clear stream that supplied me with drink, and the trees that shaded me with their foliage. I was delighted when I first discovered that a pleasant sound, which often saluted my ears, proceeded from the throats of the little winged animals who had often intercepted the light from my eyes. I began also to observe, with greater accuracy, the forms that surrounded me, and to perceive the boundaries of the radiant roof of light which canopied me. Sometimes I tried to imitate the pleasant songs of the birds, but was unable.

Sometimes I wished to express my sensations in my own mode, but the uncouth and inarticulate sounds which broke from me frightened me into silence again.

'The moon had disappeared from the night, and again, with a lessened form, shewed itself, while I still remained in the forest. My sensations had, by this time, become distinct, and my mind received every day additional ideas. My eyes became accustomed to the light, and to perceive objects in their right forms; I distinguished the insect from the herb, and, by degrees, one herb from another. I found that the sparrow uttered none but harsh notes, whilst those of the blackbird and thrush were sweet and enticing.

'One day, when I was oppressed by cold, I found a fire which had been left by some wandering beggars, and was overcome with delight at the warmth I experienced from it. In my joy I thrust my hand into the live embers, but quickly drew it out again with a cry of pain. How strange, I thought, that the same cause should produce such opposite effects! I examined the materials of the fire, and to my joy found it to be composed of wood. I quickly collected some branches; but they were wet, and would not burn. I was pained at this, and sat still watching the operation of the fire. The wet wood which I had placed near the heat dried, and itself became inflamed. I reflected on this; and, by touching the various branches, I discovered the cause, and busied myself in collecting a great quantity of wood, that I might dry it, and have a plentiful supply of fire. When night came on, and brought sleep with it, I was in the greatest fear lest my fire should be extinguished. I covered it carefully with dry wood and leaves, and placed wet branches upon it; and then, spreading my cloak, I lay on the ground, and sunk into sleep.

'It was morning when I awoke, and my first care was to visit the fire. I uncovered it, and a gentle breeze quickly fanned it into a flame. I observed this also, and contrived a fan of branches, which roused the embers when they were nearly extinguished. When night came again, I found, with pleasure, that the fire gave light as well as heat; and that the discovery of this element was useful to me in my food; for I found some of the offals that the travellers had left had been roasted, and tasted much more savoury than the berries I gathered from the trees.* I tried, therefore, to dress my food in the same manner, placing it on the live embers. I found that the berries were spoiled by this operation, and the nuts and roots much improved.

'Food, however, became scarce; and I often spent the whole day searching in vain for a few acorns to assuage the pangs of hunger. When I found this, I resolved to quit the place that I had hitherto inhabited, to seek for one where the few wants I experienced would be more easily satisfied. In this emigration, I exceedingly lamented the loss of the fire which I had obtained through accident, and knew not how to re-produce it. I gave several hours to the serious consideration of this difficulty; but I was obliged to relinquish all attempt to supply it; and, wrapping myself up in my cloak, I struck across the wood towards the setting sun. I passed three days in these rambles, and at length discovered the open country. A great fall of snow had taken place the night before, and the fields were of one uniform white; the appearance was disconsolate, and I found my feet chilled by the cold damp substance that covered the ground.

'It was about seven in the morning, and I longed to obtain food and shelter; at length I perceived a small hut, on a rising ground, which had doubtless been built for the convenience of some shepherd. This was a new sight to me; and I examined the structure with great curiosity. Finding the door open, I entered. An old man sat in it, near a fire, over which he was preparing his breakfast. He turned on hearing a noise; and, perceiving me, shrieked loudly, and, quitting the hut, ran across the fields with a speed of which his debilitated form hardly appeared capable. His appearance, different from any I had ever before seen, and his flight, somewhat surprised me. But I was enchanted by the appearance of the hut: here the snow and rain could not penetrate; the ground was dry; and it presented to me then as exquisite and divine a retreat as Pandæmonium appeared to the dæmons of hell after their sufferings in the lake of fire.* I greedily devoured the remnants of the shepherd's breakfast, which consisted of bread, cheese, milk, and wine; the latter, however, I did not like. Then, overcome by fatigue, I lay down among some straw, and fell asleep.

'It was noon when I awoke; and, allured by the warmth of the sun, which shone brightly on the white ground, I determined to recommence my travels; and, depositing the remains of the peasant's breakfast in a wallet* I found, I proceeded across the fields for several hours, until at sunset I arrived at a village. How miraculous did this appear! the huts, the neater cottages, and stately houses, engaged my admiration by turns. The vegetables in the gardens, the milk and cheese that I saw placed at the windows of some of the cottages, allured my appetite. One of the best of these I entered; but I had hardly placed my foot within the door, before the children shrieked, and one of the women fainted. The whole village was roused; some fled, some attacked me, until, grievously bruised by stones and many other kinds of missile weapons, I escaped to the open country, and fearfully took refuge in a low hovel, quite bare, and making a wretched appearance after the palaces I had beheld in the village. This hovel, however, joined a cottage of a neat and pleasant appearance; but, after my late dearly-bought experience, I dared not enter it. My place of refuge was constructed of wood, but so low, that I could with difficulty sit upright in it. No wood, however, was placed on the earth, which formed the floor, but it was dry; and although the wind entered it by innumerable chinks, I found it an agreeable asylum from the snow and rain.

'Here then I retreated, and lay down, happy to have found a shelter, however miserable, from the inclemency of the season, and still more from the barbarity of man.

'As soon as morning dawned, I crept from my kennel, that I might view the adjacent cottage, and discover if I could remain in the habitation I had found. It was situated against the back of the cottage, and surrounded on the sides which were exposed by a pig-stye and a clear pool of water. One part was open, and by that I had crept in; but now I covered every crevice by which I might be perceived with stones and wood, yet in such a manner that I might move them on occasion to pass out: all the light I enjoyed came through the stye, and that was sufficient for me.

'Having thus arranged my dwelling, and carpeted it with clean straw, I retired; for I saw the figure of a man at a distance, and I remembered too well my treatment the night before, to trust myself in his power. I had first, however, provided for my sustenance for that day, by a loaf of coarse bread, which I purloined, and a cup with which I could drink, more conveniently than from my hand, of the pure water which flowed by my retreat. The floor was a little raised, so that it was kept perfectly dry, and by its vicinity to the chimney of the cottage it was tolerably warm.

'Being thus provided, I resolved to reside in this hovel, until something should occur which might alter my determination. It was indeed a paradise, compared to the bleak forest, my former residence, the rain-dropping branches, and dank earth. I ate my breakfast with pleasure, and was about to remove a plank to procure myself a little water, when I heard a step, and, looking through a small chink, I beheld a young creature, with a pail on her head, passing before my hovel. The girl was young and of gentle* demeanour, unlike what I have since found cottagers and farm-house servants to be. Yet she was meanly dressed, a coarse blue petticoat and a linen jacket being her only garb; her fair hair was plaited, but not adorned; she looked patient, yet sad. I lost sight of her; and in about a quarter of an hour she returned, bearing the pail, which was now partly filled with milk. As she walked along, seemingly incommoded by the burden, a young man met her, whose countenance expressed a deeper despondence. Uttering a few sounds with an air of melancholy, he took the pail from her head, and bore it to the cottage himself. She followed, and they disappeared. Presently I saw the young man again, with some tools in his hand, cross the field behind the cottage; and the girl was also busied, some-times in the house, and sometimes in the yard.

'On examining my dwelling, I found that one of the windows of the cottage had formerly occupied a part of it, but the panes had been filled up with wood. In one of these was a small and almost impercept-ible chink, through which the eye could just penetrate. Through this crevice, a small room was visible, white-washed and clean, but very bare of furniture. In one corner, near a small fire, sat an old man, lean-ing his head on his hands in a disconsolate attitude. The young girl was occupied in arranging the cottage; but presently she took some-thing out of a drawer, which employed her hands, and she sat down beside the old man, who, taking up an instrument, began to play, and to produce sounds, sweeter than the voice of the thrush or the night-ingale. It was a lovely sight, even to me, poor wretch! who had never beheld aught beautiful before. The silver hair and benevolent counten-ance of the aged cottager, won my reverence; while the gentle man-ners of the girl enticed my love. He played a sweet mournful air, which I perceived drew tears from the eyes of his amiable companion, of which the old man took no notice, until she sobbed audibly; he then pronounced a few sounds, and the fair creature, leaving her work, knelt at his feet. He raised her, and smiled with such kindness and affection, that I felt sensations of a peculiar and overpowering nature: they were a mixture of pain and pleasure, such as I had never before experienced, either from hunger or cold, warmth or food; and I with-drew from the window, unable to bear these emotions.

'Soon after this the young man returned, bearing on his shoulders a load of wood. The girl met him at the door, helped to relieve him of his burden, and, taking some of the fuel into the cottage, placed it on the fire; then she and the youth went apart into a nook of the cottage, and he shewed her a large loaf and a piece of cheese. She seemed pleased; and went into the garden for some roots and plants, which she placed in water, and then upon the fire. She afterwards continued her work, whilst the young man went into the garden, and appeared busily employed in digging and pulling up roots. After he had been employed thus about an hour, the young woman joined him, and they entered the cottage together.

'The old man had, in the mean time, been pensive; but, on the appearance of his companions, he assumed a more cheerful air, and they sat down to eat. The meal was quickly dispatched. The young woman was again occupied in arranging the cottage; the old man walked before the cottage in the sun for a few minutes, leaning on the arm of the youth. Nothing could exceed in beauty the contrast between these two excellent creatures. One was old, with silver hairs and a countenance beaming with benevolence and love: the younger was slight and graceful in his figure, and his features were moulded with the finest symmetry; yet his eyes and attitude expressed the utmost sadness and despondency. The old man returned to the cottage; and the youth, with tools different from those he had used in the morning, directed his steps across the fields.

'Night quickly shut in; but, to my extreme wonder, I found that the cottagers had a means of prolonging light, by the use of tapers, and was delighted to find, that the setting of the sun did not put an end to the pleasure I experienced in watching my human neighbours. In the evening, the young girl and her companion were employed in various occupations which I did not understand; and the old man again took up the instrument, which produced the divine sounds that had enchanted me in the morning. So soon as he had finished, the youth began, not to play, but to utter sounds that were monotonous, and neither resembling the harmony of the old man's instrument or the songs of the birds; I since found that he read aloud, but at that time I knew nothing of the science of words or letters.

'The family, after having been thus occupied for a short time, extinguished their lights, and retired, as I conjectured, to rest.

CHAPTER IV.

'I LAY on my straw, but I could not sleep. I thought of the occurrences of the day. What chiefly struck me was the gentle manners of these people; and I longed to join them, but dared not. I remembered too well the treatment I had suffered the night before from the barbarous villagers, and resolved, whatever course of conduct I might hereafter think it right to pursue, that for the present I would remain quietly in my hovel, watching, and endeavouring to discover the motives which influenced their actions.

'The cottagers arose the next morning before the sun. The young woman arranged the cottage, and prepared the food; and the youth departed after the first meal.

'This day was passed in the same routine as that which preceded it. The young man was constantly employed out of doors, and the girl in various laborious occupations within. The old man, whom I soon perceived to be blind, employed his leisure hours on his instrument, or in contemplation. Nothing could exceed the love and respect which the younger cottagers exhibited towards their venerable companion. They performed towards him every little office of affection and duty with gentleness; and he rewarded them by his benevolent smiles.

'They were not entirely happy. The young man and his companion often went apart, and appeared to weep. I saw no cause for their unhappiness; but I was deeply affected by it. If such lovely creatures were miserable, it was less strange that I, an imperfect and solitary being, should be wretched. Yet why were these gentle beings unhappy? They possessed a delightful house (for such it was in my eyes), and every luxury; they had a fire to warm them when chill, and delicious viands when hungry; they were dressed in excellent clothes; and, still more, they enjoyed one another's company and speech, interchanging each day looks of affection and kindness. What did their tears imply? Did they really express pain? I was at first unable to solve these questions; but perpetual attention, and time, explained to me many appearances which were at first enigmatic.

'A considerable period elapsed before I discovered one of the causes of the uneasiness of this amiable family; it was poverty: and they suffered that evil in a very distressing degree. Their nourishment consisted entirely of the vegetables of their garden, and the milk of one cow, who gave very little during the winter, when its masters could scarcely procure food to support it. They often, I believe, suffered the pangs of hunger very poignantly, especially the two younger cottagers; for several times they placed food before the old man, when they reserved none for themselves.

'This trait of kindness moved me sensibly. I had been accustomed, during the night, to steal a part of their store for my own consumption; but when I found that in doing this I inflicted pain on the cottagers, I abstained, and satisfied myself with berries, nuts, and roots, which I gathered from a neighbouring wood.

'I discovered also another means through which I was enabled to assist their labours. I found that the youth spent a great part of each day in collecting wood for the family fire; and, during the night, I often took his tools, the use of which I quickly discovered, and brought home firing sufficient for the consumption of several days.

'I remember, the first time that I did this, the young woman, when she opened the door in the morning, appeared greatly astonished on seeing a great pile of wood on the outside. She uttered some words in a loud voice, and the youth joined her, who also expressed surprise. I observed, with pleasure, that he did not go to the forest that day, but spent it in repairing the cottage, and cultivating the garden.

'By degrees I made a discovery of still greater moment. I found that these people possessed a method of communicating their experience and feelings to one another by articulate sounds. I perceived that the words they spoke sometimes produced pleasure or pain, smiles or sadness, in the minds and countenances of the hearers. This was indeed a godlike science, and I ardently desired to become acquainted with it. But I was baffled in every attempt I made for this purpose. Their pronunciation was quick; and the words they uttered, not having any apparent connexion with visible objects, I was unable to discover any clue by which I could unravel the mystery of their reference. By great application, however, and after having remained during the space of several revolutions of the moon in my hovel, I discovered the names that were given to some of the most familiar objects of discourse: I learned and applied the words *fire*, *milk*, *bread*, and *wood*. I learned also the names of the cottagers themselves. The youth and his companion had each of them several names, but the old man had only one, which was *father*. The girl was called *sister*, or *Agatha*; and the youth *Felix*, *brother*, or *son*. I cannot describe the delight I felt when I learned the ideas appropriated to each of these sounds, and was able to pronounce them. I distinguished several other words, without being able as yet to understand or apply them; such as *good*, *dearest*, *unhappy*.

'I spent the winter in this manner. The gentle manners and beauty of the cottagers greatly endeared them to me: when they were unhappy, I felt depressed; when they rejoiced, I sympathized in their joys. I saw few human beings beside them; and if any other happened to enter the cottage, their harsh manners and rude gait only enhanced to me the superior accomplishments of my friends. The old man, I could perceive, often endeavoured to encourage his children, as sometimes I found that he called them, to cast off their melancholy. He would talk in a cheerful accent, with an expression of goodness that bestowed pleasure even upon me. Agatha listened with respect, her eyes some-times filled with tears, which she endeavoured to wipe away unper-ceived; but I generally found that her countenance and tone were more cheerful after having listened to the exhortations of her father. It was not thus with Felix. He was always the saddest of the groupe; and, even to my unpractised senses, he appeared to have suffered more deeply than his friends. But if his countenance was more sor-rowful, his voice was more cheerful than that of his sister, especially when he addressed the old man.

'I could mention innumerable instances, which, although slight, marked the dispositions of these amiable cottagers. In the midst of poverty and want, Felix carried with pleasure to his sister the first lit-tle white flower that peeped out from beneath the snowy ground. Early in the morning before she had risen, he cleared away the snow that obstructed her path to the milk-house, drew water from the well, and brought the wood from the out-house, where, to his perpetual astonishment, he found his store always replenished by an invisible hand. In the day, I believe, he worked sometimes for a neighbouring farmer, because he often went forth, and did not return until dinner, yet brought no wood with him. At other times he worked in the gar-den; but, as there was little to do in the frosty season, he read to the old man and Agatha.

'This reading had puzzled me extremely at first; but, by degrees, I discovered that he uttered many of the same sounds when he read as when he talked. I conjectured, therefore, that he found on the paper signs for speech which he understood, and I ardently longed to com-prehend these also; but how was that possible, when I did not even understand the sounds for which they stood as signs? I improved, however, sensibly in this science, but not sufficiently to follow up any kind of conversation, although I applied for my whole mind to the endeavour: for I easily perceived that, although I eagerly longed to discover myself to the cottagers, I ought not to make the attempt until I had first become master of their language; which knowledge might enable me to make them overlook the deformity of my figure; for with this also the contrast perpetually presented to my eyes had made me acquainted.

'I had admired the perfect forms of my cottagers—their grace, beauty, and delicate complexions: but how was I terrified, when I viewed myself in a transparent pool!* At first I started back, unable to believe that it was indeed I who was reflected in the mirror; and when I became fully convinced that I was in reality the monster that I am, I was filled with the bitterest sensations of despondence and mortification. Alas! I did not yet entirely know the fatal effects of this miserable deformity.

'As the sun became warmer, and the light of day longer, the snow vanished, and I beheld the bare trees and the black earth. From this time Felix was more employed; and the heart-moving indications of impending famine disappeared. Their food, as I afterwards found, was coarse, but it was wholesome; and they procured a sufficiency of it. Several new kinds of plants sprung up in the garden, which they dressed; and these signs of comfort increased daily as the season advanced.

'The old man, leaning on his son, walked each day at noon, when it did not rain, as I found it was called when the heavens poured forth its waters. This frequently took place; but a high wind quickly dried the earth, and the season became far more pleasant than it had been.

'My mode of life in my hovel was uniform. During the morning I attended the motions of the cottagers; and when they were dispersed in various occupations, I slept: the remainder of the day was spent in observing my friends. When they had retired to rest, if there was any moon, or the night was star-light, I went into the woods, and collected my own food and fuel for the cottage. When I returned, as often as it was necessary, I cleared their path from the snow, and performed those offices that I had seen done by Felix. I afterwards found that these labours, performed by an invisible hand, greatly astonished them; and once or twice I heard them, on these occasions, utter the

words *good spirit*, *wonderful*; but I did not then understand the signification of these terms.

'My thoughts now became more active, and I longed to discover
the motives and feelings of these lovely creatures; I was inquisitive to
know why Felix appeared so miserable, and Agatha so sad. I thought
(foolish wretch!) that it might be in my power to restore happiness to
these deserving people. When I slept, or was absent, the forms of the
venerable blind father, the gentle Agatha, and the excellent Felix, flit-
ted before me. I looked upon them as superior beings, who would be
the arbiters of my future destiny. I formed in my imagination a thousand pictures of presenting myself to them, and their reception of me.
I imagined that they would be disgusted, until, by my gentle demeanour and conciliating words, I should first win their favour, and afterwards their love.

'These thoughts exhilarated me, and led me to apply with fresh
ardour to the acquiring the art of language. My organs were indeed
harsh, but supple; and although my voice was very unlike the soft
music of their tones, yet I pronounced such words as I understood
with tolerable ease. It was as the ass and the lap-dog;* yet surely the
gentle ass, whose intentions were affectionate, although his manners
were rude, deserved better treatment than blows and execration.

'The pleasant showers and genial warmth of spring greatly altered
the aspect of the earth. Men, who before this change seemed to have
been hid in caves, dispersed themselves, and were employed in various arts of cultivation. The birds sang in more cheerful notes, and the
leaves began to bud forth on the trees. Happy, happy earth! fit habitation* for gods, which, so short a time before, was bleak, damp, and
unwholesome. My spirits were elevated by the enchanting appearance
of nature; the past was blotted from my memory, the present was
tranquil, and the future gilded by bright rays of hope, and anticipa-
tions of joy.

CHAPTER V.

'I NOW hasten to the more moving part of my story. I shall relate
events that impressed me with feelings which, from what I was, have
made me what I am.

'Spring advanced rapidly; the weather became fine, and the skies cloudless. It surprised me, that what before was desert and gloomy should now bloom with the most beautiful flowers and verdure. My senses were gratified and refreshed by a thousand scents of delight, and a thousand sights of beauty.

'It was on one of these days, when my cottagers periodically rested from labour—the old man played on his guitar, and the children listened to him—I observed that the countenance of Felix was melancholy beyond expression: he sighed frequently; and once his father paused in his music, and I conjectured by his manner that he inquired the cause of his son's sorrow. Felix replied in a cheerful accent, and the old man was recommencing his music, when some one tapped at the door.

'It was a lady on horseback, accompanied by a countryman as a guide. The lady was dressed in a dark suit, and covered with a thick black veil. Agatha asked a question; to which the stranger only replied by pronouncing, in a sweet accent, the name of Felix. Her voice was musical, but unlike that of either of my friends. On hearing this word, Felix came up hastily to the lady; who, when she saw him, threw up her veil, and I beheld a countenance of angelic beauty and expression. Her hair of a shining raven black, and curiously braided; her eyes were dark, but gentle, although animated; her features of a regular proportion, and her complexion wondrously fair, each cheek tinged with a lovely pink.

'Felix seemed ravished with delight when he saw her, every trait of sorrow vanished from his face, and it instantly expressed a degree of ecstatic joy, of which I could hardly have believed it capable; his eyes sparkled, as his cheek flushed with pleasure; and at that moment I thought him as beautiful as the stranger. She appeared affected by different feelings; wiping a few tears from her lovely eyes, she held out her hand to Felix, who kissed it rapturously, and called her, as well as I could distinguish, his sweet Arabian. She did not appear to understand him, but smiled. He assisted her to dismount, and, dismissing her guide, conducted her into the cottage. Some conversation took place between him and his father; and the young stranger knelt at the old man's feet, and would have kissed his hand, but he raised her, and embraced her affectionately.

'I soon perceived, that although the stranger uttered articulate sounds, and appeared to have a language of her own, she was neither understood by, or herself understood, the cottagers. They made many

signs which I did not comprehend; but I saw that her presence diffused gladness through the cottage, dispelling their sorrow as the
sun dissipates the morning mists. Felix seemed peculiarly happy, and
with smiles of delight welcomed his Arabian. Agatha, the ever-gentle
Agatha, kissed the hands of the lovely stranger; and, pointing to her
brother, made signs which appeared to me to mean that he had been
sorrowful until she came. Some hours passed thus, while they, by
their countenances, expressed joy, the cause of which I did not com-
prehend. Presently I found, by the frequent recurrence of one sound
which the stranger repeated after them, that she was endeavouring
to learn their language; and the idea instantly occurred to me, that
I should make use of the same instructions to the same end. The
stranger learned about twenty words at the first lesson, most of them
indeed were those which I had before understood, but I profited by
the others.

'As night came on, Agatha and the Arabian retired early. When
they separated, Felix kissed the hand of the stranger, and said, "Good
night, sweet Safie."* He sat up much longer, conversing with his
father; and, by the frequent repetition of her name, I conjectured that
their lovely guest was the subject of their conversation. I ardently
desired to understand them, and bent every faculty towards that purpose, but found it utterly impossible.

'The next morning Felix went out to his work; and, after the usual
occupations of Agatha were finished, the Arabian sat at the feet of the
old man, and, taking his guitar, played some airs so entrancingly
beautiful, that they at once drew tears of sorrow and delight from my
eyes. She sang, and her voice flowed in a rich cadence, swelling or
dying away, like a nightingale of the woods.

'When she had finished, she gave the guitar to Agatha, who at first
declined it. She played a simple air, and her voice accompanied it
in sweet accents, but unlike the wondrous strain of the stranger. The
old man appeared enraptured, and said some words, which Agatha
endeavoured to explain to Safie, and by which he appeared to wish to
express that she bestowed on him the greatest delight by her music.

'The days now passed as peaceably as before, with the sole alteration,
that joy had taken place of sadness in the countenances of my friends.
Safie was always gay and happy; she and I improved rapidly in the
knowledge of language, so that in two months I began to comprehend
most of the words uttered by my protectors.

'In the meanwhile also the black ground was covered with herbage, and the green banks interspersed with innumerable flowers, sweet to the scent and the eyes, stars of pale radiance among the moonlight woods; the sun became warmer, the nights clear and balmy; and my nocturnal rambles were an extreme pleasure to me, although they were considerably shortened by the late setting and early rising of the sun; for I never ventured abroad during daylight, fearful of meeting with the same treatment as I had formerly endured in the first village which I entered.

'My days were spent in close attention, that I might more speedily master the language; and I may boast that I improved more rapidly than the Arabian, who understood very little, and conversed in broken accents, whilst I comprehended and could imitate almost every word that was spoken.

'While I improved in speech, I also learned the science of letters, as it was taught to the stranger; and this opened before me a wide field for wonder and delight.

'The book from which Felix instructed Safie was Volney's *Ruins of Empires*.* I should not have understood the purport of this book, had not Felix, in reading it, given very minute explanations. He had chosen this work, he said, because the declamatory style was framed in imitation of the eastern authors. Through this work I obtained a cursory knowledge of history, and a view of the several empires at present existing in the world; it gave me an insight into the manners, governments, and religions of the different nations of the earth. I heard of the slothful Asiatics; of the stupendous genius and mental activity of the Grecians; of the wars and wonderful virtue of the early Romans—of their subsequent degeneration—of the decline of that mighty empire; of chivalry, christianity, and kings. I heard of the discovery of the American hemisphere, and wept with Safie over the hapless fate of its original inhabitants.

'These wonderful narrations inspired me with strange feelings. Was man, indeed, at once so powerful, so virtuous, and magnificent, yet so vicious and base? He appeared at one time a mere scion of the evil principle, and at another as all that can be conceived of noble and godlike. To be a great and virtuous man appeared the highest honour that can befall a sensitive being; to be base and vicious, as many on record have been, appeared the lowest degradation, a condition more abject than that of the blind mole or harmless worm. For a long time

I could not conceive how one man could go forth to murder his fellow, or even why there were laws and governments; but when I heard details of vice and bloodshed, my wonder ceased, and I turned away with disgust and loathing.

'Every conversation of the cottagers now opened new wonders to me. While I listened to the instructions which Felix bestowed upon the Arabian, the strange system of human society was explained to me. I heard of the division of property, of immense wealth and squalid poverty; of rank, descent, and noble blood.

'The words induced me to turn towards myself. I learned that the possessions most esteemed by your fellow-creatures were, high and unsullied descent united with riches. A man might be respected with only one of these acquisitions; but without either he was considered, except in very rare instances, as a vagabond and a slave, doomed to waste his powers for the profit of the chosen few. And what was I? Of my creation and creator I was absolutely ignorant; but I knew that I possessed no money, no friends, no kind of property. I was, besides, endowed with a figure hideously deformed and loathsome; I was not even of the same nature as man. I was more agile than they, and could subsist upon coarser diet; I bore the extremes of heat and cold with less injury to my frame; my stature far exceeded their's. When I looked around, I saw and heard of none like me. Was I then a monster, a blot upon the earth, from which all men fled, and whom all men disowned?

'I cannot describe to you the agony that these reflections inflicted upon me; I tried to dispel them, but sorrow only increased with knowledge. Oh, that I had for ever remained in my native wood, nor known or felt beyond the sensations of hunger, thirst, and heat!

'Of what a strange nature is knowledge! It clings to the mind, when it has once seized on it, like a lichen on the rock. I wished sometimes to shake off all thought and feeling; but I learned that there was but one means to overcome the sensation of pain, and that was death— a state which I feared yet did not understand. I admired virtue and good feelings, and loved the gentle manners and amiable qualities of my cottagers; but I was shut out from intercourse with them, except through means which I obtained by stealth, when I was unseen and unknown, and which rather increased than satisfied the desire I had of becoming one among my fellows. The gentle words of Agatha, and the animated smiles of the charming Arabian, were not for me. The mild exhortations of the old man, and the lively conversation of the loved Felix, were not for me. Miserable, unhappy wretch!

'Other lessons were impressed upon me even more deeply. I heard of the difference of sexes; of the birth and growth of children; how the father doated on the smiles of the infant, and the lively sallies of the older child; how all the life and cares of the mother were wrapt up in the precious charge; how the mind of youth expanded and gained knowledge; of brother, sister, and all the various relationships which bind one human being to another in mutual bonds.

'But where were my friends and relations? No father had watched my infant days, no mother had blessed me with smiles and caresses; or if they had, all my past life was now a blot, a blind vacancy in which I distinguished nothing. From my earliest remembrance I had been as I then was in height and proportion. I had never yet seen a being resembling me, or who claimed any intercourse with me. What was I? The question again recurred, to be answered only with groans.

'I will soon explain to what these feelings tended; but allow me now to return to the cottagers, whose story excited in me such various feelings of indignation, delight, and wonder, but which all terminated in additional love and reverence for my protectors (for so I loved, in an innocent, half painful self-deceit, to call them).

CHAPTER VI.

'SOME time elapsed before I learned the history of my friends. It was one which could not fail to impress itself deeply on my mind, unfolding as it did a number of circumstances each interesting and wonderful to one so utterly inexperienced as I was.

'The name of the old man was De Lacey. He was descended from a good family in France, where he had lived for many years in affluence, respected by his superiors, and beloved by his equals. His son was bred in the service of his country; and Agatha had ranked with ladies of the highest distinction. A few months before my arrival, they had lived in a large and luxurious city, called Paris, surrounded by friends, and possessed of every enjoyment which virtue, refinement of intellect, or taste, accompanied by a moderate fortune, could afford.

'The father of Safie had been the cause of their ruin. He was a Turkish merchant, and had inhabited Paris for many years, when, for some reason which I could not learn, he became obnoxious to the government. He was seized and cast into prison the very day that Safie arrived from Constantinople to join him. He was tried, and condemned to death. The injustice of his sentence was very flagrant; all Paris was indignant; and it was judged that his religion and wealth, rather than the crime alleged against him, had been the cause of his condemnation.

'Felix had been present at the trial; his horror and indignation were uncontrollable, when he heard the decision of the court. He made, at that moment, a solemn vow to deliver him, and then looked around for the means. After many fruitless attempts to gain admittance to the prison, he found a strongly grated window in an unguarded part of the building, which lighted the dungeon of the unfortunate Mahometan;* who, loaded with chains, waited in despair the execution of the barbarous sentence. Felix visited the grate at night, and made known to the prisoner his intentions in his favour. The Turk, amazed and delighted, endeavoured to kindle the zeal of his deliverer by promises of reward and wealth. Felix rejected his offers with contempt; yet when he saw the lovely Safie, who was allowed to visit her father, and who, by her gestures, expressed her lively gratitude, the youth could not help owning to his own mind, that the captive possessed a treasure which would fully reward his toil and hazard.

'The Turk quickly perceived the impression that his daughter had made on the heart of Felix, and endeavoured to secure him more entirely in his interests by the promise of her hand in marriage, so soon as he should be conveyed to a place of safety. Felix was too delicate* to accept this offer; yet he looked forward to the probability of that event as to the consummation of his happiness.

'During the ensuing days, while the preparations were going forward for the escape of the merchant, the zeal of Felix was warmed by several letters that he received from this lovely girl, who found means to express her thoughts in the language of her lover by the aid of an old man, a servant of her father's, who understood French. She thanked him in the most ardent terms for his intended services towards her father; and at the same time she gently deplored her own fate.

'I have copies of these letters; for I found means, during my residence in the hovel, to procure the implements of writing; and the letters were often in the hands of Felix or Agatha. Before I depart, I will give them to you, they will prove the truth of my tale; but at present, as the sun is already far declined, I shall only have time to repeat the substance of them to you.

'Safie related, that her mother was a Christian Arab, seized and made a slave by the Turks; recommended by her beauty, she had won the heart of the father of Safie, who married her. The young girl spoke in high and enthusiastic terms of her mother, who, born in freedom spurned the bondage to which she was now reduced. She instructed her daughter in the tenets of her religion, and taught her to aspire to higher powers of intellect, and an independence of spirit, forbidden to the female followers of Mahomet. This lady died; but her lessons were indelibly impressed on the mind of Safie, who sickened at the prospect of again returning to Asia, and the being immured within the walls of a haram,* allowed only to occupy herself with puerile amusements, ill suited to the temper of her soul, now accustomed to grand ideas and a noble emulation for virtue. The prospect of marrying a Christian, and remaining in a country where women were allowed to take a rank in society, was enchanting to her.

'The day for the execution of the Turk was fixed; but, on the night previous to it, he had quitted prison, and before morning was distant many leagues from Paris. Felix had procured passports in the name of his father, sister, and himself. He had previously communicated his plan to the former, who aided the deceit by quitting his house, under the pretence of a journey, and concealed himself, with his daughter, in an obscure part of Paris.

'Felix conducted the fugitives through France to Lyons, and across Mont Cenis to Leghorn, where the merchant had decided to wait a favourable opportunity of passing into some part of the Turkish dominions.

'Safie resolved to remain with her father until the moment of his departure, before which time the Turk renewed his promise that she should be united to his deliverer; and Felix remained with them in expectation of that event; and in the mean time he enjoyed the society of the Arabian, who exhibited towards him the simplest and tenderest affection. They conversed with one another through the means of an interpreter, and sometimes with the interpretation of looks; and Safie sang to him the divine airs of her native country.

'The Turk allowed this intimacy to take place, and encouraged the hopes of the youthful lovers, while in his heart he had formed far other plans. He loathed the idea that his daughter should be united to a Christian; but he feared the resentment of Felix if he should appear lukewarm; for he knew that he was still in the power of his deliverer, if he should choose to betray him to the Italian state which they inhabited. He revolved a thousand plans by which he should be enabled to prolong the deceit until it might be no longer necessary, and secretly to take his daughter with him when he departed. His plans were greatly facilitated by the news which arrived from Paris.

'The government of France were greatly enraged at the escape of their victim, and spared no pains to detect and punish his deliverer. The plot of Felix was quickly discovered, and De Lacey and Agatha were thrown into prison. The news reached Felix, and roused him from his dream of pleasure. His blind and aged father, and his gentle sister, lay in a noisome dungeon, while he enjoyed the free air, and the society of her whom he loved. This idea was torture to him. He quickly arranged with the Turk, that if the latter should find a favourable opportunity for escape before Felix could return to Italy, Safie should remain as a boarder at a convent at Leghorn; and then, quitting the lovely Arabian, he hastened to Paris, and delivered himself up to the vengeance of the law, hoping to free De Lacey and Agatha by this proceeding.

'He did not succeed. They remained confined for five months before the trial took place; the result of which deprived them of their fortune, and condemned them to a perpetual exile from their native country.

'They found a miserable asylum in the cottage in Germany, where I discovered them. Felix soon learned that the treacherous Turk, for whom he and his family endured such unheard-of oppression, on discovering that his deliverer was thus reduced to poverty and impotence, became a traitor to good feeling and honour, and had quitted Italy with his daughter, insultingly sending Felix a pittance of money to aid him, as he said, in some plan of future maintenance.

'Such were the events that preyed on the heart of Felix, and rendered him, when I first saw him, the most miserable of his family. He could have endured poverty, and when this distress had been the meed* of his virtue, he would have gloried in it: but the ingratitude of the Turk, and the loss of his beloved Safie, were misfortunes more bitter and irreparable. The arrival of the Arabian now infused new life into his soul.

'When the news reached Leghorn, that Felix was deprived of his wealth and rank, the merchant commanded his daughter to think no more of her lover, but to prepare to return with him to her native country. The generous nature of Safie was outraged by this command; she attempted to expostulate with her father, but he left her angrily, reiterating his tyrannical mandate.

'A few days after, the Turk entered his daughter's apartment, and told her hastily, that he had reason to believe that his residence at Leghorn had been divulged, and that he should speedily be delivered up to the French government; he had, consequently, hired a vessel to convey him to Constantinople, for which city he should sail in a few hours. He intended to leave his daughter under the care of a confidential servant, to follow at her leisure with the greater part of his property, which had not yet arrived at Leghorn.

'When alone, Safie resolved in her own mind the plan of conduct that it would become her to pursue in this emergency. A residence in Turkey was abhorrent to her; her religion and feelings were alike adverse to it. By some papers of her father's, which fell into her hands, she heard of the exile of her lover, and learnt the name of the spot where he then resided. She hesitated some time, but at length she formed her determination. Taking with her some jewels that belonged to her, and a small sum of money, she quitted Italy, with an attendant, a native of Leghorn, but who understood the common language of Turkey, and departed for Germany.

'She arrived in safety at a town about twenty leagues from the cottage of De Lacey, when her attendant fell dangerously ill. Safie nursed her with the most devoted affection; but the poor girl died, and the Arabian was left alone, unacquainted with the language of the country, and utterly ignorant of the customs of the world. She fell, however, into good hands. The Italian had mentioned the name of the spot for which they were bound; and, after her death, the woman of the house in which they had lived took care that Safie should arrive in safety at the cottage of her lover.

CHAPTER VII.

'SUCH was the history of my beloved cottagers. It impressed me deeply. I learned, from the views of social life which it developed, to admire their virtues, and to deprecate the vices of mankind.

'As yet I looked upon crime as a distant evil; benevolence and generosity were ever present before me, inciting within me a desire to become an actor in the busy scene where so many admirable qualities were called forth and displayed. But, in giving an account of the progress of my intellect, I must not omit a circumstance which occurred in the beginning of the month of August of the same year.

'One night, during my accustomed visit to the neighbouring wood, where I collected my own food, and brought home firing for my protectors, I found on the ground a leathern portmanteau, containing several articles of dress and some books. I eagerly seized the prize, and returned with it to my hovel. Fortunately the books were written in the language the elements of which I had acquired at the cottage; they consisted of *Paradise Lost*, a volume of *Plutarch's Lives*, and the *Sorrows of Werter*.* The possession of these treasures gave me extreme delight; I now continually studied and exercised my mind upon these histories, whilst my friends were employed in their ordinary occupations.

'I can hardly describe to you the effect of these books. They produced in me an infinity of new images and feelings, that sometimes raised me to ecstacy, but more frequently sunk me into the lowest dejection. In the *Sorrows of Werter*, besides the interest of its simple and affecting story, so many opinions are canvassed, and so many lights thrown upon what had hitherto been to me obscure subjects, that I found in it a never-ending source of speculation and astonishment. The gentle and domestic manners it described, combined with lofty sentiments and feelings, which had for their object something out of self,* accorded well with my experience among my protectors, and with the wants which were for ever alive in my own bosom. But I thought Werter himself a more divine being than I had ever beheld or imagined; his character contained no pretension, but it sunk deep. The disquisitions upon death and suicide were calculated to fill me with wonder.* I did not pretend to enter into the merits of the case, yet I inclined towards the opinions of the hero, whose extinction I wept, without precisely understanding it.

'As I read, however, I applied much personally to my own feelings and condition. I found myself similar, yet at the same time strangely unlike the beings concerning whom I read, and to whose conversation I was a listener. I sympathized with, and partly understood them, but I was unformed in mind; I was dependent on none, and related to none. "The path of my departure was free;"* and there was none to lament my annihilation. My person was hideous, and my stature gigantic:

what did this mean? Who was I? What was I? Whence did I come? What was my destination? These questions continually recurred, but I was unable to solve them.

'The volume of *Plutarch's Lives* which I possessed, contained the histories of the first founders of the ancient republics. This book had a far different effect upon me from the *Sorrows of Werter*. I learned from Werter's imaginations despondency and gloom: but Plutarch taught me high thoughts; he elevated me above the wretched sphere of my own reflections, to admire and love the heroes of past ages. Many things I read surpassed my understanding and experience. I had a very confused knowledge of kingdoms, wide extents of country, mighty rivers, and boundless seas. But I was perfectly unacquainted with towns, and large assemblages of men. The cottage of my protectors had been the only school in which I had studied human nature; but this book developed new and mightier scenes of action. I read of men concerned in public affairs governing or massacring their species. I felt the greatest ardour for virtue rise within me, and abhorrence for vice, as far as I understood the signification of those terms, relative as they were, as I applied them, to pleasure and pain alone. Induced by these feelings, I was of course led to admire peaceable law-givers, Numa, Solon, and Lycurgus, in preference to Romulus and Theseus.* The patriarchal* lives of my protectors caused these impressions to take a firm hold on my mind; perhaps, if my first introduction to humanity had been made by a young soldier, burning for glory and slaughter, I should have been imbued with different sensations.

'But *Paradise Lost* excited different and far deeper emotions. I read it, as I had read the other volumes which had fallen into my hands, as a true history. It moved every feeling of wonder and awe, that the picture of an omnipotent God warring with his creatures was capable of exciting. I often referred the several situations, as their similarity struck me, to my own. Like Adam, I was created apparently united by no link to any other being in existence; but his state was far different from mine in every other respect. He had come forth from the hands of God a perfect creature, happy and prosperous, guarded by the espe- cial care of his Creator; he was allowed to converse with, and acquire knowledge from beings of a superior nature: but I was wretched, help- less, and alone. Many times I considered Satan as the fitter emblem of my condition; for often, like him, when I viewed the bliss of my protectors, the bitter gall of envy rose within me.*

'Another circumstance strengthened and confirmed these feelings. Soon after my arrival in the hovel, I discovered some papers in the pocket of the dress which I had taken from your laboratory. At first I had neglected them; but now that I was able to decypher the characters in which they were written, I began to study them with diligence. It was your journal of the four months that preceded my creation. You minutely described in these papers every step you took in the progress of your work; this history was mingled with accounts of domestic occurrences. You, doubtless, recollect these papers. Here they are. Every thing is related in them which bears reference to my accursed origin; the whole detail of that series of disgusting circumstances which produced it is set in view; the minutest description of my odious and loathsome person is given, in language which painted your own horrors, and rendered mine ineffaceable. I sickened as I read. "Hateful day when I received life!" I exclaimed in agony. "Cursed creator! Why did you form a monster so hideous that even you turned from me in disgust? God in pity made man beautiful and alluring, after his own image; but my form is a filthy type of your's, more horrid from its very resemblance. Satan had his companions, fellow-devils, to admire and encourage him; but I am solitary and detested."

'These were the reflections of my hours of despondency and solitude; but when I contemplated the virtues of the cottagers, their amiable and benevolent dispositions, I persuaded myself that when they should become acquainted with my admiration of their virtues, they would compassionate me, and overlook my personal deformity. Could they turn from their door one, however monstrous, who solicited their compassion and friendship? I resolved, at least, not to despair, but in every way to fit myself for an interview with them which would decide my fate. I postponed this attempt for some months longer; for the importance attached to its success inspired me with a dread lest I should fail. Besides, I found that my understanding improved so much with every day's experience, that I was unwilling to commence this undertaking until a few more months should have added to my wisdom.

'Several changes, in the mean time, took place in the cottage. The presence of Safie diffused happiness among its inhabitants; and I also found that a greater degree of plenty reigned there. Felix and Agatha spent more time in amusement and conversation, and were assisted in their labours by servants. They did not appear rich, but they were contented and happy; their feelings were serene and peaceful, while mine became every day more tumultuous. Increase of knowledge only discovered to me more clearly what a wretched outcast I was. I cherished hope, it is true; but it vanished, when I beheld my person reflected in water, or my shadow in the moon-shine, even as that frail image and that inconstant shade.

'I endeavoured to crush these fears, and to fortify myself for the trial which in a few months I resolved to undergo; and sometimes I allowed my thoughts, unchecked by reason, to ramble in the fields of Paradise, and dared to fancy amiable and lovely creatures sympathizing with my feelings and cheering my gloom; their angelic countenances breathed smiles of consolation. But it was all a dream: no Eve soothed my sorrows, or shared my thoughts; I was alone. I remembered Adam's supplication to his Creator;* but where was mine? he had abandoned me,* and, in the bitterness of my heart, I cursed him.

'Autumn passed thus. I saw, with surprise and grief, the leaves decay and fall, and nature again assume the barren and bleak appearance it had worn when I first beheld the woods and the lovely moon. Yet I did not heed the bleakness of the weather; I was better fitted by my conformation* for the endurance of cold than heat. But my chief delights were the sight of the flowers, the birds, and all the gay apparel of summer; when those deserted me, I turned with more attention towards the cottagers. Their happiness was not decreased by the absence of summer. They loved, and sympathized with one another; and their joys, depending on each other, were not interrupted by the casualties that took place around them. The more I saw of them, the greater became my desire to claim their protection and kindness; my heart yearned to be known and loved by these amiable creatures: to see their sweet looks turned towards me with affection, was the utmost limit of my ambition. I dared not think that they would turn them from me with disdain and horror. The poor that stopped at their door were never driven away. I asked, it is true, for greater treasures than a little food or rest; I required kindness and sympathy; but I did not believe myself utterly unworthy of it.

'The winter advanced, and an entire revolution of the seasons had taken place since I awoke into life. My attention, at this time, was solely directed towards my plan of introducing myself into the cottage of my protectors. I revolved many projects; but that on which I finally fixed was, to enter the dwelling when the blind old man should be

alone. I had sagacity enough to discover, that the unnatural hideousness of my person was the chief object of horror with those who had
formerly beheld me. My voice, although harsh, had nothing terrible
in it; I thought, therefore, that if, in the absence of his children,
I could gain the good-will and mediation of the old De Lacy,* I might,
by his means, be tolerated by my younger protectors.

'One day, when the sun shone on the red leaves that strewed the
ground, and diffused cheerfulness, although it denied warmth, Safie,
Agatha, and Felix, departed on a long country walk, and the old man,
at his own desire, was left alone in the cottage. When his children had
departed, he took up his guitar, and played several mournful, but
sweet airs, more sweet and mournful than I had ever heard him play
before. At first his countenance was illuminated with pleasure, but, as
he continued, thoughtfulness and sadness succeeded; at length, laying aside the instrument, he sat absorbed in reflection.

'My heart beat quick; this was the hour and moment of trial, which
would decide my hopes, or realize my fears. The servants were gone
to a neighbouring fair. All was silent in and around the cottage: it was
an excellent opportunity; yet, when I proceeded to execute my plan,
my limbs failed me, and I sunk to the ground. Again I rose; and,
exerting all the firmness of which I was master, removed the planks
which I had placed before my hovel to conceal my retreat. The fresh
air revived me, and, with renewed determination, I approached the
door of their cottage.

'I knocked. "Who is there?" said the old man—"Come in."

'I entered; "Pardon this intrusion," said I, "I am a traveller in want
of a little rest; you would greatly oblige me, if you would allow me to
remain a few minutes before the fire."

'"Enter," said De Lacy; "and I will try in what manner I can relieve
your wants; but, unfortunately, my children are from home, and, as
I am blind, I am afraid I shall find it difficult to procure food for you."

'"Do not trouble yourself, my kind host, I have food; it is warmth
and rest only that I need."

'I sat down, and a silence ensued. I knew that every minute was
precious to me, yet I remained irresolute in what manner to commence the interview; when the old man addressed me—

'"By your language, stranger, I suppose you are my countryman;—are you French?"

'"No; but I was educated by a French family, and understand that language only. I am now going to claim the protection of some friends, whom I sincerely love, and of whose favour I have some hopes."

' "Are these Germans?"

' "No, they are French. But let us change the subject. I am an unfortunate and deserted creature; I look around, and I have no relation or friend upon earth. These amiable people to whom I go have never seen me, and know little of me. I am full of fears; for if I fail there, I am an outcast in the world for ever."

' "Do not despair. To be friendless is indeed to be unfortunate; but the hearts of men, when unprejudiced by* any obvious self-interest, are full of brotherly love and charity. Rely, therefore, on your hopes; and if these friends are good and amiable, do not despair."

' "They are kind—they are the most excellent creatures in the world; but, unfortunately, they are prejudiced against me. I have good dispositions; my life has been hitherto harmless, and, in some degree, beneficial; but a fatal prejudice clouds their eyes, and where they ought to see a feeling and kind friend, they behold only a detestable monster."

' "That is indeed unfortunate; but if you are really blameless, cannot you undeceive them?"

' "I am about to undertake that task; and it is on that account that I feel so many overwhelming terrors. I tenderly love these friends; I have, unknown to them, been for many months in the habits of daily kindness towards them; but they believe that I wish to injure them, and it is that prejudice which I wish to overcome."

' "Where do these friends reside?"

' "Near this spot."

'The old man paused, and then continued, "If you will unreservedly confide to me the particulars of your tale, I perhaps may be of use in undeceiving them. I am blind, and cannot judge of your countenance, but there is something in your words which persuades me that you are sincere. I am poor, and an exile; but it will afford me true pleasure to be in any way serviceable to a human creature."

' "Excellent man! I thank you, and accept your generous offer. You raise me from the dust by this kindness; and I trust that, by your aid, I shall not be driven from the society and sympathy of your fellow-creatures."

' "Heaven forbid! even if you were really criminal; for that can only drive you to desperation, and not instigate you to virtue. I also am

unfortunate; I and my family have been condemned, although innocent: judge, therefore, if I do not feel for your misfortunes."

'"How can I thank you, my best and only benefactor? from your
lips first have I heard the voice of kindness directed towards me;
I shall be for ever grateful; and your present humanity assures me of
success with those friends whom I am on the point of meeting."

'"May I know the names and residence of those friends?"

'I paused. This, I thought, was the moment of decision, which was
to rob me of, or bestow happiness on me for ever. I struggled vainly
for firmness sufficient to answer him, but the effort destroyed all my
remaining strength; I sank on the chair, and sobbed aloud. At that
moment I heard the steps of my younger protectors. I had not
a moment to lose; but, seizing the hand of the old man, I cried, "Now
is the time!—save and protect me! You and your family are the friends
whom I seek. Do not you desert me in the hour of trial!"

'"Great God!" exclaimed the old man, "who are you?"

'At that instant the cottage door was opened, and Felix, Safie and
Agatha entered. Who can describe their horror and consternation on
beholding me? Agatha fainted; and Safie, unable to attend to her
friend, rushed out of the cottage. Felix darted forward, and with
supernatural force tore me from his father, to whose knees I clung: in
a transport of fury, he dashed me to the ground, and struck me violently with a stick. I could have torn him limb from limb, as the lion
rends the antelope. But my heart sunk within me as with bitter sickness, and I refrained. I saw him on the point of repeating his blow,
when, overcome by pain and anguish, I quitted the cottage, and in the
general tumult escaped unperceived to my hovel.

CHAPTER VIII.

'CURSED, cursed creator! Why did I live? Why, in that instant, did
I not extinguish the spark of existence which you had so wantonly
bestowed? I know not; despair had not yet taken possession of me; my
feelings were those of rage and revenge. I could with pleasure have
destroyed the cottage and its inhabitants, and have glutted myself
with their shrieks and misery.

'When night came, I quitted my retreat, and wandered in the wood;
and now, no longer restrained by the fear of discovery, I gave vent to

my anguish in fearful howlings. I was like a wild beast that had broken the toils;* destroying the objects that obstructed me, and ranging through the wood with a stag-like swiftness. Oh! what a miserable night I passed! the cold stars shone in mockery, and the bare trees waved their branches above me: now and then the sweet voice of a bird burst forth amidst the universal stillness. All, save I, were at rest or in enjoyment: I, like the arch fiend, bore a hell within me;* and, finding myself unsympathized with, wished to tear up the trees, spread havoc and destruction around me, and then to have sat down and enjoyed the ruin.

'But this was a luxury of sensation that could not endure; I became fatigued with excess of bodily exertion, and sank on the damp grass in the sick impotence of despair. There was none among the myriads of men that existed who would pity or assist me; and should I feel kindness towards my enemies? No: from that moment I declared everlasting war against the species, and, more than all, against him who had formed me, and sent me forth to this insupportable misery.

'The sun rose; I heard the voices of men, and knew that it was impossible to return to my retreat during that day. Accordingly I hid myself in some thick underwood, determining to devote the ensuing hours to reflection on my situation.

'The pleasant sunshine, and the pure air of day, restored me to some degree of tranquillity; and when I considered what had passed at the cottage, I could not help believing that I had been too hasty in my conclusions. I had certainly acted imprudently. It was apparent that my conversation had interested the father in my behalf, and I was a fool in having exposed my person to the horror of his children. I ought to have familiarized the old De Lacy to me, and by degrees have discovered myself to the rest of his family, when they should have been prepared for my approach. But I did not believe my errors to be irretrievable; and, after much consideration, I resolved to return to the cottage, seek the old man, and by my representations win him to my party.

'These thoughts calmed me, and in the afternoon I sank into a profound sleep; but the fever of my blood did not allow me to be visited by peaceful dreams. The horrible scene of the preceding day was for ever acting before my eyes; the females were flying, and the enraged Felix tearing me from his father's feet. I awoke exhausted; and, finding that it was already night, I crept forth from my hiding-place, and went in search of food.

'When my hunger was appeased, I directed my steps towards the well-known path that conducted to the cottage. All there was at peace. I crept into my hovel, and remained in silent expectation of the accustomed hour when the family arose. That hour past, the sun mounted high in the heavens, but the cottagers did not appear. I trembled violently, apprehending some dreadful misfortune. The inside of the cottage was dark, and I heard no motion; I cannot describe the agony of this suspence.

'Presently two countrymen passed by; but, pausing near the cottage, they entered into conversation, using violent gesticulations; but I did not understand what they said, as they spoke the language of the country,* which differed from that of my protectors. Soon after, however, Felix approached with another man: I was surprised, as I knew that he had not quitted the cottage that morning, and waited anxiously to discover, from his discourse, the meaning of these unusual appearances.

'"Do you consider," said his companion to him, "that you will be obliged to pay three months' rent, and to lose the produce of your garden? I do not wish to take any unfair advantage, and I beg therefore that you will take some days to consider of your determination."

'"It is utterly useless," replied Felix, "we can never again inhabit your cottage. The life of my father is in the greatest danger, owing to the dreadful circumstance that I have related. My wife and my sister will never recover* their horror. I entreat you not to reason with me any more. Take possession of your tenement, and let me fly from this place."

'Felix trembled violently as he said this. He and his companion entered the cottage, in which they remained for a few minutes, and then departed. I never saw any of the family of De Lacy more.

'I continued for the remainder of the day in my hovel in a state of utter and stupid* despair. My protectors had departed, and had broken the only link that held me to the world. For the first time the feelings of revenge and hatred filled my bosom, and I did not strive to controul them; but, allowing myself to be borne away by the stream, I bent my mind towards injury and death. When I thought of my friends, of the mild voice of De Lacy, the gentle eyes of Agatha, and the exquisite beauty of the Arabian, these thoughts vanished, and a gush of tears somewhat soothed me. But again, when I reflected that they had spurned and deserted me, anger returned, a rage of anger;

and, unable to injure any thing human, I turned my fury towards inanimate objects. As night advanced, I placed a variety of combustibles around the cottage; and, after having destroyed every vestige of cultivation in the garden, I waited with forced impatience until the moon had sunk to commence my operations.

'As the night advanced, a fierce wind arose from the woods, and quickly dispersed the clouds that had loitered in the heavens: the blast tore along like a mighty avalanche, and produced a kind of insanity in my spirits, that burst all bounds of reason and reflection. I lighted the dry branch of a tree, and danced with fury around the devoted cottage, my eyes still fixed on the western horizon, the edge of which the moon nearly touched.* A part of its orb was at length hid, and I waved my brand; it sunk, and, with a loud scream, I fired the straw, and heath, and bushes, which I had collected. The wind fanned the fire, and the cottage was quickly enveloped by the flames, which clung to it, and licked it with their forked and destroying tongues.

'As soon as I was convinced that no assistance could save any part of the habitation, I quitted the scene, and sought for refuge in the woods.

'And now, with the world before me, whither should I bend my steps?* I resolved to fly far from the scene of my misfortunes; but to me, hated and despised, every country must be equally horrible. At length the thought of you crossed my mind. I learned from your papers that you were my father, my creator; and to whom could I apply with more fitness than to him who had given me life? Among the lessons that Felix had bestowed upon Safie geography had not been omitted: I had learned from these the relative situations of the different countries of the earth. You had mentioned Geneva as the name of your native town; and towards this place I resolved to proceed.

'But how was I to direct myself? I knew that I must travel in a south-westerly direction to reach my destination; but the sun was my only guide. I did not know the names of the towns that I was to pass through, nor could I ask information from a single human being; but I did not despair. From you only could I hope for succour, although towards you I felt no sentiment but that of hatred. Unfeeling, heartless creator! you had endowed me with perceptions and passions, and then cast me abroad an object for the scorn and horror of mankind. But on you only had I any claim for pity and redress, and from you I determined to seek that justice which I vainly attempted to gain from any other being that wore the human form.

'My travels were long, and the sufferings I endured intense. It was late in autumn when I quitted the district where I had so long resided. I travelled only at night, fearful of encountering the visage of a human being. Nature decayed around me, and the sun became heatless; rain and snow poured around me; mighty rivers were frozen; the surface of the earth was hard, and chill, and bare, and I found no shelter. Oh, earth! how often did I imprecate curses on the cause of my being! The mildness of my nature had fled, and all within me was turned to gall and bitterness. The nearer I approached to your habitation, the more deeply did I feel the spirit of revenge enkindled in my heart. Snow fell, and the waters were hardened, but I rested not. A few incidents now and then directed me, and I possessed a map of the country; but I often wandered wide from my path. The agony of my feelings allowed me no respite: no incident occurred from which my rage and misery could not extract its food; but a circumstance that happened when I arrived on the confines of Switzerland, when the sun had recovered its warmth, and the earth again began to look green, confirmed in an especial manner the bitterness and horror of my feelings.

'I generally rested during the day, and travelled only when I was secured by night from the view of man. One morning, however, finding that my path lay through a deep wood, I ventured to continue my journey after the sun had risen; the day, which was one of the first of spring, cheered even me by the loveliness of its sunshine and the balminess of the air. I felt emotions of gentleness and pleasure, that had long appeared dead, revive within me. Half surprised by the novelty of these sensations, I allowed myself to be borne away by them; and, forgetting my solitude and deformity, dared to be happy. Soft tears again bedewed my cheeks, and I even raised my humid eyes with thankfulness towards the blessed sun which bestowed such joy upon me.

'I continued to wind among the paths of the wood, until I came to its boundary, which was skirted by a deep and rapid river, into which many of the trees bent their branches, now budding with the fresh spring. Here I paused, not exactly knowing what path to pursue, when I heard the sound of voices, that induced me to conceal myself under the shade of a cypress. I was scarcely hid, when a young girl came running towards the spot where I was concealed, laughing as if she ran from some one in sport. She continued her course along the precipitous sides of the river, when suddenly her foot slipt, and she fell into the rapid stream. I rushed from my hiding-place, and, with extreme labour from the force of the current, saved her, and dragged her to shore. She was senseless; and I endeavoured, by every means in my power, to restore animation, when I was suddenly interrupted by the approach of a rustic, who was probably the person from whom she had playfully fled. On seeing me, he darted towards me, and, tearing the girl from my arms, hastened towards the deeper parts of the wood. I followed speedily, I hardly knew why; but when the man saw me draw near, he aimed a gun, which he carried, at my body, and fired. I sunk to the ground, and my injurer, with increased swiftness, escaped into the wood.

'This was then the reward of my benevolence! I had saved a human being from destruction, and, as a recompence, I now writhed under the miserable pain of a wound, which shattered the flesh and bone. The feelings of kindness and gentleness, which I had entertained but a few moments before, gave place to hellish rage and gnashing of teeth. Inflamed by pain, I vowed eternal hatred and vengeance to all mankind. But the agony of my wound overcame me; my pulses paused, and I fainted.

'For some weeks I led a miserable life in the woods, endeavouring to cure the wound which I had received. The ball had entered my shoulder, and I knew not whether it had remained there or passed through; at any rate I had no means of extracting it. My sufferings were augmented also by the oppressive sense of the injustice and ingratitude of their infliction. My daily vows rose for revenge—a deep and deadly revenge, such as would alone compensate for the outrages and anguish I had endured.

'After some weeks my wound healed, and I continued my journey. The labours I endured were no longer to be alleviated by the bright sun or gentle breezes of spring; all joy was but a mockery, which insulted my desolate state, and made me feel more painfully that I was not made for the enjoyment of pleasure.

'But my toils now drew near a close; and, two months from this time, I reached the environs of Geneva.

'It was evening when I arrived, and I retired to a hiding-place among the fields that surround it, to meditate in what manner I should apply to you. I was oppressed by fatigue and hunger, and far too unhappy to enjoy the gentle breezes of evening, or the prospect of the sun setting behind the stupendous mountains of Jura.

'At this time a slight sleep relieved me from the pain of reflection, which was disturbed by the approach of a beautiful child, who came running into the recess I had chosen with all the sportiveness of infancy. Suddenly, as I gazed on him, an idea seized me, that this little creature was unprejudiced, and had lived too short a time to have imbibed a horror of deformity. If, therefore, I could seize him, and educate him as my companion and friend, I should not be so desolate in this peopled earth.

'Urged by this impulse, I seized on the boy as he passed, and drew him towards me. As soon as he beheld my form, he placed his hands before his eyes, and uttered a shrill scream: I drew his hand forcibly from his face, and said, "Child, what is the meaning of this? I do not intend to hurt you; listen to me."

'He struggled violently; "Let me go," he cried; "monster! ugly wretch! you wish to eat me, and tear me to pieces—You are an ogre—Let me go, or I will tell my papa."

' "Boy, you will never see your father again; you must come with me."

' "Hideous monster! let me go; My papa is a Syndic—he is M. Frankenstein—he would punish you. You dare not keep me."

' "Frankenstein! you belong then to my enemy—to him towards whom I have sworn eternal revenge; you shall be my first victim."

'The child still struggled, and loaded me with epithets which carried despair to my heart: I grasped his throat to silence him, and in a moment he lay dead at my feet.

'I gazed on my victim, and my heart swelled with exultation and hellish triumph: clapping my hands, I exclaimed, "I, too, can create desolation; my enemy is not impregnable; this death will carry despair to him, and a thousand other miseries shall torment and destroy him."

'As I fixed my eyes on the child, I saw something glittering on his breast. I took it; it was a portrait of a most lovely woman. In spite of my malignity, it softened and attracted me. For a few moments I gazed with delight on her dark eyes fringed by deep lashes, and her lovely lips; but presently my rage returned: I remembered that I was for ever deprived of the delights that such beautiful creatures could bestow; and that she whose resemblance I contemplated would, in regarding me, have changed that air of divine benignity to one expressive of disgust and affright.

'Can you wonder that such thoughts transported me with rage? I only wonder that at that moment, instead of venting my sensations in exclamations and agony, I did not rush among mankind, and perish in the attempt to destroy them.

'While I was overcome by these feelings, I left the spot where I had committed the murder, and was seeking a more secluded hiding-place, when I perceived a woman passing near me. She was young, not indeed so beautiful as her whose portrait I held, but of an agreeable aspect, and blooming in the loveliness of youth and health. Here, I thought, is one of those whose smiles are bestowed on all but me; she shall not escape: thanks to the lessons of Felix, and the sanguinary* laws of man, I have learned how to work mischief. I approached her unperceived, and placed the portrait securely in one of the folds of her dress.

'For some days I haunted the spot where these scenes had taken place; sometimes wishing to see you, sometimes resolved to quit the world and its miseries for ever. At length I wandered towards these mountains, and have ranged through their immense recesses, consumed by a burning passion which you alone can gratify. We may not part until you have promised to comply with my requisition.* I am alone, and miserable; man will not associate with me; but one as deformed and horrible as myself would not deny herself to me. My companion must be of the same species, and have the same defects. This being you must create.'

CHAPTER IX.

THE being finished speaking, and fixed his looks upon me in expectation of a reply. But I was bewildered, perplexed, and unable to arrange my ideas sufficiently to understand the full extent of his proposition. He continued—

'You must create a female for me, with whom I can live in the interchange of those sympathies necessary for my being. This you alone can do; and I demand it of you as a right which you must not refuse.'*

The latter part of his tale had kindled anew in me the anger that had died away while he narrated his peaceful life among the cottagers, and, as he said this, I could no longer suppress the rage that burned within me.

'I do refuse it,' I replied; 'and no torture shall ever extort a consent from me. You may render me the most miserable of men, but you shall never make me base in my own eyes. Shall I create another like yourself, whose joint wickedness might desolate the world. Begone! I have answered you; you may torture me, but I will never consent.'

'You are in the wrong,' replied the fiend; 'and, instead of threatening, I am content to reason with you. I am malicious because I am miserable; am I not shunned and hated by all mankind? You, my creator, would tear me to pieces, and triumph; remember that, and tell me why I should pity man more than he pities me? You would not call it murder, if you could precipitate me into one of those ice-rifts, and destroy my frame, the work of your own hands. Shall I respect man, when he contemns* me? Let him live with me in the interchange of kindness, and, instead of injury, I would bestow every benefit upon him with tears of gratitude at his acceptance. But that cannot be; the human senses are insurmountable barriers to our union. Yet mine shall not be the submission of abject slavery. I will revenge my injuries: if I cannot inspire love, I will cause fear; and chiefly towards you my arch-enemy, because my creator, do I swear inextinguishable hatred. Have a care: I will work at your destruction, nor finish until I desolate your heart, so that you curse the hour of your birth.'*

A fiendish rage animated him as he said this; his face was wrinkled into contortions too horrible for human eyes to behold; but presently he calmed himself, and proceeded—

'I intended to reason. This passion is detrimental to me; for you do not reflect that you are the cause of its excess. If any being felt emotions of benevolence towards me, I should return them an hundred and an hundred fold; for that one creature's sake, I would make peace with the whole kind! But I now indulge in dreams of bliss that cannot be realized. What I ask of you is reasonable and moderate; I demand a creature of another sex, but as hideous as myself: the gratification is small, but it is all that I can receive, and it shall content me. It is true, we shall be monsters, cut off from all the world; but on that account we shall be more attached to one another. Our lives will not be happy, but they will be harmless, and free from the misery I now feel. Oh! my creator, make me happy; let me feel gratitude towards you for one benefit! Let me see that I excite the sympathy of some existing thing; do not deny me my request!'

I was moved. I shuddered when I thought of the possible consequences of my consent; but I felt that there was some justice in his argument. His tale, and the feelings he now expressed, proved him to be a creature of fine sensations; and did I not, as his maker, owe him all the portion of happiness that it was in my power to bestow? He saw my change of feeling, and continued—

'If you consent, neither you nor any other human being shall ever see us again: I will go to the vast wilds of South America. My food is not that of man; I do not destroy the lamb and the kid, to glut my appetite; acorns and berries afford me sufficient nourishment.* My companion will be of the same nature as myself, and will be content with the same fare. We shall make our bed of dried leaves; the sun will shine on us as on man, and will ripen our food. The picture I present to you is peaceful and human, and you must feel that you could deny it only in the wantonness of power and cruelty. Pitiless as you have been towards me, I now see compassion in your eyes; let me seize the favourable moment, and persuade you to promise what I so ardently desire.'

'You propose,' replied I, 'to fly from the habitations of man, to dwell in those wilds where the beasts of the field will be your only companions. How can you, who long for the love and sympathy of man, persevere in this exile? You will return, and again seek their kindness, and you will meet with their detestation; your evil passions will be renewed, and you will then have a companion to aid you in the task of destruction. This may not be; cease to argue the point, for I cannot consent.'

'How inconstant are your feelings! but a moment ago you were moved by my representations, and why do you again harden yourself to my complaints? I swear to you, by the earth which I inhabit, and by you that made me, that, with the companion you bestow, I will quit the neighbourhood of man, and dwell, as it may chance, in the most savage of places. My evil passions will have fled, for I shall meet with sympathy; my life will flow quietly away, and, in my dying moments, I shall not curse my maker.'

His words had a strange effect upon me. I compassionated him, and sometimes felt a wish to console him; but when I looked upon him, when I saw the filthy mass that moved and talked, my heart sickened, and my feelings were altered to those of horror and hatred. I tried to stifle these sensations; I thought, that as I could not sympathize with him, I had no right to withhold from him the small portion of happiness which was yet in my power to bestow.

'You swear,' I said, 'to be harmless; but have you not already shewn a degree of malice that should reasonably make me distrust you? May not even this be a feint that will increase your triumph by affording a wider scope for your revenge?'

'How is this? I thought I had moved your compassion, and yet you still refuse to bestow on me the only benefit that can soften my heart, and render me harmless. If I have no ties and no affections, hatred and vice must be my portion; the love of another will destroy the cause of my crimes, and I shall become a thing, of whose existence every one will be ignorant. My vices are the children of a forced solitude that I abhor; and my virtues will necessarily arise when I live in communion with an equal. I shall feel the affections of a sensitive being, and become linked to the chain of existence and events, from which I am now excluded.'

I paused some time to reflect on all he had related, and the various arguments which he had employed. I thought of the promise of virtues which he had displayed on the opening of his existence, and the subsequent blight of all kindly feeling by the loathing and scorn which his protectors had manifested towards him. His power and threats were not omitted in my calculations: a creature who could exist in the ice caves of the glaciers, and hide himself from pursuit among the ridges of inaccessible precipices, was a being possessing faculties it would be vain to cope with. After a long pause of reflection, I concluded, that the justice due both to him and my fellow-creatures demanded of me that I should comply with his request. Turning to him, therefore, I said—

'I consent to your demand, on your solemn oath to quit Europe for ever, and every other place in the neighbourhood of man, as soon as I shall deliver into your hands a female who will accompany you in your exile.'

'I swear,' he cried, 'by the sun, and by the blue sky of heaven, that if you grant my prayer, while they exist you shall never behold me again. Depart to your home, and commence your labours: I shall watch their progress with unutterable anxiety; and fear not but that when you are ready I shall appear.'

Saying this, he suddenly quitted me, fearful, perhaps, of any change in my sentiments. I saw him descend the mountain with greater speed than the flight of an eagle, and quickly lost him among the undulations of the sea of ice.

His tale had occupied the whole day; and the sun was upon the verge of the horizon when he departed. I knew that I ought to hasten my descent towards the valley, as I should soon be encompassed in darkness; but my heart was heavy, and my steps slow. The labour of winding among the little paths of the mountains, and fixing my feet firmly as I advanced, perplexed me, occupied as I was by the emotions which the occurrences of the day had produced. Night was far advanced, when I came to the half-way resting-place, and seated myself beside the fountain. The stars shone at intervals, as the clouds passed from over them; the dark pines rose before me, and every here and there a broken tree lay on the ground: it was a scene of wonderful solemnity, and stirred strange thoughts within me. I wept bitterly; and, clasping my hands in agony, I exclaimed, 'Oh! stars, and clouds, and winds, ye are all about to mock me: if ye really pity me, crush sensation and memory; let me become as nought; but if not, depart, depart and leave me in darkness.'

These were wild and miserable thoughts; but I cannot describe to you how the eternal twinkling of the stars weighed upon me, and how I listened to every blast of wind, as if it were a dull ugly siroc* on its way to consume me.

Morning dawned before I arrived at the village of Chamounix; but my presence, so haggard and strange, hardly calmed the fears of my family, who had waited the whole night in anxious expectation of my return.

The following day we returned to Geneva. The intention of my father in coming had been to divert my mind, and to restore me to my lost tranquillity; but the medicine had been fatal. And, unable to account for the excess of misery I appeared to suffer, he hastened to return home, hoping the quiet and monotony of a domestic life would by degrees alleviate my sufferings from whatsoever cause they might spring.

For myself, I was passive in all their arrangements; and the gentle affection of my beloved Elizabeth was inadequate to draw me from the depth of my despair. The promise I had made to the dæmon weighed upon my mind, like Dante's iron cowl on the heads of the hellish hypocrites.* All pleasures of earth and sky passed before me like a dream, and that thought only had to me the reality of life. Can you wonder, that sometimes a kind of insanity possessed me, or that I saw continually about me a multitude of filthy animals inflicting on me incessant torture, that often extorted screams and bitter groans?

By degrees, however, these feelings became calmed. I entered again into the every-day scene of life, if not with interest, at least with some degree of tranquillity.

END OF VOL. II.

VOLUME III

CHAPTER I.

DAY after day, week after week, passed away on my return to Geneva; and I could not collect the courage to recommence my work. I feared the vengeance of the disappointed fiend, yet I was unable to overcome my repugnance to the task which was enjoined me. I found that I could not compose a female without again devoting several months to profound study and laborious disquisition. I had heard of some discoveries having been made by an English philosopher,* the knowledge of which was material to my success, and I sometimes thought of obtaining my father's consent to visit England for this purpose; but I clung to every pretence of delay, and could not resolve to interrupt my returning tranquillity. My health, which had hitherto declined, was now much restored; and my spirits, when unchecked by the memory of my unhappy promise, rose proportionably. My father saw this change with pleasure, and he turned his thoughts towards the best method of eradicating the remains of my melancholy, which every now and then would return by fits, and with a devouring blackness overcast the approaching sunshine. At these moments I took refuge in the most perfect solitude. I passed whole days on the lake alone in a little boat, watching the clouds, and listening to the rippling of the waves, silent and listless. But the fresh air and bright sun seldom failed to restore me to some degree of composure; and, on my return, I met the salutations of my friends with a readier smile and a more cheerful heart.

It was after my return from one of these rambles that my father, calling me aside, thus addressed me:—

'I am happy to remark, my dear son, that you have resumed your former pleasures, and seem to be returning to yourself. And yet you are still unhappy, and still avoid our society. For some time I was lost in conjecture as to the cause of this; but yesterday an idea struck me, and if it is well founded, I conjure* you to avow it. Reserve on such a point would be not only useless, but draw down treble misery on us all.'

I trembled violently at this exordium,* and my father continued—

'I confess, my son, that I have always looked forward to your marriage with your cousin as the tie of our domestic comfort, and the stay of my declining years. You were attached to each other from your earliest infancy; you studied together, and appeared, in dispositions and tastes, entirely suited to one another. But so blind is the experience of man, that what I conceived to be the best assistants to my plan may have entirely destroyed it. You, perhaps, regard her as your sister, without any wish that she might become your wife. Nay, you may have met with another whom you may love; and, considering yourself as bound in honour to your cousin, this struggle may occasion the poignant misery which you appear to feel.'

'My dear father, re-assure yourself. I love my cousin tenderly and sincerely. I never saw any woman who excited, as Elizabeth does, my warmest admiration and affection. My future hopes and prospects are entirely bound up in the expectation of our union.'

'The expression of your sentiments on this subject, my dear Victor, gives me more pleasure than I have for some time experienced. If you feel thus, we shall assuredly be happy, however present events may cast a gloom over us. But it is this gloom, which appears to have taken so strong a hold of your mind, that I wish to dissipate. Tell me, therefore, whether you object to an immediate solemnization of the marriage. We have been unfortunate, and recent events have drawn us from that everyday tranquillity befitting my years and infirmities. You are younger; yet I do not suppose, possessed as you are of a competent fortune, that an early marriage would at all interfere with any future plans of honour and utility that you may have formed. Do not suppose, however, that I wish to dictate happiness to you, or that a delay on your part would cause me any serious uneasiness. Interpret my words with candour, and answer me, I conjure you, with confidence and sincerity.'

I listened to my father in silence, and remained for some time incapable of offering any reply. I revolved rapidly in my mind a multitude of thoughts, and endeavoured to arrive at some conclusion. Alas! to me the idea of an immediate union with my cousin was one of horror and dismay. I was bound by a solemn promise, which I had not yet fulfilled, and dared not break; or, if I did, what manifold miseries might not impend over me and my devoted family! Could I enter into a festival with this deadly weight yet hanging round my neck, and bowing me to the ground.* I must perform my engagement, and let the monster depart with his mate, before I allowed myself to enjoy the delight of an union from which I expected peace.

I remembered also the necessity imposed upon me of either journeying to England, or entering into a long correspondence with those philosophers of that country, whose knowledge and discoveries were of indispensable use to me in my present undertaking. The latter method of obtaining the desired intelligence was dilatory and unsatisfactory: besides, any variation was agreeable to me, and I was delighted with the idea of spending a year or two in change of scene and variety of occupation, in absence from my family; during which period some event might happen which would restore me to them in peace and happiness: my promise might be fulfilled, and the monster have departed; or some accident might occur to destroy him, and put an end to my slavery for ever.

These feelings dictated my answer to my father. I expressed a wish to visit England; but, concealing the true reasons of this request, I clothed my desires under the guise of wishing to travel and see the world before I sat down for life within the walls of my native town.

I urged my entreaty with earnestness, and my father was easily induced to comply; for a more indulgent and less dictatorial parent did not exist upon earth. Our plan was soon arranged. I should travel to Strasburgh, where Clerval would join me. Some short time would be spent in the towns of Holland, and our principal stay would be in England. We should return by France; and it was agreed that the tour should occupy the space of two years.

My father pleased himself with the reflection, that my union with Elizabeth should take place immediately on my return to Geneva. 'These two years,' said he, 'will pass swiftly, and it will be the last delay that will oppose itself to your happiness. And, indeed, I earnestly desire that period to arrive, when we shall all be united, and neither hopes or fears arise to disturb our domestic calm.'

'I am content,' I replied, 'with your arrangement. By that time we shall both have become wiser, and I hope happier, than we at present are.' I sighed; but my father kindly forbore to question me further concerning the cause of my dejection. He hoped that new scenes, and the amusement of travelling, would restore my tranquillity.

I now made arrangements for my journey; but one feeling haunted me, which filled me with fear and agitation. During my absence I should leave my friends unconscious of the existence of their enemy, and unprotected from his attacks, exasperated as he might be by my departure. But he had promised to follow me wherever I might go; and would he not accompany me to England? This imagination was dreadful in itself, but soothing, inasmuch as it supposed the safety of my friends. I was agonized with the idea of the possibility that the reverse of this might happen. But through the whole period during which I was the slave of my creature, I allowed myself to be governed by the impulses of the moment; and my present sensations strongly intimated that the fiend would follow me, and exempt my family from the danger of his machinations.

It was in the latter end of August that I departed, to pass two years of exile. Elizabeth approved of the reasons of my departure, and only regretted that she had not the same opportunities of enlarging her experience, and cultivating her understanding. She wept, however, as she bade me farewell, and entreated me to return happy and tranquil. 'We all,' said she, 'depend upon you; and if you are miserable, what must be our feelings?'

I threw myself into the carriage that was to convey me away, hardly knowing whither I was going, and careless of what was passing around. I remembered only, and it was with a bitter anguish that I reflected on it, to order that my chemical instruments should be packed to go with me: for I resolved to fulfil my promise while abroad, and return, if possible, a free man. Filled with dreary imaginations, I passed through many beautiful and majestic scenes; but my eyes were fixed and unobserving. I could only think of the bourne* of my travels, and the work which was to occupy me whilst they endured.

After some days spent in listless indolence, during which I traversed many leagues, I arrived at Strasburgh, where I waited two days for Clerval. He came: Alas, how great was the contrast between us! He was alive to every new scene; joyful when he saw the beauties of the setting sun, and more happy when he beheld it rise, and recommence a new day. He pointed out to me the shifting colours of the landscape, and the appearances of the sky. 'This is what it is to live;' he cried, 'now I enjoy existence! But you, my dear Frankenstein, wherefore are you desponding and sorrowful?' In truth, I was occupied by gloomy thoughts, and neither saw the descent of the evening star, nor the golden sun-rise reflected in the Rhine.—And you, my friend, would be far more amused with the journal of Clerval, who observed the scenery with an eye of feeling and delight, than to listen to my reflections.

I, a miserable wretch, haunted by a curse that shut up every avenue to enjoyment.

We had agreed to descend the Rhine in a boat from Strasburgh to Rotterdam,* whence we might take shipping for London. During this voyage, we passed by many willowy islands, and saw several beautiful towns. We staid a day at Manheim, and, on the fifth from our departure from Strasburgh, arrived at Mayence. The course of the Rhine below Mayence becomes much more picturesque. The river descends rapidly, and winds between hills, not high, but steep, and of beautiful forms. We saw many ruined castles standing on the edges of precipices, surrounded by black woods, high and inaccessible. This part of the Rhine, indeed, presents a singularly variegated landscape. In one spot you view rugged hills, ruined castles overlooking tremendous precipices, with the dark Rhine rushing beneath; and, on the sudden turn of a promontory, flourishing vineyards, with green sloping banks, and a meandering river, and populous towns, occupy the scene.

We travelled at the time of the vintage, and heard the song of the labourers, as we glided down the stream. Even I, depressed in mind, and my spirits continually agitated by gloomy feelings, even I was pleased. I lay at the bottom of the boat, and, as I gazed on the cloudless blue sky, I seemed to drink in a tranquillity to which I had long been a stranger. And if these were my sensations, who can describe those of Henry? He felt as if he had been transported to Fairy-land, and enjoyed a happiness seldom tasted by man. 'I have seen,' he said, 'the most beautiful scenes of my own country; I have visited the lakes of Lucerne and Uri, where the snowy mountains descend almost perpendicularly to the water, casting black and impenetrable shades, which would cause a gloomy and mournful appearance, were it not for the most verdant islands that relieve the eye by their gay appearance; I have seen this lake agitated by a tempest, when the wind tore up whirlwinds of water, and gave you an idea of what the water-spout must be on the great ocean, and the waves dash with fury the base of the mountain, where the priest and his mistress were overwhelmed by an avalanche, and where their dying voices are still said to be heard amid the pauses of the nightly wind;* I have seen the mountains of La Valais, and the Pays de Vaud: but this country, Victor, pleases me more than all those wonders. The mountains of Switzerland are more majestic and strange; but there is a charm in the banks of this divine river, that I never before saw equalled. Look at that castle which overhangs yon precipice; and that also on the island, almost concealed amongst the foliage of those lovely trees; and now that group of labourers coming from among their vines; and that village half-hid in the recess of the mountain. Oh, surely, the spirit that inhabits and guards this place has a soul more in harmony with man, than those who pile* the glacier, or retire to the inaccessible peaks of the mountains of our own country.'

Clerval! beloved friend! even now it delights me to record your words, and to dwell on the praise of which you are so eminently deserving. He was a being formed in the 'very poetry of nature[1].' His wild and enthusiastic imagination was chastened by the sensibility of his heart. His soul overflowed with ardent affections, and his friendship was of that devoted and wondrous nature that the worldly-minded teach us to look for only in the imagination. But even human sympathies were not sufficient to satisfy his eager mind. The scenery of external nature, which others regard only with admiration, he loved with ardour:

> ——————'The sounding cataract
> Haunted *him* like a passion: the tall rock,
> The mountain, and the deep and gloomy wood,
> Their colours and their forms, were then to him
> An appetite: a feeling, and a love,
> That had no need of a remoter charm,
> By thought supplied, or any interest
> Unborrowed from the eye[2].'

And where does he now exist? Is this gentle and lovely being lost for ever? Has this mind so replete with ideas, imaginations fanciful and magnificent, which formed a world, whose existence depended on the life of its creator; has this mind perished? Does it now only exist in my memory? No, it is not thus; your form so divinely wrought, and beaming with beauty, has decayed, but your spirit still visits and consoles your unhappy friend.

Pardon this gush of sorrow; these ineffectual words are but a slight tribute to the unexampled worth of Henry, but they soothe my heart, overflowing with the anguish which his remembrance creates. I will proceed with my tale.

---

[1] Leigh Hunt's 'Rimini.'*
[2] Wordsworth's 'Tintern Abbey'.*

Beyond Cologne we descended to the plains of Holland; and we resolved to post* the remainder of our way; for the wind was contrary, and the stream of the river was too gentle to aid us.

Our journey here lost the interest arising from beautiful scenery; but we arrived in a few days at Rotterdam, whence we proceeded by sea to England. It was on a clear morning, in the latter days of December, that I first saw the white cliffs of Britain. The banks of the Thames presented a new scene; they were flat, but fertile, and almost every town was marked by the remembrance of some story. We saw Tilbury Fort, and remembered the Spanish armada;* Gravesend, Woolwich, and Greenwich, places which I had heard of even in my country.

At length we saw the numerous steeples of London, St. Paul's towering above all, and the Tower famed in English history.

CHAPTER II.

LONDON was our present point of rest; we determined to remain several months in this wonderful and celebrated city. Clerval desired the intercourse of* the men of genius and talent who flourished at this time; but this was with me a secondary object; I was principally occupied with the means of obtaining the information necessary for the completion of my promise, and quickly availed myself of the letters of introduction that I had brought with me, addressed to the most distinguished natural philosophers.

If this journey had taken place during my days of study and happiness, it would have afforded me inexpressible pleasure. But a blight had come over my existence, and I only visited these people for the sake of the information they might give me on the subject in which my interest was so terribly profound. Company was irksome to me; when alone, I could fill my mind with the sights of heaven and earth; the voice of Henry soothed me, and I could thus cheat myself into a transitory peace. But busy uninteresting joyous faces brought back despair to my heart. I saw an insurmountable barrier placed between me and my fellow-men; this barrier was sealed with the blood of William and Justine; and to reflect on the events connected with those names filled my soul with anguish.

But in Clerval I saw the image of my former self; he was inquisitive, and anxious to gain experience and instruction. The difference of manners which he observed was to him an inexhaustible source of instruction and amusement. He was for ever busy; and the only check to his enjoyments was my sorrowful and dejected mien. I tried to conceal this as much as possible, that I might not debar him from the pleasures natural to one who was entering on a new scene of life, undisturbed by any care or bitter recollection. I often refused to accompany him, alleging another engagement, that I might remain alone. I now also began to collect the materials necessary for my new creation, and this was to me like the torture of single drops of water continually falling on the head. Every thought that was devoted to it was an extreme anguish, and every word that I spoke in allusion to it caused my lips to quiver, and my heart to palpitate.

After passing some months in London, we received a letter from a person in Scotland, who had formerly been our visitor at Geneva. He mentioned the beauties of his native country, and asked us if those were not sufficient allurements to induce us to prolong our journey as far north as Perth, where he resided. Clerval eagerly desired to accept this invitation; and I, although I abhorred society, wished to view again mountains and streams, and all the wondrous works with which Nature adorns her chosen dwelling-places.

We had arrived in England at the beginning of October,* and it was now February. We accordingly determined to commence our journey towards the north at the expiration of another month. In this expedition we did not intend to follow the great road to Edinburgh, but to visit Windsor, Oxford, Matlock,* and the Cumberland lakes, resolving to arrive at the completion of this tour about the end of July. I packed my chemical instruments, and the materials I had collected, resolving to finish my labours in some obscure nook in the northern highlands of Scotland.

We quitted London on the 27th of March, and remained a few days at Windsor, rambling in its beautiful forest. This was a new scene to us mountaineers; the majestic oaks, the quantity of game, and the herds of stately deer, were all novelties to us.

From thence we proceeded to Oxford.* As we entered this city, our minds were filled with the remembrance of the events that had been transacted there more than a century and a half before. It was here that Charles I had collected his forces. This city had remained faithful to him, after the whole nation had forsaken his cause to join the standard of parliament and liberty. The memory of that unfortunate king, and his companions, the amiable Falkland,* the insolent Gower,* his queen, and son,* gave a peculiar interest to every part of the city, which they might be supposed to have inhabited. The spirit of elder days found a dwelling here, and we delighted to trace its footsteps. If these feelings had not found an imaginary gratification, the appearance of the city had yet in itself sufficient beauty to obtain our admiration. The colleges are ancient and picturesque; the streets are almost magnificent; and the lovely Isis,* which flows beside it through meadows of exquisite verdure, is spread forth into a placid expanse of waters, which reflects its majestic assemblage of towers, and spires, and domes, embosomed among aged trees.

I enjoyed this scene; and yet my enjoyment was embittered both by the memory of the past, and the anticipation of the future. I was formed for peaceful happiness. During my youthful days discontent never visited my mind; and if I was ever overcome by *ennui*,* the sight of what is beautiful in nature, or the study of what is excellent and sublime in the productions of man, could always interest my heart, and communicate elasticity to my spirits. But I am a blasted tree; the bolt has entered my soul; and I felt then that I should survive to exhibit, what I shall soon cease to be—a miserable spectacle of wrecked humanity, pitiable to others, and abhorrent to myself.

We passed a considerable period at Oxford, rambling among its environs, and endeavouring to identify every spot which might relate to the most animating epoch of English history. Our little voyages of discovery were often prolonged by the successive objects that presented themselves. We visited the tomb of the illustrious Hampden, and the field on which that patriot fell.* For a moment my soul was elevated from its debasing and miserable fears to contemplate the divine ideas of liberty and self-sacrifice, of which these sights were the monuments and the remembrancers. For an instant I dared to shake off my chains, and look around me with a free and lofty spirit; but the iron had eaten into my flesh, and I sank again, trembling and hopeless, into my miserable self.

We left Oxford with regret, and proceeded to Matlock, which was our next place of rest. The country in the neighbourhood of this village resembled, to a greater degree, the scenery of Switzerland; but every thing is on a lower scale, and the green hills want the crown of distant white Alps, which always attend on the piny mountains of my native country. We visited the wondrous cave, and the little cabinets of natural history, where the curiosities are disposed in the same manner

as in the collections at Servox and Chamounix.* The latter name
made me tremble, when pronounced by Henry; and I hastened to quit
Matlock, with which that terrible scene was thus associated.

From Derby still journeying northward, we passed two months in
Cumberland and Westmoreland.* I could now almost fancy myself
among the Swiss mountains. The little patches of snow which yet lingered on the northern sides of the mountains, the lakes, and the dashing of the rocky streams, were all familiar and dear sights to me. Here
also we made some acquaintances, who almost contrived to cheat me
into happiness. The delight of Clerval was proportionably greater than
mine; his mind expanded in the company of men of talent,* and he
found in his own nature greater capacities and resources than he could
have imagined himself to have possessed while he associated with his
inferiors. 'I could pass my life here,' said he to me; 'and among these
mountains I should scarcely regret Switzerland and the Rhine.'

But he found that a traveller's life is one that includes much pain
amidst its enjoyments. His feelings are for ever on the stretch;* and
when he begins to sink into repose, he finds himself obliged to quit
that on which he rests in pleasure for something new, which again
engages his attention, and which also he forsakes for other novelties.

We had scarcely visited the various lakes of Cumberland and Westmoreland, and conceived an affection for some of the inhabitants,
when the period of our appointment with our Scotch friend approached,
and we left them to travel on. For my own part I was not sorry. I had
now neglected my promise for some time, and I feared the effects of
the dæmon's disappointment. He might remain in Switzerland, and
wreak his vengeance on my relatives. This idea pursued me, and tormented me at every moment from which I might otherwise have
snatched repose and peace. I waited for my letters with feverish impatience: if they were delayed, I was miserable, and overcome by a thousand fears; and when they arrived, and I saw the superscription of
Elizabeth or my father, I hardly dared to read and ascertain my fate.
Sometimes I thought that the fiend followed me, and might expedite
my remissness by murdering my companion. When these thoughts
possessed me, I would not quit Henry for a moment, but followed
him as his shadow, to protect him from the fancied rage of his destroyer.
I felt as if I had committed some great crime, the consciousness of
which haunted me. I was guiltless, but I had indeed drawn down
a horrible curse upon my head, as mortal as that of crime.

I visited Edinburgh with languid eyes and mind; and yet that city might have interested the most unfortunate being. Clerval did not like it so well as Oxford; for the antiquity of the latter city was more pleasing to him. But the beauty and regularity of the new town of Edinburgh, its romantic castle, and its environs, the most delightful in the world, Arthur's Seat, St. Bernard's Well, and the Pentland Hills,* compensated him for the change, and filled him with cheerfulness and admiration. But I was impatient to arrive at the termination of my journey.

We left Edinburgh in a week, passing through Coupar, St. Andrews, and along the banks of the Tay, to Perth, where our friend expected us. But I was in no mood to laugh and talk with strangers, or enter into their feelings or plans with the good humour expected from a guest; and accordingly I told Clerval that I wished to make the tour of Scotland alone. 'Do you,' said I, 'enjoy yourself, and let this be our rendezvous. I may be absent a month or two; but do not interfere with my motions, I entreat you: leave me to peace and solitude for a short time; and when I return, I hope it will be with a lighter heart, more congenial to your own temper.'

Henry wished to dissuade me; but, seeing me bent on this plan, ceased to remonstrate. He entreated me to write often. 'I had rather be with you,' he said, 'in your solitary rambles, than with these Scotch people, whom I do not know: hasten then, my dear friend, to return, that I may again feel myself somewhat at home, which I cannot do in your absence.'

Having parted from my friend, I determined to visit some remote spot of Scotland, and finish my work in solitude. I did not doubt but that the monster followed me, and would discover himself to me when I should have finished, that he might receive his companion.

With this resolution I traversed the northern highlands, and fixed on one of the remotest of the Orkneys as the scene [of my] labours. It was a place fitted for such a work, being hardly more than a rock, whose high sides were continually beaten upon by the waves. The soil was barren, scarcely affording pasture for a few miserable cows, and oatmeal for its inhabitants, which consisted of five persons, whose gaunt and scraggy limbs gave tokens of their miserable fare. Vegetables and bread, when they indulged in such luxuries, and even fresh water, was to be procured from the main land, which was about five miles distant.*

On the whole island there were but three miserable huts, and one of these was vacant when I arrived. This I hired. It contained but two rooms, and these exhibited all the squalidness of the most miserable penury. The thatch had fallen in, the walls were unplastered, and the door was off its hinges. I ordered it to be repaired, bought some furniture, and took possession; an incident which would, doubtless, have occasioned some surprise, had not all the senses of the cottagers been benumbed by want and squalid poverty. As it was, I lived ungazed at and unmolested, hardly thanked for the pittance of food and clothes which I gave; so much does suffering blunt even the coarsest sensations of men.

In this retreat I devoted the morning to labour; but in the evening, when the weather permitted, I walked on the stony beach of the sea, to listen to the waves as they roared, and dashed at my feet. It was a monotonous, yet ever-changing scene. I thought of Switzerland; it was far different from this desolate and appalling landscape. Its hills are covered with vines, and its cottages are scattered thickly in the plains. Its fair lakes reflect a blue and gentle sky; and, when troubled by the winds, their tumult is but as the play of a lively infant, when compared to the roarings of the giant ocean.

In this manner I distributed my occupations when I first arrived; but, as I proceeded in my labour, it became every day more horrible and irksome to me. Sometimes I could not prevail on myself to enter my laboratory for several days; and at other times I toiled day and night in order to complete my work. It was indeed a filthy process in which I was engaged. During my first experiment, a kind of enthusiastic frenzy had blinded me to the horror of my employment; my mind was intently fixed on the sequel* of my labour, and my eyes were shut to the horror of my proceedings. But now I went to it in cold blood, and my heart often sickened at the work of my hands.

Thus situated, employed in the most detestable occupation, immersed in a solitude where nothing could for an instant call my attention from the actual scene in which I was engaged, my spirits became unequal;* I grew restless and nervous. Every moment I feared to meet my persecutor. Sometimes I sat with my eyes fixed on the ground, fearing to raise them lest they should encounter the object which I so much dreaded to behold. I feared to wander from the sight of my fellow-creatures, lest when alone he should come to claim his companion.

In the mean time I worked on, and my labour was already considerably advanced. I looked towards its completion with a tremulous and eager hope, which I dared not trust myself to question, but which was intermixed with obscure forebodings of evil, that made my heart sicken in my bosom.

CHAPTER III.

I SAT one evening in my laboratory; the sun had set, and the moon was just rising from the sea; I had not sufficient light for my employment, and I remained idle, in a pause of consideration of whether I should leave my labour for the night, or hasten its conclusion by an unremitting attention to it. As I sat, a train of reflection occurred to me, which led me to consider the effects of what I was now doing. Three years before I was engaged in the same manner, and had created a fiend whose unparalleled barbarity had desolated my heart, and filled it for ever with the bitterest remorse. I was now about to form another being, of whose dispositions I was alike ignorant; she might become ten thousand times more malignant than her mate, and delight, for its own sake, in murder and wretchedness. He had sworn to quit the neighbourhood of man, and hide himself in deserts;* but she had not; and she, who in all probability was to become a thinking and reasoning animal, might refuse to comply with a compact made before her creation. They might even hate each other; the creature who already lived loathed his own deformity, and might he not conceive a greater abhorrence for it when it came before his eyes in the female form? She also might turn with disgust from him to the superior beauty of man; she might quit him, and he be again alone, exasperated by the fresh provocation of being deserted by one of his own species.

Even if they were to leave Europe, and inhabit the deserts of the new world, yet one of the first results of those sympathies for which the dæmon thirsted would be children, and a race of devils would be propagated upon the earth,* who might make the very existence of the species of man a condition precarious and full of terror. Had I a right, for my own benefit, to inflict this curse upon everlasting generations? I had before been moved by the sophisms* of the being I had created; I had been struck senseless by his fiendish threats: but now, for the first time, the wickedness of my promise burst upon me; I shuddered to think that future ages might curse me as their pest, whose selfishness had not hesitated to buy its own peace at the price perhaps of the existence of the whole human race.

I trembled, and my heart failed within me; when, on looking up, I saw, by the light of the moon, the dæmon at the casement. A ghastly grin wrinkled his lips as he gazed on me, where I sat fulfilling the task which he had allotted to me. Yes, he had followed me in my travels; he had loitered in forests, hid himself in caves, or taken refuge in wide and desert heaths; and he now came to mark my progress, and claim the fulfilment of my promise.

As I looked on him, his countenance expressed the utmost extent of malice and treachery. I thought with a sensation of madness on my promise of creating another like to him, and, trembling with passion, tore to pieces the thing on which I was engaged. The wretch saw me destroy the creature on whose future existence he depended for happiness, and, with a howl of devilish despair and revenge, withdrew.

I left the room, and, locking the door, made a solemn vow in my own heart never to resume my labours; and then, with trembling steps, I sought my own apartment. I was alone; none were near me to dissipate the gloom, and relieve me from the sickening oppression of the most terrible reveries.

Several hours passed, and I remained near my window gazing on the sea; it was almost motionless, for the winds were hushed, and all nature reposed under the eye of the quiet moon. A few fishing vessels alone specked the water, and now and then the gentle breeze wafted the sound of voices, as the fishermen called to one another. I felt the silence, although I was hardly conscious of its extreme profundity, until my ear was suddenly arrested by the paddling of oars near the shore, and a person landed close to my house.

In a few minutes after, I heard the creaking of my door, as if some one endeavoured to open it softly. I trembled from head to foot; I felt a presentiment of who it was, and wished to rouse one of the peasants who dwelt in a cottage not far from mine; but I was overcome by the sensation of helplessness, so often felt in frightful dreams, when you in vain endeavour to fly from an impending danger, and was rooted to the spot.

Presently I heard the sound of footsteps along the passage; the door opened, and the wretch whom I dreaded appeared. Shutting the door, he approached me, and said, in a smothered voice—

'You have destroyed the work which you began; what is it that you intend? Do you dare to break your promise? I have endured toil and misery: I left Switzerland with you; I crept along the shores of the

Rhine, among its willow islands, and over the summits of its hills. I have dwelt many months in the heaths of England, and among the deserts of Scotland. I have endured incalculable fatigue, and cold, and hunger; do you dare destroy my hopes?'

'Begone! I do break my promise; never will I create another like yourself, equal in deformity and wickedness.'

'Slave, I before reasoned with you, but you have proved yourself unworthy of my condescension. Remember that I have power; you believe yourself miserable, but I can make you so wretched that the light of day will be hateful to you. You are my creator, but I am your master;—obey!'

'The hour of my weakness is past, and the period* of your power is arrived. Your threats cannot move me to do an act of wickedness; but they confirm me in a resolution of not creating you a companion in vice. Shall I, in cool blood, set loose upon the earth a dæmon, whose delight is in death and wretchedness. Begone! I am firm, and your words will only exasperate my rage.'

The monster saw my determination in my face, and gnashed his teeth in the impotence of anger. 'Shall each man,' cried he, 'find a wife for his bosom, and each beast have his mate, and I be alone? I had feelings of affection, and they were requited by detestation and scorn. Man, you may hate; but beware! Your hours will pass in dread and misery, and soon the bolt will fall which must ravish from you your happiness for ever. Are you to be happy, while I grovel in the intensity of my wretchedness? You can blast my other passions; but revenge remains—revenge, henceforth dearer than light or food! I may die; but first you, my tyrant and tormentor, shall curse the sun that gazes on your misery. Beware; for I am fearless, and therefore powerful. I will watch with the wiliness of a snake, that I may sting with its venom. Man, you shall repent of the injuries you inflict.'

'Devil, cease; and do not poison the air with these sounds of malice. I have declared my resolution to you, and I am no coward to bend beneath words. Leave me; I am inexorable.'

'It is well. I go; but remember, I shall be with you on your wedding-night.'

I started forward, and exclaimed, 'Villain! before you sign my death-warrant, be sure that you are yourself safe.'

I would have seized him; but he eluded me, and quitted the house with precipitation: in a few moments I saw him in his boat, which shot across the waters with an arrowy swiftness, and was soon lost amidst the waves.

All was again silent; but his words rung in my ears. I burned with rage to pursue the murderer of my peace, and precipitate him into the ocean. I walked up and down my room hastily and perturbed, while my imagination conjured up a thousand images to torment and sting me. Why had I not followed him, and closed* with him in mortal strife? But I had suffered him to depart, and he had directed his course towards the main land. I shuddered to think who might be the next victim sacrificed to his insatiate revenge. And then I thought again of his words—'*I will be with you on your wedding-night.*' That then was the period fixed for the fulfilment of my destiny. In that hour I should die, and at once satisfy and extinguish his malice. The prospect did not move me to fear; yet when I thought of my beloved Elizabeth,—of her tears and endless sorrow, when she should find her lover so barbarously snatched from her,—tears, the first I had shed for many months, streamed from my eyes, and I resolved not to fall before my enemy without a bitter struggle.

The night passed away, and the sun rose from the ocean; my feelings became calmer, if it may be called calmness, when the violence of rage sinks into the depths of despair. I left the house, the horrid scene of the last night's contention, and walked on the beach of the sea, which I almost regarded as an insuperable barrier between me and my fellow-creatures; nay, a wish that such should prove the fact stole across me. I desired that I might pass my life on that barren rock, wearily it is true, but uninterrupted by any sudden shock of misery. If I returned, it was to be sacrificed, or to see those whom I most loved die under the grasp of a dæmon whom I had myself created.

I walked about the isle like a restless spectre, separated from all it loved, and miserable in the separation. When it became noon, and the sun rose higher, I lay down on the grass, and was overpowered by a deep sleep. I had been awake the whole of the preceding night, my nerves were agitated, and my eyes inflamed by watching and misery. The sleep into which I now sunk refreshed me; and when I awoke, I again felt as if I belonged to a race of human beings like myself, and I began to reflect upon what had passed with greater composure; yet still the words of the fiend rung in my ears like a death-knell, they appeared like a dream, yet distinct and oppressive as a reality.

The sun had far descended, and I still sat on the shore, satisfying my appetite, which had become ravenous, with an oaten cake, when I saw a fishing-boat land close to me, and one of the men brought me a packet; it contained letters from Geneva, and one from Clerval, entreating me to join him. He said that nearly a year had elapsed since we had quitted Switzerland, and France was yet unvisited. He entreated me, therefore, to leave my solitary isle, and meet him at Perth, in a week from that time, when we might arrange the plan of our future proceedings. This letter in a degree recalled me to life, and I determined to quit my island at the expiration of two days.

Yet, before I departed, there was a task to perform, on which I shuddered to reflect: I must pack my chemical instruments; and for that purpose I must enter the room which had been the scene of my odious work, and I must handle those utensils, the sight of which was sickening to me. The next morning, at day-break, I summoned sufficient courage, and unlocked the door of my laboratory. The remains of the half-finished creature, whom I had destroyed, lay scattered on the floor, and I almost felt as if I had mangled the living flesh of a human being.* I paused to collect myself, and then entered the chamber. With trembling hand I conveyed the instruments out of the room; but I reflected that I ought not to leave the relics of my work to excite the horror and suspicion of the peasants, and I accordingly put them into a basket, with a great quantity of stones, and laying them up, determined to throw them into the sea that very night; and in the mean time I sat upon the beach, employed in cleaning and arranging my chemical apparatus.

Nothing could be more complete than the alteration that had taken place in my feelings since the night of the appearance of the dæmon. I had before regarded my promise with a gloomy despair, as a thing that, with whatever consequences, must be fulfilled; but I now felt as if a film had been taken from before my eyes, and that I, for the first time, saw clearly. The idea of renewing my labours did not for one instant occur to me; the threat I had heard weighed on my thoughts, but I did not reflect that a voluntary act of mine could avert it. I had resolved in my own mind, that to create another like the fiend I had first made would be an act of the basest and most atrocious selfishness; and I banished from my mind every thought that could lead to a different conclusion.

Between two and three in the morning the moon rose; and I then, putting my basket aboard a little skiff, sailed out about four miles from the shore. The scene was perfectly solitary: a few boats were returning towards land, but I sailed away from them. I felt as if I was about the commission of a dreadful crime, and avoided with shuddering anxiety any encounter with my fellow-creatures. At one time the moon, which had before been clear, was suddenly overspread by a thick cloud, and I took advantage of the moment of darkness, and cast my basket into the sea; I listened to the gurgling sound as it sunk, and then sailed away from the spot. The sky became clouded; but the air was pure, although chilled by the north-east breeze that was then rising. But it refreshed me, and filled me with such agreeable sensations, that I resolved to prolong my stay on the water, and fixing the rudder in a direct position, stretched myself at the bottom of the boat. Clouds hid the moon, every thing was obscure, and I heard only the sound of the boat, as its keel cut through the waves; the murmur lulled me, and in a short time I slept soundly.

I do not know how long I remained in this situation, but when I awoke I found that the sun had already mounted considerably. The wind was high, and the waves continually threatened the safety of my little skiff. I found that the wind was north-east, and must have driven me far from the coast from which I had embarked. I endeavoured to change my course, but quickly found that if I again made the attempt the boat would be instantly filled with water. Thus situated, my only resource was to drive before the wind. I confess that I felt a few sensations of terror. I had no compass with me, and was so little acquainted with the geography of this part of the world that the sun was of little benefit to me. I might be driven into the wide Atlantic, and feel all the tortures of starvation, or be swallowed up in the immeasurable waters that roared and buffeted around me. I had already been out many hours, and felt the torment of a burning thirst,* a prelude to my other sufferings. I looked on the heavens, which were covered by clouds that flew before the wind only to be replaced by others: I looked upon the sea, it was to be my grave. 'Fiend,' I exclaimed, 'your task is already fulfilled!' I thought of Elizabeth, of my father, and of Clerval; and sunk into a reverie, so despairing and frightful, that even now, when the scene is on the point of closing before me for ever, I shudder to reflect on it.

Some hours passed thus; but by degrees, as the sun declined towards the horizon, the wind died away into a gentle breeze, and the sea became free from breakers. But these gave place to a heavy swell; I felt sick, and hardly able to hold the rudder, when suddenly I saw a line of high land towards the south.

Almost spent, as I was, by fatigue, and the dreadful suspense I endured for several hours, this sudden certainty of life rushed like a flood of warm joy to my heart, and tears gushed from my eyes.

How mutable are our feelings, and how strange is that clinging love we have of life even in the excess of misery! I constructed another sail with a part of my dress, and eagerly steered my course towards the land. It had a wild and rocky appearance; but as I approached nearer, I easily perceived the traces of cultivation. I saw vessels near the shore, and found myself suddenly transported back to the neighbour-hood of civilized man. I eagerly traced the windings of the land, and hailed a steeple which I at length saw issuing from behind a small promontory. As I was in a state of extreme debility, I resolved to sail directly towards the town as a place where I could most easily procure nourishment. Fortunately I had money with me. As I turned the promontory, I perceived a small neat town and a good harbour, which I entered, my heart bounding with joy at my unexpected escape.

As I was occupied in fixing the boat and arranging the sails, several people crowded towards the spot. They seemed very much surprised at my appearance; but, instead of offering me any assistance, whis-pered together with gestures that at any other time might have pro-duced in me a slight sensation of alarm. As it was, I merely remarked that they spoke English; and I therefore addressed them in that lan-guage: 'My good friends,' said I, 'will you be so kind as to tell me the name of this town, and inform me where I am?'

'You will know that soon enough,' replied a man with a gruff voice. 'May be you are come to a place that will not prove much to your taste; but you will not be consulted as to your quarters, I promise you.'

I was exceedingly surprised on receiving so rude an answer from a stranger; and I was also disconcerted on perceiving the frowning and angry countenances of his companions. 'Why do you answer me so roughly?' I replied: 'surely it is not the custom of Englishmen to receive strangers so inhospitably.'

'I do not know,' said the man, 'what the custom of the English may be; but it is the custom of the Irish to hate villains.'*

While this strange dialogue continued, I perceived the crowd rap-idly increase. Their faces expressed a mixture of curiosity and anger, which annoyed, and in some degree alarmed me. I inquired the way to the inn; but no one replied. I then moved foward, and a murmuring sound arose from the crowd as they followed and surrounded me; when an ill-looking man approaching, tapped me on the shoulder, and said, 'Come, Sir, you must follow me to Mr. Kirwin's, to give an account of yourself.'

'Who is Mr. Kirwin?* Why am I to give an account of myself? Is not this a free country?'

'Aye, Sir, free enough for honest folks. Mr. Kirwin is a magistrate; and you are to give an account of the death of a gentleman who was found murdered here last night.'

This answer startled me; but I presently recovered myself. I was innocent; that could easily be proved: accordingly I followed my conductor in silence, and was led to one of the best houses in the town. I was ready to sink from fatigue and hunger; but, being surrounded by a crowd, I thought it politic to rouse all my strength, that no physical debility might be construed into apprehension or conscious guilt. Little did I then expect the calamity that was in a few moments to overwhelm me, and extinguish in horror and despair all fear of ignominy or death.

I must pause here; for it requires all my fortitude to recall the memory of the frightful events which I am about to relate, in proper detail, to my recollection.

CHAPTER IV.

I was soon introduced into the presence of the magistrate, an old benevolent man, with calm and mild manners. He looked upon me, however, with some degree of severity; and then, turning towards my conductors, he asked who appeared as witnesses on this occasion.

About half a dozen men came forward; and one being selected by the magistrate, he deposed, that he had been out fishing the night before with his son and brother-in-law, Daniel Nugent, when, about ten o'clock, they observed a strong northerly blast rising, and they accordingly put in for port. It was a very dark night, as the moon had not yet risen; they did not land at the harbour, but, as they had been accustomed, at a creek about two miles below. He walked on first, carrying a part of the fishing tackle, and his companions followed him at some distance. As he was proceeding along the sands, he struck his foot against something, and fell all his length on the ground. His companions came up to assist him; and, by the light of their lantern, they found that he had fallen on the body of a man, who was to all appearance dead. Their first supposition was, that it was the corpse of some person who had been drowned, and was thrown on shore by the waves; but, upon examination, they found that the clothes were not wet, and even that the body was not then cold. They instantly carried it to the cottage of an old woman near the spot, and endeavoured, but in vain, to restore it to life. He appeared to be a handsome young man, about five and twenty years of age. He had apparently been strangled; for there was no sign of any violence, except the black mark of fingers on his neck.

The first part of this deposition did not in the least interest me; but when the mark of the fingers was mentioned, I remembered the murder of my brother, and felt myself extremely agitated; my limbs trembled, and a mist came over my eyes, which obliged me to lean on a chair for support. The magistrate observed me with a keen eye, and of course drew an unfavourable augury from my manner.

The son confirmed his father's account: but when Daniel Nugent was called, he swore positively that, just before the fall of his companion, he saw a boat, with a single man in it, at a short distance from the shore; and, as far as he could judge by the light of a few stars, it was the same boat in which I had just landed.

A woman deposed, that she lived near the beach, and was standing at the door of her cottage, waiting for the return of the fishermen, about an hour before she heard of the discovery of the body, when she saw a boat, with only one man in it, push off from that part of the shore where the corpse was afterwards found.

Another woman confirmed the account of the fishermen having brought the body into her house; it was not cold. They put it into a bed, and rubbed it; and Daniel went to the town for an apothecary, but life was quite gone.

Several other men were examined concerning my landing; and they agreed, that, with the strong north wind that had arisen during the night, it was very probable that I had beaten about for many hours, and had been obliged to return nearly to the same spot from which I had departed. Besides, they observed that it appeared that I had brought the body from another place, and it was likely, that as I did not appear to know the shore, I might have put into the harbour ignorant of the distance of the town of —— from the place where I had deposited the corpse.

Mr. Kirwin, on hearing this evidence, desired that I should be taken into the room where the body lay for interment, that it might be observed what effect the sight of it would produce upon me. This idea was probably suggested by the extreme agitation I had exhibited when the mode of the murder had been described. I was accordingly conducted, by the magistrate and several other persons, to the inn. I could not help being struck by the strange coincidences that had taken place during this eventful night; but, knowing that I had been conversing with several persons in the island I had inhabited about the time that the body had been found, I was perfectly tranquil as to the consequences of the affair.

I entered the room where the corpse lay, and was led up to the coffin. How can I describe my sensations on beholding it? I feel yet parched with horror, nor can I reflect on that terrible moment without shuddering and agony, that faintly reminds me of the anguish of the recognition. The trial, the presence of the magistrate and witnesses, passed like a dream from my memory, when I saw the lifeless form of Henry Clerval stretched before me. I gasped for breath; and, throwing myself on the body, I exclaimed, 'Have my murderous machinations deprived you also, my dearest Henry, of life? Two I have already destroyed; other victims await their destiny: but you, Clerval, my friend, my benefactor'—

The human frame could no longer support the agonizing suffering that I endured, and I was carried out of the room in strong convulsions.

A fever succeeded to this. I lay for two months on the point of death: my ravings, as I afterwards heard, were frightful; I called myself the murderer of William, of Justine, and of Clerval. Sometimes I entreated my attendants to assist me in the destruction of the fiend by whom I was tormented; and, at others, I felt the fingers of the monster already grasping my neck, and screamed aloud with agony and terror. Fortunately, as I spoke my native language, Mr. Kirwin alone understood me; but my gestures and bitter cries were sufficient to affright the other witnesses.

Why did I not die? More miserable than man ever was before, why did I not sink into forgetfulness and rest? Death snatches away many blooming children, the only hopes of their doating parents: how many brides and youthful lovers have been one day in the bloom of health and hope, and the next a prey for worms and the decay of the tomb! Of what materials was I made, that I could thus resist so many shocks, which, like the turning of the wheel, continually renewed the torture.

But I was doomed to live; and, in two months, found myself as awaking from a dream, in a prison, stretched on a wretched bed, surrounded by gaolers, turnkeys, bolts, and all the miserable apparatus of a dungeon. It was morning, I remember, when I thus awoke to understanding: I had forgotten the particulars of what had happened, and only felt as if some great misfortune had suddenly overwhelmed me; but when I looked around, and saw the barred windows, and the squalidness of the room in which I was, all flashed across my memory, and I groaned bitterly.

This sound disturbed an old woman who was sleeping in a chair beside me. She was a hired nurse, the wife of one of the turnkeys, and her countenance expressed all those bad qualities which often characterize that class. The lines of her face were hard and rude, like that of persons accustomed to see without sympathizing in sights of misery. Her tone expressed her entire indifference; she addressed me in English, and the voice struck me as one that I had heard during my sufferings:

'Are you better now, Sir?' said she.

I replied in the same language, with a feeble voice, 'I believe I am; but if it be all true, if indeed I did not dream, I am sorry that I am still alive to feel this misery and horror.'

'For that matter,' replied the old woman, 'if you mean about the gentleman you murdered, I believe that it were better for you if you were dead, for I fancy it will go hard with you; but you will be hung when the next sessions come on. However, that's none of my business, I am sent to nurse you, and get you well; I do my duty with a safe conscience, it were well if every body did the same.'

I turned with loathing from the woman who could utter so unfeeling a speech to a person just saved, on the very edge of death; but I felt languid, and unable to reflect on all that had passed. The whole series of my life appeared to me as a dream; I sometimes doubted if indeed it were all true, for it never presented itself to my mind with the force of reality.

As the images that floated before me became more distinct, I grew feverish; a darkness pressed around me; no one was near me who soothed me with the gentle voice of love; no dear hand supported me.

The physician came and prescribed medicines, and the old woman prepared them for me; but utter carelessness was visible in the first, and the expression of brutality was strongly marked in the visage of the second. Who could be interested in the fate of a murderer, but the hangman who would gain his fee?

These were my first reflections; but I soon learned that Mr. Kirwin had shewn me extreme kindness. He had caused the best room in the prison to be prepared for me (wretched indeed was the best); and it was he who had provided a physician and a nurse. It is true, he seldom came to see me; for, although he ardently desired to relieve the sufferings of every human creature, he did not wish to be present at the agonies and miserable ravings of a murderer. He came, therefore, sometimes to see that I was not neglected; but his visits were short, and at long intervals.

One day, when I was gradually recovering, I was seated in a chair, my eyes half open, and my cheeks livid like those in death, I was overcome by gloom and misery, and often reflected I had better seek death than remain miserably pent up only to be let loose in a world replete with wretchedness. At one time I considered whether I should not declare myself guilty, and suffer the penalty of the law, less innocent than poor Justine had been. Such were my thoughts, when the door of my apartment was opened, and Mr. Kirwin entered. His countenance expressed sympathy and compassion; he drew a chair close to mine, and addressed me in French—

'I fear that this place is very shocking to you; can I do any thing to make you more comfortable?'

'I thank you; but all that you mention is nothing to me: on the whole earth there is no comfort which I am capable of receiving.'

'I know that the sympathy of a stranger can be but of little relief to one borne down as you are by so strange a misfortune. But you will, I hope, soon quit this melancholy abode; for, doubtless, evidence can easily be brought to free you from the criminal charge.'

'That is my least concern: I am, by a course of strange events, become the most miserable of mortals. Persecuted and tortured as I am and have been, can death be any evil to me?'

'Nothing indeed could be more unfortunate and agonizing than the strange chances that have lately occurred. You were thrown, by some surprising accident, on this shore, renowned for its hospitality; seized immediately, and charged with murder. The first sight that was presented to your eyes was the body of your friend, murdered in so unaccountable a manner, and placed, as it were, by some fiend across your path.'

As Mr. Kirwin said this, notwithstanding the agitation I endured on this retrospect of my sufferings, I also felt considerable surprise at the knowledge he seemed to possess concerning me. I suppose some astonishment was exhibited in my countenance; for Mr. Kirwin hastened to say—

'It was not until a day or two after your illness that I thought of examining your dress, that I might discover some trace by which I could send to your relations an account of your misfortune and illness. I found several letters, and, among others, one which I discovered from its commencement to be from your father. I instantly wrote to Geneva: nearly two months have elapsed since the departure of my letter.—But you are ill; even now you tremble: you are unfit for agitation of any kind.'

'This suspense is a thousand times worse than the most horrible event: tell me what new scene of death has been acted, and whose murder I am now to lament.'

'Your family is perfectly well,' said Mr. Kirwin, with gentleness; 'and some one, a friend, is come to visit you.'

I know not by what chain of thought the idea presented itself, but it instantly darted into my mind that the murderer had come to mock at my misery, and taunt me with the death of Clerval, as a new incitement for me to comply with his hellish desires. I put my hand before my eyes, and cried out in agony—

'Oh! take him away! I cannot see him; for God's sake, do not let him enter!'

Mr. Kirwin regarded me with a troubled countenance. He could not help regarding my exclamation as a presumption of my guilt, and said, in rather a severe tone—

'I should have thought, young man, that the presence of your father would have been welcome, instead of inspiring such violent repugnance.'

'My father!' cried I, while every feature and every muscle was relaxed from anguish to pleasure. 'Is my father, indeed, come? How kind, how very kind. But where is he, why does he not hasten to me?'

My change of manner surprised and pleased the magistrate; perhaps he thought that my former exclamation was a momentary return of delirium, and now he instantly resumed his former benevolence.

He rose, and quitted the room with my nurse, and in a moment my father entered it.

Nothing, at this moment, could have given me greater pleasure than the arrival of my father. I stretched out my hand to him, and cried—

'Are you then safe—and Elizabeth—and Ernest?'

My father calmed me with assurances of their welfare, and endeavoured, by dwelling on these subjects so interesting to my heart, to raise my desponding spirits; but he soon felt that a prison cannot be the abode of cheerfulness. 'What a place is this that you inhabit, my son!' said he, looking mournfully at the barred windows, and wretched appearance of the room. 'You travelled to seek happiness, but a fatality seems to pursue you. And poor Clerval—'

The name of my unfortunate and murdered friend was an agitation too great to be endured in my weak state; I shed tears.

'Alas! yes, my father,' replied I; 'some destiny of the most horrible kind hangs over me, and I must live to fulfil it, or surely I should have died on the coffin of Henry.'

We were not allowed to converse for any length of time, for the precarious state of my health rendered every precaution necessary that could insure tranquillity. Mr. Kirwin came in, and insisted that my strength should not be exhausted by too much exertion. But the appearance of my father was to me like that of my good angel, and I gradually recovered my health.

As my sickness quitted me, I was absorbed by a gloomy and black melancholy, that nothing could dissipate. The image of Clerval was for ever before me, ghastly and murdered. More than once the agitation into which these reflections threw me made my friends dread a dangerous relapse. Alas! why did they preserve so miserable and detested a life? It was surely that I might fulfil my destiny, which is now drawing to a close. Soon, oh, very soon, will death extinguish these throbbings, and relieve me from the mighty weight of anguish that bears me to the dust; and, in executing the award of justice, I shall also sink to rest. Then the appearance of death was distant, although the wish was ever present to my thoughts; and I often sat for hours motionless and speechless, wishing for some mighty revolution that might bury me and my destroyer in its ruins.*

The season of the assizes* approached. I had already been three months in prison; and although I was still weak, and in continual danger of a relapse, I was obliged to travel nearly a hundred miles to the county-town, where the court was held. Mr. Kirwin charged himself with every care of collecting witnesses, and arranging my defence. I was spared the disgrace of appearing publicly as a criminal, as the case was not brought before the court that decides on life and death. The grand jury rejected the bill, on its being proved that I was on the Orkney Islands at the hour the body of my friend was found, and a fortnight after my removal I was liberated from prison.

My father was enraptured on finding me freed from the vexations of a criminal charge, that I was again allowed to breathe the fresh atmosphere, and allowed to return to my native country. I did not participate in these feelings; for to me the walls of a dungeon or a palace were alike hateful. The cup of life was poisoned for ever; and although the sun shone upon me, as upon the happy and gay of heart, I saw around me nothing but a dense and frightful darkness, penetrated by no light but the glimmer of two eyes that glared upon me.* Sometimes they were the expressive eyes of Henry, languishing in death, the dark orbs nearly covered by the lids, and the long black lashes that fringed them; sometimes it was the watery clouded eyes of the monster, as I first saw them in my chamber at Ingolstadt.

My father tried to awaken in me the feelings of affection. He talked of Geneva, which I should soon visit—of Elizabeth, and Ernest; but these words only drew deep groans from me. Sometimes, indeed, I felt a wish for happiness; and thought, with melancholy delight, of my beloved cousin; or longed, with a devouring *maladie du pays*,* to see once more the blue lake and rapid Rhone, that had been so dear to me in early childhood: but my general state of feeling was a torpor, in which a prison was as welcome a residence as the divinest scene in nature; and these fits were seldom interrupted, but by paroxysms of anguish and despair. At these moments I often endeavoured to put an end to the existence I loathed; and it required unceasing attendance and vigilance to restrain me from committing some dreadful act of violence.

I remember, as I quitted the prison, I heard one of the men say, 'He may be innocent of the murder, but he has certainly a bad conscience.' These words struck me. A bad conscience! yes, surely I had one. William, Justine, and Clerval, had died through my infernal machinations; 'And whose death,' cried I, 'is to finish the tragedy? Ah! my father, do not remain in this wretched country; take me where I may forget myself, my existence, and all the world.'

My father easily acceded to my desire; and, after having taken leave of Mr. Kirwin, we hastened to Dublin. I felt as if I was relieved from a heavy weight, when the packet* sailed with a fair wind from Ireland, and I had quitted for ever the country which had been to me the scene of so much misery.

It was midnight. My father slept in the cabin; and I lay on the deck, looking at the stars, and listening to the dashing of the waves. I hailed the darkness that shut Ireland from my sight, and my pulse beat with a feverish joy, when I reflected that I should soon see Geneva. The past appeared to me in the light of a frightful dream; yet the vessel in which I was, the wind that blew me from the detested shore of Ireland, and the sea which surrounded me, told me too forcibly that I was deceived by no vision, and that Clerval, my friend and dearest companion, had fallen a victim to me and the monster of my creation. I repassed, in my memory, my whole life; my quiet happiness while residing with my family in Geneva, the death of my mother, and my departure for Ingolstadt. I remembered shuddering at the mad enthusiasm that hurried me on to the creation of my hideous enemy, and I called to mind the night during which he first lived. I was unable to pursue the train of thought; a thousand feelings pressed upon me, and I wept bitterly.

Ever since my recovery from the fever I had been in the custom of taking every night a small quantity of laudanum;* for it was by means of this drug only that I was enabled to gain the rest necessary for the preservation of life. Oppressed by the recollection of my various misfortunes, I now took a double dose, and soon slept profoundly. But sleep did not afford me respite from thought and misery; my dreams presented a thousand objects that scared me. Towards morning I was possessed by a kind of night-mare; I felt the fiend's grasp in my neck, and could not free myself from it; groans and cries rung in my ears. My father, who was watching over me, perceiving my restlessness, awoke me, and pointed to the port of Holyhead, which we were now entering.

CHAPTER V.

WE had resolved not to go to London, but to cross the country to Portsmouth, and thence to embark for Havre.* I preferred this plan principally because I dreaded to see again those places in which

I had enjoyed a few moments of tranquillity with my beloved Clerval. I thought with horror of seeing again those persons whom we had been accustomed to visit together, and who might make inquiries concerning an event, the very remembrance of which made me again feel the pang I endured when I gazed on his lifeless form in the inn at ——.

As for my father, his desires and exertions were bounded to the again seeing me* restored to health and peace of mind. His tenderness and attentions were unremitting; my grief and gloom was obstinate, but he would not despair. Sometimes he thought that I felt deeply the degradation of being obliged to answer a charge of murder, and he endeavoured to prove to me the futility of pride.

'Alas! my father,' said I, 'how little do you know me. Human beings, their feelings and passions, would indeed be degraded, if such a wretch as I felt pride. Justine, poor unhappy Justine, was as innocent as I, and she suffered the same charge; she died for it; and I am the cause of this—I murdered her. William, Justine, and Henry—they all died by my hands.'

My father had often, during my imprisonment, heard me make the same assertion; when I thus accused myself, he sometimes seemed to desire an explanation, and at others he appeared to consider it as caused by delirium, and that, during my illness, some idea of this kind had presented itself to my imagination, the remembrance of which I preserved in my convalescence. I avoided explanation, and maintained a continual silence concerning the wretch I had created. I had a feeling that I should be supposed mad, and this for ever chained my tongue, when I would have given the whole world to have confided the fatal secret.

Upon this occasion my father said, with an expression of unbounded wonder, 'What do you mean, Victor? are you mad? My dear son, I entreat you never to make such an assertion again.'

'I am not mad,' I cried energetically; 'the sun and the heavens, who have viewed my operations, can bear witness of my truth. I am the assassin of those most innocent victims; they died by my machinations. A thousand times would I have shed my own blood, drop by drop, to have saved their lives; but I could not, my father, indeed I could not sacrifice the whole human race.'

The conclusion of this speech convinced my father that my ideas were deranged, and he instantly changed the subject of our conversation, and endeavoured to alter the course of my thoughts. He wished as much as possible to obliterate the memory of the scenes that had taken place in Ireland, and never alluded to them, or suffered me to speak of my misfortunes.

As time passed away I became more calm: misery had her dwelling in my heart, but I no longer talked in the same incoherent manner of my own crimes; sufficient for me was the consciousness of them. By the utmost self-violence, I curbed the imperious voice of wretchedness, which sometimes desired to declare itself to the whole world; and my manners were calmer and more composed than they had ever been since my journey to the sea of ice.*

We arrived at Havre on the 8th of May, and instantly proceeded to Paris, where my father had some business which detained us a few weeks. In this city, I received the following letter from Elizabeth:—

'*To* VICTOR FRANKENSTEIN.

'MY DEAREST FRIEND,

'It gave me the greatest pleasure to receive a letter from my uncle dated at Paris; you are no longer at a formidable distance, and I may hope to see you in less than a fortnight. My poor cousin, how much you must have suffered! I expect to see you looking even more ill than when you quitted Geneva. This winter has been passed most miserably, tortured as I have been by anxious suspense; yet I hope to see peace in your countenance, and to find that your heart is not totally devoid of comfort and tranquillity.

'Yet I fear that the same feelings now exist that made you so miserable a year ago, even perhaps augmented by time. I would not disturb you at this period, when so many misfortunes weigh upon you; but a conversation that I had with my uncle previous to his departure renders some explanation necessary before we meet.

'Explanation! you may possibly say; what can Elizabeth have to explain? If you really say this, my questions are answered, and I have no more to do than to sign myself your affectionate cousin. But you are distant from me, and it is possible that you may dread, and yet be pleased with this explanation; and, in a probability of this being the case, I dare not any longer postpone writing what, during your absence, I have often wished to express to you, but have never had the courage to begin.

'You well know, Victor, that our union had been the favourite plan of your parents ever since our infancy. We were told this when young, and taught to look forward to it as an event that would certainly take place. We were affectionate playfellows during childhood, and, I believe, dear and valued friends to one another as we grew older. But as brother and sister often entertain a lively affection towards each other, without desiring a more intimate union, may not such also be our case? Tell me, dearest Victor. Answer me, I conjure you, by our mutual happiness, with simple truth—Do you not love another?

'You have travelled; you have spent several years of your life at Ingolstadt; and I confess to you, my friend, that when I saw you last autumn so unhappy, flying to solitude, from the society of every crea-ture, I could not help supposing that you might regret our connexion, and believe yourself bound in honour to fulfil the wishes of your par-ents, although they opposed themselves to your inclinations. But this is false reasoning. I confess to you, my cousin, that I love you, and that in my airy dreams of futurity you have been my constant friend and companion. But it is your happiness I desire as well as my own, when I declare to you, that our marriage would render me eternally miser-able, unless it were the dictate of your own free choice. Even now I weep to think, that, borne down as you are by the cruelest misfor-tunes, you may stifle, by the word *honour*, all hope of that love and happiness which would alone restore you to yourself. I, who have so interested an affection for you, may increase your miseries ten-fold, by being an obstacle to your wishes. Ah, Victor, be assured that your cousin and playmate has too sincere a love for you not to be made miserable by this supposition. Be happy, my friend; and if you obey me in this one request, remain satisfied that nothing on earth will have the power to interrupt my tranquillity.

'Do not let this letter disturb you; do not answer it tomorrow, or the next day, or even until you come, if it will give you pain. My uncle will send me news of your health; and if I see but one smile on your lips when we meet, occasioned by this or any other exertion of mine, I shall need no other happiness.

'ELIZABETH LAVENZA.

'Geneva, May 18th, 17—.'

This letter revived in my memory what I had before forgotten, the threat of the fiend—'*I will be with you on your wedding-night!*' Such was my sentence, and on that night would the dæmon employ every art to destroy me, and tear me from the glimpse of happiness which prom-ised partly to console my sufferings. On that night he had determined to consummate* his crimes by my death. Well, be it so; a deadly strug-gle would then assuredly take place, in which if he was victorious, I should be at peace, and his power over me be at an end. If he were vanquished, I should be a free man. Alas! what freedom? such as the peasant enjoys when his family have been massacred before his eyes, his cottage burnt, his lands laid waste, and he is turned adrift, home-less, pennyless, and alone, but free. Such would be my liberty, except that in my Elizabeth I possessed a treasure; alas! balanced by those horrors of remorse and guilt, which would pursue me until death.

Sweet and beloved Elizabeth! I read and re-read her letter, and some softened feelings stole into my heart, and dared to whisper paradisaical dreams of love and joy; but the apple was already eaten, and the angel's arm bared to drive me from all hope. Yet I would die to make her happy. If the monster executed his threat, death was inevitable; yet, again, I considered whether my marriage would hasten my fate. My destruction might indeed arrive a few months sooner; but if my torturer should suspect that I postponed it, influenced by his menaces, he would surely find other, and perhaps more dreadful means of revenge. He had vowed *to be with me on my wedding-night*, yet he did not con-sider that threat as binding him to peace in the mean time; for, as if to shew me that he was not yet satiated with blood, he had murdered Clerval immediately after the enunciation of his threats. I resolved, therefore, that if my immediate union with my cousin would conduce either to her's or my father's happiness, my adversary's designs against my life should not retard it a single hour.

In this state of mind I wrote to Elizabeth. My letter was calm and affectionate. 'I fear, my beloved girl,' I said, 'little happiness remains for us on earth; yet all that I may one day enjoy is concentered in you. Chase away your idle fears; to you alone do I consecrate my life, and my endeavours for contentment. I have one secret, Elizabeth, a dread-ful one; when revealed to you, it will chill your frame with horror, and then, far from being surprised at my misery, you will only wonder that I survive what I have endured. I will confide this tale of misery and terror to you the day after our marriage shall take place; for, my sweet cousin, there must be perfect confidence between us. But until then, I conjure you, do not mention or allude to it. This I most earnestly entreat, and I know you will comply.'

In about a week after the arrival of Elizabeth's letter, we returned to Geneva. My cousin welcomed me with warm affection; yet tears were in her eyes, as she beheld my emaciated frame and feverish cheeks. I saw a change in her also. She was thinner, and had lost much of that heavenly vivacity that had before charmed me; but her gentleness, and soft looks of compassion, made her a more fit companion for one blasted and miserable as I was.

The tranquillity which I now enjoyed did not endure. Memory brought madness with it; and when I thought on what had passed, a real insanity possessed me; sometimes I was furious, and burnt with rage, sometimes low and despondent. I neither spoke or looked, but sat motionless, bewildered by the multitude of miseries that overcame me.

Elizabeth alone had the power to draw me from these fits; her gentle voice would soothe me when transported by passion, and inspire me with human feelings when sunk in torpor. She wept with me, and for me. When reason returned, she would remonstrate, and endeavour to inspire me with resignation. Ah! it is well for the unfortunate to be resigned, but for the guilty there is no peace. The agonies of remorse poison the luxury there is otherwise sometimes found in indulging the excess of grief.

Soon after my arrival my father spoke of my immediate marriage with my cousin. I remained silent.

'Have you, then, some other attachment?'

'None on earth. I love Elizabeth, and look forward to our union with delight. Let the day therefore be fixed; and on it I will consecrate myself, in life or death, to the happiness of my cousin.'

'My dear Victor, do not speak thus. Heavy misfortunes have befallen us; but let us only cling closer to what remains, and transfer our love for those whom we have lost to those who yet live. Our circle will be small, but bound close by the ties of affection and mutual misfortune. And when time shall have softened your despair, new and dear objects of care will be born to replace those of whom we have been so cruelly deprived.'

Such were the lessons of my father. But to me the remembrance of the threat returned: nor can you wonder, that, omnipotent as the fiend had yet been in his deeds of blood, I should almost regard him as invincible; and that when he had pronounced the words, '*I shall be with you on your wedding-night*,' I should regard the threatened fate as unavoidable. But death was no evil to me, if the loss of Elizabeth were balanced with it; and I therefore, with a contented and even cheerful countenance, agreed with my father, that if my cousin would consent, the ceremony should take place in ten days, and thus put, as I imagined, the seal to my fate.

Great God! if for one instant I had thought what might be the hellish intention of my fiendish adversary, I would rather have banished myself for ever from my native country, and wandered a friendless outcast over the earth, than have consented to this miserable marriage. But, as if possessed of magic powers, the monster had blinded me to his real intentions; and when I thought that I prepared only my own death, I hastened that of a far dearer victim.

As the period fixed for our marriage drew nearer, whether from cowardice or a prophetic feeling, I felt my heart sink within me. But I concealed my feelings by an appearance of hilarity, that brought smiles and joy to the countenance of my father, but hardly deceived the ever-watchful and nicer* eye of Elizabeth. She looked forward to our union with placid contentment, not unmingled with a little fear, which past misfortunes had impressed, that what now appeared certain and tangible happiness, might soon dissipate into an airy dream, and leave no trace but deep and everlasting regret.

Preparations were made for the event; congratulatory visits were received; and all wore a smiling appearance. I shut up, as well as I could, in my own heart the anxiety that preyed there, and entered with seeming earnestness into the plans of my father, although they might only serve as the decorations of my tragedy. A house was purchased for us near Cologny, by which we should enjoy the pleasures of the country; and yet be so near Geneva as to see my father every day; who would still reside within the walls, for the benefit of Ernest, that he might follow his studies at the schools.

In the mean time I took every precaution to defend my person, in case the fiend should openly attack me. I carried pistols and a dagger constantly about me, and was ever on the watch to prevent artifice; and by these means gained a greater degree of tranquillity. Indeed, as the period approached, the threat appeared more as a delusion, not to be regarded as worthy to disturb my peace, while the happiness I hoped for in my marriage wore a greater appearance of certainty, as the day fixed for its solemnization drew nearer, and I heard it continually spoken of as an occurrence which no accident could possibly prevent.

Elizabeth seemed happy; my tranquil demeanour contributed greatly to calm her mind. But on the day that was to fulfil my wishes and my destiny, she was melancholy, and a presentiment of evil pervaded her;

and perhaps also she thought of the dreadful secret, which I had promised to reveal to her the following day. My father was in the mean time
overjoyed, and, in the bustle of preparation, only observed in the
melancholy of his niece the diffidence of a bride.

After the ceremony was performed, a large party assembled at my
father's; but it was agreed that Elizabeth and I should pass the afternoon and night at Evian, and return to Cologny the next morning. As
the day was fair, and the wind favourable, we resolved to go by water.

Those were the last moments of my life during which I enjoyed the
feeling of happiness. We passed rapidly along: the sun was hot, but we
were sheltered from its rays by a kind of canopy, while we enjoyed the
beauty of the scene, sometimes on one side of the lake, where we saw
Mont Salêve, the pleasant banks of Montalègre, and at a distance,
surmounting all, the beautiful Mont Blânc, and the assemblage of
snowy mountains that in vain endeavour to emulate her; sometimes
coasting the opposite banks, we saw the mighty Jura opposing its dark
side to the ambition that would quit its native country, and an almost
insurmountable barrier to the invader who should wish to enslave it.*

I took the hand of Elizabeth: 'You are sorrowful, my love. Ah! if you
knew what I have suffered, and what I may yet endure, you would
endeavour to let me taste the quiet, and freedom from despair, that
this one day at least permits me to enjoy.'

'Be happy, my dear Victor,' replied Elizabeth; 'there is, I hope,
nothing to distress you; and be assured that if a lively joy is not painted
on my face, my heart is contented. Something whispers to me not to
depend too much on the prospect that is opened before us; but I will
not listen to such a sinister voice. Observe how fast we move along,
and how the clouds which sometimes obscure, and sometimes rise
above the dome of Mont Blânc, render this scene of beauty still more
interesting. Look also at the innumerable fish that are swimming in
the clear waters, where we can distinguish every pebble that lies at the
bottom. What a divine day! how happy and serene all nature appears!'

Thus Elizabeth endeavoured to divert her thoughts and mine from
all reflection upon melancholy subjects. But her temper was fluctuating; joy for a few instants shone in her eyes, but it continually gave
place to distraction and reverie.

The sun sunk lower in the heavens; we passed the river Drance,
and observed its path through the chasms of the higher, and the glens
of the lower hills. The Alps here come closer to the lake, and we

approached the amphitheatre of mountains which forms its eastern boundary.*The spire of Evian shone under the woods that surrounded it, and the range of mountain above mountain by which it was overhung.

The wind, which had hitherto carried us along with amazing rapidity, sunk at sunset to a light breeze; the soft air just ruffled the water, and caused a pleasant motion among the trees as we approached the shore, from which it wafted the most delightful scent of flowers and hay. The sun sunk beneath the horizon as we landed; and as I touched the shore, I felt those cares and fears revive, which soon were to clasp me, and cling to me for ever.

CHAPTER VI.

IT was eight o'clock when we landed; we walked for a short time on the shore, enjoying the transitory light, and then retired to the inn, and contemplated the lovely scene of waters, woods, and mountains, obscured in darkness, yet still displaying their black outlines.

The wind, which had fallen in the south, now rose with great violence in the west. The moon had reached her summit in the heavens, and was beginning to descend; the clouds swept across it swifter than the flight of the vulture, and dimmed her rays, while the lake reflected the scene of the busy heavens, rendered still busier by the restless waves that were beginning to rise. Suddenly a heavy storm of rain descended.

I had been calm during the day; but so soon as night obscured the shapes of objects, a thousand fears arose in my mind. I was anxious and watchful, while my right hand grasped a pistol which was hidden in my bosom; every sound terrified me; but I resolved that I would sell my life dearly, and not relax the impending conflict until my own life, or that of my adversary, were extinguished.

Elizabeth observed my agitation for some time in timid and fearful silence; at length she said, 'What is it that agitates you, my dear Victor? What is it you fear?'

'Oh! peace, peace, my love,' replied I, 'this night, and all will be safe: but this night is dreadful, very dreadful.'

I passed an hour in this state of mind, when suddenly I reflected how dreadful the combat which I momentarily expected would be to my wife, and I earnestly entreated her to retire, resolving not to join her until I had obtained some knowledge as to the situation of my enemy.

She left me, and I continued some time walking up and down the passages of the house, and inspecting every corner that might afford a retreat to my adversary. But I discovered no trace of him, and was beginning to conjecture that some fortunate chance had intervened to prevent the execution of his menaces; when suddenly I heard a shrill and dreadful scream. It came from the room into which Elizabeth had retired. As I heard it, the whole truth rushed into my mind, my arms dropped, the motion of every muscle and fibre was suspended; I could feel the blood trickling in my veins, and tingling in the extremities of my limbs. This state lasted but for an instant; the scream was repeated, and I rushed into the room.

Great God! why did I not then expire! Why am I here to relate the destruction of the best hope, and the purest creature of earth. She was there, lifeless and inanimate, thrown across the bed, her head hanging down, and her pale and distorted features half covered by her hair.* Every where I turn I see the same figure—her bloodless arms and relaxed form flung by the murderer on its bridal bier. Could I behold this, and live? Alas! life is obstinate, and clings closest where it is most hated. For a moment only did I lose recollection; I fainted.

When I recovered, I found myself surrounded by the people of the inn; their countenances expressed a breathless terror: but the horror of others appeared only as a mockery, a shadow of the feelings that oppressed me. I escaped from them to the room where lay the body of Elizabeth, my love, my wife, so lately living, so dear, so worthy. She had been moved from the posture in which I had first beheld her; and now, as she lay, her head upon her arm, and a handkerchief thrown across her face and neck, I might have supposed her asleep. I rushed towards her, and embraced her with ardour; but the deathly languor and coldness of the limbs told me, that what I now held in my arms had ceased to be the Elizabeth whom I had loved and cherished. The murderous mark of the fiend's grasp was on her neck, and the breath had ceased to issue from her lips.

While I still hung over her in the agony of despair, I happened to look up. The windows of the room had before been darkened; and I felt a kind of panic on seeing the pale yellow light of the moon illuminate the chamber. The shutters had been thrown back; and, with a sensa-tion of horror not to be described, I saw at the open window a figure the most hideous and abhorred. A grin was on the face of the monster; he seemed to jeer, as with his fiendish finger he pointed towards the corpse of my wife. I rushed towards the window, and drawing a pistol from my bosom, shot; but he eluded me, leaped from his station, and, running with the swiftness of lightning, plunged into the lake.*

The report of the pistol brought a crowd into the room. I pointed to the spot where he had disappeared, and we followed the track with boats; nets were cast, but in vain. After passing several hours, we returned hopeless, most of my companions believing it to have been a form conjured by my fancy. After having landed, they proceeded to search the country, parties going in different directions among the woods and vines.

I did not accompany them; I was exhausted: a film covered my eyes, and my skin was parched with the heat of fever. In this state I lay on a bed, hardly conscious of what had happened; my eyes wandered round the room, as if to seek something that I had lost.

At length I remembered that my father would anxiously expect the return of Elizabeth and myself, and that I must return alone. This reflection brought tears into my eyes, and I wept for a long time; but my thoughts rambled to various subjects, reflecting on my misfortunes, and their cause. I was bewildered in a cloud of wonder and horror. The death of William, the execution of Justine, the murder of Clerval, and lastly of my wife; even at that moment I knew not that my only remaining friends were safe from the malignity of the fiend; my father even now might be writhing under his grasp, and Ernest might be dead at his feet. This idea made me shudder, and recalled me to action. I started up, and resolved to return to Geneva with all possible speed.

There were no horses to be procured, and I must return by the lake; but the wind was unfavourable, and the rain fell in torrents. However, it was hardly morning, and I might reasonably hope to arrive by night. I hired men to row, and took an oar myself, for I had always experienced relief from mental torment in bodily exercise. But the overflowing misery I now felt, and the excess of agitation that I endured, rendered me incapable of any exertion. I threw down the oar; and, leaning my head upon my hands, gave way to every gloomy idea that arose. If I looked up, I saw the scenes which were familiar to me in my happier time, and which I had contemplated but the day before in the company of her who was now but a shadow and a recollection. Tears streamed from my eyes. The rain had ceased for a moment, and I saw the fish play in the waters as they had done a few hours before; they had then been observed by Elizabeth. Nothing is so painful to the human mind as a great and sudden change. The sun might shine, or the clouds might lour; but nothing could appear to me as it had done the day before. A fiend had snatched from me every hope of future happiness: no creature had ever been so miserable as I was; so frightful an event is single in the history of man.

But why should I dwell upon the incidents that followed this last overwhelming event. Mine has been a tale of horrors; I have reached their *acme*, and what I must now relate can but be tedious to you. Know that, one by one, my friends were snatched away; I was left desolate. My own strength is exhausted; and I must tell, in a few words, what remains of my hideous narration.

I arrived at Geneva. My father and Ernest yet lived; but the former sunk under the tidings that I bore. I see him now, excellent and venerable old man! his eyes wandered in vacancy, for they had lost their charm and their delight—his niece, his more than daughter, whom he doated on with all that affection which a man feels, who, in the decline of life, having few affections, clings more earnestly to those that remain. Cursed, cursed be the fiend that brought misery on his grey hairs, and doomed him to waste in wretchedness! He could not live under the horrors that were accumulated around him; an apoplectic fit was brought on, and in a few days he died in my arms.

What then became of me? I know not; I lost sensation, and chains and darkness were the only objects that pressed upon me. Sometimes, indeed, I dreamt that I wandered in flowery meadows and pleasant vales with the friends of my youth; but awoke, and found myself in a dungeon. Melancholy followed, but by degrees I gained a clear conception of my miseries and situation, and was then released from my prison. For they had called me mad; and during many months, as I understood, a solitary cell had been my habitation.

But liberty had been a useless gift to me had I not, as I awakened to reason, at the same time awakened to revenge. As the memory of past misfortunes pressed upon me, I began to reflect on their cause—the monster whom I had created, the miserable dæmon whom I had sent abroad into the world for my destruction. I was possessed by a maddening rage when I thought of him, and desired and ardently prayed that I might have him within my grasp to wreak a great and signal revenge on his cursed head.

Nor did my hate long confine itself to useless wishes; I began to reflect on the best means of securing him; and for this purpose, about a month after my release, I repaired to a criminal judge in the town, and told him that I had an accusation to make; that I knew the destroyer of my family; and that I required him to exert his whole authority for the apprehension of the murderer.

The magistrate listened to me with attention and kindness: 'Be assured, sir,' said he, 'no pains or exertions on my part shall be spared to discover the villain.'

'I thank you,' replied I; 'listen, therefore, to the deposition that I have to make. It is indeed a tale so strange, that I should fear you would not credit it, were there not something in truth which, however wonderful,* forces conviction. The story is too connected to be mistaken for a dream, and I have no motive for falsehood.' My manner, as I thus addressed him, was impressive, but calm; I had formed in my own heart a resolution to pursue my destroyer to death; and this purpose quieted my agony, and provisionally reconciled me to life. I now related my history briefly, but with firmness and precision, marking the dates with accuracy, and never deviating into invective or exclamation.

The magistrate appeared at first perfectly incredulous, but as I continued he became more attentive and interested; I saw him sometimes shudder with horror, at others a lively surprise, unmingled with disbelief, was painted on his countenance.

When I had concluded my narration, I said, 'This is the being whom I accuse, and for whose detection and punishment I call upon you to exert your whole power. It is your duty as a magistrate, and I believe and hope that your feelings as a man will not revolt from the execution of those functions on this occasion.'

This address caused a considerable change in the physiognomy of my auditor. He had heard my story with that half kind of belief that is given to a tale of spirits and supernatural events; but when he was called upon to act officially in consequence, the whole tide of his incredulity returned. He, however, answered mildly, 'I would willingly afford you every aid in your pursuit; but the creature of whom you speak appears to have powers which would put all my exertions to defiance. Who can follow an animal which can traverse the sea of ice, and inhabit caves and dens, where no man would venture to intrude? Besides, some months have elapsed since the commission of his crimes, and no one can conjecture to what place he has wandered, or what region he may now inhabit.'

'I do not doubt that he hovers near the spot which I inhabit; and if he has indeed taken refuge in the Alps, he may be hunted like the chamois, and destroyed as a beast of prey. But I perceive your thoughts: you do not credit my narrative, and do not intend to pursue my enemy with the punishment which is his desert.'

As I spoke, rage sparkled in my eyes; the magistrate was intimidated; 'You are mistaken,' said he, 'I will exert myself; and if it is in my power to seize the monster, be assured that he shall suffer punishment proportionate to his crimes. But I fear, from what you have yourself described to be his properties, that this will prove impracticable, and that, while every proper measure is pursued, you should endeavour to make up your mind to disappointment.'

'That cannot be; but all that I can say will be of little avail. My revenge is of no moment to you; yet, while I allow it to be a vice, I confess that it is the devouring and only passion of my soul. My rage is unspeakable, when I reflect that the murderer, whom I have turned loose upon society, still exists. You refuse my just demand: I have but one resource; and I devote myself, either in my life or death, to his destruction.'

I trembled with excess of agitation as I said this; there was a phrenzy in my manner, and something, I doubt not, of that haughty fierceness, which the martyrs of old are said to have possessed. But to a Genevan magistrate, whose mind was occupied by far other ideas than those of devotion and heroism, this elevation of mind had much the appearance of madness. He endeavoured to soothe me as a nurse does a child, and reverted to my tale as the effects of delirium.

'Man,' I cried, 'how ignorant art thou in thy pride of wisdom! Cease; you know not what it is you say.'

I broke from the house angry and disturbed, and retired to meditate on some other mode of action.

CHAPTER VII.

MY present situation was one in which all voluntary thought was swallowed up and lost. I was hurried away by fury; revenge alone endowed me with strength and composure; it modelled my feelings, and allowed me to be calculating and calm, at periods when otherwise delirium or death would have been my portion.

My first resolution was to quit Geneva for ever; my country, which, when I was happy and beloved, was dear to me, now, in my adversity, became hateful. I provided myself with a sum of money, together with a few jewels which had belonged to my mother, and departed.

And now my wanderings began, which are to cease but with life.* I have traversed a vast portion of the earth, and have endured all the hardships which travellers, in deserts and barbarous countries, are wont to meet. How I have lived I hardly know; many times have I stretched my failing limbs upon the sandy plain, and prayed for death. But revenge kept me alive; I dared not die, and leave my adversary in being.

When I quitted Geneva, my first labour was to gain some clue by which I might trace the steps of my fiendish enemy. But my plan was unsettled; and I wandered many hours around the confines of the town, uncertain what path I should pursue. As night approached, I found myself at the entrance of the cemetery where William, Elizabeth, and my father, reposed. I entered it, and approached the tomb which marked their graves. Every thing was silent, except the leaves of the trees, which were gently agitated by the wind; the night was nearly dark; and the scene would have been solemn and affecting even to an uninterested observer. The spirits of the departed seemed to flit around, and to cast a shadow, which was felt but seen not, around the head of the mourner.

The deep grief which this scene had at first excited quickly gave way to rage and despair. They were dead, and I lived; their murderer also lived, and to destroy him I must drag out my weary existence. I knelt on the grass, and kissed the earth, and with quivering lips exclaimed, 'By the sacred earth on which I kneel, by the shades* that wander near me, by the deep and eternal grief that I feel, I swear; and by thee, O Night, and by the spirits that preside over thee, I swear to pursue the dæmon, who caused this misery, until he or I shall perish in mortal conflict. For this purpose I will preserve my life: to execute this dear revenge, will I again behold the sun, and tread the green herbage of earth, which otherwise should vanish from my eyes for ever. And I call on you, spirits of the dead; and on you, wandering ministers of vengeance, to aid and conduct me in my work. Let the cursed and hellish monster drink deep of agony; let him feel the despair that now torments me.'

I had begun my adjuration with solemnity, and an awe which almost assured me that the shades of my murdered friends heard and approved my devotion; but the furies* possessed me as I concluded, and rage choked my utterance.

I was answered through the stillness of night by a loud and fiendish laugh. It rung on my ears long and heavily; the mountains re-echoed it, and I felt as if all hell surrounded me with mockery and laughter. Surely in that moment I should have been possessed by phrenzy, and have destroyed my miserable existence, but that my vow was heard, and that I was reserved for vengeance. The laughter died away; when a well-known and abhorred voice, apparently close to my ear, addressed me in an audible whisper—'I am satisfied: miserable wretch! you have determined to live, and I am satisfied.'

I darted towards the spot from which the sound proceeded; but the devil eluded my grasp. Suddenly the broad disk of the moon arose, and shone full upon his ghastly and distorted shape, as he fled with more than mortal speed.

I pursued him; and for many months this has been my task. Guided by a slight clue, I followed the windings of the Rhone, but vainly. The blue Mediterranean appeared; and, by a strange chance, I saw the fiend enter by night, and hide himself in a vessel bound for the Black Sea. I took my passage in the same ship; but he escaped, I know not how.

Amidst the wilds of Tartary and Russia, although he still evaded me, I have ever followed in his track. Sometimes the peasants, scared by this horrid apparition, informed me of his path; sometimes he himself, who feared that if I lost all trace I should despair and die, often left some mark to guide me. The snows descended on my head, and I saw the print of his huge step on the white plain. To you first entering on life, to whom care is new, and agony unknown, how can you understand what I have felt, and still feel? Cold, want, and fatigue, were the least pains which I was destined to endure; I was cursed by some devil, and carried about with me my eternal hell;* yet still a spirit of good followed and directed my steps, and, when I most murmured,* would suddenly extricate me from seemingly insurmountable difficulties. Sometimes, when nature, overcome by hunger, sunk under the exhaustion, a repast was prepared for me in the desert, that restored and inspirited me. The fare was indeed coarse, such as the peasants of the country ate; but I may not doubt that it was set there by the spirits that I had invoked to aid me. Often, when all was dry, the heavens cloudless, and I was parched by thirst, a slight cloud would bedim the sky, shed the few drops that revived me, and vanish.

I followed, when I could, the courses of the rivers; but the dæmon generally avoided these, as it was here that the population of the country chiefly collected. In other places human beings were seldom seen; and I generally subsisted on the wild animals that crossed my path. I had money with me, and gained the friendship of the villagers by distributing it, or bringing with me some food that I had killed, which, after taking a small part, I always presented to those who had provided me with fire and utensils for cooking.

My life, as it passed thus, was indeed hateful to me, and it was during sleep alone that I could taste joy. O blessed sleep! often, when most miserable, I sank to repose, and my dreams lulled me even to rapture. The spirits that guarded me had provided these moments, or rather hours, of happiness, that I might retain strength to fulfil my pilgrimage. Deprived of this respite, I should have sunk under my hardships. During the day I was sustained and inspirited by the hope of night: for in sleep I saw my friends, my wife, and my beloved country; again I saw the benevolent countenance of my father, heard the silver tones of my Elizabeth's voice, and beheld Clerval enjoying health and youth. Often, when wearied by a toilsome march, I persuaded myself that I was dreaming until night should come, and that I should then enjoy reality in the arms of my dearest friends. What agonizing fondness did I feel for them! how did I cling to their dear forms, as sometimes they haunted even my waking hours, and persuade myself that they still lived! At such moments vengeance, that burned within me, died in my heart, and I pursued my path towards the destruction of the dæmon, more as a task enjoined by heaven, as the mechanical impulse of some power of which I was unconscious, than as the ardent desire of my soul.

What his feelings were whom I pursued, I cannot know. Sometimes, indeed, he left marks in writing on the barks of the trees, or cut in stone,* that guided me, and instigated my fury. 'My reign is not yet over,' (these words were legible in one of these inscriptions); 'you live, and my power is complete. Follow me; I seek the everlasting ices of the north, where you will feel the misery of cold and frost, to which I am impassive. You will find near this place, if you follow not too tardily, a dead hare;* eat, and be refreshed. Come on, my enemy; we have yet to wrestle for our lives; but many hard and miserable hours must you endure, until that period shall arrive.'

Scoffing devil! Again do I vow vengeance; again do I devote thee, miserable fiend, to torture and death. Never will I omit my search, until he or I perish; and then with what ecstacy shall I join my Elizabeth, and those who even now prepare for me the reward of my tedious toil and horrible pilgrimage.

As I still pursued my journey to the northward, the snows thickened, and the cold increased in a degree almost too severe to support. The peasants were shut up in their hovels, and only a few of the most hardy ventured forth to seize the animals whom starvation had forced from their hiding-places to seek for prey. The rivers were covered with ice, and no fish could be procured; and thus I was cut off from my chief article of maintenance.

The triumph of my enemy increased with the difficulty of my labours. One inscription that he left was in these words: 'Prepare! your toils only begin: wrap yourself in furs, and provide food, for we shall soon enter upon a journey where your sufferings will satisfy my everlasting hatred.'

My courage and perseverance were invigorated by these scoffing words; I resolved not to fail in my purpose; and, calling on heaven to support me, I continued with unabated fervour to traverse immense deserts, until the ocean appeared at a distance, and formed the utmost boundary of the horizon. Oh! how unlike it was to the blue seas of the south! Covered with ice, it was only to be distinguished from land by its superior wildness and ruggedness. The Greeks wept for joy when they beheld the Mediterranean from the hills of Asia, and hailed with rapture the boundary of their toils.* I did not weep; but I knelt down, and, with a full heart, thanked my guiding spirit for conducting me in safety to the place where I hoped, notwithstanding my adversary's gibe, to meet and grapple with him.

Some weeks before this period I had procured a sledge and dogs, and thus traversed the snows with inconceivable speed. I know not whether the fiend possessed the same advantages; but I found that, as before I had daily lost ground in the pursuit, I now gained on him; so much so, that when I first saw the ocean, he was but one day's journey in advance, and I hoped to intercept him before he should reach the beach. With new courage, therefore, I pressed on, and in two days arrived at a wretched hamlet on the seashore. I inquired of the inhabitants concerning the fiend, and gained accurate information. A gigantic monster, they said, had arrived the night before, armed with a gun and many pistols; putting to flight the inhabitants of a solitary cottage, through fear of his terrific appearance. He had carried off their store of winter food, and, placing it in a sledge, to draw which he had seized on a numerous drove of trained dogs, he had harnessed them, and the same night, to the joy of the horror-struck villagers, had pursued his journey across the sea in a direction that led to no land; and they conjectured that he must speedily be destroyed by the breaking of the ice, or frozen by the eternal frosts.

On hearing this information, I suffered a temporary access of despair. He had escaped me; and I must commence a destructive and almost endless journey across the mountainous ices of the ocean,— amidst cold that few of the inhabitants could long endure, and which I, the native of a genial and sunny climate, could not hope to survive. Yet at the idea that the fiend should live and be triumphant, my rage and vengeance returned, and, like a mighty tide, overwhelmed every other feeling. After a slight repose, during which the spirits of the dead hovered round,* and instigated me to toil and revenge, I prepared for my journey.

I exchanged my land sledge for one fashioned for the inequalities of the frozen ocean; and, purchasing a plentiful stock of provisions, I departed from land.

I cannot guess how many days have passed since then; but I have endured misery, which nothing but the eternal sentiment of a just retribution burning within my heart could have enabled me to support. Immense and rugged mountains of ice often barred up my passage, and I often heard the thunder of the ground sea, which threatened my destruction. But again the frost came, and made the paths of the sea secure.

By the quantity of provision which I had consumed I should guess that I had passed three weeks in this journey; and the continual protraction of hope, returning back upon the heart, often wrung bitter drops of despondency and grief from my eyes. Despair had indeed almost secured her prey, and I should soon have sunk beneath this misery; when once, after the poor animals that carried me had with incredible toil gained the summit of a sloping ice mountain, and one sinking under his fatigue died, I viewed the expanse before me with anguish, when suddenly my eye caught a dark speck upon the dusky plain. I strained my sight to discover what it could be, and uttered a wild cry of ecstacy when I distinguished a sledge, and the distorted proportions of a well-known form within. Oh! with what a burning gush did hope revisit my heart! warm tears filled my eyes, which I hastily wiped away, that they might not intercept the view I had of the dæmon; but still my sight was dimmed by the burning drops, until, giving way to the emotions that oppressed me, I wept aloud.

But this was not the time for delay; I disencumbered the dogs of their dead companion, gave them a plentiful portion of food; and, after an hour's rest, which was absolutely necessary, and yet which was bitterly irksome to me, I continued my route. The sledge was still visible; nor did I again lose sight of it, except at the moments when for a short time some ice rock concealed it with its intervening crags. I indeed perceptibly gained on it; and when, after nearly two days' journey, I beheld my enemy at no more than a mile distant, my heart bounded within me.

But now, when I appeared almost within grasp of my enemy, my hopes were suddenly extinguished, and I lost all trace of him more utterly than I had ever done before. A ground sea was heard; the thunder of its progress, as the waters rolled and swelled beneath me, became every moment more ominous and terrific. I pressed on, but in vain. The wind arose; the sea roared; and, as with the mighty shock of an earthquake, it split, and cracked with a tremendous and overwhelming sound. The work was soon finished: in a few minutes a tumultuous sea rolled between me and my enemy, and I was left drifting on a scattered piece of ice, that was continually lessening, and thus preparing for me a hideous death.

In this manner many appalling hours passed; several of my dogs died; and I myself was about to sink under the accumulation of distress, when I saw your vessel riding at anchor, and holding forth to me hopes of succour and life. I had no conception that vessels ever came so far north, and was astounded at the sight. I quickly destroyed part of my sledge to construct oars; and by these means was enabled, with infinite fatigue, to move my ice-raft in the direction of your ship. I had determined, if you were going southward, still to trust myself to the mercy of the seas, rather than abandon my purpose. I hoped to induce you to grant me a boat with which I could still pursue my enemy. But your direction was northward. You took me on board when my vigour was exhausted, and I should soon have sunk under my multiplied hardships into a death, which I still dread,—for my task is unfulfilled.

Oh! when will my guiding spirit, in conducting me to the dæmon, allow me the rest I so much desire; or must I die, and he yet live? If I do, swear to me, Walton, that he shall not escape; that you will seek him, and satisfy my vengeance in his death. Yet, do I dare ask you to undertake my pilgrimage, to endure the hardships that I have undergone? No; I am not so selfish. Yet, when I am dead, if he should appear; if the ministers of vengeance should conduct him to you, swear that he shall not live—swear that he shall not triumph over my accumulated woes, and live to make another such a wretch as I am. He is eloquent and persuasive; and once his words had even power over my heart: but trust him not. His soul is as hellish as his form, full of treachery and fiend-like malice. Hear him not; call on the manes* of William, Justine, Clerval, Elizabeth, my father, and of the wretched Victor, and thrust your sword into his heart. I will hover near, and direct the steel aright

WALTON, *in continuation.*

August 26th, 17—.

You have read this strange and terrific story, Margaret; and do you not feel your blood congealed with horror, like that which even now curdles mine? Sometimes, seized with sudden agony, he could not continue his tale; at others, his voice broken, yet piercing, uttered with difficulty the words so replete with agony. His fine and lovely eyes were now lighted up with indignation, now subdued to downcast sorrow, and quenched in infinite wretchedness. Sometimes he commanded his countenance and tones, and related the most horrible incidents with a tranquil voice, suppressing every mark of agitation; then, like a volcano bursting forth, his face would suddenly change to an expression of the wildest rage, as he shrieked out imprecations on his persecutor.

His tale is connected,* and told with an appearance of the simplest truth; yet I own to you that the letters of Felix and Safie, which he shewed me, and the apparition of the monster, seen from our ship, brought to me a greater conviction of the truth of his narrative than his asseverations,* however earnest and connected. Such a monster has then really existence; I cannot doubt it; yet I am lost in surprise and admiration. Sometimes I endeavoured to gain from Frankenstein the particulars of his creature's formation; but on this point he was impenetrable.

'Are you mad, my friend?' said he, 'or whither does your senseless curiosity lead you? Would you also create for yourself and the world a demoniacal enemy? Or to what do your questions tend? Peace, peace! learn my miseries, and do not seek to increase your own.'

Frankenstein discovered that I made notes concerning his history: he asked to see them, and then himself corrected and augmented them in many places; but principally in giving the life and spirit to the conversations he held with his enemy. 'Since you have preserved my narration,' said he, 'I would not that a mutilated one should go down to posterity.'

Thus has a week passed away, while I have listened to the strangest tale that ever imagination formed. My thoughts, and every feeling of my soul, have been drunk up by the interest for my guest, which this tale, and his own elevated and gentle manners have created. I wish to soothe him; yet can I counsel one so infinitely miserable, so destitute of every hope of consolation, to live? Oh, no! the only joy that he can now know will be when he composes his shattered feelings to peace and death. Yet he enjoys one comfort, the offspring of solitude and delirium: he believes, that, when in dreams he holds converse with his friends, and derives from that communion consolation for his miseries, or excitements to his vengeance, that they are not the creations of his fancy, but the real beings who visit him from the regions of a remote world. This faith gives a solemnity to his reveries that render them to me almost as imposing and interesting as truth.

Our conversations are not always confined to his own history and misfortunes. On every point of general literature he displays unbounded knowledge, and a quick and piercing apprehension. His eloquence is forcible and touching; nor can I hear him, when he relates a pathetic incident, or endeavours to move the passions of pity or love, without tears. What a glorious creature must he have been in the days of his prosperity, when he is thus noble and godlike in ruin. He seems to feel his own worth, and the greatness of his fall.

'When younger,' said he, 'I felt as if I were destined for some great enterprise. My feelings are profound; but I possessed a coolness of judgment that fitted me for illustrious achievements. This sentiment of the worth of my nature supported me, when others would have been oppressed; for I deemed it criminal to throw away in useless grief those talents that might be useful to my fellow-creatures. When I reflected on the work I had completed, no less a one than the

creation of a sensitive and rational animal, I could not rank myself with
the herd of common projectors. But this feeling, which supported me
in the commencement of my career, now serves only to plunge me lower
in the dust. All my speculations and hopes are as nothing; and, like
the archangel who aspired to omnipotence, I am chained in an eternal
hell.* My imagination was vivid, yet my powers of analysis and application were intense; by the union of these qualities I conceived the
idea, and executed the creation of a man. Even now I cannot recollect,
without passion, my reveries while the work was incomplete. I trod
heaven in my thoughts, now exulting in my powers, now burning with
the idea of their effects. From my infancy I was imbued with high
hopes and a lofty ambition; but how am I sunk! Oh! my friend, if you
had known me as I once was, you would not recognize me in this state
of degradation. Despondency rarely visited my heart; a high destiny
seemed to bear me on, until I fell, never, never again to rise.'

Must I then lose this admirable being? I have longed for a friend;
I have sought one who would sympathize with and love me. Behold,
on these desert seas I have found such a one; but, I fear, I have gained
him only to know his value, and lose him. I would reconcile him to
life, but he repulses the idea.

'I thank you, Walton,' he said, 'for your kind intentions towards so
miserable a wretch; but when you speak of new ties, and fresh affections, think you that any can replace those who are gone? Can any man
be to me as Clerval was; or any woman another Elizabeth? Even where
the affections are not strongly moved by any superior excellence, the
companions of our childhood always possess a certain power over our
minds, which hardly any later friend can obtain. They know our
infantine dispositions, which, however they may be afterwards modified, are never eradicated; and they can judge of our actions with
more certain conclusions as to the integrity of our motives. A sister or
a brother can never, unless indeed such symptoms have been shewn
early, suspect the other of fraud or false dealing, when another friend,
however strongly he may be attached, may, in spite of himself, be
invaded with suspicion. But I enjoyed friends, dear not only through
habit and association, but from their own merits; and, wherever I am,
the soothing voice of my Elizabeth, and the conversation of Clerval,
will be ever whispered in my ear. They are dead; and but one feeling
in such a solitude can persuade me to preserve my life. If I were engaged
in any high undertaking or design, fraught with extensive utility to

my fellow-creatures, then could I live to fulfil it. But such is not my destiny; I must pursue and destroy the being to whom I gave existence; then my lot on earth will be fulfilled, and I may die.'

September 2d.

MY BELOVED SISTER,

I write to you, encompassed by peril, and ignorant whether I am ever doomed to see again dear England, and the dearer friends that inhabit it. I am surrounded by mountains of ice, which admit of no escape, and threaten every moment to crush my vessel. The brave fellows, whom I have persuaded to be my companions, look towards me for aid; but I have none to bestow. There is something terribly appalling in our situation, yet my courage and hopes do not desert me. We may survive; and if we do not, I will repeat the lessons of my Seneca,* and die with a good heart.

Yet what, Margaret, will be the state of your mind? You will not hear of my destruction, and you will anxiously await my return. Years will pass, and you will have visitings of despair, and yet be tortured by hope. Oh! my beloved sister, the sickening failings of your heart-felt expectations are, in prospect, more terrible to me than my own death. But you have a husband, and lovely children; you may be happy: heaven bless you, and make you so!

My unfortunate guest regards me with the tenderest compassion. He endeavours to fill me with hope; and talks as if life were a possession which he valued. He reminds me how often the same accidents have happened to other navigators, who have attempted this sea, and, in spite of myself, he fills me with cheerful auguries. Even the sailors feel the power of his eloquence: when he speaks, they no longer despair; he rouses their energies, and, while they hear his voice, they believe these vast mountains of ice are mole-hills, which will vanish before the resolutions of man. These feelings are transitory; each day's expectation delayed fills them with fear, and I almost dread a mutiny caused by this despair.

September 5th.

A scene has just passed of such uncommon interest, that although it is highly probable that these papers may never reach you, yet I cannot forbear recording it.

We are still surrounded by mountains of ice, still in imminent danger of being crushed in their conflict. The cold is excessive, and many of my unfortunate comrades have already found a grave amidst this scene of desolation. Frankenstein has daily declined in health: a feverish fire still glimmers in his eyes; but he is exhausted, and, when suddenly roused to any exertion, he speedily sinks again into apparent lifelessness.

I mentioned in my last letter the fears I entertained of a mutiny. This morning, as I sat watching the wan countenance of my friend— his eyes half closed, and his limbs hanging listlessly,—I was roused by half a dozen of the sailors, who desired admission into the cabin. They entered; and their leader addressed me. He told me that he and his companions had been chosen by the other sailors to come in deputation to me, to make me a demand, which, in justice, I could not refuse. We were immured in ice, and should probably never escape; but they feared that if, as was possible, the ice should dissipate, and a free passage be opened, I should be rash enough to continue my voyage, and lead them into fresh dangers, after they might happily have surmounted this. They desired, therefore, that I should engage with a solemn promise, that if the vessel should be freed, I would instantly direct my course southward.

This speech troubled me. I had not despaired; nor had I yet conceived the idea of returning, if set free. Yet could I, in justice, or even in possibility, refuse this demand? I hesitated before I answered; when Frankenstein, who had at first been silent, and, indeed, appeared hardly to have force enough to attend, now roused himself; his eyes sparkled, and his cheeks flushed with momentary vigour. Turning towards the men, he said— *exploration at cost*

'What do you mean? What do you demand of your captain? Are you then so easily turned from your design? Did you not call this a glorious expedition? and wherefore was it glorious? Not because the way was smooth and placid as a southern sea, but because it was full of dangers and terror; because, at every new incident, your fortitude was to be called forth, and your courage exhibited; because danger and death surrounded, and these dangers you were to brave and overcome. For this was it a glorious, for this was it an honourable undertaking. You were hereafter to be hailed as the benefactors of your species; your name adored, as belonging to brave men who encountered death for honour and the benefit of mankind. And now, behold, with the first imagination of danger, or, if you will, the first mighty and terrific trial of your courage, you shrink away, and are content to be handed down as men who had not strength enough to endure cold and peril; and so, poor souls, they were chilly, and returned to their warm firesides. Why, that requires not this preparation; ye need not have come thus far, and dragged your captain to the shame of a defeat, merely to prove yourselves cowards. Oh! be men, or be more than men. Be steady to your purposes, and firm as a rock. This ice is not made of such stuff as your hearts might be; it is mutable, cannot withstand you, if you say that it shall not. Do not return to your families with the stigma of disgrace marked on your brows. Return as heroes who have fought and conquered, and who know not what it is to turn their backs on the foe.'*

He spoke this with a voice so modulated to the different feelings expressed in his speech, with an eye so full of lofty design and heroism, that can you wonder that these men were moved. They looked at one another, and were unable to reply. I spoke; I told them to retire, and consider of what had been said: that I would not lead them further north, if they strenuously desired the contrary; but that I hoped that, with reflection, their courage would return.

They retired, and I turned towards my friend; but he was sunk in languor, and almost deprived of life. *able to lie*

How all this will terminate, I know not; but I had rather die, than return shamefully,—my purpose unfulfilled. Yet I fear such will be my fate; the men, unsupported by ideas of glory and honour, can never willingly continue to endure their present hardships.

September 7th.

The die is cast; I have consented to return, if we are not destroyed. Thus are my hopes blasted by cowardice and indecision; I come back ignorant and disappointed. It requires more philosophy than I possess, to bear this injustice with patience.

September 12th.

It is past; I am returning to England. I have lost my hopes of utility and glory;—I have lost my friend. But I will endeavour to detail these bitter circumstances to you, my dear sister; and, while I am wafted towards England, and towards you, I will not despond.

September 9th,* the ice began to move, and roarings like thunder were heard at a distance, as the islands split and cracked in every direction. We were in the most imminent peril; but, as we could only remain passive, my chief attention was occupied by my unfortunate guest, whose illness increased in such a degree, that he was entirely confined to his bed. The ice cracked behind us, and was driven with force towards the north; a breeze sprung from the west, and on the 11th the passage towards the south became perfectly free. When the sailors saw this, and that their return to their native country was apparently assured, a shout of tumultuous joy broke from them, loud and long-continued. Frankenstein, who was dozing, awoke, and asked the cause of the tumult. 'They shout,' I said, 'because they will soon return to England.'

'Do you then really return?'

'Alas! yes; I cannot withstand their demands. I cannot lead them unwillingly to danger, and I must return.'

'Do so, if you will; but I will not. You may give up your purpose; but mine is assigned to me by heaven, and I dare not. I am weak; but surely the spirits who assist my vengeance will endow me with sufficient strength.' Saying this, he endeavoured to spring from the bed, but the exertion was too great for him; he fell back, and fainted.

It was long before he was restored; and I often thought that life was entirely extinct. At length he opened his eyes, but he breathed with difficulty, and was unable to speak. The surgeon gave him a composing draught, and ordered us to leave him undisturbed. In the mean time he told me, that my friend had certainly not many hours to live.

His sentence was pronounced; and I could only grieve, and be patient. I sat by his bed watching him; his eyes were closed, and I thought he slept; but presently he called to me in a feeble voice, and, bidding me come near, said—'Alas! the strength I relied on is gone; I feel that I shall soon die, and he, my enemy and persecutor, may still be in being. Think not, Walton, that in the last moments of my existence I feel that burning hatred, and ardent desire of revenge, I once expressed, but I feel myself justified in desiring the death of my adversary. During these last days I have been occupied in examining my past conduct; nor do I find it blameable. In a fit of enthusiastic madness I created a rational creature, and was bound towards him, to assure, as far as was in my power, his happiness and well-being. This was my duty; but there was another still paramount to that. My duties towards my fellow-creatures had greater claims to my attention, because they included a greater proportion of happiness or misery. Urged by this view, I refused, and I did right in refusing, to create a companion for the first creature. He shewed unparalleled malignity and selfishness, in evil: he destroyed my friends; he devoted to destruction beings who possessed exquisite sensations, happiness, and wisdom; nor do

I know where this thirst for vengeance may end. Miserable himself, that he may render no other wretched, he ought to die. The task of his destruction was mine, but I have failed. When actuated by selfish and vicious motives, I asked you to undertake my unfinished work; and I renew this request now, when I am only induced by reason and virtue.

'Yet I cannot ask you to renounce your country and friends, to fulfil this task; and now, that you are returning to England, you will have little chance of meeting with him. But the consideration of these points, and the well-balancing of what you may esteem your duties, I leave to you; my judgment and ideas are already disturbed by the near approach of death. I dare not ask you to do what I think right, for I may still be misled by passion.

'That he should live to be an instrument of mischief disturbs me; in other respects this hour, when I momentarily expect my release, is the only happy one which I have enjoyed for several years. The forms of the beloved dead flit before me, and I hasten to their arms. Farewell, Walton! Seek happiness in tranquillity, and avoid ambition, even if it be only the apparently innocent one of distinguishing yourself in science and discoveries. Yet why do I say this? I have myself been blasted in these hopes, yet another may succeed.'

His voice became fainter as he spoke; and at length, exhausted by his effort, he sunk into silence. About half an hour afterwards he attempted again to speak, but was unable; he pressed my hand feebly, and his eyes closed for ever, while the irradiation of a gentle smile passed away from his lips.

Margaret, what comment can I make on the untimely extinction of this glorious spirit? What can I say, that will enable you to understand the depth of my sorrow? All that I should express would be inadequate and feeble. My tears flow; my mind is overshadowed by a cloud of disappointment But I journey towards England, and I may there find consolation.

I am interrupted. What do these sounds portend? It is midnight; the breeze blows fairly, and the watch on deck scarcely stir. Again; there is a sound as of a human voice, but hoarser; it comes from the cabin where the remains of Frankenstein still lie. I must arise, and examine. Good night, my sister.

Great God! what a scene has just taken place! I am yet dizzy with the remembrance of it. I hardly know whether I shall have the power to detail it; yet the tale which I have recorded would be incomplete without this final and wonderful catastrophe.

I entered the cabin, where lay the remains of my ill-fated and admirable friend. Over him hung a form which I cannot find words to describe; gigantic in stature, yet uncouth and distorted in its proportions. As he hung over the coffin, his face was concealed by long locks of ragged hair; but one vast hand was extended, in colour and apparent texture like that of a mummy. When he heard the sound of my approach, he ceased to utter exclamations of grief and horror, and sprung towards the window. Never did I behold a vision so horrible as his face, of such loathsome, yet appalling hideousness. I shut my eyes involuntarily, and endeavoured to recollect what were my duties with regard to this destroyer. I called on him to stay.

He paused, looking on me with wonder; and, again turning towards the lifeless form of his creator, he seemed to forget my presence, and every feature and gesture seemed instigated by the wildest rage of some uncontrollable passion.

'That is also my victim!' he exclaimed; 'in his murder my crimes are consummated; the miserable series of my being is wound to its close! Oh, Frankenstein! generous and self-devoted being! what does it avail that I now ask thee to pardon me? I, who irretrievably destroyed thee by destroying all thou lovedst. Alas! he is cold; he may not answer me.'

His voice seemed suffocated; and my first impulses, which had suggested to me the duty of obeying the dying request of my friend, in destroying his enemy, were now suspended by a mixture of curiosity and compassion. I approached this tremendous being; I dared not again raise my looks upon his face, there was something so scaring and unearthly in his ugliness. I attempted to speak, but the words died away on my lips. The monster continued to utter wild and incoherent self-reproaches. At length I gathered resolution to address him, in a pause of the tempest of his passion: 'Your repentance,' I said, 'is now superfluous. If you had listened to the voice of conscience, and heeded the stings of remorse, before you had urged your diabolical vengeance to this extremity, Frankenstein would yet have lived.'

'And do you dream?' said the dæmon; 'do you think that I was then dead to agony and remorse?—He,' he continued, pointing to the corpse, 'he suffered not more in the consummation of the deed;—oh! not the ten-thousandth portion of the anguish that was mine during the lingering detail of its execution. A frightful selfishness hurried me on, while my heart was poisoned with remorse. Think ye that the groans of Clerval were music to my ears? My heart was fashioned to be susceptible of love and sympathy; and, when wrenched by misery to vice and hatred, it did not endure the violence of the change without torture, such as you cannot even imagine.

'After the murder of Clerval, I returned to Switzerland, heart-broken and overcome. I pitied Frankenstein; my pity amounted to horror: I abhorred myself. But when I discovered that he, the author at once of my existence and of its unspeakable torments, dared to hope for happiness; that while he accumulated wretchedness and despair upon me, he sought his own enjoyment in feelings and passions from the indulgence of which I was for ever barred, then impotent envy and bitter indignation filled me with an insatiable thirst for vengeance. I recollected my threat, and resolved that it should be accomplished. I knew that I was preparing for myself a deadly torture; but I was the slave, not the master of an impulse, which I detested, yet could not disobey. Yet when she died!—nay, then I was not miserable. I had cast off all feeling, subdued all anguish to riot in the excess of my despair. Evil thenceforth became my good.* Urged thus far, I had no choice but to adapt my nature to an element which I had willingly chosen. The completion of my demoniacal design became an insatiable passion. And now it is ended; there is my last victim!'

I was at first touched by the expressions of his misery; yet when I called to mind what Frankenstein had said of his powers of eloquence and persuasion, and when I again cast my eyes on the lifeless form of my friend, indignation was rekindled within me. 'Wretch!' I said, 'it is well that you come here to whine over the desolation that you have made. You throw a torch into a pile of buildings, and when they are consumed you sit among the ruins, and lament the fall. Hypocritical fiend! if he whom you mourn still lived, still would he be the object, again would he become the prey of your accursed vengeance. It is not pity that you feel; you lament only because the victim of your malignity is withdrawn from your power.'

'Oh, it is not thus—not thus,' interrupted the being; 'yet such must be the impression conveyed to you by what appears to be the purport of my actions. Yet I seek not a fellow-feeling in my misery. No sympathy may I ever find. When I first sought it, it was the love of virtue, the feelings of happiness and affection with which my whole being

overflowed, that I wished to be participated. But now, that virtue has
become to me a shadow, and that happiness and affection are turned
into bitter and loathing despair, in what should I seek for sympathy?
I am content to suffer alone, while my sufferings shall endure: when
I die, I am well satisfied that abhorrence and opprobrium should load
my memory. Once my fancy was soothed with dreams of virtue, of
fame, and of enjoyment. Once I falsely hoped to meet with beings,
who, pardoning my outward form, would love me for the excellent
qualities which I was capable of bringing forth. I was nourished with
high thoughts of honour and devotion. But now vice, has degraded
me beneath the meanest animal. No crime, no mischief, no malignity,
no misery, can be found comparable to mine. When I call over* the
frightful catalogue of my deeds, I cannot believe that I am he whose
thoughts were once filled with sublime and transcendant visions of
the beauty and the majesty of goodness. But it is even so; the fallen
angel becomes a malignant devil. Yet even that enemy of God and
man had friends and associates in his desolation; I am quite alone.

'You, who call Frankenstein your friend, seem to have a knowledge
of my crimes and his misfortunes. But, in the detail which he gave
you of them, he could not sum up the hours and months of misery
which I endured, wasting in impotent passions. For whilst I destroyed
his hopes, I did not satisfy my own desires. They were for ever ardent
and craving; still I desired love and fellowship, and I was still spurned.
Was there no injustice in this? Am I to be thought the only criminal,
when all human kind sinned against me? Why do you not hate Felix,
who drove his friend from his door with contumely?* Why do you not
execrate the rustic who sought to destroy the saviour of his child?
Nay, these are are virtuous and immaculate beings? I, the miserable
and the abandoned, am an abortion,* to be spurned at, and kicked,
and trampled on. Even now my blood boils at the recollection of this
injustice.

'But it is true that I am a wretch. I have murdered the lovely and
the helpless; I have strangled the innocent as they slept, and grasped
to death his throat who never injured me or any other living thing.
I have devoted my creator, the select specimen of all that is worthy of
love and admiration among men, to misery; I have pursued him even
to that irremediable ruin. There he lies, white and cold in death. You
hate me; but your abhorrence cannot equal that with which I regard
myself. I look on the hands which executed the deed; I think on the

heart in which the imagination of it was conceived, and long for the moment when they will meet my eyes, when it will haunt my thoughts, no more.

'Fear not that I shall be the instrument of future mischief. My work is nearly complete. Neither your's nor any man's death is needed to consummate the series of my being, and accomplish that which must be done; but it requires my own. Do not think that I shall be slow to perform this sacrifice. I shall quit your vessel on the ice-raft which brought me hither, and shall seek the most northern extremity of the globe; I shall collect my funeral pile, and consume to ashes this miserable frame, that its remains may afford no light to any curious and unhallowed wretch, who would create such another as I have been.* I shall die. I shall no longer feel the agonies which now consume me, or be the prey of feelings unsatisfied, yet unquenched. He is dead who called me into being; and when I shall be no more, the very remembrance of us both will speedily vanish. I shall no longer see the sun or stars, or feel the winds play on my cheeks. Light, feeling, and sense, will pass away; and in this condition must I find my happiness. Some years ago, when the images which this world affords first opened upon me, when I felt the cheering warmth of summer, and heard the rustling of the leaves and the chirping of the birds, and these were all to me, I should have wept to die; now it is my only consolation. Polluted by crimes, and torn by the bitterest remorse, where can I find rest but in death?

'Farewell! I leave you, and in you the last of human kind whom these eyes will ever behold. Farewell, Frankenstein! If thou wert yet alive, and yet cherished a desire of revenge against me, it would be better satiated in my life than in my destruction. But it was not so; thou didst seek my extinction, that I might not cause greater wretchedness; and if yet, in some mode unknown to me, thou hast not yet ceased to think and feel, thou desirest not my life for my own misery. Blasted as thou wert, my agony was still superior to thine; for the bitter sting of remorse may not cease to rankle in my wounds until death shall close them for ever.

'But soon,' he cried, with sad and solemn enthusiasm, 'I shall die, and what I now feel be no longer felt. Soon these burning miseries will be extinct. I shall ascend my funeral pile triumphantly, and exult in the agony of the torturing flames. The light of that conflagration will fade away; my ashes will be swept into the sea by the winds. My spirit will sleep in peace; or if it thinks, it will not surely think thus. Farewell.'

He sprung from the cabin-window, as he said this, upon the ice-raft which lay close to the vessel. He was soon borne away by the waves, and lost in darkness and distance.

THE END.

APPENDIX A

AUTHOR'S INTRODUCTION TO THE STANDARD NOVELS EDITION (1831)

THE Publishers of the Standard Novels,* in selecting 'Frankenstein' for one of their series, expressed a wish that I should furnish them with some account of the origin of the story. I am the more willing to comply, because I shall thus give a general answer to the question, so very frequently asked me—'How I, then a young girl, came to think of, and to dilate upon, so very hideous an idea?' It is true that I am very averse to bringing myself forward in print; but as my account will only appear as an appendage to a former production, and as it will be confined to such topics as have connection with my authorship alone, I can scarcely accuse myself of a personal intrusion.

It is not singular that, as the daughter of two persons of distinguished literary celebrity, I should very early in life have thought of writing. As a child I scribbled; and my favourite pastime, during the hours given me for recreation, was to 'write stories.' Still I had a dearer pleasure than this, which was the formation of castles in the air—the indulging in waking dreams—the following up trains of thought, which had for their subject the formation of a succession of imaginary incidents. My dreams were at once more fantastic and agreeable than my writings. In the latter I was a close imitator—rather doing as others had done than putting down the suggestions of my own mind. What I wrote was intended at least for one other eye—my childhood's companion and friend;* but my dreams were all my own; I accounted for them to nobody; they were my refuge when annoyed—my dearest pleasure when free.

I lived principally in the country as a girl, and passed a considerable time in Scotland.* I made occasional visits to the more picturesque parts; but my habitual residence was on the blank and dreary northern shores of the Tay, near Dundee. Blank and dreary on retrospection I call them; they were not so to me then. They were the eyry* of freedom, and the pleasant region where unheeded I could commune with the creatures of my fancy. I wrote then—but in a most common-place style. It was beneath the trees of the grounds belonging to our house, or on the bleak sides of the woodless mountains near, that my true compositions, the airy flights of my imagination, were born and fostered. I did not make myself the heroine of my tales. Life appeared to me too common-place an affair as regarded myself. I could not figure to myself that romantic woes or wonderful events would ever be my lot; but I was not confined to my own identity, and I could people the hours with creations far more interesting to me at that age than my own sensations.

After this my life became busier, and reality stood in place of fiction. My husband, however, was from the first, very anxious that I should prove myself worthy of my parentage, and enrol myself on the page of fame. He was for ever inciting me to obtain literary reputation, which even on my own part I cared for then, though since I have become infinitely indifferent to it. At this time he desired that I should write, not so much with the idea that I could produce any thing worthy of notice, but that he might himself judge how far I possessed the promise of better things hereafter. Still I did nothing. Travelling, and the cares of a family, occupied my time; and study, in the way of reading, or improving my ideas in communication with his far more cultivated mind, was all of literary employment that engaged my attention.

In the summer of 1816, we visited Switzerland, and became the neighbours of Lord Byron. At first we spent our pleasant hours on the lake, or wandering on its shores; and Lord Byron, who was writing the third canto of Childe Harold, was the only one among us who put his thoughts upon paper. These, as he brought them successively to us, clothed in all the light and harmony of poetry, seemed to stamp as divine the glories of heaven and earth, whose influences we partook with him.

But it proved a wet, ungenial summer, and incessant rain often confined us for days to the house. Some volumes of ghost stories, translated from the German into French, fell into our hands. There was the History of the Inconstant Lover, who, when he thought to clasp the bride to whom he had pledged his vows, found himself in the arms of the pale ghost of her whom he had deserted. There was the tale of the sinful founder of his race,* whose miserable doom it was to bestow the kiss of death on all the younger sons of his fated house, just when they reached the age of promise. His gigantic, shadowy form, clothed like the ghost in Hamlet, in complete armour, but with the beaver up, was seen at midnight, by the moon's fitful beams, to advance slowly along the gloomy avenue. The shape was lost beneath the shadow of the castle walls; but soon a gate swung back, a step was heard, the door of the chamber opened, and he advanced to the couch of the blooming youths, cradled in healthy sleep. Eternal sorrow sat upon his face as he bent down and kissed the forehead of the boys, who from that hour withered like flowers snapt upon the stalk. I have not seen these stories since then; but their incidents are as fresh in my mind as if I had read them yesterday.

'We will each write a ghost story,' said Lord Byron; and his proposition was acceded to. There were four of us.* The noble author began a tale, a fragment of which he printed at the end of his poem of Mazeppa.* Shelley, more apt to embody ideas and sentiments in the radiance of brilliant imagery, and in the music of the most melodious verse that adorns our language, than to invent the machinery of a story, commenced one founded on the experiences of his early life. Poor Polidori had some terrible idea about a skull-headed lady, who was so punished for peeping through a key-hole*—what to see I forget—something very shocking and wrong of course; but when she was reduced to a worse condition than the renowned Tom of Coventry,* he did not know what to do with her, and was obliged to dispatch her to the tomb of the Capulets,* the only place for which she was fitted. The illustrious poets also, annoyed by the platitude of prose, speedily relinquished their uncongenial task.

I busied myself *to think of a story*,—a story to rival those which had excited us to this task. One which would speak to the mysterious fears of our nature, and awaken thrilling horror—one to make the reader dread to look round, to curdle the blood, and quicken the beatings of the heart.* If I did not accomplish these things, my ghost story would be unworthy of its name. I thought and pondered—vainly. I felt that blank incapability of invention which is the greatest misery of authorship, when dull Nothing replies to our anxious invocations. *Have you thought of a story?* I was asked each morning, and each morning I was forced to reply with a mortifying negative.

Every thing must have a beginning, to speak in Sanchean phrase;* and that beginning must be linked to something that went before. The Hindoos give the world an elephant to support it, but they make the elephant stand upon a tortoise.* Invention, it must be humbly admitted, does not consist in creating out of void, but out of chaos;* the materials must, in the first place, be afforded: it can give form to dark, shapeless substances, but cannot bring into being the substance itself. In all matters of discovery and invention, even of those that appertain to the imagination, we are continually reminded of the story of Columbus and his egg.* Invention consists in the capacity of seizing on the capabilities of a subject, and in the power of moulding and fashioning ideas suggested to it.

Many and long were the conversations between Lord Byron and Shelley, to which I was a devout but nearly silent listener. During one of these, various philosophical doctrines were discussed, and among others the nature of the principle of life, and whether there was any probability of its ever being discovered and communicated.* They talked of the experiments of Dr. Darwin, (I speak not of what the Doctor really did, or said that he did, but, as more to my purpose, of what was then spoken of as having been done by him,) who preserved a piece of vermicelli in a glass case, till by some extraordinary means it began to move with voluntary motion.* Not thus, after all, would life be given. Perhaps a corpse would be reanimated; galvanism* had given token of such things: perhaps the component parts of a creature might be manufactured, brought together, and endued with vital warmth.

Night waned upon this talk, and even the witching hour had gone by, before we retired to rest. When I placed my head on my pillow, I did not sleep, nor could I be said to think. My imagination, unbidden,* possessed and guided me, gifting the successive images that arose in my mind with a vividness far beyond the usual bounds of reverie. I saw—with shut eyes, but acute mental vision—I saw the pale student of unhallowed arts kneeling beside the thing he had put together. I saw the hideous phantasm of a man stretched out, and then, on the working of some powerful engine, show signs of life, and stir with an uneasy, half vital motion. Frightful must it be; for supremely frightful would be the effect of any human endeavour to mock the stupendous mechanism of the Creator of the world.* His success would terrify the artist; he would rush away from his odious handywork,* horror-stricken. He would hope that, left to itself, the slight spark of life which he had communicated would fade; that this thing, which had received such imperfect animation, would subside into dead matter; and he might sleep in the belief that the silence of the grave would quench forever the transient existence of the hideous corpse which he had looked upon as the cradle of life. He sleeps; but he is awakened; he opens his eyes; behold, the horrid thing stands at his bedside, opening his curtains and looking on him with yellow, watery, but speculative eyes.

I opened mine in terror. The idea so possessed my mind, that a thrill of fear ran through me, and I wished to exchange the ghastly image of my fancy for the realities around. I see them still; the very room, the dark *parquet*,* the closed shutters, with the moonlight struggling through, and the sense I had that the glassy lake and white high Alps were beyond. I could not so easily get rid of my hideous phantom; still it haunted me. I must try to think of something else. I recurred to my ghost story,—my tiresome unlucky ghost story! O! if I could only contrive one which would frighten my reader as I myself had been frightened that night!

Swift as light and as cheering was the idea that broke in upon me. 'I have found it! What terrified me will terrify others; and I need only describe the spectre which had haunted my midnight pillow.' On the morrow I announced that I had *thought of a story*. I began that day with the words, *It was on a dreary night of November*,* making only a transcript of the grim terrors of my waking dream.

At first I thought but of a few pages—of a short tale; but Shelley urged me to develope the idea at greater length. I certainly did not owe the suggestion of one incident, nor scarcely of one train of feeling, to my husband,* and yet but for his incitement, it would never have taken the form in which it was presented to the world. From this declaration I must except the preface.* As far as I can recollect, it was entirely written by him.

And now, once again, I bid my hideous progeny go forth and prosper. I have affection for it, for it was the offspring of happy days, when death and grief were but words, which found no true echo in my heart. Its several pages speak of many a walk, many a drive, and many a conversation, when I was not alone; and my companion was one who, in this world, I shall never see more. But this is for myself; my readers have nothing to do with these associations.

I will add but one word as to the alterations I have made. They are principally those of style. I have changed no portion of the story nor introduced any new ideas or circumstances. I have mended the language where it was so bald as to interfere with the interest of the narrative; and these changes occur almost exclusively in the beginning of the first volume. Throughout they are entirely confined to such parts as are mere adjuncts to the story, leaving the core and substance of it untouched.*

M.W.S.

London, October 15. 1831.

APPENDIX B

THE THIRD EDITION (1831):
SUBSTANTIVE CHANGES

THIS Appendix outlines the significant changes between the 1818 text of *Frankenstein*, composed by Mary Shelley in 1816–17 and edited by Percy Shelley, and the third edition of 1831. Only significantly rewritten passages are included; changes in individual words and phrases are not recorded here.[1]

For this final lifetime edition, Shelley rewrote the first two chapters and in doing so turned them into three chapters. She presented Victor's education as accidental and fateful—after his early flirtation with alchemy he learns about electricity, for example, from a friend of the family rather than from his father. She removed much scientific detail, and so instead of researching natural philosophy and debating vitalism, Victor aspires to Romantic idealism in seeking 'the inner spirit of nature and the mysterious soul of man . . . the metaphysical, or, in its highest sense, the physical secrets of the world' (p. 185).[2] His language accordingly becomes more spiritual: he refers to the 'guardian angel of my life' (p. 187) and his 'soul . . . grappling with a palpable enemy' (p. 188)—an enemy that leads him to his ominous tutors at Ingolstadt and a 'return to my ancient studies' (p. 189). Led thus to forbidden knowledge by an evil providence or doom, Victor is partly absolved of individual responsibility: his monomania is allayed and he is presented as a less culpable and more principled character, more attuned to fellow beings and alive to the risks attached to Walton's ambitions. Victor is also, to a degree, sentimentalized—as are Walton, Elizabeth, and his father. Elizabeth is no longer Victor's cousin and is also presented as less forthright in her language and opinions if rather more ethereal in her appearance. Meanwhile, the whole Frankenstein family is in better health and there is now no tang of decaying aristocracy that so fascinates many writers of the Gothic. There are also more minor changes: Victor's parents have visited Lake Como and Elizabeth has property there—perhaps a memory of the Shelleys' intention in 1818 to settle there—and several

---

[1] For the sake of consistency I have adopted Marilyn Butler's selection of passages (see Butler (ed.), *Frankenstein or The Modern Prometheus: The 1818 Text* (London: William Pickering, 1993; repr. Oxford: Oxford University Press, 1994), 200–28, with certain revisions); for a full account of the 1831 changes see James Rieger (ed.), *Frankenstein or The Modern Prometheus: The 1818 Text (with Variant Readings, an Introduction, and Notes)* (Chicago: Chicago University Press, 1982).

[2] See Butler (ed.), *Frankenstein*, 198–200.

passages of picturesque scenery are elaborated consistent with the style that characterizes Shelley's novel *The Last Man* (1826). The 1831 version is therefore less urgent, more reflective, and more compassionate— mourning, perhaps, an earlier, more impassioned era.

The page numbers before each substantive variant refer to the present edition. Catchwords for the 1818 reading are given first and are distinguished from the 1831 reading by a square bracket, thus]. The 1831 edition was printed in one volume and consequently renumbers the chapters as a single sequence.

VOLUME I

11 He is, indeed...moreover, heroically generous.] This circumstance, added to his well known integrity and dauntless courage, made me very desirous to engage him. A youth passed in solitude, my best years spent under your gentle and feminine fosterage, has so refined the groundwork of my character, that I cannot overcome an intense dis- taste to the usual brutality exercised on board ship: I have never believed it to be necessary; and when I heard of a mariner equally noted for his kindliness of heart, and the respect and obedience paid to him by his crew, I felt myself peculiarly fortunate in being able to secure his ser- vices. I heard of him first in rather a romantic manner, from a lady who owes to him the happiness of her life. This, briefly, is his story.

has passed all...not suppose that,] is wholly uneducated: he is as silent as a Turk, and a kind of ignorant carelessness attends him, which, while it renders his conduct the more astonishing, detracts from the interest and sympathy which otherwise he would command.
    Yet do not suppose,

for my safety.] for my safety, or if I should come back to you as worn and woful as the 'Ancient Mariner?' You will smile at my allusion; but I will disclose a secret. I have often attributed my attachment to, my passionate enthusiasm for, the dangerous mysteries of ocean, to that production of the most imaginative of modern poets. There is some- thing at work in my soul, which I do not understand. I am practically industrious—pains-taking; a workman to execute with perseverance and labour:—but besides this, there is a love for the marvellous, a belief in the marvellous, intertwined in all my projects, which hurries me out of the common pathways of men, even to the wild sea and unvisited regions I am about to explore.
    But to return to dearer considerations.

13 Remember me to...Most affectionately yours,] But success *shall* crown my endeavours. Wherefore not? Thus far I have gone, tracing a secure way over the pathless seas: the very stars themselves being

witnesses and testimonies of my triumph. Why not still proceed over
the untamed yet obedient element? What can stop the determined
heart and resolved will of man?

My swelling heart involuntarily pours itself out thus. But I must
finish. Heaven bless my beloved sister!

16–17 asked me many…a possible acquisition.] frequently conversed with
me on mine, which I have communicated to him without disguise. He
entered attentively into all my arguments in favour of my eventual
success, and into every minute detail of the measures I had taken to
secure it. I was easily led by the sympathy which he evinced, to use the
language of my heart; to give utterance to the burning ardour of my
soul; and to say, with all the fervour that warmed me, how gladly
I would sacrifice my fortune, my existence, my every hope, to the fur-
therance of my enterprise. One man's life or death were but a small
price to pay for the acquirement of the knowledge which I sought; for
the dominion I should acquire and transmit over the elemental foes of
our race. As I spoke, a dark gloom spread over my listener's countenance. At first I perceived that he tried to suppress his emotion; he
placed his hands before his eyes; and my voice quivered and failed me,
as I beheld tears trickle fast from between his fingers,—a groan burst
from his heaving breast. I paused;—at length he spoke, in broken
accents:—'Unhappy man! Do you share my madness? Have you drank
also of the intoxicating draught? Hear me,—let me reveal my tale, and
you will dash the cup from your lips!'

Such words, you may imagine, strongly excited my curiosity; but
the paroxysm of grief that had seized the stranger overcame his weakened powers, and many hours of repose and tranquil conversation
were necessary to restore his composure.

Having conquered the violence of his feelings, he appeared to despise
himself for being the slave of passion; and quelling the dark tyranny of
despair, he led me again to converse concerning myself personally. He
asked me the history of my earlier years. The tale was quickly told: but it
awakened various trains of reflection. I spoke of my desire of finding
a friend—of my thirst for a more intimate sympathy with a fellow mind
than had ever fallen to my lot; and expressed my conviction that a man
could boast of little happiness, who did not enjoy this blessing.

'I agree with you,' replied the stranger; 'we are unfashioned creatures, but half made up, if one wiser, better, dearer than ourselves—such
a friend ought to be—do not lend his aid to perfectionate our weak and
faulty natures.

17 Will you laugh at…for repeating them.] Will you smile at the enthusiasm I express concerning this divine wanderer? You would not, if you

saw him. You have been tutored and refined by books and retirement from the world, and you are, therefore, somewhat fastidious; but this only renders you the more fit to appreciate the extraordinary merits of this wonderful man. Sometimes I have endeavoured to discover what quality it is which he possesses, that elevates him so immeasurably above any other person I ever knew. I believe it to be an intuitive discernment; a quick but never-failing power of judgment; a penetration into the causes of things, unequalled for clearness and precision; add to this a facility of expression, and a voice whose varied intonations are soul-subduing music.

if you are...do not doubt] when I reflect that you are pursuing the same course, exposing yourself to the same dangers which have rendered me what I am, I imagine that you may deduce an apt moral from my tale; one that may direct you if you succeed in your undertaking, and console you in case of failure. Prepare to hear of occurrences which are usually deemed marvellous. Were we among the tamer scenes of nature, I might fear to encounter your unbelief, perhaps your ridicule; but many things will appear possible in these wild and mysterious regions, which would provoke the laughter of those unacquainted with the ever-varied powers of nature:—nor can I doubt but

18 some future day!] some future day! Even now, as I commence my task, his full-toned voice swells in my ears; his lustrous eyes dwell on me with all their melancholy sweetness; I see his thin hand raised in animation, while the lineaments of his face are irradiated by the soul within. Strange and harrowing must be his story; frightful the storm which embraced the gallant vessel on its course, and wrecked it—thus!

19 and it was...down to posterity.] a variety of circumstances had prevented his marrying early, nor was it until the decline of life that he became a husband and the father of a family.

grieved also for...endeavour to persuade] bitterly deplored the false pride which led his friend to a conduct so little worthy of the affection that united them. He lost no time in endeavouring to seek him out, with the hope of persuading

20 When my father...I feel pleasure.] There was a considerable difference between the ages of my parents, but this circumstance seemed to unite them only closer in bonds of devoted affection. There was a sense of justice in my father's upright mind, which rendered it necessary that he should approve highly to love strongly. Perhaps during former years he had suffered from the late-discovered unworthiness of one beloved,. and so was disposed to set a greater value on tried worth. There was

a show of gratitude and worship in his attachment to my mother, differing wholly from the doating fondness of age, for it was inspired by reverence for her virtues, and a desire to be the means of, in some degree, recompensing her for the sorrows she had endured, but which gave inexpressible grace to his behaviour to her. Every thing was made to yield to her wishes and her convenience. He strove to shelter her, as a fair exotic is sheltered by the gardener, from every rougher wind, and to surround her with all that could tend to excite pleasurable emotion in her soft and benevolent mind. Her health, and even the tranquillity of her hitherto constant spirit, had been shaken by what she had gone through. During the two years that had elapsed previous to their marriage my father had gradually relinquished all his public functions; and immediately after their union they sought the pleasant climate of Italy, and the change of scene and interest attendant on a tour through that land of wonders, as a restorative for her weakened frame.

From Italy they visited Germany and France. I, their eldest child, was born at Naples, and as an infant accompanied them in their rambles. I remained for several years their only child. Much as they were attached to each other, they seemed to draw inexhaustible stores of affection from a very mine of love to bestow them upon me. My mother's tender caresses, and my father's smile of benevolent pleasure while regarding me, are my first recollections. I was their plaything and their idol, and something better—their child, the innocent and helpless creature bestowed on them by Heaven, whom to bring up to good, and whose future lot it was in their hands to direct to happiness or misery, according as they fulfilled their duties towards me. With this deep consciousness of what they owed towards the being to which they had given life, added to the active spirit of tenderness that animated both, it may be imagined that while during every hour of my infant life I received a lesson of patience, of charity, and of self-control, I was so guided by a silken cord, that all seemed but one train of enjoyment to me.

For a long time I was their only care. My mother had much desired to have a daughter, but I continued their single offspring. When I was about five years old, while making an excursion beyond the frontiers of Italy, they passed a week on the shores of the Lake of Como.* Their benevolent disposition often made them enter the cottages of the poor. This, to my mother, was more than a duty; it was a necessity, a passion,—remembering what she had suffered, and how she had been relieved,—for her to act in her turn the guardian angel to the afflicted. During one of their walks a poor cot in the foldings of a vale attracted their notice, as being singularly disconsolate, while the number of half-clothed children gathered about it, spoke of penury in its worst shape. One day, when my father had gone by himself to Milan, my mother, accompanied by me, visited this abode. She found a peasant and his wife, hard working, bent down by care and labour, distributing a scanty meal to five hungry babes. Among these there was one which attracted my mother far above all the rest. She appeared of a different stock. The four others were dark-eyed, hardy little vagrants; this child was thin, and very fair. Her hair was the brightest living gold, and, despite the poverty of her clothing, seemed to set a crown of distinction on her head. Her brow was clear and ample, her blue eyes cloudless, and her lips and the moulding of her face so expressive of sensibility and sweetness, that none could behold her without looking on her as of a distinct species, a being heaven-sent, and bearing a celestial stamp in all her features.

The peasant woman, perceiving that my mother fixed eyes of wonder and admiration on this lovely girl, eagerly communicated her history. She was not her child, but the daughter of a Milanese nobleman. Her mother was a German, and had died on giving her birth. The infant had been placed with these good people to nurse: they were better off then. They had not been long married, and their eldest child was but just born. The father of their charge was one of those Italians nursed in the memory of the antique glory of Italy,—one among the *schiavi ognor frementi*,* who exerted himself to obtain the liberty of his country. He became the victim of its weakness. Whether he had died, or still lingered in the dungeons of Austria, was not known. His property was confiscated, his child became an orphan and a beggar. She continued with her foster parents, and bloomed in their rude abode, fairer than a garden rose among dark-leaved brambles.

When my father returned from Milan, he found playing with me in the hall of our villa, a child fairer than pictured cherub—a creature who seemed to shed radiance from her looks, and whose form and motions were lighter than the chamois of the hills. The apparition was soon explained. With his permission my mother prevailed on her rustic guardians to yield their charge to her. They were fond of the sweet orphan. Her presence had seemed a blessing to them; but it would be unfair to her to keep her in poverty and want, when Providence afforded her such powerful protection. They consulted their village priest, and the result was, that Elizabeth Lavenza* became the inmate of my parents' house—my more than sister—the beautiful and adored companion of all my occupations and my pleasures.

Every one loved Elizabeth. The passionate and almost reverential attachment with which all regarded her became, while I shared it, my pride and my delight. On the evening previous to her being brought to my home, my mother had said playfully,—'I have a pretty present for my Victor—to-morrow he shall have it.' And when, on the morrow, she presented Elizabeth to me as her promised gift, I, with childish seriousness, interpreted her words literally, and looked upon Elizabeth as mine—mine to protect, love, and cherish. All praises bestowed on her, I received as made to a possession of my own. We called each other familiarly by the name of cousin. No word, no expression could body forth the kind of relation in which she stood to me—my more than sister, since till death she was to be mine only.

CHAPTER II.

[*Chapters renumbered from this point.*]

We were brought up together; there was not quite a year difference in our ages. I need not say that we were strangers to any species of disunion or dispute. Harmony was the soul of our companionship, and the diversity and contrast that subsisted in our characters drew us nearer together. Elizabeth was of a calmer and more concentrated disposition; but, with all my ardour, I was capable of a more intense application, and was more deeply smitten with the thirst for knowledge. She busied herself with following the aerial creations of the poets; and in the majestic and wondrous scenes which surrounded our Swiss home—the sublime shapes of the mountains; the changes of the seasons; tempest and calm; the silence of winter, and the life and turbulence of our Alpine summers,—she found ample scope for admiration and delight. While my companion contemplated with a serious and satisfied spirit the magnificent appearances of things, I delighted in investigating their causes. The world was to me a secret which I desired to divine. Curiosity, earnest research to learn the hidden laws of nature, gladness akin to rapture, as they were unfolded to me, are among the earliest sensations I can remember.

On the birth of a second son, my junior by seven years, my parents gave up entirely their wandering life, and fixed themselves in their native country. We possessed a house in Geneva, and a *campagne** on Belrive, the eastern shore of the lake, at the distance of rather more than a league from the city. We resided principally in the latter, and the lives of my parents were passed in considerable seclusion. It was my temper to avoid a crowd, and to attach myself fervently to a few. I was indifferent, therefore, to my schoolfellows in general; but I united myself in the bonds of the closest friendship to one among them. Henry Clerval was the son of a merchant of Geneva. He was a boy of singular talent and fancy. He loved enterprise, hardship, and even danger, for its own sake. He was deeply read in books of chivalry and romance. He composed heroic songs, and began to write many a tale of enchantment and knightly adventure. He tried to make us act plays, and to enter into masquerades, in which the characters were drawn from the heroes of Roncesvalles,* of the Round Table of King Arthur, and the chivalrous train who shed their blood to redeem the holy sepulchre from the hands of the infidels.*

No human being could have passed a happier childhood than myself. My parents were possessed by the very spirit of kindness and indulgence. We felt that they were not the tyrants to rule our lot according to their caprice, but the agents and creators of all the many delights which we enjoyed. When I mingled with other families, I distinctly discerned how peculiarly fortunate my lot was, and gratitude assisted the development of filial love.

My temper was sometimes violent, and my passions vehement; but by some law in my temperature* they were turned, not towards childish pursuits, but to an eager desire to learn, and not to learn all things indiscriminately. I confess that neither the structure of languages, nor the code of governments, nor the politics of various states, possessed attractions for me. It was the secrets of heaven and earth that I desired to learn; and whether it was the outward substance of things, or the inner spirit of nature and the mysterious soul of man that occupied me, still my enquiries were directed to the metaphysical, or, in its highest sense, the physical secrets of the world.

Meanwhile Clerval occupied himself, so to speak, with the moral relations of things. The busy stage of life, the virtues of heroes, and the actions of men, were his theme; and his hope and his dream was to become one among those whose names are recorded in story, as the gallant and adventurous benefactors of our species. The saintly soul of Elizabeth shone like a shrine-dedicated lamp in our peaceful home. Her sympathy was ours; her smile, her soft voice, the sweet glance of her celestial eyes, were ever there to bless and animate us. She was the living spirit of love to soften and attract: I might have become sullen in my study, rough through the ardour of my nature, but that she was there to subdue me to a semblance of her own gentleness. And Clerval—could aught ill entrench on the noble spirit of Clerval?—yet he might not have been so perfectly humane, so thoughtful in his generosity—so full of kindness and tenderness amidst his passion for adventurous exploit, had she not unfolded to him the real loveliness of beneficence, and made the doing good the end and aim of his soaring ambition.

I feel exquisite pleasure

23 with my imagination . . . from modern discoveries.] have contented my imagination, warmed as it was, by returning with greater ardour to my former studies.

23 few beside myself; . . . undisturbed by reality; and] few beside myself.
    I have described myself as always having been embued with a fervent
    longing to penetrate the secrets of nature. In spite of the intense labour
    and wonderful discoveries of modern philosophers, I always came from
    my studies discontented and unsatisfied. Sir Isaac Newton is said to
    have avowed that he felt like a child picking up shells beside the great
    and unexplored ocean of truth.* Those of his successors in each branch
    of natural philosophy with whom I was acquainted, appeared even to
    my boy's apprehensions, as tyros* engaged in the same pursuit.
        The untaught peasant beheld the elements around him, and was
    acquainted with their practical uses. The most learned philosopher
    knew little more. He had partially unveiled the face of Nature, but her
    immortal lineaments were still a wonder and a mystery. He might dis-
    sect, anatomise, and give names; but, not to speak of a final cause,
    causes in their secondary and tertiary grades were utterly unknown to
    him. I had gazed upon the fortifications and impediments that seemed
    to keep human beings from entering the citadel of nature, and rashly
    and ignorantly I had repined.
        But here were books, and here were men who had penetrated deeper
    and knew more. I took their word for all that they averred, and
    I became their disciple. It may appear strange that such should arise in
    the eighteenth century; but while I followed the routine of education
    in the schools of Geneva, I was, to a great degree, self taught with
    regard to my favourite studies. My father was not scientific, and I was
    left to struggle with a child's blindness, added to a student's thirst for
    knowledge. Under the guidance of my new preceptors,

24 The natural phænomena . . . in my mind.] [No new paragraph.] And thus
    for a time I was occupied by exploded systems, mingling, like an unadept,
    a thousand contradictory theories, and floundering desperately in a very
    slough of multifarious knowledge, guided by an ardent imagination and
    childish reasoning, till an accident again changed the current of my ideas.

24–25 The catastrophe of . . . of each other.] Before this I was not unacquainted
    with the more obvious laws of electricity. On this occasion a man of
    great research in natural philosophy was with us, and, excited by this
    catastrophe, he entered on the explanation of a theory which he had
    formed on the subject of electricity and galvanism, which was at once
    new and astonishing to me. All that he said threw greatly into the
    shade Cornelius Agrippa, Albertus Magnus, and Paracelsus, the lords
    of my imagination; but by some fatality the overthrow of these men
    disinclined me to pursue my accustomed studies. It seemed to me as if
    nothing would or could ever be known. All that had so long engaged
    my attention suddenly grew despicable. By one of those caprices of the

mind, which we are perhaps most subject to in early youth, I at once gave up my former occupations; set down natural history and all its progeny as a deformed and abortive creation; and entertained the greatest disdain for a would-be science, which could never even step within the threshold of real knowledge. In this mood of mind I betook myself to the mathematics, and the branches of study appertaining to that science, as being built upon secure foundations, and so worthy of my consideration.

Thus strangely are our souls constructed, and by such slight ligaments are we bound to prosperity or ruin. When I look back, it seems to me as if this almost miraculous change of inclination and will was the immediate suggestion of the guardian angel of my life—the last effort made by the spirit of preservation to avert the storm that was even then hanging in the stars, and ready to envelope me. Her victory was announced by an unusual tranquillity and gladness of soul, which followed the relinquishing of my ancient and latterly tormenting studies. It was thus that I was to be taught to associate evil with their prosecution, happiness with their disregard.

It was a strong effort of the spirit of good; but it was ineffectual. Destiny was too potent, and her immutable laws had decreed my utter and terrible destruction.

26 her favourite was...infection was past. The] the life of her favourite was menaced, she could no longer control her anxiety. She attended her sick bed,—her watchful attentions triumphed over the malignity of the distemper,—Elizabeth was saved, but the

27 This period was...forgetful of herself.] It appeared to me sacrilege so soon to leave the repose, akin to death, of the house of mourning, and to rush into the thick of life. I was new to sorrow, but it did not the less alarm me. I was unwilling to quit the sight of those that remained to me; and, above all, I desired to see my sweet Elizabeth in some degree consoled.

She indeed veiled her grief, and strove to act the comforter to us all. She looked steadily on life, and assumed its duties with courage and zeal. She devoted herself to those whom she had been taught to call her uncle and cousins. Never was she so enchanting as at this time, when she recalled the sunshine of her smiles and spent them upon us. She forgot even her own regret in her endeavours to make us forget.

I had taken...have accompanied me.] Clerval spent the last evening with us. He had endeavoured to persuade his father to permit him to accompany me, and to become my fellow student; but in vain. His father was a narrow-minded trader, and saw idleness and ruin in the aspirations and ambition of his son. Henry deeply felt the misfortune of being debarred from a liberal education. He said little; but when he spoke, I read in his kindling eye and in his animated glance a restrained but firm resolve, not to be chained to the miserable details of commerce.

We sat late. We could not tear ourselves away from each other, nor persuade ourselves to say the word 'Farewell!' It was said; and we retired under the pretence of seeking repose, each fancying that the other was deceived: but when at morning's dawn I descended to the carriage which was to convey me away, they were all there—my father again to bless me, Clerval to press my hand once more, my Elizabeth to renew her entreaties that I would write often, and to bestow the last feminine attentions on her playmate and friend.

28 professors, and among . . . upon those subjects.] professors. Chance— or rather the evil influence, the Angel of Destruction, which asserted omnipotent sway over me from the moment I turned my reluctant steps from my father's door—led me first to Mr. Krempe, professor of natural philosophy. He was an uncouth man, but deeply embued in the secrets of his science. He asked me several questions concerning my progress in the different branches of science appertaining to natural philosophy. I replied carelessly; and, partly in contempt, mentioned the names of my alchymists as the principal authors I had studied.

29 of his doctrine.] of his pursuits. In rather a too philosophical and con- nected a strain, perhaps, I have given an account of the conclusions I had come to concerning them in my early years. As a child, I had not been content with the results promised by the modern professors of natural science. With a confusion of ideas only to be accounted for by my extreme youth, and my want of a guide on such matters, I had retrod the steps of knowledge along the paths of time, and exchanged the dis- coveries of recent enquirers for the dreams of forgotten alchymists.

30 I departed highly . . . the same evening.] Such were the professor's words—rather let me say such the words of fate, enounced* to destroy me. As he went on, I felt as if my soul were grappling with a palpable enemy; one by one the various keys were touched which formed the mechanism of my being: chord after chord was sounded, and soon my mind was filled with one thought, one conception, one purpose. So much has been done, exclaimed the soul of Frankenstein,—more, far more, will I achieve: treading in the steps already marked, I will pioneer a new way, explore unknown powers, and unfold to the world the deepest mysteries of creation.

I closed not my eyes that night. My internal being was in a state of insurrection and turmoil; I felt that order would thence arise, but I had no power to produce it. By degrees, after the morning's dawn, sleep came. I awoke, and my yesternight's thoughts were as a dream. There only remained a resolution to return to my ancient studies, and to devote myself to a science for which I believed myself to possess a natural talent. On the same day, I paid M. Waldman a visit.

30 and I, at the same time,] I expressed myself in measured terms, with the modesty and deference due from a youth to his instructor, without letting escape (inexperience in life would have made me ashamed) any of the enthusiasm which stimulated my intended labours. I

31 It was, perhaps . . . and resolution, now] In a thousand ways he smoothed for me the path of knowledge, and made the most abstruse enquiries clear and facile* to my apprehension. My application was at first fluctuating and uncertain; it gained strength as I proceeded, and soon

36 a disease that . . . away such symptoms;] the fall of a leaf startled me, and I shunned my fellow-creatures as if I had been guilty of a crime. Sometimes I grew alarmed at the wreck I perceived that I had become; the energy of my purpose alone sustained me: my labours would soon end, and I believed that exercise and amusement would then drive away incipient disease;

42–43 'into my hands . . . remember Justine Moritz?] into my hands. It was from my own Elizabeth:—

'My dearest Cousin,

'You have been ill, very ill, and even the constant letters of dear kind Henry are not sufficient to reassure me on your account. You are forbidden to write—to hold a pen; yet one word from you, dear Victor, is necessary to calm our apprehensions. For a long time I have thought that each post would bring this line, and my persuasions have restrained my uncle from undertaking a journey to Ingolstadt. I have prevented his encountering the inconveniences and perhaps dangers of so long a journey; yet how often have I regretted not being able to perform it myself! I figure to myself that the task of attending on your sick bed has devolved on some mercenary old nurse, who could never guess your wishes, nor minister to them with the care and affection of your poor cousin. Yet that is over now: Clerval writes that indeed you are getting better. I eagerly hope that you will confirm this intelligence soon in your own handwriting.

'Get well—and return to us. You will find a happy, cheerful home, and friends who love you dearly. Your father's health is vigorous, and he asks but to see you,—but to be assured that you are well; and not a care will ever cloud his benevolent countenance. How pleased you would be to remark the improvement of our Ernest! He is now sixteen, and full of activity and spirit. He is desirous to be a true Swiss, and to enter into foreign service; but we cannot part with him, at least until his elder brother return to us. My uncle is not pleased with the idea of a military career in a distant country; but Ernest never had your powers of application. He looks upon study as an odious fetter;—his time is spent in the open air, climbing the hills or rowing on the lake. I fear that he will become an idler, unless we yield the point, and permit him to enter on the profession which he has selected.

'Little alteration, except the growth of our dear children, has taken place since you left us. The blue lake, and snow-clad mountains, they never change;—and I think our placid home, and our contented hearts are regulated by the same immutable laws. My trifling occupations take up my time and amuse me, and I am rewarded for any exertions by seeing none but happy, kind faces around me. Since you left us, but one change has taken place in our little household. Do you remember on what occasion Justine Moritz entered our family?

44–45 yet I cannot...my dearest cousin.] but my anxiety returns upon me as I conclude. Write, dearest Victor,—one line—one word will be a blessing to us. Ten thousand thanks to Henry for his kindness, his affection, and his many letters: we are sincerely grateful. Adieu! my cousin; take care of yourself; and, I entreat you, write!

46 Clerval was no natural...my own part, idleness] Clerval had never sympathised in my tastes for natural science; and his literary pursuits differed wholly from those which had occupied me. He came to the university with the design of making himself complete master of the oriental languages, as thus he should open a field for the plan of life he had marked out for himself. Resolved to pursue no inglorious career, he turned his eyes toward the East, as affording scope for his spirit of enterprise. The Persian, Arabic, and Sanscrit languages engaged his attention, and I was easily induced to enter on the same studies. Idleness

of the orientalists.] of the orientalists. I did not, like him, attempt a critical knowledge of their dialects, for I did not contemplate making any other use of them than temporary amusement. I read merely to understand their meaning, and they well repaid my labours.

50 raise my spirits...His friends] say a few words of consolation; he could only express his heartfelt sympathy. 'Poor William!' said he, 'dear lovely child, he now sleeps with his angel mother! Who that had seen him bright and joyous in his young beauty, but must weep over his untimely loss! To die so miserably; to feel the murderer's grasp! How much more a murderer, that could destroy such radiant innocence! Poor little fellow! one only consolation have we; his friends

53–54 But we are...'She indeed requires consolation;] You come to us now to share a misery which nothing can alleviate; yet your presence will, I hope, revive our father, who seems sinking under his misfortune; and your persuasions will induce poor Elizabeth to cease her vain and tormenting self-accusations.—Poor William! he was our darling and our pride!'

Tears, unrestrained, fell from my brother's eyes; a sense of mortal agony crept over my frame. Before, I had only imagined the wretchedness of my desolated home; the reality came on me as a new, and a not less terrible, disaster. I tried to calm Ernest; I enquired more minutely concerning my father, and her I named my cousin.

'She most of all,' said Ernest, 'requires consolation;

55 to convict her; . . . an evil result.] to convict her. My tale was not one to announce publicly; its astounding horror would be looked upon as madness by the vulgar. Did any one indeed exist, except I, the creator, who would believe, unless his senses convinced him, in the existence of the living monument of presumption and rash ignorance which I had let loose upon the world?

made great alterations . . . slight and graceful.] altered her since I last beheld her; it had endowed her with loveliness surpassing the beauty of her childish years. There was the same candour, the same vivacity, but it was allied to an expression more full of sensibility and intellect.

57 Unable to rest or sleep,] Most of the night she spent here watching; towards morning she believed that she slept for a few minutes; some steps disturbed her, and she awoke. It was dawn, and

59 When I returned home,] This was strange and unexpected intelligence; what could it mean? Had my eyes deceived me? and was I really as mad as the whole world would believe me to be, if I disclosed the object of my suspicions? I hastened to return home, and

61 dear girl; . . . I never can] dear girl. Do not fear. I will proclaim, I will prove your innocence. I will melt the stony hearts of your enemies by my tears and prayers. You shall not die!—You, my play-fellow, my companion, my sister, perish on the scaffold! No! no! I never could

'Dear, sweet Elizabeth . . . increase of misery.'] Justine shook her head mournfully. 'I do not fear to die,' she said; 'that pang is past. God raises my weakness, and gives me courage to endure the worst. I leave a sad and bitter world; and if you remember me, and think of me as of one unjustly condemned, I am resigned to the fate awaiting me. Learn from me, dear lady, to submit in patience to the will of Heaven!'

62 As we returned . . . I then endured.] And on the morrow Justine died. Elizabeth's heart-rending eloquence failed to move the judges from their settled conviction in the criminality of the saintly sufferer. My passionate and indignant appeals were lost upon them. And when I received their cold answers, and heard the harsh unfeeling reasoning

of these men, my purposed avowal died away on my lips. Thus I might proclaim myself a madman, but not revoke the sentence passed upon my wretched victim. She perished on the scaffold as a murderess!

From the tortures of my own heart, I turned to contemplate the deep and voiceless grief of my Elizabeth. This also was my doing! And my father's woe, and the desolation of that late so smiling home—all was the work of my thrice-accursed hands! Ye weep, unhappy ones; but these are not your last tears! Again shall you raise the funeral wail, and the sound of your lamentations shall again and again be heard! Frankenstein, your son, your kinsman, your early, much-loved friend; he who would spend each vital drop of blood for your sakes—who has no thought nor sense of joy, except as it is mirrored also in your dear countenances—who would fill the air with blessings, and spend his life in serving you—he bids you weep—to shed countless tears; happy beyond his hopes, if thus inexorable fate be satisfied, and if the destruction pause before the peace of the grave have succeeded to your sad torments!

Thus spoke my prophetic soul, as, torn by remorse, horror, and despair, I beheld those I loved spend vain sorrow upon the graves of William and Justine, the first hapless victims to my unhallowed arts.

VOLUME II

63 to reason with...to immoderate grief.] by arguments deduced from the feelings of his serene conscience and guiltless life, to inspire me with fortitude, and awaken in me the courage to dispel the dark cloud which brooded over me.

65 She had become...of human life.] The first of those sorrows which are sent to wean us from the earth, had visited her, and its dimming influence quenched her dearest smiles.

66 Be calm, my...we ascended still] Dear Victor, banish these dark passions. Remember the friends around you, who centre all their hopes in you. Have we lost the power of rendering you happy? Ah! while we love—while we are true to each other, here in this land of peace and beauty, your native country, we may reap every tranquil blessing,—what can disturb our peace?'

And could not such words from her whom I fondly prized before every other gift of fortune, suffice to chase away the fiend that lurked in my heart? Even as she spoke I drew near to her, as if in terror; lest at that very moment the destroyer had been near to rob me of her.

Thus not the tenderness of friendship, nor the beauty of earth, nor of heaven, could redeem my soul from woe: the very accents of love were ineffectual. I was encompassed by a cloud which no beneficial influence could penetrate. The wounded deer dragging its fainting limbs to some untrodden brake, there to gaze upon the arrow which had pierced it, and to die—was but a type of me.

Sometimes I could cope with the sullen despair that overwhelmed me: but sometimes the whirlwind passions of my soul drove me to seek, by bodily exercise and by change of place, some relief from my intolerable sensations. It was during an access of this kind that I suddenly left my home, and bending my steps towards the near Alpine valleys, sought in the magnificence, the eternity of such senses, to forget myself and my ephemeral, because human, sorrows. My wanderings were directed towards the valley of Chamounix. I had visited it frequently during my boyhood. Six years had passed since then: *I* was a wreck—but nought had changed in those savage and enduring scenes.

I performed the first part of my journey on horseback. I afterwards hired a mule, as the more sure-footed, and least liable to receive injury on these rugged roads. The weather was fine: it was about the middle of the month of August, nearly two months after the death of Justine; that miserable epoch from which I dated all my woe. The weight upon my spirit was sensibly lightened as I plunged yet deeper in the ravine of Arve. The immense mountains and precipices that overhung me on every side—the sound of the river raging among the rocks, and the dashing of the waterfalls around, spoke of a power mighty as Omnipotence—and I ceased to fear, or to bend before any being less almighty than that which had created and ruled the elements, here displayed in their most terrific guise. Still, as I ascended

67 During this journey...pallid lightning.] A tingling long-lost sense of pleasure often came across me during this journey. Some turn in the road, some new object suddenly perceived and recognised, reminded me of days gone by, and were associated with the light-hearted gaiety of boyhood. The very winds whispered in soothing accents, and maternal nature bade me weep no more. Then again the kindly influence ceased to act—I found myself fettered again to grief, and indulging in all the misery of reflection. Then I spurred on my animal, striving so to forget the world, my fears, and, more than all, myself—or, in a more desperate fashion, I alighted, and threw myself on the grass, weighed down by horror and despair.

At length I arrived at the village of Chamounix. Exhaustion succeeded to the extreme fatigue both of body and of mind which I had endured. For a short space of time I remained at the window, watching the pallid lightnings

ran below my window.] pursued its noisy way beneath. The same lulling sounds acted as a lullaby to my too keen sensations: when I placed my head upon my pillow, sleep crept over me; I felt it as it came, and blest the giver of oblivion.

67 The next day...valley until evening.] I SPENT the following day
    roaming through the valley. I stood beside the sources of the Arveiron,
    which take their rise in a glacier, that with slow pace is advancing down
    from the summit of the hills, to barricade the valley. The abrupt sides
    of vast mountains were before me; the icy wall of the glacier overhung
    me; a few shattered pines were scattered around; and the solemn
    silence of this glorious presence-chamber of imperial Nature was
    broken only by the brawling waves, or the fall of some vast fragment,
    the thunder sound of the avalanche, or the cracking, reverberated
    along the mountains of the accumulated ice, which, through the silent
    working of immutable laws, was ever and anon rent and torn, as if it
    had been but a plaything in their hands.

67–68 I returned in...to go alone,] I retired to rest at night; my slumbers,
    as it were, waited on and ministered to by the assemblance of grand
    shapes which I had contemplated during the day. They congregated
    round me; the unstained snowy mountain-top, the glittering pinnacle,
    the pine woods, and ragged bare ravine; the eagle, soaring amidst the
    clouds—they all gathered round me, and bade me be at peace.

    Where had they fled when the next morning I awoke? All of soul-
    inspiriting* fled with sleep, and dark melancholy clouded every
    thought. The rain was pouring in torrents, and the thick mists hid the
    summits of the mountains, so that I even saw not the faces of those
    mighty friends. Still I would penetrate their misty veil, and seek them in
    their cloudy retreats. What were rain and storm to me? My mule was
    brought to the door, and I resolved to ascend

106 when I perceived...She was young,] I entered a barn which had appeared
    to me to be empty. A woman was sleeping on some straw; she was young;
    all but me...lessons of Felix,] And then I bent over her, and whispered
    "Awake, fairest, thy lover is near—he who would give his life but to
    obtain one look of affection from thine eyes: my beloved, awake!"

    'The sleeper stirred; a thrill of terror ran through me. Should she
    indeed awake, and see me, and curse me, and denounce the murderer?
    Thus would she assuredly act, if her darkened eyes opened, and she
    beheld me. The thought was madness; it stirred the fiend within me—not
    I, but she shall suffer: the murder I have committed because I am for ever
    robbed of all that she could give me, she shall atone. The crime had its
    source in her: be hers the punishment! Thanks to the lessons of Felix

110–111 but my presence...degree of tranquillity.] I took no rest, but
    returned immediately to Geneva. Even in my own heart I could give no
    expression to my sensations—they weighed on me with a mountain's
    weight, and their excess destroyed my agony beneath them. Thus

I returned home, and entering the house, presented myself to the family. My haggard and wild appearance awoke intense alarm; but I answered no question, scarcely did I speak. I felt as if I were placed under a ban—as if I had no right to claim their sympathies—as if never more might I enjoy companionship with them. Yet even thus I loved them to adoration; and to save them, I resolved to dedicate myself to my most abhorred task. The prospect of such an occupation made every other circumstance of existence pass before me like a dream; and that thought only had to me the reality of life.

VOLUME III

113 could not resolve...My health,] shrunk from taking the first step in an undertaking whose immediate necessity began to appear less absolute to me. A change indeed had taken place in me: my health,

114 your cousin,] our dear Elizabeth
     your cousin] Elizabeth
     with my cousin] with my Elizabeth

115 any variation was...some accident might] I had an insurmountable aversion to the idea of engaging myself in my loathsome task in my father's house, while in habits of familiar intercourse with those I loved. I knew that a thousand fearful accidents might occur, the slightest of which would disclose a tale to thrill all connected with me with horror. I was aware also that I should often lose all self-command, all capacity of hiding the harrowing sensations that would possess me during the progress of my unearthly occupation. I must absent myself from all I loved while thus employed. Once commenced, it would quickly be achieved, and I might be restored to my family in peace and happiness. My promise fulfilled, the monster would depart for ever. Or (so my fond fancy imaged) some accident might meanwhile

the guise of...restore my tranquillity.] a guise which excited no suspicion, while I urged my desire with an earnestness that easily induced my father to comply. After so long a period of an absorbing melancholy, that resembled madness in its intensity and effects, he was glad to find that I was capable of taking pleasure in the idea of such a journey, and he hoped that change of scene and varied amusement would, before my return, have restored me entirely to myself.

The duration of my absence was left to my own choice; a few months, or at most a year, was the period contemplated. One paternal kind precaution he had taken to ensure my having a companion. Without previously communicating with me, he had, in concert with Elizabeth, arranged that Clerval should join me at Strasburgh. This interfered with the solitude I coveted for the prosecution of my task; yet at the commencement of my journey the presence of my friend could in no way be an impediment, and truly I rejoiced that thus I should be saved many hours of lonely, maddening reflection. Nay, Henry might stand between me and the intrusion of my foe. If I were alone, would he not at times force his abhorred presence on me, to remind me of my task, or to contemplate its progress?

To England, therefore, I was bound, and it was understood that my union with Elizabeth should take place immediately on my return. My father's age rendered him extremely averse to delay. For myself, there was one reward I promised myself from my detested toils—one consolation for my unparalleled sufferings; it was the prospect of that day when, enfranchised from my miserable slavery, I might claim Elizabeth, and forget the past in my union with her.

116 end of August...be our feelings?'] end of September that I again quitted my native country. My journey had been my own suggestion, and Elizabeth, therefore, acquiesced: but she was filled with disquiet at the idea of my suffering, away from her, the inroads of misery and grief. It had been her care which provided me a companion in Clerval—and yet a man is blind to a thousand minute circumstances, which call forth a woman's sedulous attention. She longed to bid me hasten my return,—a thousand conflicting emotions rendered her mute, as she bade me a tearful silent farewell.

120 amusement.] amusement. He was also pursuing an object he had long had in view. His design was to visit India, in the belief that he had in his knowledge of its various languages, and in the views he had taken of its society, the means of materially assisting the progress of European colonisation and trade.* In Britain only could he further the execution of his plan.

121 Gower] Goring

129 nearly a year...our future proceedings.] he was wearing away his time fruitlessly where he was; that letters from the friends he had formed in London desired his return to complete the negotiation they had entered into for his Indian enterprise. He could not any longer delay his departure; but as his journey to London might be followed, even sooner than he now conjectured, by his longer voyage, he entreated me to bestow as much of my society on him as I could spare. He besought me, therefore, to leave my solitary isle, and to meet him at Perth, that we might proceed southwards together.

139–140 I remember, as...It was midnight.] Yet one duty remained to me, the recollection of which finally triumphed over my selfish despair. It was necessary that I should return without delay to Geneva, there to watch over the lives of those I so fondly loved; and to lie in wait for the murderer, that if any chance led me to the place of his concealment, or if he dared again to blast me by his presence, I might, with unfailing aim, put an end to the existence of the monstrous Image which I had endued with the mockery of a soul still more monstrous. My father still desired to delay our departure, fearful that I could not sustain the fatigues of a journey: for I was a shattered wreck,—the shadow of a human being. My strength was gone. I was a mere skeleton; and fever night and day preyed upon my wasted frame.

Still, as I urged our leaving Ireland with such inquietude and impatience, my father thought it best to yield. We took our passage on board a vessel bound for Havre-de-Grace,* and sailed with a fair wind from the Irish shores. It was midnight.

140 awoke me...were now entering.] awoke me; the dashing waves were around: the cloudy sky above; the fiend was not here: a sense of security, a feeling that a truce was established between the present hour and the irresistible, disastrous future, imparted to me a kind of calm forgetfulness, of which the human mind is by its structure peculiarly susceptible.

140–141 We had resolved...he would not] THE voyage came to an end. We landed, and proceeded to Paris. I soon found that I had overtaxed my strength, and that I must repose before I could continue my journey. My father's care and attentions were indefatigable; but he did not know the origin of my sufferings, and sought erroneous methods to remedy the incurable ill. He wished me to seek amusement in society. I abhorred the face of man. Oh, not abhorred! they were my brethren, my fellow beings, and I felt attracted even to the most repulsive among them, as to creatures of an angelic nature and celestial mechanism. But I felt that I had no right to share their intercourse. I had unchained an enemy among them, whose joy it was to shed their blood, and to revel in their groans. How they would, each and all, abhor me, and hunt me from the world, did they know my unhallowed acts, and the crimes which had their source in me!

My father yielded at length to my desire to avoid society, and strove by various arguments to banish my

141 for ever chained my tongue, . . . fatal secret.] in itself would for ever have chained my tongue. But, besides, I could not bring myself to disclose a secret which would fill my hearer with consternation, and make fear and unnatural horror the inmates of his breast. I checked, therefore, my impatient thirst for sympathy, and was silent when I would have given the world to have confided the fatal secret. Yet still words

like those I have recorded, would burst uncontrollably from me. I could offer no explanation of them; but their truth in part relieved the burden of my mysterious woe.

142 DEAREST FRIEND,] dear Friend,

and I have . . . your affectionate cousin.] and all my doubts satisfied.

143 my cousin,] my friend,

144 My cousin] The sweet girl

145 my cousin.] Elizabeth.

146 A house was . . . at the schools.] Through my father's exertions, a part of the inheritance of Elizabeth had been restored to her by the Austrian government. A small possession on the shores of Como belonged to her. It was agreed that, immediately after our union, we should proceed to Villa Lavenza, and spend our first days of happiness beside the beautiful lake near which it stood.

147 pass the afternoon . . . go by water.] commence our journey by water, sleeping that night at Evian, and continuing our voyage on the following day. The day was fair, the wind favourable, all smiled on our nuptial embarkation.

150 did not accompany them; I was exhausted:] attempted to accompany them, and proceeded a short distance from the house; but my head whirled round, my steps were like those of a drunken man, I fell at last in a state of utter exhaustion;

At length I . . . a long time;] After an interval, I arose, and, as if by instinct, crawled into the room where the corpse of my beloved lay. There were women weeping around*—I hung over it, and joined my sad tears to theirs—all this time no distinct idea presented itself to my mind;

151 niece,] Elizabeth,

163 We may survive . . . good heart. Yet what,] Yet it is terrible to reflect that the lives of all these men are endangered through me. If we are lost, my mad schemes are the cause.
    And what,

APPENDIX C

ON *FRANKENSTEIN*
BY PERCY BYSSHE SHELLEY

THE novel of 'Frankenstein; or the Modern Prometheus,' is undoubtedly, as a mere story, one of the most original and complete productions of the day. We debate with ourselves in wonder, as we read it, what could have been the series of thoughts—what could have been the peculiar experiences that awakened them—which conduced, in the author's mind, to the astonishing combinations of motives and incidents, and the startling catastrophe, which compose this tale. There are, perhaps, some points of subordinate importance, which prove that it is the author's first attempt. But in this judgment, which requires a very nice discrimination, we may be mistaken; for it is conducted throughout with a firm and steady hand. The interest gradually accumulates and advances towards the conclusion with the accelerated rapidity of a rock rolled down a mountain. We are led breathless with suspense and sympathy, and the heaping up of incident on incident, and the working of passion out of passion. We cry 'hold, hold! enough!'—but there is yet something to come; and, like the victim whose history it relates, we think we can bear no more, and yet more is to be borne. Pelion is heaped on Ossa, and Ossa on Olympus.* We climb Alp after Alp, until the horizon is seen blank, vacant, and limitless; and the head turns giddy, and the ground seems to fail under our feet.

This novel rests its claim on being a source of powerful and profound emotion. The elementary feelings of the human mind are exposed to view; and those who are accustomed to reason deeply on their origin and tendency will, perhaps, be the only persons who can sympathize, to the full extent, in the interest of the actions which are their result. But, founded on nature as they are, there is perhaps no reader, who can endure anything beside a new love story, who will not feel a responsive string touched in his inmost soul. The sentiments are so affectionate and so innocent—the characters of the subordinate agents in this strange drama are clothed in the light of such a mild and gentle mind—the pictures of domestic manners are of the most simple and attaching character: the pathos* is irresistible and deep. Nor are the crimes and malevolence of the single Being, though indeed withering and tremendous, the offspring of any unaccountable propensity to evil, but flow irresistibly from certain causes fully adequate to their production. They are the children, as it were, of Necessity and Human Nature. In this the direct moral of the book consists; and it is perhaps the most important, and of the most universal application, of any moral that can be enforced by example. Treat a person ill, and he will become wicked. Requite affection with scorn;—let one being be selected, for whatever cause, as the refuse of his kind—divide him, a social being, from society, and you impose upon him the irresistible obligations—malevolence and selfishness. It is thus that, too often in society, those who are best qualified to be its benefactors and its ornaments, are branded by some accident with scorn, and changed, by neglect and solitude of heart, into a scourge and a curse.

The Being in 'Frankenstein' is, no doubt, a tremendous creature. It was impossible that he should not have received among men that treatment which led to the consequences of his being a social nature. He was an abortion* and an anomaly; and though his mind was such as its first impressions framed it, affectionate and full of moral sensibility, yet the circumstances of his existence are so monstrous and uncommon, that, when the consequences of them became developed in action, his original goodness was gradually turned into inextinguishable misanthropy and revenge. The scene between the Being and the blind De Lacey in the cottage, is one of the most profound and extraordinary instances of pathos that we ever recollect. It is impossible to read this dialogue,—and indeed many others of a somewhat similar character,—without feeling the heart suspend its pulsations with wonder, and the 'tears stream down the cheeks.'* The encounter and argument between Frankenstein and the Being on the sea of ice, almost approaches, in effect, to the expostulations of Caleb Williams with Falkland.* It reminds us, indeed, somewhat of the style and character of that admirable writer, to whom the author has dedicated his work, and whose productions he seems to have studied.

There is only one instance, however, in which we detect the least approach to imitation; and that is the conduct of the incident of Frankenstein's landing in Ireland. The general character of the tale, indeed, resembles nothing that ever preceded it. After the death of Elizabeth, the story, like a stream which grows at once more rapid and profound as it proceeds, assumes an irresistible solemnity, and the magnificent energy and swiftness of a tempest.

The churchyard scene, in which Frankenstein visits the tombs of his family, his quitting Geneva, and his journey through Tartary* to the shores of the Frozen Ocean, resemble at once the terrible reanimation of a corpse and the supernatural career of a spirit. The scene in the cabin of Walton's ship—the more than mortal enthusiasm and grandeur of the Being's speech over the dead body of his victim—is an exhibition of intellectual and imaginative power, which we think the reader will acknowledge has seldom been surpassed.

EXPLANATORY NOTES

1 [title page] *Frankenstein*: probably derived from Burg Frankenstein (castle of the Franks' rock) near Darmstadt; the Shelleys had visited the region in 1814 (25 August–5 September). There was a story attached to the castle that the alchemist Johann Konrad Dippel (1673–1724), who was born there, had been involved in bodysnatching in investigating reanimation (see Joe Nickell, *Adventures in Paranormal Investigation* (Lexington, KY: University Press of Kentucky, 2007), 162–5). François-Félix Nogaret's *Le Miroir des événements actuels, ou La Belle au plus offrant: Histoire à deux visages* ('The Looking-Glass of Actuality, or Beauty to the Highest Bidder: A Two-Faced Tale') is a short idealist novel from 1790 describing a human being created by an inventor—an inventor named Frankénsteïn (see Julia Douthwaite, *The Frankenstein of 1790 and Other Lost Chapters from Revolutionary France* (Chicago: University of Chicago Press, 2012), 59–97).

[title page] *Prometheus*: the 'forethinker', demigod and Titan, trickster and craftsman. Prometheus was both the 'bearer of sacred fire' (*pyrphoros*) and 'the maker' (*plasticator*) (see Introduction, pp. xxviii–xxxii). He duped the gods by offering a sacrifice of bones wrapped in fat in order to keep the best part, the meat, for those on earth—of whom he is consistently the guardian. Zeus retaliated by revoking the holy gift of fire, which Prometheus then stole back. He was punished by being chained to a rock in the Caucasus and having his liver torn out by an eagle during the day, the organ regenerating through the night to allow the hideous cycle to be repeated. (Another version has Zeus creating Pandora, the bringer of evils into the world, as punishment for Prometheus' offence.) The myth of 'the maker' reworked Prometheus' seizure of fire as the expropriation of divine powers, enabling Prometheus to create mankind from clay. Johann Wolfgang von Goethe's poem 'Prometheus' (first published 1785) presented Prometheus as a defiant artist-rebel of obvious appeal to the emerging generation of Romantic poets (see Carl Kerényi, *Prometheus: Archetypal Image of Human Existence*, trans. Ralph Manheim (1963; Princeton: Princeton University Press, 1991)); Lord Byron, meanwhile, identified Napoleon with Prometheus in *Childe Harold's Pilgrimage* (1812–18) (see Harold Bloom, 'Napoleon and Prometheus: The Romantic Myth of Organic Energy', *Yale French Studies*, 26, *The Myth of Napoleon* (1960), 79–82).

[epigraph] *Did I request thee . . . promote me?*: John Milton, *Paradise Lost* (1667), x. 743–5. These plaintive lines are spoken by Adam.

3 [dedication] WILLIAM GODWIN: Shelley's father, the radical philosopher and novelist (1756–1836). *Enquiry Concerning Political Justice* was an uncompromising political thesis published in 1793; *Caleb Williams*, a novel, followed a year later (see Introduction, pp. xii–xiii).

PREFACE

The Preface was written by Percy Shelley, presumably on 14 May 1817 when
Mary Shelley recorded in her journal 'S[helley]. . . . corrects F. write Preface—
Finis' (*The Journals of Mary Shelley: 1814–1844*, 2 vols. ed. Paula R. Feldman and
Diana Scott-Kilvert (Oxford: Clarendon Press, 1987), i. 169). On 28 November
Percy reminded the publisher to send him a proof of the Preface (see William
St Clair, *The Godwins and the Shelleys: The Biography of a Family* (London:
Faber and Faber, 1989), 554 n. 25)—this was exactly a month after the proofs
of the text itself had been completed (see *The Letters of Percy Bysshe Shelley*,
ed. Frederick. L. Jones, 2 vols. (Oxford: Clarendon Press, 1964), i. 565).

5 *Dr Darwin*: Erasmus Darwin (1731–1802), poet and natural scientist,
and author of *The Botanic Garden* (1791), *Zoonomia* (1794–6), and *The
Temple of Nature* (1803)—the last, an annotated poem, was an influence
on *Frankenstein* (see notes to pp. 113 and 175). Darwin's grandson Charles
shared his interest in natural selection and evolution, and went on to write
On the Origin of Species (1859) and *The Descent of Man* (1871).

the physiological writers of Germany: the Jena circle of Johann Wilhelm Ritter,
Friedrich Wilhelm Joseph Schelling, Karl Wilhelm Friedrich von Schlegel,
and others inspired by Gottfried Wilhelm Leibniz's *Monadology* (1714),
which argues that the natural sciences should be concerned with core processes of flow and medium (such as electromagnetism), rather than treating
matter as inert and mechanistic. Ritter had a meteorically brilliant career
before his early death in 1810, possibly hastened by madness and his predilection for performing galvanic experiments upon himself (see Richard
Holmes, *The Age of Wonder: How the Romantic Generation Discovered the
Beauty and Terror of Science* (London: HarperPress, 2008), 305–36). Percy
Shelley may also have had in mind Johann Friedrich's Blumenbach's classification of five human races, refined by Karl Rudolphi into a theory of human
species and subsequently developed by Friedrich Tiedemann. Blumenbach
was a pioneer of comparative anatomy, and, along with the Swedish anatomical physicians Rudolphi and Tiedemann, was cited by William Lawrence
in his lectures, published as *An Introduction to Comparative Anatomy and
Physiology* in 1816. Blumenbach's 1805 textbook on the subject (*Handbuch
der vergleichenden Anatomie*) was later translated by Lawrence in 1827.

supernatural terrors: there is, arguably, nothing supernatural about the tale
at all (see Introduction, p. l).

casual conversation: that between the three ill-fated friends George Gordon,
Lord Byron (1788–1824), Percy Shelley (1792–1822), and John Polidori
(1795–1821).

any philosophical doctrine of whatever kind: a guarded defence—possibly
against accusations of atheism—that distances the characters from the
author.

6 *some German stories of ghosts*: the book was *Fantasmagoriana, ou Recueil
d'histoires d'apparitions de spectres, revenans, fantômes, etc.; Traduit de*

l'allemand, par un amateur, trans. Jean Baptiste Benoit Eyriès, 2 vols. (F. Schoell: Paris, 1812).

agreed to each write a story: being Byron, Polidori, and Percy Shelley (posing as Shelley) (see Introduction, pp. xvii–xviii).

VOLUME I

7   *Mrs. SAVILLE*: Margaret Walton Saville shares her initials with Mary Wollstonecraft Shelley.

St. Petersburgh: major port on the Baltic Sea, seat of the Romanov dynasty, and at the time the Russian capital.

Dec. 11th, 17—: possibly 1796. The novel begins as an epistolary travel narrative, dominated by physical geography and climate.

my day dreams become more fervent and vivid: Shelley suggests that Walton is prey to hallucinations, immediately casting doubt on his reliability as a narrator.

snow and frost are banished: in classical accounts the extreme north (*Ultima Thule*) was a clement region (see Percy Shelley, 'The Revolt of Islam' (1818), I. xlviii–liv).

8   *the secret of the magnet*: Walton's expedition to the magnetic North Pole is, like Victor's researches, in pursuit of invisible electromagnetic forces.

various voyages . . . arriving at the North Pacific Ocean: attempts to discover the fabled North-West Passage through the Arctic (see Introduction, p. xxviii; also alluded to by Milton in *Paradise Lost* (1667), x. 290–3). Walton is transfixed by the idea of the North, though it is also a proverbial place of exile, and literally hellish: the ninth circle of Dante's *Inferno* is a frozen lake, and Milton's hell has ice-cold regions:

> Beyond this flood a frozen Continent
> Lies dark and wild, beat with perpetual storms
> Of whirlwind and dire hail, which on firm land
> Thaws not, but gathers heap, and ruin seems
> Of ancient pile; all else deep snow and ice.
>
> (ii. 587–91)

I also became a poet . . . Paradise of my own creation: Walton's poetic ambitions are inspired by William Wordsworth (1770–1850) and Samuel Taylor Coleridge (1772–1834); see note to p. 118.

9   *dignity*: rank (*OED*).

Archangel: northern Russian port on the Northern Dvina River near the White Sea.

10   *I shall commit . . . communication of feeling*: despite a year spent writing poetry, Walton has lost faith in the written word.

romantic: in literature, romances were fantastical, often supernatural, narratives, peopled by sentimental and extravagant characters.

10 *keeping*: maintaining the harmony of a composition (*OED*): according to William Gilpin, '*Keeping* . . . proportions a proper degree of strength to the near and distant parts, in respect to each other' (*An Essay upon Prints* (2nd edn., London, 1768), 19).

   sense: sensitivity.

11 *shroud*: a set of ropes forming part of the rigging (*OED*).

12 *'the land of mist and snow'*: Samuel Taylor Coleridge, 'The Rime of the Ancyent Marinere' (in William Wordsworth and Samuel Taylor Coleridge, *Lyrical Ballads, with A Few Other Poems*, first published by Biggs and Cottle of Bristol, in 1798), ll. 130, 383, and 408; the Mariner shoots the albatross and is cursed. Shelley heard Coleridge recite the poem when she was aged only 9.

13 *inequalities*: irregularity of surface (*OED*); see also p. 158.

   ground sea: a heavy sea of large, rising waves (*OED*); see also pp. 158, 159.

14 *a sledge . . . on a large fragment of ice*: the extract on 'Labrador' in *Omniana, or Horæ Otiosiores* (London: Longman, Hurst, Rees, Orme, and Brown, 1812), collected by Samuel Taylor Coleridge and Robert Southey and read by Shelley, includes an account of the 'Esquimaux' riding on sledges pulled by lupine dogs, and a spectacular report of the ice cracking:

   > the large fields of ice, raising themselves out of the water, striking against each other, and plunging into the deep, with a violence not to be described, and a noise like the discharge of innumerable batteries of heavy guns. The darkness of the night, the roaring of the wind and sea, and the dashing of the waves and ice against the rocks, filled the travellers with sensations of awe and horror. (i. 164–87, at 172)

   capitulated: negotiated (*OED*).

15 *impatient of*: unable to endure (*OED*).

   dæmon: Shelley deliberately spells the word in this way from the earliest extant draft (see Charles E. Robinson (ed.), *Frankenstein* (Oxford: Bodleian Library, 2008), 100, 296), mixing meanings of both demon (an evil or malevolent spirit) and daemon (an attendant supernatural figure of inspiration; such daemons could also haunt and terrorize their human hosts) (*OED*). The ancient Greek derivation of the word daemon (δαίω) means to kindle a fire or burn with life and also to be torn apart, and is thus etymologically linked to Prometheus; it is also associated with craft and with rebellion (see Nick Groom, *The Forger's Shadow: How Forgery Changed the Course of Literature* (London: Picador, 2003), 187–94).

16 *humour*: disposition (*OED*).

17 *You have hope, and the world before you*: alluding bleakly to one of the final lines of Milton's *Paradise Lost*, 'The world was all before them' (xii. 646).

19 *syndics*: the four elected chief magistrates who governed Geneva.

   Lucerne: German-speaking Catholic town in central Switzerland. Shelley's account of her visit is given in her *History of a Six Weeks' Tour through a Part of France, Switzerland, Germany, and Holland* (London: T. Hookham, Jun., and C. & J. Ollier, 1817), published anonymously eight weeks before *Frankenstein* appeared.

the Reuss: river running through Lucerne from Lake Lucerne.

20 *plain work*: plain needlework (*OED*, citing this instance).

21 *books of chivalry and romance*: a literary taste for medievalist Gothic.

Orlando, Robin Hood, Amadis, and St George: *Orlando Furioso* by Ludovico Ariosto, an epic fantasy published in 1532; John Hoole's translation (1783) was admired by both Robert Southey and Sir Walter Scott. Ballads of Robin Hood and St George were popular throughout the period, and a selection appear in Thomas Percy's *Reliques of Ancient English Poetry* (5th edn., 1812), and the Robin Hood ballads were also edited by the radical and antiquarian Joseph Ritson in 1795; Scott was inspired by both Percy's and Ritson's collections. *Amadis de Gaul* was an influential jointly authored Spanish chivalric romance dating from the fourteenth century and popular with English readers; it was translated by Southey in 1803.

22 *Natural philosophy*: physical sciences.

genius: tutelary spirit (*OED*), a daemon.

Thonon: Thonon-les-Bains, a French Alpine town on the shores of Lake Geneva.

Cornelius Agrippa: Henricus Cornelius Agrippa of Cologne (1486–1535), the leading esotericist of the Renaissance and author of *De Occulta Philosophia Libri Tres* (published in 1533), an influential treatise of practical magic. In Christopher Marlowe's play *Doctor Faustus* (written 1588–9), Faustus declares his intention to become 'as cunning as Agrippa was' (I. i. 119).

23 *chimerical*: filled with idle fancies and wild dreams (*OED*).

Paracelsus and Albertus Magnus: Paracelsus (Theophrastus Bombast von Hohenheim, 1493–1541), Swiss physician, alchemist, and mystic. His Rosicrucian cosmology of magical creatures (*Ex Libro de Nymphis, Sylvanis, Pygmaeis, Salamandris, et Gigantibus etc*, 1566) provided the supernatural machinery for Alexander Pope's poem *The Rape of the Lock* (1714). Paracelsus believed not only that the imagination was physically creative, but also that male alchemists could actually create artificial human beings (*homunculi*) independent of female reproduction (*De Rerum Natura*, 1584); see Franz Hartmann, *The Life of Philippus Theophrastus Bombast of Hohenheim known by the name of Paracelsus and the Substance of his Teachings* (2nd edn., London: Kegan Paul, Trench, Trübner & Co., n.d. [1896]), 256–7. Albertus Magnus (b. 1193 or 1206, d. 1280), St Albert of Cologne, a Dominican friar known as 'Doctor Universalis' for his comprehensive commentary of Aristotelian philosophy. Albertus is reputed to have constructed a brass head able to answer questions.

philosopher's stone . . . elixir of life: the two great ambitions of alchemy were to discover the philosopher's stone that would turn base metals into gold, and the elixir of eternal youth. Both are bequeathed to the protagonist of

William Godwin's novel *St Leon* (1799). The chemist, inventor, and writer Humphry Davy (1778–1829) discusses these dreams of alchemy in his 'Discourse Introductory to a Course of Lectures in Chemistry' (*The Collected Works of Sir Humphry Davy, Bart. LL.D., F.R.S.*, ed. John Davy, 9 vols. (London: Smith, Elder, and Co., 1839–40), ii. 321) (see Introduction, p. xx).

23 *raising of ghosts or devils*: in 'Hymn to Intellectual Beauty', written at the same time Shelley began *Frankenstein*, Percy Shelley claims that 'While yet a boy I sought for ghosts' and had 'Hopes of high talk with the departed dead' (ll. 49, 52).

24 *effects of steam*: the first railway journey undertaken by a steam locomotive was made in Wales in 1804.

some experiments on an air-pump: in the acclaimed painting *An Experiment on a Bird in the Air Pump* (1768), Joseph Wright of Derby depicted a natural scientist evacuating air from a jar containing a live bird. This experiment was first conducted by Robert Boyle in the seventeenth century and became a staple of popular scientific demonstrations, often performed before large audiences. The air would be pumped out and the bird would begin to expire; sometimes air was released back into the jar to revive it, sometimes not.

Belrive: Bellerive, a hamlet on the western edge of Lake Geneva, about four miles from where the Shelleys stayed when visiting Byron in 1816.

Jura: mountain range marking the border between Switzerland and France.

fluid: one of several subtle, imponderable and all-pervading substances, whose assumed existence accounts for the phenomena of heat, magnetism, and electricity (*OED*; see Introduction, pp. xxvi–xxvii).

25 *boron . . . oxyds*: in chemistry, boron is one of the elementary bodies, a non-metallic solid not fusible at any known temperature (*OED*); it was first identified by Davy in 1807. Oxides are compounds with the element oxygen.

Pliny and Buffon: Pliny the Elder (AD 23–79), naturalist and compiler of the encyclopedic and miscellaneous *Historia Naturalis*, influential in the Middle Ages and Renaissance; Percy Shelley was said to have translated the first fifteen books before he left school, which may have helped to inspire his subsequent vegetarianism. Georges-Louis Leclerc, comte de Buffon (1707–88), French naturalist and celebrated author of the first 36 vols. of *Histoire naturelle, générale et particulière* (1749–88), completed after his death in another 8 vols. (1788–1802).

William: the name of Shelley's father, her half-brother, and her own son.

university of Ingolstadt: Bavarian university founded in 1472 and trans-ferred to Landshut in 1800. For centuries Ingolstadt was renowned for its Medical School, but by the end of the eighteenth century it was also notorious as the home of the Illuminati, a secret society founded by Adam Weishaupt in May 1776. Initially a humanitarian scientific Enlightenment group, the Illuminati also had esoteric and occult interests, and were feared by some to be an international conspiracy of ultra-rationalists and republicans, ultimately responsible for inspiring the Jacobins; by 1784 they had already been outlawed. In Abbé Augustin Barruel's 1797 history, *Memoirs Illustrating the History of Jacobinism*—a favourite of Percy Shelley's—the Illuminati and their legacy are described as monstrous, and Weishaupt (alleged among other things to be an incestuous child-murderer) as being 'like the sinister owl . . . which glides in the shadow of the night'. For Barruel, 'this baleful Sophist will be remembered in history only as the Demon' (see Peter Dale Scott, 'Vital Artifice: Mary, Percy, and the Psychopolitical Identity of *Frankenstein*', in George Levine and U. C. Knoepflmacher (eds.), *The Endurance of Frankenstein: Essays on Mary Shelley's Novel* (Berkeley and Los Angeles: University of California Press, 1979), 172–202, at 179).

26 *meeting you in another world*: alluding to Goethe, *The Sorrows of Young Werther* (1774), bk. i, 10 September. The popularity of Werther's death scene inspired such attractions as a life-size waxwork vignette (see the broadsheet *At Mrs. Salmon's Royal Wax-Work, in Fleet-Street* (London: *c.*1785?), in the 4th room).

27 *the spoiler*: time, as used figuratively by Charles Lamb (1775–1834), essayist and poet, in his *Elia* essay 'My Relations' (1821).

imperious: imperative (*OED*).

chaise: general term for a light carriage (*OED*).

'old familiar faces': the title of Lamb's poem beginning 'Where are they gone, the old familiar faces? | I had a mother, but she died and left me, | Died prematurely in a day of horrors—' (1798).

29 *sentences*: opinions (*OED*).

the sweetest I had ever heard: the portrait of Waldman is reminiscent of Godwin, nicknamed by Lamb 'the Professor'; it may also be influenced by the anatomist John Abernethy who, Robert Christison remembered, was renowned for his 'pure thoughts, sound reasoning, beautiful language, and noble delivery' (*The Life of Sir Robert Christison, Bart.*, 2 vols. (London and Edinburgh: William Blackwood and Sons, 1885–6), i. 199; see Introduction, pp. xx, xxv–xxvi.

cursory: rapid and informal.

They penetrate . . . her hiding places: M. Waldman's lecture follows Davy's argument in his 'Discourse Introductory to a Course of Lectures in Chemistry' (21 January 1802), in which he admonishes the practices of chemical physiology: 'Instead of slowly endeavouring to lift up the veil concealing the wonderful phenomena of living nature; full of ardent imaginations, they have vainly and presumptuously attempted to tear it asunder' ('Discourse', in *Works*, ii. 314). Similarly, in his 'Introductory Lecture to the Chemistry of Nature' (31 January 1807), Davy considers that concerning 'chemical operations, as far as they are connected with the powers of living systems . . . as yet, little has been effected; and the materials, though important, are few and slender. The skirt only of the veil which conceals these mysterious and sublime processes has been lifted up, and the grand view is as yet known' (*Works*, viii. 175–6).

30 *mock the invisible world with its own shadows*: a reference to phantasmagoria and other audiovisual spectacles.

    peculiar: particular (*OED*).

    mathematics: not pure mathematics, but physical sciences involving geometry, such as optics and astronomy (*OED*).

31 *applied so closely*: assiduously and attentively devoted [myself to] (*OED*).

32 *principle*: fundamental source; a primary element, force, or law (*OED*).

    physiology: functional processes of a living organism or system (*OED*).

    To examine the causes of life . . . death: according to Davy, 'the study of the simple and unvarying agencies of dead matter ought surely to precede investigations concerning the mysterious and complicated powers of life' ('Discourse', in *Works*, ii. 313–14). The mystic alchemist Paracelsus had also studied putrefaction, categorizing it as a form of generation: see note to p. 175.

33 *the Arabian . . . seemingly ineffectual, light*: on Sinbad the Sailor's fourth voyage in the popular collection of Oriental tales *Arabian Nights Entertainments* (or *The Thousand and One Nights*, first published in English *c*.1708), he is interred in a mass grave with the dead body of his wife, but eventually escapes the burial chamber by following a faint light that leads him to freedom.

34 *ideal bounds*: imaginary or fancied limits (*OED*).

    if I could bestow . . . corruption: for Davy, the discipline of chemistry included 'the conversion of dead matter into living matter by vegetable organs' ('Discourse', in *Works*, ii. 311).

    confinement: the word was used of pregnant women awaiting childbirth (*OED*).

    pursued nature to her hiding places: see note to p. 29.

35 *filthy*: both disgustingly foul and morally corrupt (*OED*); the word occurs several times in the text. For a perhaps discomforting analogy see also S. A. D. Tissot, *Onanism*, trans. A. Hume (London, 1766): 'The masturbator, entirely devoted to his filthy meditations, is subject to the same disorders as the man of letters who fixes his attention upon a single question' (75).

36 *alloy*: undesirable or degrading elements (*OED*).

    America . . . Mexico and Peru: 'Was it the charity of your gospel that led you to exterminate whole nations in America, and to destroy the empires of Mexico and Peru[?]' (Constantin François Volney, *The Ruins: or A Survey of the Revolutions of Empire*, trans. James Marshall (5th edn., London: Thomas Tegg, 1811), 176; see here p. 86).

    IT was on a dreary night of November: in her Introduction to the 1831 edition, Shelley claims that these were the first words of the novel she wrote (see Appendix A, p. 176).

instruments of life: bioscientific apparatus, which Shelley later implied was electrical equipment—'Perhaps a corpse would be reanimated; galvanism had given token of such things: perhaps the component parts of a creature might be manufactured, brought together, and endued with vital warmth' (Appendix A, p. 176; see Introduction, pp. xxvi–xxvii).

the rain pattered dismally against the panes: dissecting rooms were cold and eerily quiet places, any sounds muffled by the sawdust spread upon the floor to absorb blood and bodily fluids (see Florent Palluault, 'Medical Students in England and France, 1815–1858: A Comparative Study', DPhil thesis (University of Oxford, 2003), 106).

37 *I had selected his features as beautiful*: this was the technique of the ancient Greek painter Zeuxis, who depicted Helen of Troy by taking the best bits of the virgins of Crotona, as well as that recommended by the society portrait artist Sir Joshua Reynolds, to create 'ideal beauty' (see James Heffernan, *Cultivating Picturacy: Visual Art and Verbal Interventions* (Waco, TX: Baylor University Press, 2006), 187).

his hair was of a lustrous black . . . and straight black lips: for the relationship of the Being to early depictions of vampires and to vampirology more generally, see Nick Groom, *The Vampire: A New History* (New Haven and London: Yale University Press, 2018), 119–23; see also note to p. 52.

aspect: appearance, look (*OED*).

monster: from the Latin *monstrare*, meaning 'to show'; the word was used against political radicals such as Godwin (for a discussion, see Chris Baldick, *In Frankenstein's Shadow: Myth, Monstrosity, and Nineteenth-Century Writing* (Oxford: Clarendon Press, 1987), 10–29 and *passim*).

38 *mummy*: in addition to the preserved carcases of ancient Egypt, 'mummy' also described mortal remains or a pulpy mass, as well as a sovereign remedy; the maternal meaning is only first recorded in the late eighteenth century and is unlikely to be implied here (*OED*). Shelley uses the image again at the end of the novel (see p. 168), specifically to mean mummified or embalmed flesh.

Dante: the Italian poet Dante Alighieri (1265–1321) populated the *Inferno*, the account of hell that begins his *Divina commedia*, with allegorical monsters.

hardly: violently, strenuously (*OED*).

Ancient Mariner: Coleridge, 'The Ancyent Marinere', ll. 451–6.

diligences: public stagecoaches (*OED*).

39 *Dutch school-master in The Vicar of Wakefield*: *The Vicar of Wakefield* (1766), a novel by Oliver Goldsmith (?1728–74), includes a Dutch school-master who concludes his boast of ignorance by declaring 'as I don't know Greek, I do not believe there is any good in it' (vol. ii, ch. 1).

watching: sleepless (*OED*).

43 *the beauty of Angelica*: Angelica, heroine of Ariosto's *Orlando Furioso*, the object of Orlando's love, and the cause of his madness; there are

allusions to Angelica in both Milton's *Paradise Lost* and Wordsworth's *The Prelude* (1805).

48 *Plainpalais*: a quarter of Geneva outside the city wall. Shelley described it in her *History of a Six Weeks' Tour* as 'the promenade of the Genevese, a grassy plain planted with a few trees, and called Plainpalais' (1 June 1816).

50 *Stoics*: Athenian philosophy popular in ancient Rome *c*.100 BC–*c*.AD 200 and revived in the Renaissance, based on the efficacy of reason in governing the emotions. The *Distichs of Cato* was a collection of Stoic maxims highly admired in the Middle Ages.

Cato: Marcus Porcius Cato Uticensis (95–46 BC), known as Cato the Younger; Plutarch recorded in his *Lives of the Noble Greeks and Romans* that when his older brother Caepio died he was mourned by Cato in extravagant style.

cabriole: cabriolet, a light, two-wheeled one-horse chaise or carriage with a hood, later shortened to the familiar 'cab' (*OED*).

Lausanne: Swiss city on Lake Geneva.

'the palaces of nature': from Lord Byron, *Childe Harold's Pilgrimage* (III. lxii. 591 (1816)); belief in the restorative effects of natural environments developed alongside medical advances as an early example of 'green wellbeing'.

Mont Blanc: at 15,774 feet the highest peak in the Alps; Percy Shelley's poem 'Mont Blanc' ('Lines written in the Vale of Chamouni') was written in Switzerland as Mary Shelley was beginning *Frankenstein*.

51 *terrific*: terrifying, awe-inspiring, sublime (*OED*). In *Childe Harold's Pilgrimage*, Byron describes the Alpine storm of 13 June 1816, a few days before *Frankenstein* was begun:

> The sky is changed!—and such a change! Oh Night,
> And Storm, and Darkness, ye are wondrous strong,
> Yet lovely in your strength, as is the light
> Of a dark eye in Woman! Far along,
> From peak to peak, the rattling crags among
> Leaps the live thunder! Not from one lone cloud,
> But every mountain now hath found a tongue,
> And Jura answers, through her misty shroud,
> Back to the joyous Alps, who call to her aloud!
>   (III. xcii. ll. 860–8)

Mont Salève: the Salève, the 'Balcony of Geneva', 4,524 feet high.

the Môle: an impressive pyramidal mountain twelve miles from Geneva, rising to 6,112 feet.

52 *vampire*: as well as the more familiar meaning of a supernaturally reanimated corpse sucking the blood of its victims, the word was also used figuratively, especially in politics, to describe malignant and loathsome persons who prey ruthlessly upon others (*OED*); on 20 November 1814,

Harriet Shelley wrote that her husband had been jointly seduced by Godwin's philosophy and his bewitching daughter Mary: 'In short, the man I once loved is dead. This is a vampire. His character is blasted for ever' (*Letters of Percy Bysshe Shelley*, ed. Jones, i. 421, 992). *Frankenstein* was conceived within a few nights of Polidori's tale 'The Vampyre' (published 1819); there are vampires too in Southey's poem *Thalaba the Destroyer* (1801) and Byron's *The Giaour* (1813), and the Being exhibits vampiric characteristics (see note to p. 37).

The trial began: the style of this passage is based on popular 'Newgate' crime literature: see Nick Groom (ed.), *The Bloody Register*, 4 vols. (London: Routledge, 1999).

58 *indecent*: unseemly, unbecoming (*OED*).

tedious: painful (*OED*).

59 *ballots*: balls or tokens for a secret vote.

60 *Ever since I was condemned . . . I continued obdurate*: anti-Catholic sentiments are typical of many Gothic novels of the period.

evil hour: in Milton's *Paradise Lost*, Eve takes the forbidden fruit 'in evil hour' (ix. 780).

62 *never-dying worm*: in Milton's *Paradise Lost*, Christ refers to the 'undying worm' of hell (vi. 739; see Mark 9:44).

I bore a hell within me: in Milton's *Paradise Lost*, Satan has 'hell within him, for within him hell | He brings' (iv. 20–1; see also Satan's lines, iv. 73–5, and ix. 467—'a hot hell that always in him burns').

VOLUME II

63 *blasted*: stricken by supernatural agency or the wrath or curse of heaven, blighted (*OED*).

64 *signal*: remarkable, striking (*OED*).

66 *Chamounix*: Chamonix is a village on the northern side of Mont Blanc. The Shelleys visited during their trip to Switzerland in the summer of 1816 (21–7 July) when Shelley was drafting *Frankenstein*; they were greeted by a thunderous avalanche and spellbound by the icefields and moving glaciers (*Journals of Shelley*, ed. Feldman and Scott-Kilvert, i. 112-14; see note to p. 50). Of the glacier Le Mer de Glace, Shelley wrote on 25 July, 'This is the most desolate place in the world—iced mountains surround it—no sign of vegetation appears except on the place from which [we] view the scene—we went on the ice—it is traversed by irregular crevices whose sides of ice appear blue while the surface is of a dirty white' (*Journals of Shelley*, ed. Feldman and Scott-Kilvert, i. 119; see note to p. 142).

Arve: a tributary of the Rhône fed by glaciers.

sublime: the mind's inexpressible encounter with the infinite, inspiring the imagination with overwhelming feelings of beauty and terror; a defining Romantic experience.

66 *domes*: convex rounded summits of mountains; an inaugural usage.

67 *picturesque*: the cult of the picturesque regarded landscapes in artistic terms to discover transcendent and elevating sublimity within natural environments.

   Servox: Shelley later described this valley in more detail at the climax of her novel *The Last Man* (London: Henry Colburn, 1826), concluding with a quotation from her mother's *Letters written during a Short Residence in Sweden, Norway, and Denmark* (1796):

> We left the fair margin of the beauteous lake of Geneva, and entered the Alpine ravines; tracing to its source the brawling Arve, through the rock-bound valley of Servox, beside the mighty waterfalls, and under the shadow of the inaccessible mountains, we travelled on; while the luxuriant walnut-tree gave place to the dark pine, whose musical branches swung in the wind, and whose upright forms had braved a thousand storms—till the verdant sod, the flowery dell, and shrubbery hill were exchanged for the sky-piercing, untrodden, seedless rock, 'the bones of the world, waiting to be clothed with every thing necessary to give life and beauty.' (vol. iii, ch. 8, p. 163)

   aiguilles: Alpine peaks; Byron first used the term in his *Journal* entry for 17 September 1816.

   littleness: pettiness (*OED*).

68 *awful*: solemnly or sublimely impressive (*OED*).

   necessary beings: a veiled reference to Godwin's 'doctrine of necessity' described in chapter 5 of his *Enquiry Concerning Political Justice* (1793), which argues that what appears to be human free will is actually contingent on historical and contextual circumstances.

69 *We rest . . . endure but mutability!*: Percy Shelley, 'Mutability' (published with *Alastor*, 1816), ll. 9–16.

70 *insect*: this contemptuous insult was usually addressed to trivial nobodies obsessed with fashion (*OED*); in contrast, Victor uses it to emphasize that the Being is anything but human. Bizarrely, though, Victor earlier describes Elizabeth as 'playful as a summer insect' (p. 21).

   Do your duty . . . rest of mankind: the Being offers a social contract to Victor, based on a Godwinian notion of individual responsibility.

   devoted: the word means attached to a person or cause, but also doomed or consigned to evil (*OED*); it is repeated several times in the narrative, often—and disconcertingly—carrying both senses.

   creature: a created thing (promoting well-being), and, simultaneously, a despicable or subservient person, or an animal (*OED*); the Being is again using a deliberately slippery term.

71 *misery made me a fiend . . . I shall again be virtuous*: in *An Historical and Moral View of the Origin and Progress of the French Revolution* (London, 1794), Wollstonecraft argued that oppression and subjugation foment

parricidal rebellion—'whilst despotism and superstition exist, the convulsions, which the regeneration of man occasions, will always bring forward the vices they have engendered, to devour their parents' (259).

caves of ice: alluding to Coleridge's visionary poem 'Kubla Khan', l. 36 (printed 1816).

72 *A strange multiplicity of sensations . . . operations of my various senses*: the Being's original state conforms to Davy's thinking that 'Man, in what is called a state of nature, is a creature of almost pure sensation' ('Discourse', in *Works*, ii. 318). This gradually emerging sentience also mirrors Volney's proposition of the original state of Man:

> IN the origin of things, man, formed equally naked both as to body and mind, found himself thrown by chance upon a land confused and savage. An orphan, deserted by the unknown power that had produced him, he saw no supernatural beings at hand to advertise him of wants that he owed merely to his senses, and inform him of duties springing solely from those wants. Like other animals, without experience of the past, without knowledge of the future, he wandered in forests, guided and governed purely by the affections of his nature. By the pain of hunger he was directed to seek food, and he provided for his subsistence; by the inclemencies of the weather, the desire was excited of covering his body, and he made himself cloathing: by the attraction of a powerful pleasure, he approached a fellow-being, and perpetuated his species. . . . Thus the impressions he received from external objects, awakening his faculties, developed by degrees his understanding, and began to instruct his profound ignorance; his wants called forth his industry; his dangers formed his mind to courage; he learned to distinguish useful from pernicious plants, to resist the elements, to seize upon his prey, to defend his life; and his misery was alleviated. (*The Ruins* (5th edn., 1811), 21–2)

This materialist philosophy continues in Volney's appendix to *The Ruins*, 'The Law of Nature, or Principles of Morality, deduced from the Physical Constitution of Mankind and the Universe', which includes a dialogue on parenting.

74 *the offals . . . the berries I gathered from the trees*: in his lengthy notes to *Queen Mab* (published 1813), Percy Shelley argued that one consequence of Prometheus' theft of fire was cooking, in order to make meat more palatable.

75 *Pandæmonium . . . lake of fire*: in Milton's *Paradise Lost*, the devils lie 'Grovelling and prostrate on yon lake of fire' (i. 280) before they are roused by Satan to build the diabolical city of Pandemonium (i. 674–775).

wallet: a bag for holding provisions, clothing, books, and the like when travelling (*OED*).

77 *gentle*: honourable, courteous (*OED*).

82 *transparent pool!*: in Milton's *Paradise Lost*, Eve likewise sees her reflection in a pool, 'As I bent down to look, just opposite, | A shape within the

watery gleam appeared | Bending to look on me, I started back' (iv. 460–2);
but the Being's experience is in stark contrast to that of Eve, who admires
herself (see Introduction, p. xlv).

83 *the ass and the lap-dog*: in La Fontaine's *Fables* (bk. iv, fable 5) the ass is
chastised for frolicking like a little dog (see also Aesop's *Fables*).

fit habitation: 'Hell their fit habitation fraught with fire' (Milton, *Paradise
Lost*, vi. 876).

85 *Safie*: the name may allude to *sophia* (wisdom) (see Introduction, p. xxxiii).

86 *Volney's Ruins of Empires*: Constantin François Volney (1775–1820), philosopher and statesman, author of *Les Ruines, ou Méditation sur les révolu-
tions des empires* (Paris, 1791). Beginning with a survey of the ruins of
Palmyra, Volney links the rise and fall of human empires to religious systems of thought and belief, focused on the Middle East. The account was
popular with early nineteenth-century English and American political
radicals, and was covertly translated by Thomas Jefferson in 1802. Volney's
text arguably provides the Being with a materialist and mechanistic
philosophy, and a global perspective on human governance and power:

> Man is governed, like the world of which he forms a part, by natural
> laws, regular in their operation, consequent in their effects, immutable
> in their essence; and these laws, the common source of good and evil,
> are neither written in the distant stars, nor concealed in mysterious
> codes: inherent in the nature of all terrestrial beings, identified with their
> existence, they are at all times and in all places present to the human
> mind; they act upon the senses, inform the intellect, and annex to every
> action its punishment and its reward. Let man study these laws, let him
> understand his own nature, and the nature of the beings that surround
> him, and he will know the springs of his destiny, the causes of his evils,
> and the remedies to be applied. (*The Ruins* (5th edn., 1811), 19)

It is ironic that Volney was writing when the French Revolution was dramatically escalating, whereas Shelley is writing after the final defeat of
Napoleon; curiously, Volney barely mentions the British Empire.

89 *Mahometan*: Muslim (term derived from 'Muhammad', and now archaic:
see *OED*). Percy Shelley's Spenserian political love poem 'The Revolt of
Islam' was written in 1817 and dedicated to 'Mary———' [i.e. Wollstonecraft
Shelley]; it was published in December of that year as *Laon and Cythna*,
promptly suppressed, revised, and then republished in January 1818 as
The Revolt of Islam.

delicate: sensitive to what is proper or modest (*OED*).

90 *haram*: a sanctuary sacred to Muslims (*OED*).

91 *meed*: recompense (*OED*).

93 *Paradise Lost . . . Plutarch's Lives . . . Sorrows of Werter*: Milton's *Paradise
Lost* (1667); Plutarch's *Lives of the Noble Greeks and Romans* (also known
as *Parallel Lives*), consisting of some fifty biographies, translated into

English by John Dryden and others in 1683; and Goethe's *Die Leiden des jungen Werthers* ['The Sorrows of Young Werther'] (Leipzig, 1774). Shelley had read or reread these three books in 1815, and Percy read aloud from *Paradise Lost* while she was composing *Frankenstein* (see Introduction and Note on the Text, pp. xviii, li). The Being evidently acquires these texts as French translations.

out of self: other than self-regard.

fill me with wonder: in imitation of an episode in the novel in which Werther points a pistol at his head (12 August); there was widely believed to be a spate of copycat suicides across Europe following the publication of Goethe's novel. Although the lethal impact of the book has been exaggerated, it did undoubtedly inspire an international craze for 'Wertherism' in fashion, merchandise, and attitudes.

"The path . . . was free": Percy Shelley, 'Mutability', l. 14, slightly revised (see note to p. 69).

94 *Numa, Solon, and Lycurgus . . . Romulus and Theseus*: Numa Pompilius (715–673 BC), legendary king of Rome, who according to Plutarch cultivated an aura of superstition to keep the populace in order; Solon (*c*.640/635–*c*.561/560 BC), Athenian statesman and propagandist poet; Lycurgus of Sparta (sometime between 1100 and 600 BC), mythical and semi-divine founder of the Spartan virtues of parity, military prowess, and asceticism; Romulus (before fourth century BC), mythical founder and first king of Rome, famously raised by a wolf; and Theseus, mythical and semi-divine founder and first king of Athens, and slayer of the Cretan Minotaur. All five are included in Plutarch's *Lives of the Noble Greeks and Romans*.

patriarchal: family structure organized around the eldest males.

the bitter gall of envy rose within me: Satan's envy is described in book IV of *Paradise Lost*, 'Thus while he spake, each passion dimmed his face | Thrice changed with pale, ire, envy and despair' (iv. 114–15).

96 *Adam's supplication to his Creator*: in Milton's *Paradise Lost*, Adam's request for 'human consort' (viii. 379–97).

he had abandoned me: Rousseau's novel *Émile* (1762) begins with a warning against isolating fellow beings:

> our species does not admit to being formed halfway . . . a man abandoned to himself in the midst of other men from birth would be the most disfigured of all. Prejudices, authority, necessity, example, all the social institutions in which we find ourselves submerged would stifle nature in him and put nothing in its place. Nature there would be like a shrub that chance had caused to be born in the middle of a path and that the passers-by soon cause to perish by bumping into it from all sides and bending it in every direction. (Jean-Jacques Rousseau, *Émile, or On Education*, ed. and trans. Allan Bloom (New York: Basic Books, 1979), 37)

96 Between 1815 and 1817, Shelley read and reread Rousseau's *Confessions*, *Émile*, *Julie or The New Héloïse*, and *Essay on the Origin of Language*.

conformation: constitution (more precisely, disposition of parts: *OED*).

97 *De Lacy*: from this point in the text the spelling of the name changes, possibly due to Percy's corrections to the proof sheets made from 24 September 1817. The 1823 edition corrected by Godwin reverts to 'De Lacey' throughout.

98 *unprejudiced by*: not predisposed to (*OED*).

100 *toils*: nets used in hunting to ensnare the quarry (*OED*).

bore a hell within me: in Vol. I, Ch. vii these words are spoken by Victor; see note to p. 62.

101 *language of the country*: German.

recover: be reconciled with (*OED*).

stupid: stupefied, insensible (*OED*).

102 *the moon nearly touched*: possibly a bitter allusion to Wordsworth's 'Lucy' poem, 'Strange fits of passion I have known' (*Lyrical Ballads*, 1802).

with the world before me . . . bend my steps?: alluding to the last lines of Milton's *Paradise Lost* (xii. 646–9); see note to p. 17.

106 *sanguinary*: bloodthirsty (*OED*).

requisition: request, necessary condition (*OED*).

a right which you must not refuse: the language and philosophy of rights was central to British radicalism and the thinking of Godwin and Wollstonecraft.

107 *contemns*: despises (*OED*).

you curse the hour of your birth: see Job's curse against the day he was born (Job 3:1–26).

108 *acorns and berries . . . sufficient nourishment*: in *Paradise Lost*, Adam and Eve enjoy a vegetarian diet in the Garden of Eden (v. 303–7, 321–49, 479–86). In *Queen Mab*, Percy Shelley argued that 'man resembles frugivorous animals in everything, and carnivorous in nothing' (notes to canto viii); he also advocated temperance (see note to p. 74).

110 *siroc*: sirocco, an oppressively hot and blighting wind over the Mediterranean, characterized as moist and depressing in southern Europe (*OED*).

the hellish hypocrites: in Dante's *Inferno*, the hypocrites wear radiant gilded cowls lined with lead (xxiii. 58–67).

VOLUME III

113 *an English philosopher*: depending on the dating of the events in the novel, Shelley may have had in mind the Scottish surgeon John Hunter (1728–93), the English natural philosopher and poet Erasmus Darwin (1731–1802), the English philosopher Joseph Priestley (1733–1804), the English man of science Edward Jenner (1749–1823), or the Cornish chemist Humphry Davy (1778–1829).

conjure: beseech, implore (*OED*).

114 *exordium*: beginning, especially of a discourse (*OED*).

this deadly weight . . . to the ground: Coleridge, 'The Ancyent Marinere', ll. 138, 283.

116 *bourne*: ultimate point (*OED*).

117 *the Rhine . . . from Strasburgh to Rotterdam*: part of the journey undertaken by the Shelleys in August and September 1814, described in *History of a Six Weeks' Tour*.

the priest and his mistress . . . nightly wind: in her *History of a Six Weeks' Tour*, Shelley recorded that

> The summits of several of the mountains that enclose the lake to the south are covered by eternal glaciers; of one of these, opposite Brunen, they tell the story of a priest and his mistress, who, flying from persecution, inhabited a cottage at the foot of the snows. One winter night an avalanche overwhelmed them, but their plaintive voices are still heard in stormy nights, calling for succour from the peasant. (48–9)

118 *pile*: journey across (a usage otherwise unrecorded).

Leigh Hunt's 'Rimini': Hunt's Story of Rimini (1816) is derived from Dante's story of Paolo and Francesca's adulterous love that condemns them to Hell (*Inferno*, v. 79–138); Hunt describes Paolo as 'formed in the very nature of poetry' (l. 47).

Wordsworth's 'Tintern Abbey': 'Lines Written a few miles above Tintern Abbey, on revisiting the Banks of the Wye, during a tour, July 13, 1798' (*Lyrical Ballads*, 1798), ll. 77–84; Shelley twice revises 'me' to 'him'. The account of the creative imagination that immediately follows ('which formed a world, whose existence depended on the life of its creator') is indebted to both Wordsworth's and Coleridge's visionary conception of poetry.

119 *post*: travel with relays of horses (*OED*).

Tilbury Fort . . . Spanish armada: seventeenth-century coastal fortification on the Thames Estuary, developed from earlier defences built by Henry VIII; in 1588 Queen Elizabeth rallied her army at Tilbury against the Spanish Armada.

intercourse of: social communication or conversation with (*OED*); the sexual meaning is first recorded in 1803.

120 *beginning of October*: a discrepancy, as at the end of the final chapter Victor claims that it was 'in the latter days of December, that I first saw the white cliffs of Britain'. This error remains in the 1831 edition (140).

Matlock: Matlock Bath, a spa town in the Derbyshire Peak District later dubbed the 'English Switzerland'.

From thence we proceeded to Oxford: Mary and Percy visited Oxford together in September 1815.

121 *Falkland*: Lucius Cary, 2nd Viscount Falkland (1609/10–43), Royalist politician and writer who, despairing of the Civil War, was killed at the

Battle of Newbury when he deliberately rode into Parliamentarian cross-fire. Falkland inspired Godwin's archetypal Cavalier of the same name in *Caleb Williams* (1794).

121 *Gower*: George Goring, Baron Goring (1608–57), Royalist general with a reputation for raffish behaviour and deft strategy; in the Earl of Clarendon's *History of the Rebellion* (published 1702) he is presented as wavering in his support for the king and putting self-interest before country. The name was corrected in the third edition of 1831.

his queen, and son: Henrietta Maria of France (1609–69) and Charles (1630–85), later Charles II.

Isis: the River Thames, so called in Oxford.

ennui: mental weariness and dissatisfaction caused by lack of interest in one's surroundings or activities (*OED*).

the tomb of the illustrious Hampden . . . that patriot fell: John Hampden (1595–1643), Parliamentarian politician and colonel, and a key strategist on the battlefield. He was fatally wounded at the Battle of Chalgrove Field as the Royalists advanced on Oxford and is buried at Great Hampden, some 23 miles from the city. Thomas Gray remembered him in his 'Elegy Written in a Country Churchyard' (1753), and Shelley's mention is a reminder of the brutal history of English political progress that frequently haunts the Gothic.

122 *wondrous cave . . . Servox and Chamounix*: there are several caves and caverns (some originally lead mines) in the vicinity of Matlock Bath, notably Masson Low and High Tor, that became established as popular tourist destinations later in the nineteenth century. Percy Shelley wrote to Thomas Love Peacock on 22 July 1816 that he and Mary had visited copper and lead mines at Servox. A cabinet was a small room set aside to display *objets d'art* or curiosities; by the time Shelley was writing the word was already archaic.

Cumberland and Westmoreland: the Lake District.

men of talent: this suggests (if anachronistically) the Lake Poets—Wordsworth, Coleridge, and Southey.

on the stretch: tense (*OED*).

123 *Arthur's Seat, St Bernard's Well, . . . the Pentland Hills*: Arthur's Seat is a summit of 823 feet, about a mile from Edinburgh Castle; St Bernard's Well is a natural spring discovered in Edinburgh in 1760 and reputed to cure illnesses and benefit health; and the Pentland Hills run south-west from Edinburgh. Shelley lived in Dundee for several months in 1812–13 (see Appendix A, p. 173 and note).

five miles distant: there are over seventy islands in the Orkney archipelago, of which only about two-thirds have been permanently inhabited at some point. Orkney is far closer to the Arctic Circle than it is to Geneva.

124 *sequel*: consequence (*OED*, which notes the rarity of this usage).

unequal: disturbed (*OED*).

125 *deserts*: uninhabited wildernesses (*OED*).

a race of devils . . . the earth: Victor's fear of multiplying Beings seems influenced by Caliban's boast to Prospero in Shakespeare's *The Tempest* concerning his thwarted sexual assault of Miranda, 'Thou didst prevent me; I had peopled else | This isle with Calibans' (I. ii. 352–3).

sophisms: deliberately specious and fallacious arguments (*OED*).

127 *period*: end, conclusion (*OED*).

128 *closed*: engaged in hand-to-hand combat (*OED*).

129 *mangled the living flesh of a human being*: the destruction of the female Being may draw on the prurient public interest excited by the autopsies of women. The post-mortem examination of the prophetess Joanne Southcott in 1814 was reported at length in Hunt's *Examiner* (1815), and an account of the dissection of the 'Hottentot Venus', a South African Khoisan woman by the name of Saartjie Baartman, who had arrived in London in 1810 as an erotic sideshow, was published in 1816 and her body parts publicly displayed (see Tim Marshall, *Murdering to Dissect: Grave-Robbing, Frankenstein and the Anatomy of Literature* (Manchester: Manchester University Press, 1995), 188–200; and Peter Kitson, *Romantic Literature, Race, and Colonial Encounter* (Basingstoke: Palgrave Macmillan, 2008), 83).

130 *burning thirst*: Coleridge, 'The Ancyent Marinere', ll. 131–4.

131 *the Irish to hate villains*: Ireland is over 300 miles from Orkney as the crow flies, so Orkney may be a mistake for the Inner Hebrides archipelago, which is only about 30 nautical miles from the northern Irish coast.

132 *Kirwin*: a name possibly alluding to Richard Kirwan (1733–1812), Irish chemist, climatologist, and mineralogist (see Marilyn Butler (ed.), *Frankenstein or The Modern Prometheus: The 1818 Text* (1993; repr. Oxford: Oxford University Press, 1994), 259 n.).

138 *bury me and my destroyer in its ruins*: Volney's *Ruins* begins by contemplating the ruins of Palmyra, a touchstone for the collapse of civilization, remarking 'who knows but that hereafter, some traveller like myself will sit down upon the banks of the Seine, the Thames, or the Zuyder sea, . . . who knows but he will sit down solitary, amid silent ruins, and weep a people inurned, and their greatness changed into an empty name?' (*The Ruins* (5th edn., 1811), 7–8; see also Robert Wood and James Dawkins, *The Ruins of Palmyra, otherwise Tedmor, in the Desart* (London, 1753)).

assizes: sessions held periodically in British and Irish counties to administer civil and criminal justice (*OED*).

139 *two eyes that glared upon me*: 'two eyes, | Two starry eyes, hung in the gloom of thought' (Percy Shelley, *Alastor*, ll. 489–90).

maladie du pays: homesickness (*OED*); considered at the time to be a Swiss national characteristic.

140 *packet*: packet-boat, the regular mailboat (*OED*).

laudanum: opium dissolved in alcohol, the word coined by Paracelsus (*OED*); Coleridge and later Thomas De Quincey were addicted to the drug.

Havre: Le Havre, French town at the estuary of the River Seine estuary and Channel coast; at the time it was the second largest port in France.

141 *bounded to the again seeing me*: i.e. limited to the fact of seeing me again; a peculiar construction, present in the manuscript but revised in the 1831 edition (see Robinson (ed.), *Frankenstein*, 207, 392).

142 *sea of ice*: alluding to the Mer de Glace (literally, 'sea of ice') glacier, near Chamonix and Mont Blanc. The Shelleys visited the glacier on 25 July 1816. Percy described the expedition thus:

> In these regions every thing changes & is in motion. This vast mass of ice has one general progress which ceases neither day nor night. It breaks & rises forever; its undulations sink whilst others rise. From the precipices which surround it the echo of rocks which fall from their aerial summits, or of the ice & snow scarcely ceases for one moment. One would think that Mont Blanc was a living being & that the frozen blood forever circulated slowly thro' his stony veins. (*Letters of Percy Bysshe Shelley*, ed. Jones, i. 358)

The account was published in Shelley's *History of a Six Weeks' Tour*.

144 *consummate*: make perfect (*OED*).

146 *nicer*: more sensitive, more acute (*OED*).

147 *ambition . . . enslave it*: among the Swiss who left for France were the philosopher Rousseau, the financier and statesman Jacques Necker, and Necker's daughter Anne Louise Germaine, afterwards renowned as Mme de Staël—intellectual *salonnière* and writer. The French Revolutionary Army later invaded Switzerland in 1798; according to Butler, 'the plot . . . re-enacts the dying stages of the Genevan republic. Its death unwittingly brought on by the intellectual over-reaching, selfishness, and exclusivity of its ruling order' (Butler (ed.), *Frankenstein*, 259 n.).

148 *The Alps . . . eastern boundary*: the Chablais Massif.

149 *She was there . . . covered by her hair*: Elizabeth's prostrate corpse is reminiscent of the drugged and deranged female form in Henry Fuseli's renowned painting *The Nightmare*, first exhibited in 1782 (see Maryanne C. Ward, 'A Painting of the Unspeakable: Henry Fuseli's *The Nightmare* and the Creation of Mary Shelley's *Frankenstein*', *Journal of the Midwest Modern Language Association*, 33 (2000), 20–31). Fuseli, a Swiss national who settled in London in 1779, painted Wollstonecraft's portrait; for her part, she idolized him to the extent that she proposed she should move in with him and his wife in a ménage à trois.

150 *drawing a pistol . . . plunged into the lake*: the supposed assassination attempt on Percy Shelley at Tan-Yr-Allt in Wales seems to have influenced Victor's

chaotic attempt to shoot the Being (see Richard Holmes, *Shelley: The Pursuit* (New York: New York Review of Books, 1994), 187–8).

152 *wonderful*: full of wonder, exciting astonishment (*OED*).

154 *my wanderings . . . cease but with life*: most of Percy Shelley's poem *Alastor* concerns the wanderings of the Poet; 'wildly he wandered on, | Day after day, a weary waste of hours, | Bearing within his life the brooding care | That ever fed on its decaying flame' (ll. 244–7).

shades: spectres, phantoms (*OED*, noting that this is a rare usage).

155 *furies*: frenzied rage approaching madness; the word is derived from the avenging deities of classical mythology, and this passion is sometimes linked to daemonic poetic inspiration (*OED*).

my eternal hell: 'Which way I fly is hell; my self am hell' (Milton's *Paradise Lost*, iv. 75), and 'a hot hell that always in him burns' (ix. 467: see note to p. 62).

murmured: inarticulately complained (*OED*).

156 *marks in writing . . . cut in stone*: the idea that nature constituted a vast 'book' was a theological cornerstone for centuries—put simply, 'the great BOOK OF NATURE . . . proves the existence, the power, and the goodness of GOD in every page of it' (Sarah Trimmer, *An Easy Introduction to the Knowledge of Nature, and Reading the Holy Scriptures* (10th edn., London, 1799), 141). The deism and Neoplatonism of Romantic writers was steeped in such assumptions; however, Victor's (possibly deluded) divination of the environment not only literalizes the concept but also gives it an uncanny twist as it is the Being—not God—who is writing himself into the world.

a dead hare: under the ruthless 'Black Act' (the Criminal Law Act of 1723 and subsequent legislation), still in force in 1818, it was a capital offence in England unlawfully to hunt hare; there may be a critique of the 'Bloody Code' here in that it appeared to make little distinction between multiple homicide and poaching.

157 *The Greeks . . . their toils*: in *Anabasis*, his account of a military expedition to Persia, the Greek cavalry commander and historian Xenophon (*c*.430–*c*.354 BC) describes 'The March of the Ten Thousand'. Xenophon himself led the retreat of his army of mercenaries to Trapezus (Trebizond) on the Black Sea and the relative safety of Greek coastal settlements, which they hailed with the famous cry, 'Thalassa, thalassa!' ('The sea, the sea!').

158 *the spirits of the dead hovered round*: alluding to Ossian via Goethe, *Werther*, bk. ii, 12 September.

160 *manes*: revered spirits of the dead demanding to be propitiated (*OED*).

connected: sequential and coherent (*OED*).

asseverations: i.e. assertions.

162 *chained in an eternal hell*: 'there to dwell | In adamantine chains and penal fire' (Milton, *Paradise Lost*, i. 47–8); see Introduction, p. xxix.

163 *Seneca*: the Stoic philosopher Lucius Annaeus Seneca, the Younger (*c*.5 or 4 BC–AD 65), was implicated in a plot to assassinate the emperor Nero and instructed to commit suicide; the popular account of his death describes him slitting his wrists while lying in a warm bath.

165 *'What do you mean? . . . turn their backs on the foe'*: reminiscent of the speech made by Ulysses to convince his crew to join him on his fatal voyage; Dante encounters Ulysses in hell, forever interned in a fissure as a counsellor of fraud (*Inferno*, xxvi. 112–20).

   September 9th: the 1818 edition erroneously gives the date as September 19th—a compositorial error as the manuscript has September 9th; the date was restored in the 1823 edition (see Robinson (ed.), *Frankenstein*, 238, 252 n., 422).

169 *Evil thenceforth became my good*: 'Evil be thou my good' (Milton, *Paradise Lost*, iv. 110).

170 *call over*: list, enumerate (*OED*).

   contumely: insolent reproach or abuse (*OED*).

   abortion: in addition to the literal meaning of an aborted foetus the word is also used figuratively for a person or thing not properly formed (*OED*). This is one of the revisions made by Percy Shelley; Shelley had originally written 'the devil' (see Robinson (ed.), *Frankenstein*, 243, 428).

171 *consume to ashes . . . as I have been*: the Being cremates himself to prevent his own body from being preserved by the Arctic permafrost and subsequently anatomized. Cremation was not legalized in Britain until 1885, and the Being is therefore planning an act that is both strongly associated with paganism and evokes practices concerning the disposal of monstrous supernatural beings such as vampires.

APPENDIX A

Shelley's digressive account of the events at the Villa Diodati is generally supported by Polidori's version of events, except on the matter of Polidori's own story and Shelley's exclusion of Clairmont from the company of writers.

173 *publishers of the Standard Novels*: *Frankenstein* was number nine in the single-volume budget series, published by Henry Colburn and Richard Bentley, and was bound with Friedrich Schiller's *The Ghost-Seer* (1787–9) in a run of 4,020 copies. Shelley received £30 for the copyright (see Robinson (ed.), *Frankenstein*, 443 n.).

   companion and friend: possibly Isabel Baxter, later married to Shelley's brother-in-law David Booth.

   Scotland: Shelley stayed with the Baxter family in Dundee from June to November 1812, and June 1813 to March 1814; the Baxters were unreconstructed Jacobins—in making the arrangement Godwin seems to have wanted to stir his daughter's political sensibilities, as well as relieving her of the unhappiness of living with her stepmother (see Miranda Seymour, *Mary Shelley* (London: Faber and Faber, 2000), 70–8).

eyry: eyrie, the inaccessible nest of a bird of prey, so figuratively a human retreat in an elevated position (*OED*).

174 *tale of the sinful founder of his race*: this appears to be a vampire tale; however, like the previous narrative mentioned, it is not actually in the volume.

four of us: Mary Shelley, her husband-to-be Percy Shelley, Byron, and Polidori; Shelley omits to mention Clairmont, who appears not to have participated.

Mazeppa: 'A Fragment', published in Byron's *Mazeppa, A Poem* (London: John Murray, 1819), 59–69.

175 *skull-headed lady . . . through a keyhole*: the story, if it ever existed, is lost. However, two narratives by Polidori were inspired at the Villa Diodati: a novel, *Ernestus Berchtold; or, The Modern Oedipus* (1819), which appears to have been started around this time, and his short story 'The Vampyre' (1819), an inspired reworking of Byron's 'A Fragment', which would prove to be as influential as *Frankenstein* (see Introduction, p. xvii).

Tom of Coventry: in the eleventh century the pious Lady Godiva supposedly rode naked through Coventry so as to persuade her husband that the citizens were being unfairly taxed; Peeping Tom stole a look at her and was struck blind.

the tomb of the Capulets: the location of the final scene of mistaken death and suicide in Shakespeare's *Romeo and Juliet*.

curdle the blood . . . the heart: Shelley seeks physical rather than emotional responses (see Introduction, pp. xxiii–xxiv, xxxiv–xxxv).

Sanchean phrase: alluding to Sancho Panza, the faithful servant in Miguel de Cervantes (Saavedra)'s novel *Don Quixote of La Mancha* (1605–15), who when offered the governorship of an island decides that 'the beginning's everything' (bk. ii, ch. 33); Mary Shelley read *Don Quixote* in 1816 and Percy read parts of it aloud to her that autumn.

an elephant . . . upon a tortoise: Hindu cosmology places the elephant Maha-pudma on the back of the tortoise Chukwa, who in turn stands on an endless succession of tortoises; the belief is mentioned by the Earl of Shaftesbury in 'Advice to an Author' (Earl of Shaftesbury, 'The Moralists' (1709), in *Characteristicks of Men, Manners, Opinions, Times*, 3 vols. (5th edn., London: 1732), ii. 202; see M. K. Joseph (ed.), *Frankenstein* (Oxford: Oxford University Press, 1969), 233 n., and Introduction, pp. xxix–xxx).

chaos: a confused mass (*OED*); see Byron's poem 'Darkness' (1816)—'The World was void, | The populous and the powerful was a lump, | Seasonless, herbless, treeless, manless, lifeless— | A lump of death—a chaos of hard clay' (ll. 69–72).

175 *Columbus and his egg*: an apocryphal tale claiming that when at court and confronted with the claim that anyone could have discovered the Indies, Columbus challenged those present to stand an egg on its end; only he could do so—by crushing its end; the anecdote was accordingly taken as evidence of his lateral thinking. The story was recounted by Washington Irving in *A History of the Life and Voyages of Christopher Columbus* (1828).

Many and long . . . communicated: Polidori's diary indicates that he also discussed these matters, at least with Percy Shelley (see *The Diary of Dr. John William Polidori, 1816: Relating to Byron, Shelley, etc.*, ed. William Michael Rossetti (London: Elkin Mathews, 1911), 123).

vermicelli . . . voluntary motion: in his notes on 'Spontaneous Vitality of Microscopic Animals', Erasmus Darwin noted that within three or four days animalcules and microscopic eels could be generated from veal broth, vinegar, or a paste of flour and water ('Additional Notes', in *The Temple of Nature; or The Origin of Society: A Poem, with Philosophical Notes* (London: J. Johnson, 1803), [new pagination] 1–11, at 3; see Introduction, p. xxvi). This had also been a concern of Paracelsian alchemy, which attributed monsters to spontaneous generation. For example, 'Menstrual blood and semen exposed together to putrefaction may give rise to the basilisk, whose poison is similar to that in the eyes or breath of a menstruating woman'; rotting herbs could also generate venomous creatures such as snakes, toads, scorpions, spiders, wild bees, ants, midges, and beetles (*De Natura Rerum*; quoted in Walter Pagel, *Paracelsus: An Introduction to Philosophical Medicine in the Era of the Renaissance* (2nd edn., Basel: Karger, 1982), 116).

galvanism: named after Luigi Galvani (1737–98), anatomist and physicist who conducted electrical experiments on muscular tissue (see Introduction, p. xxvii).

176 *My imagination, unbidden*: Shelley's account of her inspiration is a mystification of her scientific and textual sources in favour of a Romantic theory of the imagination (see Butler (ed.), *Frankenstein*, 260 n.)

Creator of the world: the 1831 version introduces a more insistent religious theme, barely evident in the 1818 edition except in exclamations made by Victor and Walton.

handywork: emphasizing that the Being is the product of manual labour.

parquet: a floor geometrically patterned with inlaid blocks of wood (*OED*).

'*It was on a dreary night of November*': the beginning of Volume III, Chapter iii, p. 36.

my husband: Percy Shelley's contribution was almost entirely revising the vocabulary of the novel (see Note on the Text, pp. liii, liv, for a discussion, and Robinson's edition for a full transcript).

the preface: see note to Preface.

177 *untouched*: see Appendix B, pp. 178–9.

APPENDIX B

182 *Lake of Como*: in Lombardy, northern Italy; the Shelleys visited Lake Como in early 1818 on a fruitless quest in search of a house.

183 *schiavi ognor frementi*: 'slaves always in tumult'; i.e. the Italians (in Lombardy, the Veneto, Istria, and Dalmatia) enraged by Austrian rule (which was not introduced until 1815).

Elizabeth Lavenza: in the first edition, Elizabeth was Victor's bereaved cousin; by making her exile and adoption the consequence of political upheaval, her plight now mirrors that of Safie.

184 *campagne*: this presumably refers to a country villa, though *campagne* simply means open countryside.

185 *Roncesvalles*: the Battle of Roncevaux Pass (778) was an ambush in the Pyrenees by Basques against Charlemagne's army; the knight Roland was slain in the encounter, inspiring the eleventh-century epic *La Chanson de Roland*, Matteo Maria Boiardo's *Orlando innamorato* (1487), and Ariosto's *Orlando furioso* (1532).

chivalrous train . . . infidels: the medieval Crusades to reclaim Jerusalem.

temperature: temperament (*OED*).

186 *Sir Isaac Newton . . . ocean of truth*: shortly before he died, the mathematician and natural philosopher Sir Isaac Newton (1642–1727) is alleged to have remarked, 'I don't know what I may seem to the world, but, as to myself, I seem to have been only like a boy playing on the sea shore, and diverting myself in now and then finding a smoother pebble or a prettier shell than ordinary, whilst the great ocean of truth lay all undiscovered before me' (Joseph Spence, *Anecdotes, Observations, and Characters, of Books and Men* (London: W. H. Carpenter, 1820), 53).

tyros: novices (*OED*).

188 *enounced*: proclaimed (*OED*).

189 *facile*: easy to understand; the word had not yet acquired disparaging associations (*OED*).

194 *of soul-inspiriting*: cheering of the soul (*OED*); the compound had appeared the previous year in the *Westminster Review* (13 (1830), 460).

196 *the progress of European colonisation and trade*: see too Clerval's interest in Persian, Arabic, and Sanskrit, pp. 46, 190.

197 *Havre-de-Grace*: the French port of Le Havre, on the English Channel.

198 *There were women weeping around*: Elizabeth's corpse is surrounded by mourners, a custom that required a corpse be watched before burial to safeguard posthumous dignity.

APPENDIX C

This partisan piece was clearly written *c*.1817 as a review to promote the first edition; it was however only published well after Percy Shelley's death in *The*

Athenæum: Journal of English and Foreign Literature, Science, and the Fine Arts, 263 (10 November 1832), 730.

199 *Pelion is heaped on Ossa . . . Ossa on Olympus*: Percy Shelley is referring to the mountain range that runs across Thessaly in north-eastern central Greece to the Mediterranean Sea.

pathos: the word was first revised from 'father's' (as printed in the original review) in *The Works of Percy Bysshe Shelley in Verse and Prose*, ed. H. B. Forman, 8 vols. (London: Reeves and Turner: 1880), vii. 12 n.

200 *abortion*: Percy repeats his own telling word for the Being (see note to p. 170).

'tears stream down the cheeks': a generic sentimental reference, though there are specific instances in early texts (for example, in the Elizabethan drama *Tancred and Gismunda*, reprinted in *A Select Collection of Old Plays*, 1780).

Caleb Williams with Falkland: see note to p. 121.

Tartary: many of Percy Shelley's revisions to *Frankenstein* were daringly innovative, others were deliberately archaic; in this review the reference to Tartary as the central Asian territory extending eastwards from the Caspian Sea is a provocatively dated term.

The Oxford World's Classics Website

www.worldsclassics.co.uk

- Browse the full range of Oxford World's Classics online

- Sign up for our monthly e-alert to receive information on new titles

- Read extracts from the Introductions

- Listen to our editors and translators talk about the world's greatest literature with our Oxford World's Classics audio guides

- Join the conversation, follow us on Twitter at OWC_Oxford

- Teachers and lecturers can order inspection copies quickly and simply via our website

www.worldsclassics.co.uk

American Literature

British and Irish Literature

Children's Literature

Classics and Ancient Literature

Colonial Literature

Eastern Literature

European Literature

Gothic Literature

History

Medieval Literature

Oxford English Drama

Philosophy

Poetry

Politics

Religion

The Oxford Shakespeare

A complete list of Oxford World's Classics, including Authors in Context, Oxford English Drama, and the Oxford Shakespeare, is available in the UK from the Marketing Services Department, Oxford University Press, Great Clarendon Street, Oxford OX2 6DP, or visit the website at www.oup.com/uk/worldsclassics.

In the USA, visit www.oup.com/us/owc for a complete title list.

Oxford World's Classics are available from all good bookshops. In case of difficulty, customers in the UK should contact Oxford University Press Bookshop, 116 High Street, Oxford OX1 4BR.